Tho
A Texan's
LT THO

2005

A Texan's Luck

*Also by Jodi Thomas
in Large Print:*

The Widows of Wichita County

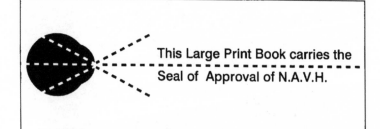

A Texan's Luck

Jodi Thomas

Published in 2005 by arrangement with
The Berkley Publishing Group,
a division of Penguin Group (USA) Inc.

Wheeler Large Print Romance.

The text of this Large Print edition is unabridged.
Other aspects of the book may vary from the original edition.

Set in 16 pt. Plantin by Elena Picard.

Printed in the United States on permanent paper.

Library of Congress Cataloging-in-Publication Data

Thomas, Jodi.
  A Texan's luck / by Jodi Thomas.
    p. cm. — (Wheeler Publishing large print romance)
  ISBN 1-58724-921-9 (lg. print : hc : alk. paper)
  1. Arranged marriage — Fiction. 2. Women pioneers —
Fiction. 3. Revenge — Fiction. 4. Texas — Fiction.   —
5. Large type books. I. Title. II. Wheeler large print
romance series.
PS3570.H5643T485 2005
813'.6—dc22   2005000382

/382

A Texan's Luck

As the Founder/CEO of NAVH, the only national health agency solely devoted to those who, although not totally blind, have an eye disease which could lead to serious visual impairment, I am pleased to recognize Thorndike Press★ as one of the leading publishers in the large print field.

Founded in 1954 in San Francisco to prepare large print textbooks for partially seeing children, NAVH became the pioneer and standard setting agency in the preparation of large type.

Today, those publishers who meet our standards carry the prestigious "Seal of Approval" indicating high quality large print. We are delighted that Thorndike Press is one of the publishers whose titles meet these standards. We are also pleased to recognize the significant contribution Thorndike Press is making in this important and growing field.

Lorraine H. Marchi, L.H.D.
Founder/CEO
NAVH

★ Thorndike Press encompasses the following imprints: Thorndike, Wheeler, Walker and Large Print Press.

Prologue

Cottonwood, Texas
1886

Captain Walker Larson gritted his teeth as Sergeant Peterson ushered in another of the prostitutes who came to complain about the evacuation order. As usual, the tall, lanky sergeant grinned at the woman as if he were guiding her into the front pew on Sunday morning.

They had a matter of hours to clear the little town before an all-out range war started, and the sergeant acted like the army was there to serve tea. Cowhands from the warring ranches were already swallowing down courage at saloons. By nightfall they would be itching to fight, and nothing Walker and his handful of men could do would stop them.

Walker frowned at the paperwork stacked on his desk. Since he moved into the abandoned sheriff's quarters, he'd seen nothing but trouble walk through the door. Why couldn't these women understand that all hell was about to break loose? They'd be better off to collect their belongings and go like most of the civilians. Trouble twisted in the streets, a building tornado, but these ladies of the night didn't seem to hear the wind.

"Captain, this one insists on seeing you right away." Peterson removed his hat and pointed her toward the only chair in the room other than the one Walker sat in behind his desk. "Says it's real important that she talk to you, sir."

Walker cleared his throat as he prepared to say what he'd said to every one of the soiled doves who had come to complain. The army had a responsibility to protect them, whether they wanted help or not. With a range war threatening, what little peace this town knew was gone. Every man seemed to have chosen a side, and it was only a matter of time before someone started the fight. No one would be safe, and the saloons, where these women roamed, were waiting powder casks.

This one was a beauty, though. Rich, walnut-colored hair he wouldn't mind folding inside his grip. And young. Far too young, Walker decided, to be in such a business. But he guessed the ones who managed to hang on to their youthful looks could demand higher prices.

She appeared wearier than the rest, as if she'd traveled a long distance. Her dusty red coat was well made but did little to hide her wares beneath. He didn't miss the fullness of her breasts or the way her jacket pulled in sharply along the waist. She had a pride about her he found even more fascinating than her beauty.

He forgot his standard speech as he raised his gaze and stared into eyes the warm brown of polished leather. She was the first woman in a long time who tempted him to visit the backstreets.

"There are no exceptions, miss. We have to evacuate you with the rest of the ladies." He felt sorry for her. She looked frightened and a little lost, as if her world were about to end. She was a master at playing the innocent, for she almost made him believe it.

"I'm not with the others," she said in little more than a whisper. "I came to see you."

He waited, wondering what she'd offer to be allowed to stay behind. Whatever it was, no matter how tempting, it wouldn't be enough for him to bend the rules. He hadn't made it to captain at twenty-five by bending.

She looked up at him with those beautiful eyes again. "The sergeant said your name was Larson . . . Frank Larson, sir."

"That's right." He nodded, finding himself wishing she had come to see him about something else. Frank was his first name, but no one but his father had ever called him that. His mother had liked her family name, Walker, best. "I'm Captain Larson," he stated, reminding her this was not a social call.

He couldn't tell if she were relieved by the information, or more frightened for some reason. He half expected her to bolt and run by the way she clung to the strings of her tattered handbag.

"And you are?" He really didn't have time to mess with learning her name, but he asked just the same.

"Mrs. Larson," she answered lifting her chin slightly. "Mrs. Frank Larson."

Walker smiled and stood. He had no idea what kind of game she was playing, but Larson was a common name. She might be married to a man who had the same name as him. That wouldn't change a thing. His job was to try to save lives. The only way he could do that was to get

10

her and all other women and children out of town. Except for a few widows and these prostitutes, most of the women had menfolk to look after them.

"Nice to meet you, Mrs. Larson. Where might your husband be?" He tried to keep his words formal as he moved around the corner of the desk. Perhaps he'd been wrong about her occupation. Maybe she was a shopkeeper's wife or a rancher's daughter who'd been separated from her family. Maybe her husband was as young as she and had joined in the fight without helping her leave town first.

Her eyebrows shot up in shock. "Why, right before me, sir."

The words hit Walker like a powerful blow to his gut. He didn't move. The tiny possibility that she spoke the truth seeped through a crack in the wall he'd spent years building around himself.

She twisted the cord of her bag about her fingers that appeared to be stained with ink.

He'd seen those kinds of stains on his father's hands many times . . . printer's ink. The clock on his cluttered desk ticked away seconds as though they both had all the time in the world.

"You must be mistaken," he said at last.

"There is no one in the room but the two of us, ma'am."

Her unsettling gaze watched him closely. "You are in the room, sir. I'm Lacy Larson, your wife."

Sergeant Peterson opened the door suddenly, following his words into the room. "Last stage will be leaving in ten minutes, Captain." Peterson had acted as doorman for the captain for two years. He jerked back a step, well aware that he'd interrupted something, even though Walker hadn't said a word. "Begging your pardon, sir."

"Hold the stage," Walker said without taking his gaze off of Lacy. "I need a few minutes with this lady."

"I don't know if I can," the sergeant mumbled. "That driver is in a powerful hurry, and don't look like he cares much what the army has to say."

Walker's cold stare shifted to Peterson. "Hold it at gunpoint if you have to, but that stage doesn't leave until this woman is on it!"

Peterson nodded and backed out of the room, closing the door behind him.

Walker turned his full attention to Lacy Larson. "You are the woman my father bailed out of jail and married me to by

12

proxy three years ago." He found it hard to believe. She must have been little more than a child at the time.

His words hadn't been a question, but she nodded in answer anyway.

"How old are you?"

"Eighteen," she answered. "How old are you?"

"Twenty-five," Walker snapped.

She watched him closely. "You seem older," she said more to herself than him. "Your father always called you his boy."

Walker walked in front of his desk, choosing his words carefully. He didn't want to frighten the lady further, but she had become far more than his responsibility as an officer of the government.

She stared at the strings of her purse.

Walker shoved paperwork aside and leaned on his desk. He crossed his long legs as he folded his arms. He stood so close to her he could touch her if he shifted. He considered himself an honest, straightforward man, but for once, he tried to think of how to be kind. She looked so frightened. He blamed his father for this mess more than her. She'd been in jail. She'd done what she thought she must to survive. But his father had paid her bail and started this whole muddle. The old man should have stayed out of his life, as well as hers. What kind of father buys his son a wife?

"I fought," Walker began, "to get the marriage annulled when I found out what my father had done. I'm a soldier, madam, I have no need or desire for a wife. You'd be better off married to someone else."

Light from the window flickered off his polished boots. She lowered her head and seemed to be focusing on the bouncing rays. He hoped he hadn't hurt her feelings by being so direct. Surely, she couldn't think he was turning her down. After all, until a few minutes ago, he'd never seen her before. She'd probably make some farmer up near Cedar Point a great wife. She was certainly a beauty, even if she did have a questionable past.

"So we have not been legally married these past three years?" she said so softly he barely heard the words.

She raised her chocolate-colored eyes to him.

Walker almost groaned aloud. He'd guess she could get about anything in this world she wanted with those eyes, but from some other man. Not him.

"Oh, we're married, all right. Thanks to the power-of-attorney letter I left my father, the marriage is as solid as if I'd signed the paper with my own hand."

"You don't want to be married to me?" She looked like it had never crossed her mind that he wouldn't want her.

Walker flinched, hating that he was hurting her. He silently swore at his father, who was a kind man but always thought he knew what was best. "It's not that I don't want *you*, it's that I don't want a wife. Any wife. And I never will."

He walked to the long, thin window that faced the dusty main street of this little town whose name he had trouble remembering. Since he had left home, his life had been a string of battles. Walker didn't want to even think about what his life might have been like if he hadn't run away from home at seventeen and kept running. He never told his father why he'd left, and he didn't plan to tell this woman who thought she was his wife.

"How is the old man?" Walker asked, realizing he hadn't heard from his father in months.

Lacy stood and walked to the window. She didn't come to his shoulder, but he sensed her nearness even before he turned around.

"Your father died three months ago."

Lacy touched his arm, offering comfort he did not know how to accept.

"He'd been ill for almost a year, but he wouldn't let me write you and tell you." She took a deep breath. "I did the best I could, moving him in with me above the print shop as he grew weaker, partly to save money, but mostly so I could check on him more often. Though he was in pain, he seemed happier there than alone at the boardinghouse."

Walker clenched his teeth and stared out the window, seeing nothing but memories.

Lacy continued, "I buried him next to your mother. I think everyone for twenty miles around came to the funeral. I'm sorry to have to tell you like this. I wrote you three letters giving all the details and even the newspaper clipping, but when I didn't hear back, I knew they hadn't caught up with you."

"There's no easy way. Straight out is fine. I knew he was failing, more crippled up every year." He faced her and was surprised to see unshed tears floating in her beautiful eyes. He covered her hand with his own, wishing he could grieve for his father as she obviously did. "Thank you for coming to tell me, but you really must go." They'd already wasted precious minutes.

"I didn't come just to tell you he died," she whispered, her bravery building with each word. "I came because I want to be your real wife."

Walker felt her fingers tremble beneath his. "Go back to Cedar Point. Sell the print shop, keep the money. I want no part of it." He didn't have time to explain. She needed to be on the stage. Even if she shared his name, she was no more to him than a stranger, a civilian. "Move away and change your name, or tell everyone I died. Get on with your life, Lacy. I've never been a part of it; I never will."

She shook her head. "No," she answered as though they talked of something debatable. "I'm not leaving today until I'm your wife. Your real wife."

Peterson tapped on the door before opening it, something Walker never remembered the sergeant doing. "The stage driver says he'll give us fifteen more —" Peterson froze as he took in the scene. The sergeant's gaze focused at the point on Walker's sleeve where Lacy's hand rested.

Walker didn't introduce Lacy; after all, Peterson would never see her again. In truth, all he needed was a few more minutes with this woman to convince her to move on with her life and forget about this

17

make-believe marriage she thought they had.

"Fifteen minutes will be fine." When Peterson didn't move, Walker added, "That is all, Sergeant."

Peterson saluted and backed out of the room.

Walker listened for the latch to snap before he gave Lacy his full attention. "What are you talking about? You are my legal wife. The only one I'll probably ever have. But, I'm setting you free from whatever bargain you made with my father."

Her hand slipped from his arm.

"I wish we had time to talk, Lacy," he added, surprised at how truly he meant the words. "I thank you for all you did for him, but you really must be on that stage. Your safety is my responsibility."

Lacy moved her head slowly back and forth.

"This is not a game or a clash of wills." Walker fought down anger. "You will be on that stage."

"Not until I'm your wife, full and proper." Her pride returned as she lifted her chin.

Walker's limited patience snapped. "What are you suggesting, Mrs. Larson, that I bed you here and now before the stage leaves?"

To his surprise, she nodded. "I'm not budging until I'm your wife. I'll not go back and wait to be a widow unless I've been a wife, even if only for fifteen minutes of my life."

It crossed his mind that he might be dealing with madness. No sane woman would want to stay in a town where trouble boiled. He frowned. No sane woman would want to bed a man she barely knew.

He decided frightening her might be his only weapon. "Well, if that is the way it has to be, Mrs. Larson, my quarters are beyond that door." He motioned with his head toward the door behind his desk. "If those are your terms, we won't be disturbed in there."

To his shock, she moved to the door.

He followed, determined to call her bluff.

She walked to the center of the small, sparsely furnished bedroom and turned up the lantern's wick, casting shadows into corners. She didn't turn around as he threw the latch, insuring their privacy.

"Go ahead and take off your clothes." He fought down a smile, knowing she'd turn and run any moment. He'd seen the fear in her eyes when she'd first entered his office. She wouldn't be able to play this game for long. "You can lay them over the chair. I'm sorry about the small bed. I'm not in the habit of entertaining company in my quarters."

Without turning around, she removed her traveling jacket and placed it over the chair. A moment later, her skirts and petticoats pooled around her ankles.

Walker swallowed, wondering how far she planned to carry this challenge. Or, how far did he?

She stepped from her shoes and turned to face him, unbuttoning her blouse as rapidly as her shaking hands could move.

He questioned how many times she'd played this game before. After all, she might look young and pure, but Walker remembered where she came from. Pure, proper ladies don't buy their way out of jail. He hadn't even bothered to ask his father what she'd been accused of or to what she'd confessed.

"Keep going," he ordered, determined to wait her out.

When her blouse parted, it took every ounce of his control not to move. Her thin camisole did little to hide the body beneath. He saw the rise and fall of her breath in the exposed flesh of her breasts. Her skin was cream from her cheek to where she tugged at the ribbons of her undergarment.

The lace and silk fell away, and she stood before him a hundred times more beautiful than any picture of a woman he'd seen over any bar. To his amazement, she stretched and pulled the combs from her hair and let the brown locks tumble. Then, as though she'd done so a hundred times, she crawled between the sheets of his bed.

Walker searched for something to say in a brain filled to the rim with the vision before him. "I thought you'd run by now."

She looked at him with frightened, determined eyes. "I'm not leaving until I'm your real wife. I promise I'll not bother you again, but I'll not step foot on that stage until this marriage, no matter how it started, is consummated."

A hundred reasons should have come to mind about why he could not do this, but not one seemed to matter. Into his world filled with war and death and pain, something perfect had fallen. Even if she were a mirage, he had to hold her this once.

Walker crossed the room, unbuttoning his uniform. He stood above her and ran his hand down the length of her body, marveling at the softness. He wanted to tell her how perfect she was, or how there had been no women in his life for years, but there was no time now. The stage would be leaving in a few minutes.

His jacket fell atop her coat as he leaned down, letting his chest press against her. The pure pleasure of her beneath him shot through him unlike anything he'd ever dreamed of experiencing. He thought of himself as a man of action whose emotions were buried years ago. Only this woman, who called herself his wife, brought them all back, an avalanche of sensation.

She didn't move. She only waited.

When he tried to kiss her, she turned her head away, and he realized what he'd been about to do was not a necessary part to this mating she wanted. Anger and relief blended, for he knew he'd never wanted to waste time kissing on the few brief encounters he'd had with women of the night. For some reason, she felt the same.

"Are you sure?" He had to know that this was what she wanted. "You'll leave as soon as I do this?"

She nodded.

He unbuttoned his trousers, reminding himself she was his wife. Though he'd never asked for the part, it was his duty to see her safe. He gripped her thigh and pulled her legs apart. Maybe this was his duty, too. She'd asked for no love. No forever. No pretense. Only this.

Walker pushed into her hard and swift, angry that he'd allowed her to call his bluff, that he hadn't been able to stop after he saw her waiting. He had no idea what game she played, but he'd do his part and be done with her.

With his second thrust, all thought vanished as her body took him in, wrapping around him. A passion strong and wild jolted through him. His senses shot in rapid fire. The fragrance of her washed over him, the feel of her, the soft sound her breathing made, the perfection of her nearness, the taste of her skin as he opened his mouth against her throat.

He wasn't prepared when his very soul shattered. He pushed into her and let out a long breath that he felt he'd held in for years. They became one, two strangers married now on paper and by action.

When he was able to form a thought, he rose a few inches off her and looked down at this woman who insisted she was his wife. Her warm brown eyes were tightly closed, her teeth biting into her fist, holding back any sound as tears streamed from the corners of her eyes into her hair.

It took a few moments to realize that the

unexpected ocean of pleasure that had washed over him like a tidal wave had held only pain for her.

Peterson pounded on the door. "Two minutes!" he yelled. "The driver threatened to shoot me if I asked him to wait any longer."

"She'll be there!" Walker shouted back as he climbed from his bed and buttoned his trousers, realizing he hadn't bothered to remove even his boots.

"I've done what you asked," he said, irritated that she seemed to be suffering through some great tragedy when she'd been the one who insisted on the mating. He glanced at her body one last time as she pushed back tears. The buckle from his uniform belt had scratched across her abdomen. "Now, you have to go, Lacy Larson. We've no more time."

Walker grabbed his jacket and turned his back, hating himself more than he had since the night he'd left Cedar Point. He thought of saying something kind to her, but there were no words. What they'd done was as far from making love as heaven from hell. He wasn't fool enough to tell himself that it was all her doing. She might be his wife. She might have insisted. She might have had a body made for love. But he'd been the one who accepted her challenge when he should have turned away.

He waited, his back to her, telling himself he would allow her a margin of privacy while she dressed. Telling himself he wasn't afraid to face her.

Walker straightened his jacket and checked to make sure all was in place in the mirror over his washstand. The reflection was the same as always. A young, professional soldier on his way up in rank, but somehow, inside, something had changed. He didn't turn around until he heard her walk to the door. He wanted to speak but could think of nothing to say. She'd gotten what she wanted; he had taken her.

He heard the latch move and the door opened, then closed behind her.

Without a word, she was gone, leaving him fuming at how he'd been manipulated by a woman not out of her teens. Maybe she'd manipulated his father also, or the old sheriff in Cedar Point.

He was back in full control, not only of his men, but of himself. He didn't need anyone. He didn't want anyone in his life. No matter what her game was, he would not play it again.

Walker had all emotion drained from his mind as he glanced around his quarters, making sure she hadn't left something that might give her reason to return. A single hairpin rested on the table, forgotten in her haste. He slipped it into his pocket and looked toward the bed.

The lantern's light caught the few drops of blood staining the white sheets where she'd lain.

The sight knocked him to his knees.

Chapter 1

Cedar Point
November 1888

Lacy folded a few dollar bills into the last pay envelope and stuffed it in the bottom drawer of her desk. She leaned back, breathing in the familiar smells of the print shop: ink, sawdust, paper, poverty. Home.

In the three years since she had taken over the shop, she managed to make the payroll every month but one. Once she'd taken all the money from the cashbox and traveled halfway across Texas to meet her husband. She shrugged. Once she'd been eighteen and a fool.

As the wind howled outside, Lacy closed her eyes, remembering how excited she'd been when she learned that Frank Walker Larson was stationed little more than a day's ride by train and then stage from her. Finally, her husband would be more than just a name on the marriage license and a few letters he'd written his father the first year he'd gone into the army.

She'd dreamed of how it would be when they met. He would be young and handsome in his uniform. She'd run into his arms, and he would tell her everything was going to be all right. After the long year of taking care of his father and keeping the shop running, Lacy would cuddle into her husband's embrace and forget all her worries.

She opened her eyes to the shadowy world of her small print shop. The real world. Her husband had been handsome, she admitted. So tall and important he took her breath away. But he hadn't welcomed her. His arms had folded around her in duty, nothing more. The Frank Larson she ran to was only a cold captain who preferred to be called Walker. And their time together had chilled her heart.

Lacy pushed away a tear as she remembered riding back on the dusty stagecoach that day. Now twenty, she was old enough to realize what a fool she had made of herself with Larson. The ride home had only prolonged her agony. Her body hurt from being used, but the dreams he killed scarred. The coach had been crowded with women wearing too much perfume and men smoking cheap cigars. When Lacy threw up in her handkerchief, the passengers decided that she would benefit from more air.

At the first stop, she was encouraged to take the seat on top of the stage. She'd pulled on her bonnet and gladly crawled into the chair tied among the luggage. As she watched the sunset that day, Lacy took the letters from her bag that Walker had written to his father years ago. She fell in love with her husband through reading his letters of adventure, memorizing every line as if it were written to her.

One by one, she watched them blow out of her hands, drifting in the wind behind the stage like dead leaves. That day she put away childhood. That day she'd given up on dreams.

Lacy stood in the dimly lit shop and pulled her shawl around her as if the wool could hug her frame. She stretched tired muscles. It was late, and tomorrow would be a busy day. Every Saturday after all the papers were sold and the flyers nailed, Lacy rode out to her friends' farm. There, she could relax for a few hours. She'd play with Bailee and Carter's children and remember how years ago when Sarah, Bailee, and she had been kicked off of a wagon train, they'd talked about what life would be like in Texas. Bailee had sworn she'd never marry, and Sarah had thought she wouldn't live to see another winter. But Lacy, then fifteen, had boasted that she would marry and have so many children she would have to start numbering them because she'd run out of names.

"Five years ago," Lacy whispered to herself as she climbed the stairs. Five years since they came to Texas half-starved, out of money, and out of luck. Bailee found her man and had three sons with another baby on the way. Sarah wrote often about her twins.

"And then there is me." Lacy walked into her small apartment above the shop. "I had a husband for fifteen minutes, once."

Her rooms welcomed her with colorful quilts she'd made and tattered books she'd collected. When she first moved in and began to learn the newspaper business, she could barely read, but Lacy studied hard. Her father-in-law never tired of helping her learn those first few years. He'd treated her like a treasure, even though she'd been little more than a ragamuffin when he'd paid her bail and married her to his son by proxy. From the first, he talked of what a grand jewel she'd be to his son when the boy finally came home from serving in the army.

On evenings like this, she missed the old man dearly. She longed for the way he always talked about Walker as if his son were still a boy, and the way he could quote every article he'd ever written as though it were only yesterday and not material from twenty years in the business. He loved telling stories of newspapermen who'd stood their ground in Western towns from Kansas City to California and had to fight, sometimes even die, for what they wrote. She missed his company.

Before Lacy could heat water for tea, someone tapped on the back door.

She lifted the old Navy Colt from the pie safe drawer and went to answer. No one ever climbed the stairs to her back door except Bailee, and she wouldn't be calling so late.

The minute she saw Sheriff Riley's stooped outline through the glass, she relaxed and set the gun aside. He'd taken a few bullets in a gun battle several years ago, and the limp made it hard for him to stand straight.

"Evening." She opened the door to a

31

cold blast of air that almost took her breath away. "Want to come in for a cup of coffee, Sheriff? It's cold enough to snow." The little porch area at the top of a narrow flight of stairs held no protection from the night, and lately, the sheriff looked little more than bone.

Riley shook his head. "Now you know I can't do that. What would folks say, a lady like yourself having a male guest after dark?"

She grinned, knowing no one would think a thing about the old man coming in from the winter night to sit a spell, but she wouldn't spoil his fun. "You know you're the only gentleman I ask inside. I'd shoot any other man who came knocking after dark, but I know you wouldn't be here if you didn't have a reason."

Riley nodded. "I'd hope so. You being a respectable lady and all. I wouldn't even bother with a trial if I found a body on this porch." Though he'd listened to their confessions of killing a robber on the road to Cedar Point five years ago, Riley had always treated Lacy, Sarah, and Bailee more like daughters than outlaws.

The sheriff, like everyone else in town, regarded her as if her husband had simply left for the day and would be back anytime.

Here, she was Mrs. Larson, and there was a solidness about it, even if there was no substance to the man she married.

Riley shifted into his coat like an aging turtle. "I just came to tell you that I got a telegram a few minutes ago saying Zeb Whitaker will be getting out of jail next week. I promised you I'd let you know the minute I heard."

Lacy fought to keep from reaching for the Colt. Big Zeb Whitaker was an old nightmare she laid aside years ago when he'd finally gone to prison. She could still feel his hands on her when he'd grabbed her and ripped the front of her dress open to see if she were woman enough to kidnap. She thought she killed him once. She would kill him for real if she had to. He was the first man Bailee, Sarah, and she met when they came to Texas, and if Zeb had his way, he would have taken their wagon and left them for dead.

"Lacy?" Riley said as though he didn't think she listened.

"Yes." She balled her fist to keep her hands from trembling.

"Rumor is he still thinks one of you three women has his stash of gold. I wouldn't be surprised if he showed up around here. I'm not too worried about

Bailee way out on the farm with Carter watching after her, and Sarah tucked away where Zeb will never find her." Riley's face wrinkled. "But you . . . with your man gone and all."

He didn't need to say more. She knew she was alone. Her man wasn't gone; Walker had never been here. Except for the one brief meeting, he was no more than a name on a piece of paper.

"I think you should leave town, Lacy." When Riley met her stare, he added quickly, "Just for a few weeks. Go see Sarah. Or maybe you have family back East you could visit. Maybe if you weren't here, he'd forget about looking you up."

Lacy wanted to scream, *Leave town with what?* There were times over the past few years when she didn't have enough money left to buy food. Once she survived on a basket of apples Bailee brought in from their farm. The two friends never discussed how Lacy was doing, but Bailee always brought apples and eggs and more from the farm, claiming she wanted to trade them for a newspaper. More often then not, Lacy swapped a ten cent paper for a week's worth of food.

Lacy didn't want the sheriff, or anyone else in town, to know how little she had.

34

They all seemed to think her invisible husband sent her money regularly. "I'll be fine here, Sheriff, don't worry about me."

Riley shook his head. "I don't know, Lacy. I'm not as spry as I used to be. I'm not sure I can face a man like Zeb Whitaker."

"He's aged, too, you know. He's probably barely getting around. Who knows, he might come back to say he's sorry for causing us so much trouble five years ago."

"Mean don't age well." The sheriff frowned. "I'd feel a lot better if your man were here."

"Walker's down on the border fighting cattle rustlers," Lacy lied. She'd been using that excuse for months now; it was time she made up another reason. "I'll be all right. I have the gun you gave me."

Mumbling to himself, Riley turned and headed down the steep stairs. Lacy knew he wasn't happy about her staying, but this was her home, her only home, and she needed to run the shop. None of the three men who worked for her could take over her job.

Duncan was almost deaf. Folks coming in to place an ad had to stand next to his good ear and yell their order. Eli's bones bothered him so much in winter that he stayed on his feet most of the day. If he sat for more than a few minutes, he seemed to rust. And, of course, Jay Boy was just a kid Lacy paid a man's wages because he supported his mother and little sister. He might be learning the business between errands, but he couldn't take over.

Lacy closed the back door and locked it. She had to stay. If Whitaker came, she'd fight, maybe even die, but she wouldn't run.

She almost wanted to laugh at the way the legend of Whitaker's gold had spread over the years. The night he'd tried to steal their wagon, they'd left him in the mud, his saddlebags heavy beside him, but with each year folks came up with theories of what might have happened to the gold. Some thought the women had it and were waiting until Whitaker died to spend it. Some decided Whitaker buried it because if he'd been caught with it, he'd serve more jail time. Even a few believed there had been no gold that rainy sunrise.

Lacy had decided a few years ago to stop trying to tell the story and just let people believe what they wanted to. They would anyway.

For the next few days she carefully locked every door and made sure the old Colt was not far from her hand. She caught herself jumping at the jingle of the front bell and waking each night when the wind rapped at her upstairs windows. As the days passed, she calmed, telling herself she was in the middle of town and had nothing to fear from an old buffalo hunter like Zeb Whitaker.

If he did come to town, he would need but one look at her shop to see that she couldn't have stolen the gold he said weighed down his saddlebags that morning. Lacy remembered seeing coins spilling out of the bags after she'd clubbed him, but she hadn't taken a single one.

One week went by, then another. Winter settled in, turning the usual mud holes in the streets to ice and frosting the air. Lacy worked in the shop by day and quilted by candlelight late into the night. She hated winter, for she never felt warm. Even standing in front of her small fire, only one side warmed, the other chilled. She tried to use the stove upstairs only when needed and conserve her wood to heat the downstairs. But winter settled in for a long stay, and the nights seemed endless as she made herself work long after dark.

Around midnight, she gave up trying to quilt. While she dressed for bed, thin bricks heated by the fire. In her gown,

Lacy carefully wrapped each brick and stuffed it beneath the covers near the bottom of her bed. Then she jumped in bed, laughing at her own attempts to keep warm.

The wind rattled the windows along the back of the apartment even more than usual, with a promise of snow.

Lacy poked her head out from beneath the quilts. She listened. The alley behind her shop sometimes sounded like a wind tunnel, dragging a howling winter into the shadows. The wooden frame of the shop below groaned. Somewhere boards popped as they shifted.

She slipped back under the blankets, hoping her breath would warm the space between the sheets.

Just as her icy toes thawed, thanks to the hot bricks, the back door rattled. The sound was muffled by a towel she'd placed to keep out the draft, but she thought she heard the creak of the door handle.

Lacy hesitated, weighing fear against being cold. The Colt rested on the dresser not three feet away, but the journey would cost her the little body heat she'd managed to trap beneath the covers.

She told herself no one would try to break in tonight. It was too cold. In the years she'd lived alone above the shop, no one had ever tried to break in. Once a drunk fell into the front windows downstairs, but he hadn't intended to enter. This was a quiet little town most of the time where folks felt safe. Crime rarely paid a call.

But what better time than tonight, with the wind blowing and no one brave enough to investigate a scream?

At the third rattle of the door, Lacy jumped from the bed and ran for the Colt. As her hand touched the handle of the gun, a cold wind barreled through her apartment. The back door swung wide open, clamoring against the wall.

Lacy held the weapon in both hands and faced the wind. She might freeze, but she'd protect to the death what was hers.

A tall figure in a dark wool coat stood before her wearing a hat low, blocking his face from view. He filled the opening. The short cape of his coat flapped in the wind like a flag.

She raised the gun and tightened her finger around the trigger.

The stranger stomped into her kitchen as if he had a right to be there. Swearing at the storm, he raised a gloved hand to shove the door closed. The dove-colored gauntlet shone pale in the moonlight.

Leveling the gun to his chest, she stepped forward. Only the yellow braiding of his hat cords kept her from firing.

"Cavalry," she whispered, remembering that only army cavalry wore yellow on their uniforms. "Infantry wear blue, artillery wear scarlet," she repeated her facts as if writing an article and not facing an intruder.

The trespasser glanced up. Icy blue eyes stared from beneath the shade of his wide-brimmed hat.

"Walker!" She almost didn't recognize him. His chin was covered by a short, black beard, but even in the shadow of his hat, she would never forget those eyes. Cold, heartless eyes, that asked nothing and gave even less.

He jerked his hat off and tossed it on the kitchen table. "Shoot me, Lacy, if that's what you plan to do, or put that old cannon away. I'm in no mood to waste time being threatened by my own wife."

Lacy blinked as if he might disappear.

Walker unbuttoned his coat and hung it on a peg behind the door as though he knew it would be there waiting for him.

He was slightly thicker, she thought. Ten pounds, maybe twenty. His hair was longer, curling over the stiff collar of his uniform jacket. But he was no less handsome, no less frightening.

"What are you doing here?" she asked without lowering the gun.

He glanced at the Colt, then faced her directly. "Let's get something straight right now, dear wife. I have no desire to be in this town. In fact, if I had my way, I'd never step foot within a hundred miles of Cedar Point."

He pulled off his gloves and tossed them atop his hat. "But it seems Sheriff Riley knows someone who is acquainted with my superior officer. He sent a letter two weeks ago demanding I come home to protect my wife from a man she has apparently confessed to killing once."

Lacy wasn't sure if she were more upset that he came home unwillingly to protect her, or that Sheriff Riley had interfered. At this point, if she had only one bullet, it would be a toss-up which one to shoot. "I didn't ask him to have you come. I can take care of myself."

Walker looked at the gun. "I can see that."

She lowered the Colt. "You've no need to stay. You can return to your post, wherever that is. I'll be fine."

The deep frown didn't lift. "Would that I could," he answered as if arguing with her. "But it seems I've been given thirty days' leave and was forced to take it."

"Thirty days," Lacy echoed. Thirty days with Walker would be an eternity. The few minutes she'd spent with him two years ago had taken her months to recover from. He hurt her. He humiliated her. And worst of all, he'd done exactly what she'd asked of him. He'd made her his wife in more than name.

"Don't look so terrified. I spent three days getting here, and it will take me the same amount of hard riding to return, so you've only twenty-four days of the hell of my company."

"You can't stay here!" Lacy looked around her little apartment crowded with her things. With her life.

"I can't stay anywhere else." His gaze followed hers. He didn't look any happier to be here than she was to have him. "What kind of guard would be posted outside the perimeter? Plus, if I remember this town, within hours everyone will know I've arrived, and it would look strange for a husband to stay at the boardinghouse when his wife sleeps alone."

The little warmth in her body turned to

ice. "You're not sleeping with me!"

For the first time, his frown spread into a smile. "I don't remember your being of such a mind the last time we were together. If memory serves, you were the one who insisted on sharing my quarters."

"The only time we were together," Lacy corrected. "The only time we will ever be together. You don't want a wife, remember?"

"I remember." He watched her carefully.

"Maybe we are divorced," she added. "Maybe I've told everyone you died."

"You haven't," he answered too matter-of-factly to be guessing. "And stop shivering with fright. I'm not here to attack you, Lacy. I'm here to protect you."

Chapter 2

Lacy wrapped a quilt around her as Walker brought in his supplies. The midnight wind blew through the open doorway, the chill no more welcome than him.

Other than the saddle and two leather bags that took up half her kitchen floor, he brought two Winchesters, a gun belt, two Colts, and several boxes of shells. Shoving aside the glass birds Lacy kept on the windowsill, Walker stacked extra rounds for the guns on the ledge. He fully loaded each rifle and positioned one near the back door and the other a few feet from the opening in the living area that led down to the shop below.

"These rooms were used for storage when I was a kid." Walker talked as he worked. "My brother and I used to play up here. If I remember right, no one can get up the front stairs from the shop without boards creaking. It's the back that will need guarding."

Lacy really didn't care what the captain figured, but it surprised her to learn Walker had a brother. The boy must have died in childhood, for her father-in-law had never mentioned him.

Watching Walker closely, she tried to stay as far away from him as the tiny rooms allowed. She didn't need her usually invisible husband to play the part of protector. If Zeb Whitaker was dumb enough to show his face in town, the locks on both doors would keep him out, the old weapon the sheriff had given her would be accurate enough to shoot the huge buffalo hunter.

Her little kitchen took on the look of a fortress. The weapons should have calmed her, made her feel safer, but panic climbed across Lacy's spine. Walker was a man she hardly knew, a man she had to fight to keep from hating. Yet suddenly he seemed to think he belonged in her quiet world.

She wanted to remind him there was no room for him in her apartment, but he didn't look as if he planned to leave. In fact, he moved about, rearranging things, shoving her quilting frames into corners, clearing papers off tables, checking the locks on windows. Despite both their names on a marriage license and the few minutes they'd once spent together, he

45

could be anyone. He could even be worse than Zeb Whitaker for all she knew.

Pulling the blanket tighter around her as if the material could somehow protect her, Lacy thought she knew all she needed to know about Captain Larson.

She knew she wanted him gone.

Two years ago when they'd met, she'd been an eighteen-year-old, frightened and alone. Now, at twenty, she was a business-woman used to making her own way, used to protecting herself.

The only thing she didn't know was how to make him leave. Fear of Zeb Whitaker seemed preferable to having Captain Walker living with her. The old buffalo hunter who had been released from jail and was believed to be heading in her direction seemed only an old nightmare she could thrust into a corner of her thoughts. But the captain, all six feet of him, was here, rearranging her life.

He grabbed a pile of papers containing all the articles she'd written over the past three months and dropped them near the kitchen stove as though he planned to use them to light the fire.

"Don't move those." She circled behind him, correcting the damage. "I'm saving those."

Walker glanced around. "Appears you save pretty much everything, wife. This place wouldn't seem so small if it were cleared out."

Lacy slammed the papers back in their original place. She wanted to tell him to go away. That he was one thing in her life she would love to clear out. "Don't touch my things," was all that anger would allow past her lips.

He glanced at her, his cold, blue eyes narrowing slightly as he studied her. "Don't worry, Lacy. If you're lucky, Whitaker will kill me and make you a widow."

"I don't want . . ." she whispered. She couldn't finish; he'd almost read her thoughts.

His laughter didn't ring true. "Don't wish me dead then, dear wife?"

"No, it's not that." She met his stare. "I wouldn't mind being a widow, but I don't like the thought of Zeb Whitaker getting close enough to me to have to step over you."

"Thanks for the consideration, but I'm not that easy to kill." Walker reached around the door and retrieved the last of his gear from the landing. The small bag looked like the old leather pouches Lacy had seen pony express riders carry years ago. The case might hold a few books, but it was too small to replace a saddlebag. One advantage of the heavy leather though might be that it looked waterproof.

She couldn't help but wonder what this last bag might hold.

When he finally closed the door, he dropped it beside the saddle and faced her. He looked more tired than angry. "Have you got anything to eat? I know it's late, but I haven't had food since I broke camp before dawn."

"You want me to cook for you at this hour?" Lacy answered before she thought about how ridiculous her question sounded. Of course he'd want food and, after all, she was his wife, and that is what wives did for their husbands. They cooked . . . among other things.

Lacy closed her eyes. She had already done the "among other things" two years ago when she demanded he bed her before she would leave his office. But once for "among other things" was enough. Never again.

She opened one eye. Her not-so-loving husband was still there and waiting for food. If he knew her cooking skills, he might decide to go to bed hungry. She thought of telling him she was probably the worst cook in the county, but he'd find out soon enough.

Walker looked like he might yell at her to step lively, as if she were one of his troops. He might be cold and tired, maybe a little worried, but he was not an easy man to feel sorry for. There didn't appear to be an ounce of softness in him. She wished he'd disappear as quickly as he'd walked into her life.

Without waiting for an answer, he knelt over one of his saddlebags and pulled out a bag of coffee. He moved to the sink and tried to pump water.

Lacy took pity on him. "The pipes may already be frozen, but there's water in the coffeepot." She'd learned the first winter that if she wanted coffee at dawn, she'd better make sure she had water drawn before sundown. The thought crossed her mind to help, but there didn't seem enough room in the kitchen for two. She slipped into the only chair at the table, her chair, and watched him.

Walker banged around in the space until he had the fire built up and coffee on, then he pulled out her supply of food from the small cool box: four eggs and a half loaf of bread. Glancing at her, he raised an eyebrow silently, asking if she minded.

Lacy shook her head, then watched as he cooked the eggs with far more skill than she could have. He drank her half jar of milk while he worked, and when he set the plate of food on the table, he silently offered her a cup of coffee.

She took the cup, careful not to touch his fingers.

He lifted the other chair from the wall and sat across the table from her.

Lacy had taken the chair down a hundred times when people visited or during the months her father-in-law stayed with her. But she still remembered the day she'd hammered nails in the wall and told her friend, Bailee, that someday her husband would come home and take the chair down; until then, she'd eat alone. She'd been fifteen when she married him by proxy. Young enough to believe in dreams of love.

The silence closed in around her. "I didn't know you had a brother. I can't remember your father ever talking of him."

"More likely, he never talked about me," Walker said between bites. "My brother was the one Dad thought would take over the business. I heard he died in a gunfight in Abilene years ago." Walker spoke without emotion, as though he barely remembered him.

When he said no more, Lacy couldn't think of anything to add. She knew little of this man and wanted to know even less than she did.

Lacy curled her feet into the chair and hugged the blanket around her as she studied Walker Larson and tried to figure out this husband of hers who acted as if he belonged in her world.

Hard, she decided. *A man molded of stone.* His body looked all muscle and bone, his eyes colder than the north wind. She tried to think of the boy his father had told her about before the old man died, but the stories had dulled with time. And many, she recalled the old man's words, were simply about "my boy," so they could have been about Walker's brother.

It bothered her that the pieces of Walker's childhood she thought she knew might be about another. For she had so few real memories of this man she'd been married to for almost five years. And now she guessed even some of them were not true.

All she could remember was the way he'd spread atop her and entered her body without one word of kindness or love. The memory of his cold belt buckle scraping against her stomach as her cheeks burned with fear and embarrassment. The anger in his words when he'd ordered her to dress and be on the stage as soon as possible.

"Stop looking at me like that, Lacy." His voice snapped in the air like a whip.

She caught herself before she shrank away and disappeared into the quilt. She would not be afraid of him. She feared too many things in her life already. "Like what?" Lacy spoke her thoughts. "Like a woman looking at a man who raped her?"

Walker stood suddenly and tossed his empty plate into the sink. "I didn't rape you."

"It couldn't be called making love, Captain." She'd called him Captain in her mind since the day they'd been together. Somehow that made what they'd done less personal. He no longer had a name.

Walker spread his arms out, gripping the counter. He lowered his head for a moment. His strong shoulders looked as if they bore a heavy weight.

Lacy wondered if she'd stepped too far. She didn't know him well enough to push, but he might as well learn now that she was not the dreamer she'd been the only time they'd met.

When he faced her, he was once more in complete control. Only his blue eyes reflected the sparks of anger her words had caused. "All right, Lacy, if that's how it's going to be, let's get it out in the open tonight. I hoped you'd wait till morning, but bad news never ages well."

He hadn't bothered to tell her how tired he was; she could see it in his gaze. He probably thought she wouldn't care any more about that than she did about him being hungry, and he'd be right. Except his last words caught her off guard. His father used to say the same thing about bad news.

She looked for a hint of the old man in the captain but could see none. The kindness of the father hadn't been inherited.

Lacy stood, tripping on the corners of her blanket. "You're right. We can wait till morning." She would just as soon wait forever. She wasn't sure she could tell him how humiliated she'd been that day he'd taken her so coldly in the back room of his office. If she told him, she'd have to relive something she'd spent two years trying to forget.

Quickly, she moved to the tiny main room. "You can sleep in here." She pointed to the small couch by the room's only window. "Or the rug is comfortable. I slept there when your father was too ill to live at the boardinghouse and moved in with me."

He followed her. "You should have written me about my father."

When she faced him once more, he lowered his voice and added, "I didn't know how he died. Sheriff Riley sent word about how you took care of him those last months, nursing him and running the paper. I thank you for that."

"There is no need." She backed toward her bedroom door. "I loved him. He was like a real father to me."

Walker probably couldn't understand how close she'd felt to the old man who'd paid her way out of jail and adopted her as his daughter-in-law. He'd treated her like a jewel, and she'd loved him for always being so kind. Staring at the son he'd always talked about, she wondered how the old man could have been so wrong about his child. He'd said his son would cherish her.

Walker took a step toward her room but stopped when she raised her hand as though to block any advance.

He growled for a second. "I only planned to make sure the window was locked," he snapped.

"I can do it." She turned away.

"Lacy?"

She looked back at him, her knuckles whitening as she gripped the door to her bedroom.

"We *will* talk about what happened between us in the morning."

Disappearing into her bedroom, she stood against the door for a moment as if preparing to brace for an attack. She wasn't sure if his words were a promise or a threat.

Slowly, she made her fingers relax from the fists they'd curled into. If the captain wanted to come into her bedroom, there would be no way to stop him, but from the sounds beyond the door, he appeared more interested in sleep.

She smiled suddenly as she drew the heavy curtains over the window and checked the lock on a window she never opened. Any intruder who could jump the fifteen feet to the window might prove to be more than even Captain Larson could handle.

After shoving the dresser against the door, Lacy crawled beneath the covers and tried to stop shivering long enough to fall asleep. But the coffee and the excitement wouldn't let her relax. She liked her quiet life. She loved running the paper and sewing at night. Why did he have to come home and ruin everything?

Home, she thought. This was her home, not his. She'd never had a place she felt she belonged, but she planned to fight for this one. She'd been moving and running most of her life, but here she'd make a stand. Not even Zeb Whitaker would frighten her away.

The echoes of a song children had made up about her drifted through her mind: "Lacy, Lacy, pretty and poor. Nobody's daughter anymore. Lacy, Lacy, dirty and wild. Just an orphan, nobody's child." She'd been passed around between neighbors so much as a child, when folks asked where she was from she always thought of saying, "The back of a wagon."

Closing her eyes, she drifted to sleep.

Walker stomped around in the tiny living room telling himself she might appreciate him being quiet, but that was probably all the ungrateful woman would appreciate. She hadn't bothered to thank him for riding three days to get to her.

He tugged off his wet boots and moved them close enough to the fire to dry by morning. She'd looked like she'd gladly kill him when he entered, and then she hadn't said three words to him before she accused him of rape. This wasn't going to be an easy assignment.

The tiny cooking stove in the kitchen was the only heat, and it hardly warmed the living space. He could guess how cold her bedroom must be with its northern exposure. Not that he cared, he reminded himself. He was here to keep her alive. No harm would come to her on his watch. He'd told her two years ago he had no room in his life for a wife, and nothing had changed.

"Nothing," he mumbled as he unpacked. Except that he couldn't forget the way she'd felt, or smelled . . . or how she'd fought back tears when he'd made her his wife in more than name only. She'd haunted him like a plague through waking and dreaming since that day. Maybe spending a few weeks with her would finally clear his mind of the memory of the way she'd felt beneath him.

He sat on what he thought was one of the chairs covered by a colorful quilt and tumbled to the floor. Rolling quickly back to his feet, he lifted the material and found only a wooden box beneath quilts pinned to look like arms of a chair. He examined the other furnishings. With the quilts they both looked like chairs, but they were simply frames and not even sturdy ones.

Marching to the couch, he lifted the layers of patchwork quilts and found only boxes stacked up beneath. They did look strong enough to hold his weight, but little more. Except for the kitchen table and chairs, and a stool, it appeared all the furniture was make-believe.

How fitting, he thought, *fake furniture in a fake marriage.*

Spreading out his bedroll on the rug, Walker tried to relax and get some sleep, but the knowledge that she probably shivered behind the closed door bothered him. Other things also worried him. He'd been sending her half of his salary since he'd learned they were married, but there was a sparseness about the way she lived that even the colorful quilts couldn't hide. The little food in the cupboard, the lack of firewood, the absence of furnishings. She was barely surviving when she should have been able to live comfortably on his money plus the amount the paper brought in.

A cat crawled out from beneath the stool and stared at him.

"Great," Walker mumbled and rolled over. "On top of everything else, she has a cat!"

Another pair of feline eyes stared at him

from a shelf, watching him as if considering him little more than prey.

"I hate cats," he mumbled and pulled his army-issue blanket over his head.

Chapter 3

Lacy awoke to the sound of a door closing. She pulled her blanket down just enough to see that she'd overslept. Not that it mattered. Duncan and Jay Boy would pick up the papers and start selling them without her help. Eli, because his joints hurt too badly to go outside in the weather, would hopefully be downstairs in time to open if anyone needed to place an ad for next week. She didn't have to be in the shop early; they all knew about the hidden key.

Holding on to as much of the covers as she could, she stood, shuffled to the window, and pulled back the heavy curtain. Never a morning person, Lacy usually had to let the sun slap her hard to pull her from sleep. She hated mornings, feeling she could easily go the rest of her life without ever seeing the sun rise.

A full day greeted her, pushing the memory of her dreams aside. From the number of people milling about, it had to be past eight. Clouds still blocked any brightness from the sun, but the threat of snow didn't keep the folks of Cedar Point from Saturday morning activities. Several farmers were already setting up their wagons in the empty space between the saloon and the sheriff's office. Unless Sheriff Riley posted notice of a hanging, everyone agreed that Saturday was trading day.

This late in the season, farmers brought in mostly vegetables from their root cellars and canned goods along with eggs and salted hams. Usually the Church Women's League had a table of handmade items for sale: crocheted pot holders and bits of lace women had donated as part of their dues. Crocheted Bible covers had been a hot seller last spring, but now the leftovers were beginning to yellow. Another month, and the lacy Christmas angels would replace the covers on the table.

The merchants on Main Street, from the saloon to the blacksmith, hauled their wares outside for display. Miss Julie Stauffer's small table by the hotel was already stacked with fresh cinnamon-raisin rolls. She was the hotel owner's daughter and a beauty. Though her rolls weren't the best, single men lined up every Saturday to

61

buy them and visit. More than one cow-hand had gotten sick eating too many.

Lacy grinned. Only the undertaker seemed left out of the trading. Even the barber had been known to take a chicken in exchange for a whole family's haircuts. Another hour, and everyone for miles around would be in town exchanging and talking. Lacy hurried to the chest of drawers and dressed as fast as she could.

Saturday excitement always tickled her. Today she'd sell her papers and find the news she'd need for next week's space. If she were lucky, several folks would be in to place small ads.

As she pulled her dress over her head, a noise came from the other room. For a second, she thought one of her cats had knocked something off one of the shelves he always crowded onto. Probably Andy. He was always climbing into small spaces between books and along windowsills.

Then she remembered she had company. How could she have forgotten?

Walker! Last night's nightmare apparently still lurked beyond the door.

A cat yelped suddenly in pain.

Without thinking of how she must look, Lacy pushed the dresser aside and ran out of her bedroom. If he'd hurt one of her cats, she'd kill him straight out and explain her actions later.

She almost collided with a wall of wool uniform before she brought herself to a sudden stop. He stood just beyond her door, his fist raised to the level of her face. For a moment, they both stared, truly surprised to see the other so close.

Lacy, recovering first, stepped back. "What are you doing? Have you hurt my cats?"

Walker looked frustrated, which she was beginning to think must be his natural expression. "I was about to knock on your door to see if you were up, but I accidentally stepped on a mangy excuse for an animal and the thing responded like a doorbell."

Lacy noticed Andy several feet away, licking his tail.

"Try not to kill my cats while you're here protecting me." She lifted her chin and stepped back, attempting to put more space between them.

The back of her head hit the doorjamb.

Walker moved closer, but Lacy stopped him. "Don't," she said with one hand raised while the other rubbed the back of her head.

"I was only —"

She stood her ground. "Don't touch me."

He retreated a safe distance. "I didn't plan to hurt you," he said. "And as for that cat, he looks like a few freight wagons have already run over him."

She glanced at Andy. Half his tail was missing along with one ear. His short fur was a mixture of black and brown, making him look muddy. She held out her arms to him, but the cat showed no interest in needing comfort from her.

"Is your head all right? Maybe you should sit down." He glanced at the furniture and looked like he was reconsidering his offer.

For the first time, she noticed he was fully dressed in his uniform, with boots newly polished. He made a striking figure in dark blue, but she knew better than anyone else that no heart beat beneath the uniform.

She stopped rubbing her sore head and tried to pull her hair into some kind of order. "You're leaving?" It was a hope more than a question.

"No. I always get up an hour before dawn." His voice lowered as he talked, as if once more pulling himself into complete control. "Since I consumed your store of food last night, I went down and restocked your supply." When she didn't thank him, he added, "I also made breakfast."

"You cooked?"

He pointed to the kitchen and waited for her to lead the way. "It's a necessary skill I learned years ago."

Lacy tiptoed into the kitchen, aware that he followed. She smelled coffee and Julie Stauffer's rolls. Food covered the tiny kitchen table. Bacon, eggs, pancakes, bread, and several jars of canned fruit.

"I didn't know what you liked." His words were matter-of-fact. "So, I picked up a little of everything as the farmers set up on the street." He pulled out her chair and waited.

"Thank you," she whispered as she took a seat.

He moved to the other chair. "I thought we could talk while we eat."

When her chin shot up, he added, "About our routine."

He passed her the eggs. "There are a few rules we need to go over to make everything run smoothly for the next few weeks. I believe in laying the groundwork first. That sets everything in order so that we both know where we stand."

She filled her plate, thankful that he

wasn't planning to talk about the last time they were together. She usually didn't eat much on Friday, knowing that she'd be going to Bailee and Carter's house for supper on Saturday. Her stomach groaned as she tasted food while waiting for him to pass more.

His words were slow, measured, while they ate, as if he feared he might frighten her again. He listed the routine he was used to and the one he expected her to follow while he was here. They'd rise before dawn and have lights out an hour after sunset. He expected the office downstairs and the apartment to be locked at all times. She could carry a key around her neck and leave a note on the door for anyone with business to knock and identify themselves. She was to go nowhere without him and, from this morning on, alter her routine so that no one on the outside could assume her whereabouts at any one time. No one, with the exception of him, was to be told her planned movements.

Lacy had finished most of her plate of food when he finally stopped talking. She leaned back and took a long drink, letting the warm coffee slide down her throat and warm her all the way to her toes. She thought of telling him to go away, but he was as much trapped here with her as she was with him. The sheriff had made sure of that with one letter. If he thought it was his duty to guard her, surely she could put up with him for a few weeks. Though following a schedule would be impossible.

"Is there any point you would like me to repeat? Everything should be clear between us from the first."

"Once your leave is over, you'll go away?"

He looked up from his coffee. "Are you aware that everything you say is a question?"

"You'll leave?" She had to know there would be an end. In her life she'd learned one hard lesson. Even hell could be endured as long as she knew that one day it would end.

"I'll leave." He took a breath as though he'd thought a great deal about his next words. "I'll also sign this building and the business over to you to do with whatever you like. I want no part of it or have any wish to ever return to this town. You took care of my father. By right it should be yours."

Lacy would have argued, but she didn't believe him. Men don't hand over their inheritances. Captain Walker would be gone in a month, and her life would go on. He had no reason to keep his word to her, but she planned to be prepared when he decided he wanted the newspaper back. Many times she'd heard promises when she'd been a child. This was one of those kinds of promises, good only until he needed money or times got hard.

"Just as long as you'll leave when the month is over. That's all I ask. I'll even try to follow your rules."

"I swear," he answered simply as if they agreed on terms.

"Two other small things I'll ask while I'm here." He set his cup down and paused.

To her surprise, the cold captain looked uncomfortable.

She twisted her hair into an untidy bun and waited for the two requests. He'd already destroyed her peace. What more could he want?

"One, I think you should leave your door open at night. I half expected to find you frozen solid this morning." When she didn't agree, he added, "I give you my word not to cross that threshold during the night, so you've nothing to fear. You can even take that cannon you call a gun to bed with you if you like."

Lacy had no intention of leaving her door open, but she waited for the next small thing he planned to bring up.

"Two." He stopped staring at her hair and added as if finishing off a minor point. "You'll get rid of those two cats within the hour."

"But —"

"The subject is not open to debate," he snapped without giving her time to even think of what to say.

Chapter 4

Walker wasn't sure what he expected, but all-out war hadn't crossed his mind. She stood up from the table, thanked him for the meal, and ordered him out.

"I've only one request, one term, one rule: leave," she yelled. "Not within the hour, but now. I don't need your protection."

He didn't stand or lower his cup of coffee until she finished; then he said as calmly as he could, "You think two dumb cats are going to save your life if that old buffalo hunter comes after you?" The woman was making no sense. "They won't save you, I will. They'll only get in the way."

She'd made it to the door before his words seemed to register. She turned suddenly, her wild hair breaking free of the few pins and flying around her shoulders. Her eyes blazed in anger.

He almost dropped his cup and reached for his Colt. Warring Apache had looked at him with less rage.

"I think," she said several times louder than he felt was necessary, "that I'd rather be here with my dumb cats and take my chances than with you. So take your guns and rules and be gone."

This wife of his was clearly not in her right mind. He'd never seen anyone so quick tempered. "I've orders to —"

"I'll write you a note excusing you from making my life hell. I'm not a child, and I'm not one of your men. And, as of right now, I'm not your responsibility!"

She was out the door before he could move. By the time he reached the landing, she'd scrambled down the steps.

Walker swore as he grabbed his hat and hurried to catch up to her. This month with her might be a blessing, he told himself. If he'd known her for more than fifteen minutes, he wouldn't have wasted so many hours thinking about her. She might have a pleasant face and a body he couldn't forget, but she had the temperament of a wounded mountain lion. The woman took fire like dry kindling when all he'd been doing was laying the ground rules so their time together would go smoothly.

That was a plan he'd best abandon, he thought as he watched her storm down the alley and onto the street.

He almost laughed, giving up all hope of routine and deciding his next plan should be one of survival.

He fell into step with her as she hurried down the street. He reached for her arm, then he thought better of touching her. After all, years ago she had confessed to killing a man. She'd yelled just now as if he were near deaf, and last night she had looked like she was considering shooting him when he first entered. There was no telling what the woman would do if he touched her.

"Go away!" she whispered.

"No," he answered as he smiled at two women passing by.

They crossed the street with her skirts flying, but Walker stayed right in step. "You forgot your coat."

"I'm not cold." She stepped on the walk but left no room for him to join her. If Walker wanted to stay beside her, he'd have to march through the mud.

Polished black boots stomped in the mud as if it were his choice of path. "Lacy, this is foolish. You have to talk to me."

She stopped suddenly and turned on him. "Correction: what you meant to say is I have to listen to you. Well, I listened, and I've heard enough. I'm not a child, Captain, so I'll thank you to stop talking to me as though I were."

She twirled before he could answer and marched into the sheriff's office. He paused, considering her words. He knew she wasn't a child. He knew that fact very well.

Walker followed her. When he stepped inside, Riley looked like he'd been caught sleeping in one of the cells. The potbellied stove warmed the room, and the smell of burned coffee filled the air. The old sheriff scrubbed his face with a tobacco-stained hand.

Before the old guy could think of anything to say, Lacy stormed toward Riley. Walker watched the sheriff's eyes dart from side to side as if looking for cover. Judging from his behavior, the old man had seen Lacy on the warpath before.

Walker stopped halfway across the room and leaned against a desk loaded with papers. He couldn't help but notice Riley didn't seem the least surprised by her anger as he tucked his shirt into his trousers and adjusted his suspenders. "Now, Lacy," he mumbled as though he'd said the words a hundred times before.

"I've changed my mind," she said to the sheriff as she pointed her finger at Walker. "I don't want to be married to that man anymore. Send me to jail. Hang me. I don't care."

The old man smiled and tried again. "Now, Lacy, don't get all riled up. You know you're not going to go to prison for confessing to killing a man when that man is still alive, and I told you when you signed the license that you could change your mind if you didn't like the match."

"Well, since I didn't have to get married . . ." She glared at Walker. "I have changed my mind. I don't want to be married to him."

Riley looked at him.

Walker folded his arms over his chest and shrugged without taking his eyes off Lacy.

The sheriff scratched his chin. "You feel the same way, son?"

Walker nodded. "I never wanted to get married in the first place."

Riley shook his head as if trying to wake himself up. "Well, I don't see any reason why this marriage can't be annulled." He shrugged. "Two out of three's not bad. Bailee loves her Carter, and Sarah's crazy about her man. It's just luck of the draw not to win every time."

He moved over to his desk. "Since the marriage was never consummated, I don't see that there should be any problem ending it. I'll get the lawyer to draw up the papers and talk to the judge when he makes his rounds next week."

He looked up at Lacy, then at Walker. "The marriage is just in name only, right?"

The color drained from Lacy's face.

Walker refused to answer. If she were going to lie, he'd say nothing, but he wouldn't be the one to deny the truth.

The sheriff raised an eyebrow and frowned. "You didn't force yourself on this little lady, did you, Captain?" He reached for the weapon he'd been using as a paperweight.

"No," Walker answered, never removing his stare from Lacy.

The color returned to her face, flooding her cheeks with fire.

"Miss Lacy." The sheriff moved to stand beside her. "Did this man hurt you in any way? Did he force you into his bed? Because if he did, there's a strong likelihood you won't have to worry about an annulment; you'll be a widow before dark."

The silence in the room was so complete Walker could hear his heart beating. All she had to do was tell Riley he'd forced her, and these might be the last beats he heard. The sheriff loved her as if she were his daughter; he'd proved that in his letter to pull Walker off duty to protect her. And from the way he held his gun, he would be willing to prove it again. The old man would take her word against his.

Walker realized a quick-tempered, crazy lady held his life in her hands.

"He didn't force me," she finally said. "I forced him."

Walker closed his eyes, almost wishing she'd lied.

The sheriff's gun rattled back on the desk as he laughed. "Well now, that's different. Why don't you tell me why you don't want to be married after you liked him well enough to take him to bed?"

Walker opened his eyes, wanting to hear the answer as well.

Lacy looked like she might cry; then she lifted her chin and stared at him. "Never mind, I'll kill him myself, Sheriff."

Walker glanced at the sheriff for help. In that second, Lacy bolted, running past him and back out into the street.

He turned to follow, but Riley stepped in his path. "What did you do, son, to get her so riled up?"

"Me?" Walker was insulted the man would even ask. "Did it ever occur to you that I might be the innocent party here? I've only been in town for a few hours. She's completely insane. If I have to live

76

with her for a month, I'll be volunteering to step in front of a firing squad."

Riley smiled. "Did you figure that out before or after you slept with her?"

"We didn't have time to sleep," Walker snapped before he realized how his words sounded. "All I want is a logical woman to deal with. Is that too much to ask?"

Riley scratched his whiskery chin. "That may be, son. Can you remember the last thing you said to her before she started yelling?"

Walker rubbed the back of his neck. "I asked for a few little changes. I told her she'd have to get rid of her cats."

"That's it." Riley slapped Walker on the back. "Everyone in town knows that Lacy's crazy about animals." He hesitated a moment. "Everyone, it seems, but her husband."

Walker offered his hand. "Thank you for your time, Sheriff."

The old man gripped his hand. "You wouldn't want to tell me about how the little lady forced you to make the marriage a real one, would you?"

"I would not." Walker turned to leave. "And don't bother asking again."

The sheriff laughed. "Oh, no bother, Captain. No bother at all."

Chapter 5

Walker marched into the street with the Sheriff's words echoing in his mind. "Everyone knows Lacy loves animals," Riley said, as if he should have known how his wife felt.

Strangers knew more about her than he did. If he planned to keep her safe, he'd better start learning . . . and learn fast. So far today he'd learned she had a temper and, to give her credit, she was honest. She could have lied to the sheriff.

He noticed her talking with a few of the farmers' wives. She was the only one without a jacket. The sun fought its way through the clouds, but the day wouldn't be warm enough to go without a coat for at least another two hours.

Since she didn't seem to be going anywhere soon, Walker crossed to the print shop, hoping to find a shawl or coat for her.

To his surprise, the print shop door stood wide open. So much for security. An old man, wearing a well-worn apron over ink-stained clothes, greeted Walker with a nod.

"Can I help you?" He whittled the end of a pencil with his pocketknife.

"I'm Captain Larson."

The old man cupped one hand to his ear. "Say what?"

"I'm Walker Larson. Lacy's husband." It sounded strange identifying himself by anything other than his rank.

The old man grinned without the burden of teeth. "Figured that. Somebody said you were in town. Usually don't see anyone in a uniform unless the supply wagon from Fort Elliot comes in to pick up something at the station." The printer's devil offered his ink-stained hand. "I'm Duncan James. Been working here setting type for close to five years. Worked for your pa before Miss Lacy took over. Mighty fine man, your pa, and mighty fine wife you got there, Mr. Larson."

Gripping Duncan's hand, Walker yelled, "Nice to meet you."

Duncan smiled and moved back to his desk. When a man worked as a printer's devil, as typesetters were called, his shoulders often rounded over time. Walker would have guessed the man's occupation, even if he'd seen him outside the shop.

Walker looked around the shop. Not much had changed since he'd been a boy. The furniture and machines appeared a little more worn. Just behind the long, high counter spread the main work area of the shop with a storage room to the left and a tiny office to the right. There were several tables cluttered with supplies and lamps hanging from wide beams to offer good light if anyone had to work after dark. The large windows across the front of the shop provided enough sunlight for daytime.

Walker frowned. The windows also allowed passersby to see almost the entire shop and anyone who might be working inside.

Crossing to the office, he wasn't shocked to find it as messy with papers and bills as the apartment had been with quilts and books. This had to be Lacy's domain. He was starting to recognize his wife's trademark.

Sweaters and old shirts, probably used as dusters during the printing work, weighed down a hat tree in the corner. Walker dug through and managed to untangle a jacket. He folded it over his arm and headed back to the street, wondering if he could possibly get his wife organized in less than a month. If she started today, she might be able to have her office and quarters livable by the time he left.

Somehow he doubted she intended to make the effort. After what she'd said to Sheriff Riley, he wouldn't be surprised if she was taking up a collection to have him shot at high noon. With his luck, the folks in Cedar Point would go along with her campaign. He'd left few friends behind when he'd ridden out of town at seventeen.

Her laughter reached him before he saw her in the crowd of people. He liked the sound, realizing that a woman's laughter was something missing for most of his life. He had no memory of his mother, and women at the frontier forts were few.

She stopped laughing when she saw him moving toward her, but she didn't dart away. She simply stood, watching him as he lifted her jacket and placed it over her shoulders.

"Thank you."

He figured he'd be lucky if he had five seconds before she threatened to kill him again so he said, "The cats stay."

Lacy raised an eyebrow. "Did the sheriff tell you to say that?"

"No. He told me how much they matter to you. I still feel you'd be safer without them in the house. It's easy to blame a noise on a cat when it might be an intruder. But I can work around that problem if they're important to you."

She tilted her head and studied him as if she didn't know whether to believe him or not. She didn't seem the least bit grateful that he'd conceded, but he'd long ago become an expert at not allowing his frustrations to show.

He offered his arm.

She hesitated, then took it.

They walked down the street until they were far enough from the crowd not to be overheard. "We can work this out," Walker said as if he believed his own words.

"I don't take orders, and I don't follow schedules. You're not stepping into my life, my world, and changing everything just because of something you've been ordered to do. You're free to leave. I'm safe enough here in town. Zeb Whitaker probably forgot all about me years ago."

He thought of arguing, but he wasn't sure what she'd say. The last thing he wanted to do was go back to the fort and explain to his commander why he couldn't stay around and protect his wife for one month. Or worse yet, leave Lacy unprotected. If Zeb Whitaker got to her, he'd never forgive himself for neglecting his duty.

And that's all she was, he told himself. His duty. A duty he never asked for. But he was a man who'd never turned his back on what he knew he had to do. If he had to get along with her in order to stay and complete his mission, he would.

"All right. No orders, but I stay until my time is over." He accepted her terms and wondered if she'd ever heard of the word *compromise*. "One rule for each of us is all I ask. You allow me to protect you, and I'll try not to interfere with your life."

"Fair enough."

He placed his hand over hers as they declared a silent truce. Then, without a word, they continued walking down the street. Lacy introduced him to almost everyone they passed. A few of the people said they remembered him as a kid, but most had moved to town in the years since he'd been gone.

Lacy calmed as they moved along. She'd never had a handsome man to walk with. Not one day of her life. Captain Walker might be heartless, but one thing she couldn't deny: he was handsome in his blue wool uniform. She noticed people who'd never paid her any mind, like the ladies on the second floor of the saloon, were now looking her over. With Walker by her side, some of the men seemed more respectful, more formal, and a few of the women giggled at everything he said as if it were funny.

Walker asked her advice about which fruits and vegetables to buy, then paid for them without really asking her if she wanted or needed them. Slowly, she became aware of what he was doing. He bought one thing, sometimes more, from each vendor. In a very simple way, he was meeting everyone, making friends, paying his respects.

Only, she knew his plan would fail when he got to the church ladies' table. Lacy knew most of the women, but she was not one of their circle. She'd learned from experience that they weren't accepting of outsiders. They had always been polite but never friendly to her.

With a smile, Walker changed all that. He bragged on their work, even buying one of the crocheted Bible covers he swore his sergeant's wife would love. He had them all beaming proudly that finally someone had noticed their efforts. When he suggested they make aprons for men, the ladies of the church circle laughed so hard, folks turned to look from half a block away.

Lacy stood in awe, wondering who had taken over her husband's body. Could this be the same man who had issued one order after another since arriving? She'd seen men who were smooth talking, usually salesmen who passed through from time to time, but nothing like Walker. By the time he left the church ladies' table he could have run for mayor and won.

She expected his bossy, rude manner to return when he talked with the men. It never did. He asked each man about his work or for facts related to the town. His plan seemed so simple. He paid each man respect, showed interest in whatever they did, and in return they gave him respect back. By the time they'd finished walking the street, her anger had cooled, and Lacy decided not to kill him. If she could just put up with him for a month, folks might be a lot friendlier toward her.

She could almost see the future, everyone stopping by to ask how Walker was doing, talking about how much they enjoyed meeting him and asking when he'd be coming back. Of course then she'd have to look sad and tell them she didn't know.

Several times Walker offered his arm to her, which she accepted awkwardly at first, but she grew used to him standing next to her. He switched sides from time to time, always putting his body nearer the street. He also had a habit of brushing his hand over hers when he was talking to someone and not even looking at her. Lacy guessed he checked to make sure she was still there.

They walked back to the print shop and relieved Duncan so he could go home for lunch. The other employee, Eli, as he often did when the temperature dropped, hadn't bothered to show up. The old printer was a thin man the weather seemed to pass right through. He complained of the heat all summer and the cold all winter.

Jay Boy reported in and collected the last stack of papers. He said sales were going great for some reason; even the church ladies bought a few copies. Lacy told him to head on home when he ran out of papers; his mother would be needing him to do chores.

When Lacy finally thought to introduce him to her husband, Walker stood and offered his hand as if Jay Boy were a full-grown man.

To her shock, Walker asked for a favor. "It seems I bought way too many vegetables without realizing Lacy has no root cellar. Do you think your mom would be willing to take some off my hands? I'd really appreciate it."

Jay Boy nodded, looking at the bag. "She can make a great soup with all this."

When he'd left, Lacy faced Walker. "That was nice of you."

"He's a hard worker."

"That he is." Lacy felt awkward, suddenly aware that she was once more alone with this strange man. "I've work to do." She turned and went into her office, thankful that he didn't follow. "I have friends I usually visit on Saturday, but they won't be expecting me if the weather gets worse," she commented over her shoulder.

"Will they mind if I come along?" he asked as he leaned against the doorjamb.

Lacy thought of Carter, who never welcomed strangers, and wondered if the big, silent man would let Walker on his property. Even after being married to her friend Bailee for almost five years, Lacy still wasn't completely comfortable around the man. He watched everyone as if trying to figure out when they might try to kill him. The only person he thawed around was his wife. Lacy had seen it from the first: Bailee centered Carter's world, and the strange thing was, he did the same thing for her.

"They'll let you in." Lacy finally remembered Walker waited for an answer. "But I wouldn't make any quick moves around Carter. He doesn't warm easily to strangers."

"How long did he take to relax around you?"

Lacy smiled. "I'm still waiting."

Walker's frown almost made her laugh.

As the afternoon passed, she glanced through the open door of her office to see him sitting on a stool pulled up to the counter. After watching her a few times, he started taking ad orders without calling for her when someone walked in. She had no idea if he knew what he was doing, but he couldn't be any worse than Duncan, who left out every other word.

The folks who came stayed longer to talk than they usually did, but Lacy noticed that Walker's strength lay in encouraging them, not in talking himself.

By midafternoon, snow began to fall, and all traffic vanished. Walker stoked the stove and bent over old issues of the paper as if finding them fascinating. When she walked out of her office, she noticed he had removed his coat and looked totally relaxed. A huge pile of wood had been stacked by the fire. Lacy had no idea when he'd left to buy wood.

She stretched. "I'm about finished. You can go on up if you like. You don't have to stay here. I'm perfectly —"

She forgot what she'd been about to say when she noticed the rifle leaning against his knee and his long Colt pulled from its holster and placed a few layers beneath the paper he appeared to be reading.

"What's wrong?" Maybe he was just being cautious.

He didn't meet her gaze. His head still bent slightly toward the paper, but his gaze fixed on something beyond the windows. "Someone is watching us from across the street," he said so softly he might have been reading the words to himself. "I saw the reflection off a rifle barrel just before the sun faded. The snow's too thick to make him out, but once in a while I see a movement in the gap between the hotel and the mercantile."

Lacy fought the urge to turn and see for herself. *No one is there.* If she didn't look, she didn't have to believe. He was just trying to frighten her.

"In a few minutes it will be full dark, and

we need to be away from these windows."
Walker slowly turned the page of the
paper.

Lacy didn't argue. If they stayed downstairs longer, she needed to light the lamps.
With the lamplight, the shop would glow
through the darkness outside.

As she turned to close her office door,
she heard the sudden scrape of Walker's
stool against the wooden floor. A second
later, Walker flew into her, knocking her to
the floor. Just before she hit, he rolled,
taking the blow of their fall against his
shoulder.

Before she could scream, a bullet hit the
window and shattered the pane over them
like fine glass snow. Walker's arm covered
her face for a few heartbeats, then he was
up, pulling her with him toward the stairs
that led to the apartment.

Another shot rattled off the iron of the
printing press. Walker moved so quickly,
Lacy's feet barely touched the floor as she
ran behind him.

They made it to the landing where the
steps turned. A blast of icy air chilled the
shop as Lacy fought to breathe.

He stopped, pulling her down with him
to sit on the first step past the landing, out
of sight of the windows. "Stay here," he or-

dered, then turned without waiting for an argument and went back down the stairs.

Several minutes passed. The shop grew dark. She listened closely and thought she heard him walking around downstairs. It crossed her mind that he made no more noise than a cat on the creaky old floor of the shop.

Huddling against the railing, Lacy shivered from cold as well as fear. She never really believed, not for a minute, that Zeb would truly come after her. Not until now.

How could the old buffalo hunter think she had his gold? He must have come straight from prison. But why her? Lacy didn't want to think about the answer, but it whispered in the snowy wind. Zeb had come here first because she'd been the easiest to find. Because he must know that she lived alone, and until last night, Zeb Whitaker would have been right.

If Walker hadn't been there, she would have worked longer. She would have lit the lamp. She would already be dead.

Another round splintered into the wood below, and somewhere beyond the store, gunfire echoed in the night.

Lacy pushed harder against the wall as if she could disappear. The old Colt she'd told Walker would be all the protection she needed was half a floor away and of no use to her. If she climbed the steps, she'd be out in the open on the landing leading to her apartment door. She'd be in full view of the windows. All she could do was wait.

Only silence below. Silence and the wind.

"Walker!" Sheriff Riley's voice sounded from somewhere in the street. "You and Lacy all right?"

Lacy stood and peered through the banister, but the town beyond her broken windows seemed only a blur of blowing snow.

"We're all right!" Walker yelled back.

"Then lower your weapon," Riley answered back, "we're coming in."

The shop filled with men. They materialized from the darkness and snow. A few used the door, but most just stomped their way through the broken windows. Willard, the mercantile owner, carrying a rifle like he held his broom, led the way. Next came Joel, the new deputy, who patted his holstered gun to make sure it was there. A few cowhands who always played poker in the window of the saloon rushed in followed by Mosely, the livery owner, whose smell would remain long after he departed.

Lacy watched them relax as they all talked at once. She noticed their weapons moved to their shoulders or were lowered to point to the floor, but not one laid his gun down. These townsmen, who only told stories of wars long ago, had picked up their weapons as easily as an old knight might lift his armor and step back into a role he once lived.

Walker circled among the men, his men now, asking questions, collecting details of who saw what. Sheriff Riley seemed far more interested in getting warm than solving any crime, and his deputy watched Walker, picking up tips he'd store until needed later.

She tried to understand what they were saying, but she couldn't make herself go downstairs. The knowledge that she really was in danger made her shake more than the cold. And somehow, while he'd appeared to be visiting with the men earlier, Walker had set up his troops. They might not have caught their man tonight, but Zeb Whitaker would never again assume she was unprotected.

In what seemed like only a few minutes, the men patched the window with boards, and Walker thanked each one. She heard him locking the door and heading up the stairs.

"Lacy?" he said as he found her

clenching the railing with both hands. "Lacy? Are you all right?"

She didn't look at him. She'd been playing what-if in her mind. What if she'd been shot? What if he'd been killed? A part of her feared that if she glanced up, she'd see blood.

Without a word, he pried her fingers free, lifted her as if she were a child, and carried her up the rest of the steps. Once in the tiny apartment, he wrapped her in a quilt and sat her down in one of the kitchen chairs while he built the fire and made sure all the doors were locked.

When he returned to her, she was still shivering.

"Lacy?" He frowned.

She didn't turn. Didn't want him to see how frightened she'd been or how big a fool she'd played for not believing first the sheriff, then Walker, that there really was a danger. It had been so many years since Zeb had grabbed her and tried to kidnap her. She'd only been fifteen then, and even now the memories were more nightmare than reality.

"Lacy!" Walker snapped finally, demanding her attention as he pulled her to her feet.

She didn't answer. She was lost in a

memory of a rainy dawn . . . of Zeb Whitaker's hands grabbing at the front of her dress . . . of knowing that she wasn't strong enough to fight him as he pulled her toward the wagon and told her of what he planned to do with her. Of how he'd throw her away like trash once she was all used up.

When she didn't look at Walker, he wrapped another blanket around her and hurried to the sink to make coffee.

But the water pump was frozen, and neither of them had remembered to set out water earlier.

Lacy's teeth chattered not from the cold now, but from the returning of a nightmare. Zeb had slapped her so hard she was afraid to cry. She'd waited on the cold, rainy morning, knowing that she was about to die. Wishing that she'd die before he made good on his threats.

Walker shoved another stick of wood into the little stove as if it could somehow warm the room instantly. He walked back to Lacy and, after a moment's hesitation, wrapped his arms around her, blankets and all.

Lacy pulled away. But his hold only increased. Feeling trapped, she fought to free herself, kicking and pushing with all her strength, but the blanket and his arms wouldn't let her move. Somewhere in the back of her mind she knew he was only trying to help, but that didn't stop the panic as the memories flooded her thoughts.

She struggled, fighting harder. "Put me down!" she screamed. "Let me go!"

He dropped her so suddenly, she almost tumbled to the floor.

"I was only trying to help you get warm." He dug his hand through his dark hair, erasing any order. "You don't have to yell as if I were attacking you. I feared you might go into shock."

Lacy stumbled on the corners of the quilts as she moved backward until she hit the wall. "Don't ever grab me like that again. I don't like to be grabbed."

"But . . ." He didn't finish.

Lacy straightened, knowing that she was being unreasonable. She'd been near panic from the gunfire and the knowledge that someone really wanted to kill her. Walker had only been trying to help. But he shouldn't have captured her as if he planned to shake reason into her.

Focusing all her anger on him, she mumbled her feelings.

Almost at the door, Walker turned to

face her. "What did you say?"

There was no kindness in the man, she decided. No compassion. He was simply annoyed at her behavior. "I said." She glared at him. "Never touch me again, Captain."

Anger and confusion flickered in his eyes for only a moment before he bowed slightly. When their gaze met again, the cold formality of his stare was all she could see. They both knew she was overreacting and he was refusing to react at all.

"Don't worry, madam, I'll not make that mistake again."

Chapter 6

Walker stomped down the steps to the print shop. He couldn't remember how long it had been since he'd been so angry with himself. Grabbing Lacy and holding her off the ground wasn't the way to deal with a woman who'd just been frightened half to death. He wasn't even sure what he'd thought to accomplish other than to get her to stop shivering. Maybe he just wanted to let her know she was safe, and he thought she'd feel that way in his arms? Maybe he hoped to convince her she wasn't alone?

She'd rattled him so badly, he couldn't remember what his intentions were, but one thing was for sure, he hadn't accomplished any of those goals.

Far from being able to say he understood women, he had terrified Lacy when he'd hoped to calm her. Judging from the volume of her scream, he'd scared her into full panic. Half the town probably heard her yell.

"Add one more thing about your wife that you don't know," he mumbled and moved through the darkened shop. "Maybe she's just plain crazy." From their few times together he had little proof otherwise.

Except the townsfolk seemed willing to come to her aid. A few had even issued veiled threats that he'd better work a little harder at being a good husband. With the exception of the church ladies, everyone he met today reminded him of what a wonderful wife he had. Even dirty old Mosely mumbled that he was keeping his good eye on Walker while he was in town.

Walker folded into one of the cane chairs pulled near an old potbellied stove that clanked while it heated. Remembering back, Lacy seemed more reluctant to talk to the churchwomen than they did to her. He almost had the feeling she thought about each word before she spoke, which made no sense. Lacy had no reason to be afraid of the old biddies. As editor of the paper, she would be in a much more powerful position than the crocheting group.

Walker leaned on the counter and watched the snow through the cracks in the boards where windows had been earlier. He was not sure he ever wanted a wife, but he was certain that the last thing he needed this month was a wife who hated him. Somehow he needed to stop doing everything wrong and do something right in her eyes.

The one-eared cat he'd seen the night before walked across the counter, brushing his tail against his hand. Absently, Walker patted his head. "I take it back. I don't hate cats. At least, they rank above snakes and rats. But don't waste your time trying to get on my good side. I don't have one."

The cat purred, as if happy to hear the news.

"Having a cat might even be better than having a wife, though I've never had either until now."

The cat moved on down the counter, looking bored with his rambling.

Walker collected an armful of firewood and headed back up the stairs. No sense putting off talking to Lacy. If he had any hope of understanding her, they had to start somewhere.

He wasn't surprised to find her huddled at the kitchen table with a notepad in one hand and a pencil in the other. A tiny pair of reading glasses perched on her nose.

Blankets still wrapped around her shoulders like armor. Neither of them spoke as he dropped the firewood in the bin.

He couldn't understand why getting along with Lacy was so hard. Somewhere there had to be a middle ground. She needed him, and he'd been ordered to protect her. He'd always thought of himself as a reasonable man. He doubted one man who'd ever served under him would hesitate if asked to do so again. Dealing with a woman couldn't be that much different. He just needed to find a common place they could start from.

He reached into the storage drawer and pulled out a jar of milk and two apples, then sat down across the table from her. While she wrote, he poured them each a cup of milk and sliced the apples onto a plate. When she didn't look at him, he collected cheese and bread and added both to the meal spread between them. He was a man used to fending for himself and hoped she might accept the light supper as a peace offering.

Finally she stopped writing and propped the notebook between them. She'd printed the number twenty-four boldly on the first page.

He waited, guessing it safer to let her

make the first move.

She removed her glasses and folded them into her pocket. Her brown eyes were huge in the lamp's light as she stared at him. "One month," she said calmly. "It took you three days to get here, and it will take you three days to return to your post. That leaves twenty-four."

He agreed, thinking this an odd start to a conversation, but at least they were communicating.

She ripped the first sheet from her pad and crumpled the page marked with the twenty-four. "Twenty-three now."

Walker didn't bother to look at the pad. He knew what would be written on the next page. He sliced a piece of bread and handed it to her, then lifted his cup of milk. "To the countdown," he said.

She tapped her cup on his and drank.

They ate in silence. The kitchen warmed. She tried to put up an act, but he could sense her fright. He leaned back, allowing as much room between them as the small space permitted. "We really don't need the notebook, Lacy. Neither of us is likely to forget."

Dark walnut eyes met his. "I learned when I was a child moving around from job to job, sometimes only earning my keep, that I could endure anything if I knew it would end."

"I swear to you that in twenty-three days I'll ride out of here. This will end."

She nodded, accepting his word.

"I didn't mean to frighten you." A half-wit could have seen that what he did after the gunfire scared her more than the shooting. The woman needed to wear a sign that said, Touch at Your Own Peril.

She took a long breath. "I know."

"Maybe it would help if we understood each other a little better." He wasn't sure anything would help, but they couldn't go around yelling for three more weeks. "In prison camps during the war, there would always be a line, sometimes it was a trench, sometimes nothing more than a rope, but every soldier knew that was the point of no return. The kill line."

She raised an eyebrow in question.

"Any prisoner who crossed that point was shot, no questions, no warning. That's what I need with you. I need to know where I'm not to cross."

She watched him closely.

"Help me out a little, Lacy. We're living in such close quarters I need to know where the kill line is."

Her eyes closed. She shrank into the

blanket. For a moment he thought she might not answer. If she didn't give him some guidelines, he guessed he'd just have to go around making her mad or angry until she finally turned that old Colt the sheriff gave her on him. At the rate he was going, it would only be a matter of hours.

When she spoke, her voice was little more than a whisper. "Before I was ten, I lived with my mother on a little farm a half mile outside of town. We mostly raised chickens and sold the eggs to anyone passing."

He leaned forward as she continued, "My mother's mother was from Hungary, and even though my mom was born in Louisiana, she didn't speak English until she was almost grown, so her words sounded foreign to most folks. My father left the day I was born."

She stopped as if expecting him to say something. When he didn't, she continued. "Because my mother talked different and dressed as her mother had, everyone in the county thought she was a witch, so no one visited with us much. She died when I was ten."

She relaxed a little and took a bite of apple. "I guess you got a right to know, folks have a way of dying around me. All my family's gone." She looked so serious, he almost laughed.

"So is mine, Lacy, but I don't consider it a curse following me. Tell me about how your mother talked."

She sat still, considering his request. Walker waited.

"I saw nothing strange in the way she talked, but sometimes folks said some mean things to us. Once a man found blood in an egg we'd sold him. He said my mother had cursed him." Lacy glanced up, meeting Walker's eyes as she remembered. "I couldn't tell anything happened to him, except he got drunk and killed most of our chickens that night."

Walker imagined Lacy as a child trying to understand. "Did you mother press charges? I've been reading about the law, and I think she could have."

Lacy nodded. "The sheriff said since he didn't steal the hens, he couldn't be found guilty. We didn't know anyone else to turn to. The man went free, but we almost starved that winter."

She looked at him now with her big dark eyes liquid with unshed tears, and he fought the urge to touch her. He remembered the way he'd been drawn to her the first time he saw her, even before he knew she was his wife on paper.

Lacy lifted her chin slightly. "About me, my mother would have said, a nightmare breathes in the shadows of my world."

Without another word, she left the room.

An hour later Walker stood on the tiny back porch landing off the kitchen and smoked the last of his thin cigars. He tried to figure out what she'd been trying to tell him. He told himself he didn't like her, didn't care if he ever saw her again, but he'd never in his life felt so protective toward someone.

The icy wind whirled down the alleyway from the livery to the north. Walker turned his collar up to the chill, feeling bad weather riding full speed toward Cedar Point. He was used to cold. Used to the weather. Even used to being shot at from time to time. But he wasn't sure he'd ever get used to Lacy. Her frightened stare had turned his gut over with a shovel. All the anger he'd felt toward her had vanished when he realized someone just beyond the window took aim at her. And when she'd told him the story of her mother, he wished he could have gone back in time and protected her.

After not eating enough to keep a bird alive, she went to bed, closing her bedroom door, though he'd told her not to. He'd even heard the scrape of what must have been her dresser, blocking him out.

Not that he would cross into her room after swearing he wouldn't. But she didn't trust him, and that bothered him even more than the fact that she was afraid of him.

"Captain?" Sheriff Riley's call rattled from the bottom of the stairs. "Your wife kick you out along with the cats?"

Walker smiled. He liked the old sheriff despite his meddlesome ways. Part of Riley still thought him a boy. "I didn't think she'd take much to my smoking in the house." Walker walked down the stairs.

Riley laughed. "Last I heard, she didn't take much to you at all. I just dropped by to see if she's killed you yet."

"Not yet," Walker answered, as if not sure he had long to wait. "We did manage to have supper without a fight."

Riley nodded. "That's some progress."

Walker didn't plan on standing in the cold and talking about his marital problems, so he changed the subject. "Anyone spot Zeb Whitaker?"

Riley shook his head. "I've had both my deputies walking the streets for over an hour. Abe said his feet are so cold his toes are falling off and rolling around in his boots. He couldn't find even one person who saw a big man riding out tonight. But that old buffalo hunter is around. I swear I can smell him."

"They found nothing," Walker said as a statement.

"Nothing," Riley echoed, "but a few tracks, already mostly covered up by new snow. Whoever stood between the buildings planned on doing some damage, if not murder. He had a horse waiting at the end of the alley and was gone before we could track him from the corner where he shot."

Riley shook his head. "Maybe you should think of getting Lacy out of here."

"To where? She'd be no safer on the road. Fort Elliot might be a good place, we could be there in a day, but she'd never go with me."

"She's got a few friends —"

"I'll not put others in harm's way," Walker said before the sheriff could finish.

"I can't argue with that. Both the other two women who came into my office confessing to the murder of Zeb Whitaker five years ago are married with families now. They're in a lot safer locations than Lacy, so I'm guessing he's heading here first. The only friend Lacy has, that might take her in, is a girl down in Childress. They call her Two Bits. But she's just a kid, even if she did inherit an old house by the tracks a few months ago. She could let Lacy stay with her, but then neither one would probably be safe. Her place is off by itself."

"Lacy stays with me," Walker said, remembering the fear in her brown eyes. If he had to give up sleep for a month, he'd protect her.

Riley nodded and touched his hat in farewell. "Stay warm. We're in for a bad storm tonight." The sheriff walked away, a mangy alley dog following behind him.

Walker climbed the stairs and stepped back into the apartment kitchen as quietly as he could. The notepad still lay on the tiny table with twenty-three marked on the top page.

"Lacy stays with me," Walker said again. "For as long as necessary." He flipped the notepad over. He didn't need to be reminded of his duty.

Chapter 7

The cold woke Lacy before dawn. She felt as if she were sleeping in a mound of snow. Not even the blankets warmed her. Wrapping the covers around her, she forced her stiff body to move toward the kitchen, which she hoped would still be warm from last night's fire in the stove. The air seemed frozen, and she took shallow breaths, pressing her nose against the top of the quilt.

As soon as she opened her bedroom door, warmth rushed in. For a moment she stood, letting the heated air caress her face. Blinking, she peered around the shadowy living space covered with quilts and hand-me-down books from her father-in-law. Home, too small of a word to describe how this place wrapped around her, welcomed her, made her feel like she belonged somewhere on the planet.

The low, steady breathing of someone sleeping reached her ears, and Lacy realized she wasn't alone. Walker slept by the door leading to the shop. One of his hands lay outside his army blanket touching the rifle at his side. The barrel of the weapon pointed toward the kitchen door. The odd leather bag he'd brought in when he'd arrived was open near the lamp, and a book lay propped up as if he'd read himself to sleep.

Lacy wondered how many times he'd slept with the rifle and the book so near. She tiptoed across the room and slipped into the kitchen. As she turned up the low-burning lamp on the table, she smiled, thankful Walker had stoked the fire in her little stove sometime during the night and not let it go out. He'd also brought in two buckets of snow. One rested on the back corner of the stove; the other, still icy, sat near the sink waiting to be heated.

Glancing back to make sure he slept, she quickly put on coffee using the cold water. She collected her things from the bedroom and then placed the warm bucket of melted snow in the far corner of the kitchen. Realizing the captain could see her should he awake, she hooked a thin old blanket between two nails. Then she ducked behind the blanket curtain and stepped into her newly made dressing room.

The curtain had gaps on either side, but at least it offered her some privacy. During the months Walker's father had stayed with her, the worn blanket provided the only space for her to change since she insisted he use the bedroom. Last winter, she'd sometimes used the blanket to bathe because the wool kept out drafts and hugged in warmth.

A tub bath would have been impossible in this weather, so she began to bathe one part of her body at a time using a sliver of the soap her friend Bailee made with peach blossoms and a soft washcloth that had survived a thousand washings. Lacy tied her hair back, opened her gown, and slowly washed until she reached her legs. Bundling up the hem of her gown, she tied it at her hips and continued to wash. The warm air dried her skin, and the smell of coffee drifted around the room as the pot bubbled to life on the stove.

When she finished bathing, she let her hair tumble and reached for her brush. With long strokes she worked the tangles from her hair. She leaned forward and let her hair fall as she pulled the brush from the back of her scalp forward. The thick brown mass floated around her shoulders. For the first time since the captain had arrived, Lacy felt order slipping back into her life.

When she finished her hair and started to button her gown, she thought she heard a sound. Lacy froze and listened. A meow came from the other side of the blanket.

Lacy stretched and peeked over the blanket. Andy pawed at the back door and meowed again.

She relaxed, held her nightgown closed, and tiptoed over to let the cat out. Andy made it a foot before he realized the snow was too deep to go about his business. Lacy laughed. Leaning back behind the door, she lifted the only coat on the hook. The captain's coat.

Wrapping it around her, she stretched back out the door and brushed off most of the snow from the long flowerpot on one side of her small porch.

She reached backward into the kitchen and grabbed the bucket, now full of soapy water, and poured it over the side railing, then refilled it with fresh-fallen snow. Once the snow melted, the water wouldn't be clean enough to use for coffee, but she could wash dishes with it, and melting snow seemed far more practical than waiting for the pipes to thaw.

Dancing quickly back inside before her

feet froze, she peeked around the wall separating the two rooms to make sure Walker still slept. He'd rolled to his back, and she heard him snoring slightly, his hair in his eyes. He didn't seem all that stiff and proper asleep.

She laughed. He almost looked human.

Quickly, she removed his coat and placed it back in place, guessing he would not approve of her using his things.

She debated taking her clothes back to her bedroom to change, but the warmth behind the wool blanket won out. As fast as she could, Lacy slipped into her shift and cotton drawers, then her petticoat and her dress. Last, she laced the heavy wool vest over her blouse. Not only would it keep her warm, Lacy thought, it did a good job of hiding the fact that she was a little heavy on top.

On days like this she'd often wished she had enough money to buy material for a proper wool dress, but the thick cotton was warm enough with the vest. She had her jacket downstairs if she got cold and wool stockings her friend Sarah sent her last Christmas. Lacy warmed her toes close to the stove before slipping on the stockings, enjoying the way they wrapped around her legs to just above her knee, then tied with a thin black ribbon.

After pulling her hair back, she began breakfast. By the time she heard Walker moving in the main room, the food was almost ready.

She heard him stomp into his boots, then walk across the room. Her hand shook slightly when he filled the passage. Even though she'd heard him coming, he looked so out of place in her home, he still startled her. The dark beard covering his face had spread during the night, no longer cut in clean lines along his jaw. He rubbed his eyes with his thumb and first finger and appeared half asleep.

"Want some breakfast?" She smiled, thinking the captain didn't seem nearly as powerful just after he woke.

Walker glanced around. "I'd like to wash up, first." He reached for his saddlebags and turned to the back door. "If I remember, there's a washstand behind the hotel."

"Wait," she said a moment before he turned the knob.

Walker glanced back at her, and she realized he fully intended to step out in the blizzard with nothing on but his trousers and undershirt. If he'd collected the buckets full of snow, he already knew the weather. And since he wasn't talking of using them, he must also know that she'd bathed.

She glanced at the blanket, wondering just how much he could see from the living area.

"I'm melting more snow. You could wash up here if you like. If there was any water in the jugs behind the hotel, it'll be frozen by now." Before he could answer, she pulled a clean towel down from the shelf and pointed toward the corner where the blanket still hung between the nails. If he could not comment on her using the water he'd collected, she could offer her space.

Walker raised an eyebrow.

Lacy tried not to think about the intimacy of the act she suggested. "I used to hang the blanket when your father lived here. Otherwise I had no place to change clothes, since he slept in the bedroom."

"Very effective. Would you mind if I made use of your private dressing room, madam?"

"No." She grinned, realizing he understood about the corner being just hers. She stepped out of his way. "I'll finish breakfast."

Walker pulled back the corner of the

blanket and bent to step behind it, but his head and shoulders rose above the curtain. Again, he glanced at her with a question in his blue eyes. A question and a hint of laughter.

"It's all right. I've seen your shoulders bare before."

The second the words left her mouth, Lacy wished she could pull them back. She turned quickly, not wanting him to read her thoughts in her eyes or see the fire in her cheeks. If he said a word about the day they'd met, she swore she'd kill him. Lacy couldn't believe she'd mentioned it so casually.

Thankfully, Walker remained silent.

She heard him pull a chair beneath the blanket. When she finally glanced in his direction, he was busy unbuttoning the collarless undershirt he had slept in.

Lifting the still-cold water, she handed it around the blanket.

"Thanks." His hand laced through her fingers to take the pail.

"I'm sorry the water's not warm yet. I'm afraid I used the bucket you left on the back of the stove."

"It doesn't matter," he answered as one of his boots dropped. "I'm accustomed to cold water."

Another boot dropped, but Lacy didn't look in his direction.

She turned her full attention to breakfast, trying not to think about how warm and hard his chest had felt that day when he'd pressed it to hers and how his heart had pounded against her own.

When she peeked at the blanket, she noticed his trousers tossed across it. Then his undershirt. Then his long johns.

She almost let the eggs burn as she realized he must be nude only a few feet away. He hadn't even been nude the day they'd met. The day he'd taken her virginity.

The blanket moved as he bumped it.

Lacy tried hard to forget how near he stood.

"The water smells like peaches," he said as if trying to break the silence between them.

"Some of my soap must have clung to the sides. I didn't have any water left to rinse it out."

"I don't mind. When I'm on the trail, the bucket I use to wash waters the horses before it gets to me. Believe me, peach blossoms are a much better smell."

Lacy grinned. His back was to her, his shoulders muscular and tan. Though he was lean, there was nothing frail about him. With the lamp still burning on the table behind him, she could see the shadow of his body outlined on the blanket. Lacy told herself to look away, but she couldn't.

Then she reddened, realizing that if he'd been awake, he could have seen her outline. Thankfully, he'd been asleep, and tomorrow she'd make sure the lamp was on the other side of the blanket before she dressed.

As he pulled a clean undershirt over his head, he said, "Mind if I wait for the water to heat before I shave?"

It surprised her that he'd even ask; then she realized he was going out of his way to be polite. He was doing what he'd done at the market, acting the perfect gentleman. It wouldn't work on her, of course, but she gave him credit for trying.

"I'll put another bucket on to warm." If he could play the game, so could she. Maybe the days would pass faster if they tried to be civil to one another. The politeness of strangers would suit her fine.

He ate breakfast in his clean undershirt and trousers, but he had taken the time to buff his boots before sitting down. As soon as they finished, he shaved behind the blanket and reappeared with his uniform buttoned to his throat.

"Will we be attending church? I've no objection to accompanying you."

"No." Lacy thought of telling him she wore her best dress now, and it was barely good enough for work. Or she could tell him she swore she'd never step foot in a church years ago when they didn't want her mother to be buried in their cemetery. But she didn't know this husband of hers well enough to tell him anything. "I doubt there will be many, even in town, who attend service today."

Walker leaned against the window in the living space and stared out at Main Street covered in snow. "So, Lacy, what do you do on days like this?" He already looked bored, and they'd just started the day.

She smiled. "When weather keeps me in, I quilt or go down and work in my office. Most Saturday evenings I go to my friend, Bailee's farm. There I play with her children and visit. She's always cooking so there's lots of food. Once it gets dark, her husband Carter reads to us all. For a man who never talks, he has a great voice for reading. When the kids start falling to sleep, I help carry them up to a little loft Carter built when he added the big kitchen onto the house."

She knew she rattled on, but it seemed better than silence. As she talked she pulled out her quilting frame. "I sleep in the bedroom below the children at their house. Bailee even calls it Lacy's room, like it will always be there for me if I need it."

When Walker didn't comment, she continued, more to break the silence than in any belief that he cared. "The baby still sleeps with Carter and Bailee in their bedroom underground. Carter built it, too. He can build almost anything. In the winter, when there's not a lot to do on the farm, he builds furniture with the help of an old carpenter who winters at his place. Bailee said once that they've shipped orders as far away as Austin."

When Walker didn't say anything, she added, "I usually do my laundry the next morning, then head back to town after lunch. For the price of a paper every week, old Mr. Mosely lets me keep your dad's old gray, Dancer, at the livery. He rents him out from time to time when anyone needs a horse and buggy, so he rarely has to charge me for feed. The only other rig fit to drive in his barn is a wagon built to hold coffins he bought used from the fort a few years ago."

"I'm surprised Dancer is still alive."

Walker finally joined the conversation. "Dad had him for several years before I left. The horse that carried my father through the first year of the War Between the States was called Dancer, so I guess he called the next horse he owned the same name. After that first year, my father never rode, that I know of, except in a buggy." Walker laughed and shoved himself away from the window frame. "I never thought much about it, but my old man had two wives, both named Laura. He must have hated having to remember names."

"Your father never told me he'd been married twice."

"Before the war, his first wife died delivering my half brother, Emory. From what he said, the first Laura was the love of his life. I think Dad thought he'd get lost reporting the war and forget about her, but a year later he came home in the back of a wagon all busted up. My mom was his first wife's cousin. I think they'd both been named after the same grandmother. Anyway, she took care of him, and they married as soon as he could stand. He was forty by then, and she was still in her teens, but a wife was a necessity to a man with a small son."

Walker continued, "A year later I was

born, I was told my mother developed a cough the next winter. He brought her West to help her recover, but she slowly grew worse. I don't remember her."

Lacy had no idea what to say. She thought of saying that she was sorry his mother died, but since it had been over twenty years, the comment sounded a little belated. She decided to change the subject. "Sometimes I read your father's books on cold days."

Walker stared out the window, his arms crossed over his chest. "Sounds like an exciting life," he mumbled.

Lacy frowned. "Well, it's not riding after outlaws, keeping the frontier safe for settlers, or chasing rustlers back across the Rio, but it is my life."

He looked at her. "I wasn't finding fault, Lacy. Sometimes I wonder what it would be like to sleep in the same bed every night. What it would feel like to have whole families of friends. Folks you could watch grow up and grow old, have children and troubles and blessings."

Lacy watched, wondering if he were longing for something or just observing.

"The men I serve with, I know for a few years, until their tours of duty are over or they transfer out. If they have wives, they're usually no more to me than a picture the soldier pulls out from time to time. Sometimes I see men leave, knowing I'll never hear from them again. Sometimes I bury them and send the wife's picture back East with my condolences."

"You could quit."

He turned back to the window. "No. I can't."

She waited for him to say more, but he didn't. He continued to stare out the window while she quilted. The cats played with her thread. He went downstairs for more wood. The north wind howled. Snow continued to fall.

As she worked quietly, Walker tried reading from his thick book, then pacing, and once even napping. When all else failed, he stood over her shoulder and watched her quilt, asking question after question about a skill he had no interest in learning. Finally, he settled at the kitchen table and cleaned his rifles, which Lacy had no doubt were already spotless.

The snow let up about five, but the sky stayed gray and heavy. Walker was at his usual post beside the window. "You think anyone is out and about? I haven't seen a wagon go by all day."

Lacy laid her needle down and stretched

her back. "The saloon and the hotel are always open. I've heard Mr. Stauffer say they make a pretty good business when folks get snowed in. If you want to go for a drink, don't worry about me. I'll be fine. Not even Zeb Whitaker would ride to town to kill me on a day like this."

Walker smiled. "How about we go over to the hotel for supper?"

Lacy shook her head. "I've only eaten there a few times. It's expensive." Mrs. Abernathy, the cook for the jail, used to bring Walker's father and her supper for a fourth what the hotel charged for two meals. It hadn't been fancy, sometimes only biscuits and beans, but at least it saved Lacy cooking after working in the shop all day.

"If I can afford it, would you consider going?" Walker tried again.

"The snow's deeper than my shoes."

"I'll carry you." He laughed, excited that he'd finally thought of something to do.

Lacy had run out of excuses. "All right." She couldn't see leaving with all the food in the apartment, but if he got any more restless, he'd be talking to the cats. He was not a man used to being closed in.

Ten minutes later, they walked out the front of the print shop. Walker stepped off the porch, turned, and lifted his arms.

"Your carriage awaits," he said lightly, but she didn't miss the worry in his eyes. He wasn't at all sure she'd get so near to him. The last time she'd been in his arms, she'd been screaming.

Cautiously, she leaned into his waiting arms and allowed him to lift her off the porch.

Turning her face into the collar of his uniform, she held on tight as he trudged through the snow. For the first time since they'd met, she giggled. For him this might just be venturing out on a snowy day, but for her it was an adventure. His arms held her solid as he tested each step, and for some strange reason, Lacy felt cherished.

By the time Walker walked across the street and set her down on the porch of the hotel, they were both smiling. They dusted the snow off their shoulders, and she took his arm. He led the way into the small hotel as if it were a fine restaurant.

Everyone turned to stare. Sheriff Riley had finished his meal and was leaning back in his chair close to the fire while he finished his coffee. A family, obviously traveling, sat with their three children at the table by the window, and two salesmen sat to their left.

"Well, welcome." Mr. Stauffer seemed

truly happy to see Lacy and the captain. He rushed forward to show them to a table as if there had been more than two to choose from. "I'm really glad to see you, Miss Lacy. And you, too, Captain."

One of the salesmen nodded toward them. "Stauffer's been figuring the more folks eat tonight, the fewer leftovers he'll have to eat tomorrow morning."

Mrs. Stauffer hurried from the kitchen. She grinned at the new customers. "I'll get your food right away." She vanished behind the door once more.

Stauffer shrugged. "Afraid we ain't got but one thing on the menu tonight. Chicken pie with roasted potatoes. But you got your choice of one of three desserts included in the price."

Walker reached in his pocket of coins, knowing it was customary in most small towns to pay before the meal unless you were regular enough to have an account. "I'd like a whiskey before dinner and coffee afterward. My wife would like . . ." he glanced at her.

"I'd like tea with milk."

She spoke to Walker, and though both men had heard her request, Walker repeated, "She'll have a pot of tea with milk and honey."

He pulled out her chair and waited until she was settled before he moved to the other side of the small table. When he pulled his chair up, their knees bumped.

"Sorry," he said.

Lacy fought down a laugh. They were being so polite to one another they could have been actors in a play. She decided braving the storm for supper had been a great idea.

While Stauffer's daughter, Julie, brought her tea, Sheriff Riley stood to leave. Lacy expected him to pull up a chair and join them, but he only tipped his hat at her.

To Lacy's surprise, Walker excused himself and followed Riley out. She had time to drink her first cup of tea before he returned without commenting.

The family gathered their children and headed upstairs. The two salesmen asked the owner if he minded if they played checkers here and not the lobby since it was warmer by the fire.

Stauffer shook his head and went back to reading last week's Austin paper that a traveler must have left.

"How's your tea?" Walker asked, downing the whiskey he'd ordered.

"Hot," she answered. "Bailee first talked me into putting a little cream in it. She loves to sit down and have a cup of tea in the middle of the afternoon while the children nap. Carter orders her tea all the way from New York. They don't even carry the kind she likes in Dallas."

"Try it with honey."

Lacy stirred in a few drops and smiled as she tasted it. "This is nice," she whispered. They both knew she was talking about more than the hotel or the tea.

As they ate they talked about the places they'd both been.

He told of Mexico and frontier forts.

Lacy told him about the wagon train and how Broken-Hand Harrison had hired her to ride along and take care of a sick lady whose entire family was heading west. She hadn't turned fifteen when they left Kansas, but she figured anywhere would be better than where she came from.

When he asked questions, she told him of being kicked off the wagon train soon after the woman died and how she traveled with Bailee and Sarah south to Texas in Bailee's old wagon.

Walker asked about the morning Lacy met Zeb Whitaker, but she wouldn't tell him more than that he'd tried to steal their wagon and they'd clubbed him. She changed the subject to how Walker's father had saved her life by paying her way out of jail.

Before Julie picked up the plates, Lacy slipped the last of her chicken pie on her napkin and folded it into her purse.

Walker raised an eyebrow in question.

"For the cats," she whispered. "They don't get meat all that often."

"But won't your money get covered in crumbs?"

"I don't have any. I only brought the purse because of the cats."

He heard her laugh as he refolded his napkin and did the same. Only instead of trying to shove the cold pie into his pocket, he handed it to her. "Have you room for more?"

She giggled as if they were stealing the silver and stuffed his bounty in with hers.

By the time they stood to leave, Walker felt he'd learned more about Lacy in one hour than he'd known for five years.

"Hope you'll come back, Captain," Stauffer said as he opened the door. "Mrs. Larson."

Lacy glanced up at Mr. Stauffer. Since he'd known her he'd called her Lacy before she took over the paper and Miss Lacy afterward, but he, along with most in town, had never called her Mrs. Larson.

Walker wrapped Lacy's shawl around her. "We'll be back tomorrow night if the snow's not too deep."

Stauffer smiled. "I'll keep the little table empty until you get here."

Lacy started to argue that they could never eat out twice in a row, but Walker guided her out the door before she could mention it.

The sky seemed inky black, but the lights from the homes flickered in the snow along the street. Walker stepped off the porch. "Ready?"

She put her arm on his shoulder, and he pulled her against him. For a moment he just held her close, letting her settle in his arms. Lacy cuddled into the warmth of his wool coat. Somehow in a day they'd made peace with one another. She'd shoved the memory of their first few minutes together far back in her mind, and Walker, who'd talked to her all day, who'd been polite and attentive, seemed someone new, someone she'd just met.

His steps were surefooted as he crossed the snow. When he gently let her down at the print shop's front door, he kept his arm around her while she turned the key, then reached in front of her and opened the door. He followed her through the dark shop and up the stairs without saying a word. She went inside first, and he bolted the apartment door closed behind him. By the time he turned, she was at her bedroom door.

"Thank you for tonight." She felt suddenly nervous around a man she'd been with all day. "I can't remember when I've had such a nice dinner."

"Mrs. Stauffer's a fine cook."

Lacy hadn't been referring to the food, but she didn't know how to say more. "Well, good night."

"Lacy?" he stopped her with a word.

"Yes?"

"Leave your door open tonight."

When she didn't answer, he added, "I promise I'll not enter your room. It's too cold to lock yourself in."

"But these rooms won't stay as warm with the bedroom door open."

"I'll survive."

She told herself she trusted him. He'd never lied to her, but she'd never slept so close to a man.

"I'll make sure that old cannon of a Colt is loaded if you like."

"All right," she finally agreed. "I'll open the door after I've changed for the night."

Walker nodded once. "I'll have the Colt ready."

Chapter 8

Walker waited for Lacy to return to pick up the old gun she thought would protect her. He let one cat in, the other out. He'd taken to calling them both Andy because he couldn't remember the other cat's name. Not that it mattered. Cats didn't know their names anyway.

He made sure there was enough wood to last the night. Double-checked the locks and verified the old Colt the sheriff had given Lacy was fully loaded. He knew she'd never need it, but if he broke his word to her, she had every right to shoot him.

Finally, he dug the old law book he'd carried over half the state out of its leather bag and tried to relax. After talking with her, it would be a long while before he could even think about sleeping. He liked getting to know her. Spending time talking to a woman was something he'd never done. He'd flirted with a few officers' daughters and single sisters, but the talk had always been polite, never real. The couple of times he'd visited ladies of the evening there had been no talk at all except about the price, and he'd felt empty when he'd left.

But with Lacy, there had been no pretend. He didn't even think she knew how to flirt. She was enjoyable to listen to, but mostly he liked watching her talk. There was a gentleness about her when she wasn't all fired up over something.

Walker closed the book, realizing he hadn't read a word. He felt like a man hypnotized by a fire; one minute it warmed him, the next he knew it would burn him, but he couldn't walk away.

When she opened the door of her bedroom and poked her head out, she startled him. He felt as if his thoughts had taken form.

He'd pulled off his boots and uniform jacket and settled atop his bedroll, planning to read by lamplight. He started to stand, but she stopped him with a raised hand.

Walker didn't move, thinking she might be afraid of him coming near, but to his surprise, she opened the door wider and hurried out of the bedroom, carrying a blanket in her arms.

He fought down a smile as he noticed her bare feet at the hem of her nightgown. She wasn't the type of woman he thought of as beautiful — too short, too rounded — but he couldn't deny her charm.

"I brought you something." She knelt beside his bedroll.

Her hair hung over her shoulders in a cloud of walnut brown. He fought the urge to hold it in his hands. Instead, he held his book with a tight grip.

"When your father died, I didn't know what to do with his clothes. He had several suits. Most were worn, but some of the material was still good." She opened a quilt made of browns and blues. "So I cut all the good pieces out and made this." Her ink-stained hands spread over the gift, removing wrinkles.

Walker couldn't believe it. His father must have never thrown away a thing, for he recognized several squares. The brown trousers he always wore on Wednesdays so the dirt wouldn't show when he unloaded paper at the railroad station. The blacks he wore on printing days so that any ink smudges blended. The black coat and trousers he saved for church and funerals.

His father's life wove amid the threads of each square.

"From his trousers and vests I cut all the watch pockets out. Most of the other pockets were too frayed or stained with ink, but I don't think your father ever carried a watch."

"He didn't," Walker remembered. "He believed in working until the job was done and sleeping until he woke each morning." Walker had forgotten his father's habit. "He would have never made it in the army."

Lacy spread the blanket out. "Maybe not, but his quilt will keep you warm tonight."

"Thank you," Walker said, touched by her kindness. "But don't you need this?"

"Oh, no, I packed it away to give to you. It's good to have something to remember your father by."

He didn't have to ask. He knew she had nothing of her parents'.

"If you can't take it with you when you travel, you can leave it." She hesitated. "It will be here if you need it."

She told him far more with her offer than where he could leave the quilt. She wanted him to know that she wasn't planning on going anywhere, even though he'd once said she could sell the place and start over. This was her home, even if it would never be his.

She jumped up as if she thought she'd stayed too long. "Well, good night."

"Don't you want the Colt?"

She wavered at the door. "No. I trust you." She lifted her chin. "I want to say I'm sorry for claiming you raped me when I came to you in Cottonwood. I'm not always totally honest, even with myself, but I can't lie about that. I gave you no choice that day."

If she were being honest, so could he. "You're wrong, Lacy. I had a choice. I knew what I was doing, and I realized too late that you didn't. I could have stopped. I could have tossed you on that stage, no matter what you demanded." He noticed tears sparkling in her eyes. "I hurt you that day, and that was never my intent."

"Your father truly believed he was doing you a service when he signed your name to the marriage license and bought my freedom. Until the day he died he told me how happy you would be to have me as a wife and how much you needed me, even though you didn't know it yet."

Walker watched her closely. "Knowing the old man, he probably believed his words. It's not because of you I don't want a wife. I don't want any wife."

"I know that now. I figured it out a little too late."

"I'm glad he was good to you and that you were with him in the end. I owe you a great debt for that."

"You owe me nothing, Captain. I loved your father as if he were my own. Every day I spent with him, even to the end, was a blessing. My mother would have said, 'Treasures of time can't be put in the pocket, they have to be stored in the heart.' He gave me his time."

Walker stood and walked closer, not wanting to be a room away when he asked her simply, "Do you think we could start over, maybe even be friends?" He told himself he asked because it would make the next three weeks easier, but deep down he knew that was a lie. He wanted to know Lacy better.

"I've never had someone like you for a friend. I wouldn't know how to act or what to do."

"Someone like me?"

"You know. A man." She frowned. "Duncan and Eli are my friends, but they're also my employees, and I can't talk about anything but the shop with them. Jay

Boy is too young, and the sheriff is too old."

Walker understood. "Don't feel so bad. I've never had a woman for a friend. But I think I can handle friendship a little easier than I do being a husband."

She smiled, looking very young. Too young to be his wife. In her shapeless gown and bare feet he could almost see her as a child. Almost.

"When this is over and you go back," she asked, "if we're friends, will you write me?"

"I will. And you'll write me and let me know about everyone in town?" He thought about how he rarely went to mail call. "I'd like hearing from you. Little things, like how the sheriff's doing and what the church ladies are making new. You could even let me know if old Mosely ever takes a bath or how the paper's doing."

"And you could tell me of your travels and what the land looks like. I'd like that."

"Then we'll try friends." He offered his hand.

She placed her hand in his. "Friends."

"Thank you, Lacy. Good night." Before he gave it much thought, he leaned forward and kissed her cheek, then turned loose of her fingers. It was a polite kiss like he might have given the wife of a friend, or a farewell to a woman he'd met and danced with at a ball in the capital.

She faded into the dark room, leaving the door open.

Walker turned down the lamp and lay back on his bed.

The snow whirled in the wind, and the storm continued until morning, but at dawn the sun broke clear. Walker woke early and dressed. When Lacy came into the kitchen, he excused himself and went downstairs to allow her more privacy to dress. When he returned with more wood, she already had oatmeal boiling.

"I'll need to buy more wood from Mosely at this rate. From what I can see of the street, the town is alive today. Several wagons have already worn a rut down Main."

"We can make do without more wood," Lacy answered without turning from the stove. "I've no money this week, and I can't expect you to keep buying everything. We'll use what wood we have left to keep the downstairs warm. Some of the heat will drift up here."

Walker frowned. He'd wanted to ask about her finances, or lack of them, since he'd arrived, but didn't know how to bring it up. "Doesn't the shop still make a profit?"

Lacy nodded. "Almost every week I'm able to pay the men and Jay Boy out of the earnings and have a few dollars for me. I save back any more than that for the bad weeks or in case the press needs a part. The older the press gets, the more the parts seem to cost. Right now, thanks to the last repair, my rainy day money box is almost empty. In slow times I can make it without my two dollars a week, but the men have families to support. Even Jay Boy's mom depends on his earnings every week."

"I thought you lived on the shop?"

Lacy laughed. "I do live above it."

Walker didn't see anything funny. It appeared she worked for free, a slave to this place. How could she even think about wanting to stay here? "So you've been surviving mostly on my allotment?"

She looked up. "What allotment?"

Chapter 9

Walker stood at the bank entrance when Morris Hutchison unlocked the door. The thin, gray-headed man with a waxed mustache that stretched from ear to ear seemed nervous when Walker stormed in a few feet behind him.

"Good morning. May I help you, sir?" Morris asked as he moved behind a massive desk and checked his pocket watch.

The clock by the tellers' booths chimed the hour. "Do you remember who I am, Mr. Hutchison?"

"Of course I remember you. I heard in church yesterday that you were in town. Welcome home, Captain Larson. We kept up with you through your father for years, and now, of course, your wife tells us now and then where you're stationed."

Walker stifled his anger and took the man's bony hand. The banker hadn't melted one degree past frozen in eight years. Hutchison had to be lying about keeping up with him, because, except the once she found him in Cottonwood, Lacy would have no idea where he was stationed.

Two employees hurried in as the clock's last chime sounded. The banker greeted them with a frown, then offered Walker a seat.

"I remember the night you left town. Eight years ago last March, I believe." Hutchison took his place behind the desk. "Sheriff Riley called old Mr. Mitchell and myself to his office. You wanted everything legal before you left. I admired that in one so young."

Walker didn't want to listen to compliments, but he nodded his thank-you. In many ways, like himself, the banker was a man of order.

"You said you were never coming back, but I understand how a wife can change a man's plans." Hutchison's smile stretched his skin across already hollow cheeks. "How can I be of service to you today, Captain?"

"The money I sent home each month starting five years ago, was it delivered here as instructed?"

"Of course. I've been saving it for you in

the account we set up."

"It was for my wife."

Hutchison looked worried. "But I received no notice to that effect, and you left very strict instructions that no one could access your account, other than yourself, of course, and your father. I believe the words were even underlined in the legal document Mitchell drew up."

Walker leaned forward. "Are you telling me that you've lived in the same town with my wife for the two years since my father's death and watched her almost starve without allowing her to touch my accounts?" He tempered his ire with the fact that he had not checked on her himself. "You could have notified me of the situation."

Hutchison blanched. "First, I was following your wishes, which is what I do. Second, I'm not aware that your wife is in hard times. She pays her employees every week, I understand, and she paid for your father's funeral in cash." He steepled his hands in front of him. "And third, the one time I did inquire about you, Sheriff Riley said even your father had trouble finding you. According to the rules you drew up that night, no one was to be informed of your banking activities with the exception of your father and, to my knowledge, he never asked."

Walker's anger turned inward. He'd been so worried about his brother taking over his accounts that he'd made it impossible for Lacy to get what, by right, she should have. At first she must have been totally dependent on his father and then on the small income from the paper, which, with three employees, could never be much.

"How much is in the account?"

Hutchison opened his log and turned it so Walker could see his accounting skills. The banker seemed very proud of his bookkeeping. "From the monthly allotments you've accumulated eighteen hundred fifty-nine dollars. With interest, it has built to just over two thousand."

Walker leaned back. "Thank you, Mr. Hutchison. You've done exactly what was expected of you." He couldn't blame the banker. "Please have the two thousand transferred to an account for my wife and, in the future, any allotments coming should be deposited in that account."

"Very good, sir." Hutchison dipped his pen. "And as to the other money?"

Walker paused halfway out of his chair. "What other money?" He knew of only a few hundred dollars left in his account after he'd covered his brother's theft. He'd hoped his father would use it if an emergency arrived.

"A bank in Boston has been sending money every quarter from your mother's father's estate."

"But they sent me five thousand when he died." Walker had been sent the money a week after he'd turned seventeen and hadn't decided what to do with it before he had to cover his half brother's crime.

"Old Mitchell contacted Boston on your behalf years ago. Apparently there was a rental property that another grandson was to inherit, but he died before your grandfather. In the will, any inheritance not claimed within one year passed to the remaining grandson. Since the lawyer in Boston wasn't sure what you wanted done with the property, he continued to rent it out and sends you the income, minus his commission."

Hutchison straightened, proud of himself. "On your behalf, of course, I commissioned Mr. Mitchell to do an annual accounting, for a small fee, which I deduct out of your account each new year."

"I see." Walker nodded. The banker hadn't missed a single detail. "How much is in that account right now?" He wouldn't be surprised if it were in the red with all the fingers poking into it.

"To date, eighteen thousand, four hundred eleven dollars and seventeen cents." When Walker didn't comment, the banker added, "Enough to buy a nice-size ranch in these parts if you're interested in settling down, Captain."

"I'll think about it," Walker answered. "At the moment I'm more concerned with my wife's safety than buying property."

Walker thanked Hutchison, made a small withdrawal, collected the paperwork on Lacy's new account, and walked out of the bank without commenting further on how he planned to spend his new inheritance.

He reminded himself money didn't matter; it hadn't to him for eight years. When he'd first found out about inheriting from a grandfather he never met, Walker had been excited and full of dreams. But Emory, two years older, had been angry, seeing the twist of fate as unfair. Even when Walker offered to split the windfall with his brother, Emory hadn't been satisfied. In the end, they'd both lost.

Shoving the memory aside, Walker glanced over at the print shop. Through the one glass window left, he saw Sheriff Riley sitting on a stool drinking coffee while visiting with Duncan. The sheriff was doing a good job of watching over things and an even better job of letting everyone in town know just how near Lacy he planned to stay. He would have been more comfortable by the old stove in the center of the shop, but he must have wanted anyone passing to know he was there.

Walker decided he had a few minutes before he needed to be back on guard. He crossed to the mercantile, wanting to buy Lacy something to thank her for the quilt. But, as he looked around, he realized she needed almost everything. Chairs, dishes, food, new buckets, boots.

"May I help you, Captain?" the old owner named Willard asked. "You need anything besides glass for that shop? I went ahead and ordered that first thing this morning."

"Boots." Walker said the last thing on his mind. "My wife needs a new pair of boots."

"What size?"

Willard must have read Walker's puzzled expression, because he laughed. "Don't worry, you ain't the first man to come in here who didn't know his wife's size. I keep a list here whenever a woman buys anything. Your wife's list is short, she's not a shopper, but I seem to remember her buying a pair of shoes in here a few years back."

While he checked, Walker noticed the bolts of wool. Lacy's dress had been cotton yesterday, and so was the one she wore this morning. If she'd owned a wool dress, she would have worn it yesterday. He thought of buying material but had no idea how much she'd need. He'd bring her back later. With the snow she needed boots now.

"She's a size five," Willard yelled from the back. "We got several to choose from right now, Captain. You want them serviceable, or fashionable?"

"How about the best leather you have?"

"You got it, one pair left in her size. I order these all the way from Kansas City and usually sell out before Christmas." Willard wasn't a success for nothing. "You'll be wanting a few pair of warm stockings with that and maybe black leather gloves to match the boots."

"Wrap them up." Walker looked at the chairs hanging along one wall, but he had no idea how to pick furniture out.

"And I got some fine coats that would look nice with all this."

"I'll let my wife pick out her clothes." Walker smiled, thinking it would be interesting to watch Lacy shop. "I'll just take the boots, gloves, and stockings for now."

Willard handed him a box. "That'll be five dollars."

When Walker raised an eyebrow, Willard added, "You said you wanted the best."

He paid the man and hurried back to the shop. It seemed everyone in town milled on the street today. They'd all been huddled by the fires yesterday, and now the townsfolk wanted to talk. It took him several minutes to tramp through the snow.

Riley now stood guard outside the print shop door, his hand played with the safety strap on his holstered six-gun, his face wrinkled with worry.

Walker took the final few steps in a run. "Did something happen? Is Lacy all right?"

"She's fine. No sign of Whitaker," Riley assured him. "My guess is he's still snowed in wherever he's holed up." The old man hesitated. "But that don't mean trouble ain't come knocking. Samantha Goble is in there with your wife asking all kinds of questions about you."

Walker couldn't form words for a moment. He thought of asking the sheriff to just shoot him. He'd rather be buried than face Samantha. "How'd she know I was here?"

"She acted like she didn't. I was sitting at the counter when she waltzed in and asks if your father still owned the place. She said she didn't even know the old man was dead and got all teary-eyed over the news." Riley glanced over his shoulder, as if fearing she might appear behind him. "Not that she ever cared about one person in this town including her parents, but that woman can carry on."

Walker knew he should go inside. He'd healed from the last time he'd seen Samantha, but he needed a moment to mentally cover his scars.

The sheriff didn't seem to notice; Walker only half-listened. "When Lacy told her he'd gone on to meet his Maker, Samantha acted like she couldn't believe it." Riley grinned. "Then, our little lady told Samantha she was your wife, and I thought the woman would faint. It took both me and Duncan to keep her and the twenty pounds of fur she's wearing afloat until Jay Boy pulled up a stool."

Riley laughed. "She sure ain't much like the poor little girl who grew up here. Her parents are still barely getting by. Her dad cleans the church for extra money, but Samantha looks like a new penny whenever she visits."

"You see her often?"

"Of course. She stops by here now and again, whenever she's between husbands. Usually only spends a day or two. I heard she made it to church yesterday. Some say she got religion after her last husband died in her arms."

"Natural causes?"

"Old age, her mother told me. But she swore her daughter loved this one, even if she was mad when she found out he didn't leave her much in his will."

Walker's brain began to work. If Samantha went to church yesterday, she probably heard he was in town. In fact, if she stopped often, he'd bet she already knew about his father and probably about Lacy. He hadn't seen Samantha in years, but snakes don't grow legs, and he'd bet she hadn't changed. She wanted something, and it wouldn't be long until he found out what. He charged into the shop.

"Darling!" Samantha screamed as she jumped from her stool.

Walker met Lacy's confused stare as Samantha wrapped her arms around him and hugged him wildly, knocking the box from his arm. He jerked his head or she would have kissed him on the mouth.

Lacy's boots tumbled to the floor amid stockings and gloves.

Samantha, all powdered and perfumed, stepped back before his lack of greeting became apparent. "What's this? Women's clothing? Why Walker, I never knew you to buy a woman clothing. You must have been on an errand for your little wife. Did she send you out shopping?"

He knelt and picked up his purchases, realizing Samantha's beauty no longer affected him. "You never knew me at all, madam." His tone froze colder than the air outside. The last thing he wanted to dredge up were memories of warm summer evenings with Samantha in his arms. The perfume he once thought intoxicating now only seemed stagnant.

Turning, he offered the box to Lacy but spoke to Samantha. "Not that this is any concern of yours, Samantha, but these are a surprise for my wife."

Lacy started to protest, then glanced over at Samantha and said simply, "Thank you, dear."

Walker couldn't help but smile. Lacy wasn't fooled for one moment by Samantha's ways. She might not know the history between them, but she knew he wasn't interested in this beautiful woman who filled the room with her self-importance.

Jay Boy, however, stood with his mouth open as if the tall blonde was a one-woman parade. Duncan also watched, for once able to hear everything being said, thanks to Samantha's constant volume.

Lacy turned to step back into her tiny office, digging through the box as if it were Christmas morning.

Samantha dismissed Lacy and gave her full attention to Walker. "I was just telling your bride that I'm her sister-in-law. Or at least I guess I still am, even though I'm Emory's widow. You did know he died almost four years ago. Tragically, I'm afraid, in a gunfight."

Before Walker informed her he'd heard the fight was in defense of her honor, she added with a wave of her hand. "Oh, I'm so sorry! I didn't mean to say bride when I referred to her." She gave another graceful wave of her hand toward the office. "You two have been married, how long? Let me think. Oh yes, five years, she said. Even though this must be the first time you've bothered to come home to see your *wife* or I would have heard about it, surely." She said the word *wife* as if it dirtied her tongue.

"Lucy, isn't it?" She whispered, but still said the name loud enough for everyone to hear.

"Lacy," he corrected with a weary stare.

Samantha almost appeared sorry for him. "Such a pretty name for such a plain girl. No wonder you've never been with her."

Walker looked over Samantha's shoulder. Lacy was tugging on one of her new boots, absently revealing several inches of her leg as she did so. She might not have furs and jewels, but nothing about his wife was plain. When she glanced up, she smiled shyly, and he couldn't help but wink at her. "My *bride* manages to come to me," he said to Samantha.

Lacy covered her laughter as Samantha whirled toward the office.

"Is that true, dear?" She leaned forward as if talking to a child. "You go traipsing across the country to find him?"

Lacy stood, testing out her new boots. "I certainly do."

Samantha gave Lacy a *You should be ashamed* look, but Lacy only watched Walker and pointed at her boots.

Walker couldn't help himself; he smiled.

He turned back to the beautiful Samantha and regarded her as if she were no more than a smashed beetle.

"Well, it was nice visiting with you, Samantha," Walker said, "but if you don't plan to place an ad, I'm afraid I'll have to bid you good day. We have to get back to work. Lacy has a paper to run, and I've promised to be her slave for the day."

"But Walker," Samantha lowered her voice. "Aren't you thrilled to see me? I know you were angry when we parted years ago. I may have made a few mistakes that I've suffered long regretting, but I'm sure a part of you still loves me." She played with the hood of her coat as if hoping he'd notice that framed in fur she was far more beautiful as a woman than she'd been as a girl. "I thought you'd want to spend some time with me before my train."

Walker in return lowered his words to her. "You're wrong, Samantha. I worshiped you as only a seventeen-year-old boy can. But that died the night you left with Emory and all the money my father had spent his life saving. You married my brother, not me, and I feel we've already spent far too much time together this morning. I wouldn't want you to miss your train."

She placed one delicate hand over Walker's heart, spreading her fingers as if she could dust away any pain she'd caused. "But Emory's dead," she whined as if Walker's brother were no more than a toy that had broken.

"So is my love for you," Walker whispered as he offered his arm.

Lacy stomped out of the office in her new boots, her eyes dancing with joy.

Samantha straightened and said in a tone dripping with sugar, "I hope to visit with you again, dear sister-in-law, but I've a train to catch this morning as soon as the tracks are clear." She glanced at the boots. "Oh, by the way, those are fine boots. Nothing like you could get in Dallas or Chicago, but good enough for here."

"Thanks," Lacy said, as if the statement were a compliment.

Samantha looked back at Walker. "We had something once."

"Maybe," Walker answered. "But it's over, Samantha."

She huffed, obviously realizing she'd lost a battle. "We'll see one another again soon." Her voice was no longer warm. "I've some business to talk over with you as soon as I get back from Dallas."

"We've nothing to discuss." Walker politely offered her his arm once more and took another step toward the door.

"Oh, but dear brother, we do. By right, half of this place was Emory's, and therefore now mine."

"Not a chance." He held the door open for her. He'd burn it to the ground before he'd let her have one board of the print shop.

Before she could answer, he closed the door.

Lacy stood beside Walker watching Samantha muster her pride and try to walk across the muddy street with grace. When she'd disappeared around a freight wagon, Lacy leaned closer to him. "I thought you said you had no women friends to talk to. That one seemed mighty willing to talk."

Walker laughed. "She was never my friend. And with Samantha, one doesn't talk, one only listens."

He offered his arm just as he had to Samantha.

Lacy accepted it hesitantly. "Thank you for the boots, but you shouldn't have."

"I've something I have to talk over with you, if we could step into your office." He opened his hand to allow her to go into the tiny space first.

She did, but offered him the only chair as she closed the door.

While he explained about the money he'd put in an account for her, Walker could see Duncan and Jay Boy trying to act like they weren't watching through the closed glass of the office door. He sat while Lacy paced three steps one way and then three in the other, waving her arms and shaking her head.

She didn't want his money. Didn't want anything from him. He'd given her his name and a ticket out of jail. That was enough. He could keep the money. She would make it fine.

Walker remained calm as she stormed. He didn't plan to back down an inch. The money was rightfully hers.

"If you don't want it, I'll stack your apartment full of supplies before I leave and tell Willard to restock every month."

"He wouldn't —"

"He would if it meant a sale, and we both know it," Walker said. "So you can pick out the supplies you need and take the allotment, or I can guess what you'll need, but you're taking the money."

"No."

Walker leaned forward in the chair. "Look, I'm not easy to find. How about you agree to keep the money for that rainy day you worry about. What does it matter if you have a few dollars squirreled away or a few thousand? If you can't make the payroll one week, you'll be glad you have it."

"Can I give all the guys a raise in salary? I don't think they've had one in years."

"It's your money. Do whatever you like." He saw the crack in her armor. "But my guess is they could really use a raise, so I'd hope you'd make it a fair one. And maybe you could stock up on a few of the supplies around here. And make sure you've enough wood to last the winter." He could go on, but he didn't want to push it.

"I'd like to buy your father a proper marker. He always paid his own way. He even left me money for his funeral, but I only had enough for a wooden cross."

"Lacy, no one can tell you how to spend the money; it's yours. We'll go pick out a stone today, if it's important to you." Walker relaxed, realizing that he'd won.

"It is," she stated. "I'd like to order a few new parts for the printing press. We've been making do. And wood to last the winter is a good idea. Eli can come to work on cold days and be warm in the shop."

"You could buy a little house if you like with that much money and have somewhere to go besides upstairs after work," Walker advised.

"No. I'll not go wasting my rainy day money when I have a perfectly good place to sleep upstairs."

Walker smiled, realizing she'd finally called the account hers. "But —"

She leaned down and poked his chest, sending his chair backward a few inches. "Now don't go telling me how to spend my money, Captain," she warned with a smile.

He caught her hand and on impulse pulled her down on his lap. "As you wish."

When she tugged her hands, he let go, worried that he'd gone too far. Right now their friendship was thin glass over a turbulent sea.

But she didn't look angry, and she didn't get off his lap. For a moment she just sat and smiled, holding her bank statement as if it were gold. "Thank you," she finally said. "I'll be careful with my rainy day money. It means a lot that I won't have to worry about the men being paid. I even had to sell the furniture upstairs to make payroll once."

Then, to his total surprise, she leaned closer and kissed him on the cheek as he had her the night before. One light, friendly kiss.

Chapter 10

After Samantha left, Lacy and Walker spent the day working. Eli, Lacy's third employee, didn't come in because of the cold, so the captain took his place. Having grown up around a printing press, Walker knew each job as well or better than Lacy. She was surprised at the amount of work they got done. For the first time she understood how Walker's father, as a young man, could have run the place himself. Without three employees, and with new machines, his income would have supported a family. Walker said whenever his dad ran short on time, he drafted the sons to pitch in. Emory became an expert at disappearing, but Walker admitted that he never minded helping.

As they worked, Lacy filled him in on all that had happened in the town since she'd arrived while Walker talked about the past when Cedar Point had only been half the size.

Old Duncan even departed from his normally gloomy state and hummed out of tune now and then. Jay Boy asked Walker one question after another about the army and campaigns he'd fought. To her surprise, Walker tried hard to paint an accurate picture of army life, not blowing it up into dreams of glory as many men might have been tempted to do. When he told the boy that, more often than not, he had to do his own laundry, the army lost its appeal to Jay Boy.

The sheriff dropped by again in the afternoon and insisted on accompanying them to the mercantile. He stood in the front of the store and whispered to Walker while Lacy shopped.

At first, she was at a loss for what to buy. She needed everything and had never truly looked around the store for fear she'd start dreaming of things she couldn't afford. Finally, she decided she'd buy five items. Then tomorrow, if she wanted, she'd buy five more. In a strange way, she needed time to enjoy each.

She bought a thread box with twenty different colors of thread on big wooden spools, seven yards of wool for a new dress, white lace for the trim, a wonderful coat of navy blue, and two extra buckets for her kitchen.

If Walker thought the purchases strange, he didn't comment. He bought a few thin cigars and a pound of coffee while Riley helped with the packages. Both men seemed in a hurry to get back to the print shop. Lacy thought it might just be that they hated shopping or worse, visiting with every woman who wandered into the place.

Then she noticed the long row of windows across the front of the store and guessed why they were on edge.

When she asked, both were a little too quick to reassure her nothing was wrong.

As they walked back, Walker asked, "Is old Mitchell, the lawyer, still around?"

"Sure," Riley answered. "He only goes into the office about once a week, and the paperwork keeps piling up there, but his shingle is still out."

"If you could stay with Lacy for a few minutes, I'd like to drop by and see him."

Riley nodded as Walker left them. "Didn't know him and the old man were so close," Riley said more to himself than Lacy. "Mitchell's a good guy. Hope if we ever get another lawyer in town he's half the man."

Lacy didn't comment, but she tried to guess why Walker felt he needed to see Mitchell. All she could come up with was that somehow Samantha must have said something. Or maybe Walker simply had a question about the law; he seemed to be studying up on it.

That evening, Lacy wore her new wool coat and her boots and gloves. She'd never felt so warm and happy in her life. She debated telling Walker that she now owned her first new coat. All the others before had been hand-me-downs or bought second-hand.

But she didn't tell him. She wanted nothing to interfere with the night. After dressing carefully, she found him waiting for her at the bottom of the stairs. He'd taken the time to brush his jacket and comb his hair. They could almost be a regular married couple stepping out for dinner, except for the pistol strapped at his waist and the way his eyes watched the darkened corners.

Lacy thought of how Samantha had called her plain and knew she'd never be the kind of beauty that turned men's heads, but just for the evening she wanted to believe that she fit with her captain. In the back of her mind she knew a tall blonde belonged on his arm and not a short brunette, but she could pretend, if only for an hour.

So she smiled as she came down the stairs, and he stared up at her in a way he'd never look at Samantha. He looked like he really saw her.

When they reached the end of the shop's porch, she hesitated, not wanting to step into the slush in her new boots.

Without a word, Walker lifted her gently in his arms and carried her across the street to the hotel as he'd done the night before in the snow. His hold was secure, and solid as before, only tonight, he talked to her as they walked, comfortable with her so near after working with her most of the afternoon.

Over dinner they talked about Jay Boy and Duncan, who started working at the paper when Walker's father's hands began to curl and knot. She told him of the time they'd worked all night to print handbills for a cattle drive that needed men immediately.

She told him of stories his father told, stories he swore he'd never heard before. Accounts of the early days when an editor worked with his gun handy because anyone who didn't like the news might stop by to argue. Walker said times hadn't changed much elsewhere, but in Cedar Point most of those that might cause trouble had moved on to wilder towns like Tascosa and Mobeetie.

Lacy hardly noticed the other people in the little hotel restaurant. Mrs. Stauffer had put a cloth over their table and placed a small sign that said Reserved beside the salt. The small action made Lacy feel special.

They had their choice of day-old chicken pie or pork chops covered in applesauce. Dessert was cobbler made from canned peaches that Mrs. Stauffer reminded Lacy were from the McKoy trees. From Kansas City to Fort Worth, McKoy peaches were known as the finest.

When Lacy folded her napkin out to save the last of her pork chop, Walker covered her hand with his.

"Stop," he whispered. "If you're going to do this every night, you might as well do it right." He pulled a small leather pouch from his coat pocket. "I picked this up while you were trying on coats. It'll keep your handbag from getting greasy."

"Thanks." She accepted the gift. "You don't mind that I save the last few bites? I'm guessing it's not the proper thing to do when eating out."

"I don't mind. Everyone knows you love those cats."

Lacy drank her hot tea laced with honey and milk. She nibbled on her cobbler while the captain finished off his, then switched bowls.

When she protested, he winked and said, "Everyone knows how much I love cobbler."

She watched her very proper captain and decided he wasn't made of stone after all. Though she had reminded him several times during the day that her employees weren't his troops, he took it good-naturedly. And he might look relaxed eating, but she hadn't missed the way he'd removed his pistol belt and put it over the chair within easy reach. He'd also made sure he sat so he could see both doors. She knew Walker worried and couldn't help but think Riley must have told her husband more than he told her about Whitaker. They weren't a couple just enjoying the evening; he was a man doing his job, his duty. Nothing more.

No matter how much he'd hated having to come home, he seemed to make the best of it and to his credit had tried to make their time together bearable. She appreciated his effort and wondered if over the years he hadn't had to make the best of many trying situations.

He wasn't the monster she thought him after she'd visited him that first time. But she wouldn't be fooled into believing he would ever be truly a husband, either. He was a man who needed his space and an order to his life only the army could provide. She must never allow herself to forget that he was here, against his will, to do a job. In three weeks he'd leave, and life would go back to being as it had been before he came.

She could enjoy the dinner and dream that it was real between them, but she couldn't afford to play the fool again.

Zeb Whitaker was still out there. Once in a while Lacy caught herself holding her breath, waiting. Even though it had been five years, she still recalled the way he smelled . . . the way his beefy hands grabbed her . . . how he'd slapped her so hard she'd been afraid to scream.

But with Walker near, she felt safe tonight. She'd worry about the tomorrows after he'd gone.

The sheriff joined them for a second cup of coffee. He couldn't seem to stop grinning at them and mentioned several times that he was real glad they weren't threatening to kill one another anymore.

He told Walker he'd talked to half the

men in town. No one the size of Whitaker would ride in unnoticed again. Even the men in town who didn't know Miss Lacy very well seemed determined to help protect her. In five years she'd become one of them.

While the sheriff spoke to Walker, Lacy swirled the few leaves in her teacup. When she'd been very young, she remembered her mother and grandmother staring into their cups. Lacy couldn't help but wonder if they saw more than she did. They'd talk of the future as if it were looking back at them from the cup.

"Playing fortune-teller, tonight?" the sheriff interrupted her thoughts.

"No." She smiled. "And hush, I haven't told my husband I'm a witch yet."

The old man laughed. "More angel than witch, my dear. All the things you do around here for folks. I know those quilts didn't just appear in my jail cells."

Lacy laughed. "Maybe it was just magic."

"Which reminds me, when are you going to mix me up a love potion to use on Mrs. Abernathy? She's been cooking my breakfast for so many years that I can't think of retiring until she agrees to marry me and cook those biscuits every morning."

Lacy laughed. "You couldn't marry her.

She told me she doesn't even like you and only cooks for the money. So, don't go getting any ideas."

"She's just playing hard to get, that's all."

"Doing a pretty fair job of it," Lacy mumbled.

"But, I'm in love with those biscuits."

Lacy shook her head. "Don't you have a wife somewhere back East?"

Riley shook his head. "I wrote her after I'd been settled here about four years saying I missed her and asking her to join me. She wrote back saying she's still waiting for me to come to my senses and ride back home, and that we've had three more daughters since I've been gone. Seems even with me in Texas, she's still delivering every spring."

"So you've set your eye on Widow Abernathy?" Walker tried to hold down a laugh. "Even if she's not fond of you."

"How could she not like me?" Riley smoothed his few strands of hair back as if proving his point. "Women don't know what they want sometimes. They get mixed up and think that somehow living alone is better than living with a man."

"You don't know women very well, do you, Sheriff?" Lacy giggled.

"I know she'd like me if she got a good look. How could she not?"

"It puzzles me," Lacy answered with a straight face. "The woman must be blind to pass up a fine-looking man like you."

"That's what I think. Maybe I should have her see the doctor. Once she gets glasses, she'll change her mind."

Lacy pretended to consider the possibility. "Why don't you ask her next time she brings breakfast? Doc McClellan hasn't been all that busy of late. He could probably use the business."

Riley nodded and stood to leave. "I'll do that." He shook Walker's hand. "Keep an eye on our Lacy," he added, as if she belonged to the town.

Walker finished his coffee without speaking, but the silence that lay between them didn't seem uncomfortable. When he rose, Lacy let him help her on with her coat and they bade Mr. Stauffer good night.

Without a word, he lifted her in his arms and carried her across the street, staying in the shadows. He stood between her and the street as she unlocked the door. She felt the warmth of him just behind her.

They walked in darkness through the shop and were halfway up the stairs when

172

he touched her arm and stopped her progress.

Lacy turned on the step ahead of him. Her eyes were level with his, but she saw only the outline of his face in the shadows. "What is it? Is something wrong?" Fear danced along her spine.

"No. Nothing's wrong. I just wanted to say something before we get upstairs." He stood so close she felt his words brushed her face.

"All right."

"I'm thinking of kissing you good night, but if I do so at your bedroom door, you may fear I'm planning an advance. So I thought it proper to mention it ahead of time so you wouldn't think I had further intentions."

Lacy smiled. "And you don't?"

"No." He straightened. "I plan to leave in twenty-one days as we agreed."

"Then why kiss me?" A moment before, she would have welcomed a kiss to the end of their evening, but now, after knowing he'd analyzed it like a battle plan, the idea didn't seem so appealing. His need to qualify a simple kiss stung her pride. Just because she'd objected to being grabbed and held wrapped in a quilt when she'd been frightened didn't mean she wouldn't consider a simple kiss or any other slight show of caring. It would have been nice to have a few such memories, but not if the captain thought they had to be planned out.

"I just didn't want you to be frightened again if I came too near, or start jumping to conclusions." He would have had to have been a dead man not to sense the stiffening of her body. "I didn't want you to think I might stay, that I might want to be . . ."

". . . a real husband?" Lacy snapped, angry that they were even having the discussion. How many times did he think he had to tell her that he didn't want to be her husband?

She straightened, wishing she were taller so she could look down on him. "What makes you think I want a husband anymore, Captain? Or maybe you think because we've been civil to one another today, that I'll drag you in if you kiss me too close to the bedroom door. After all, I've forced you to my bed once before."

Walker let out a long breath. "I only sought to be polite, not have an argument with you." His cold, impersonal manner had returned.

"What made you think you wanted to

kiss me anyway?" Since she'd never been kissed, Lacy's anger molded into curiosity.

"Hell if I know," he answered.

"Maybe it's some kind of affliction you have. Maybe you should go with Mrs. Abernathy to the doctor."

"There's nothing wrong with my sight."

"Then it must be your hearing, because I made it plain we would try to be friends, not lovers."

She stormed up the last half of the stairs and went into the apartment.

"I swear," he yelled from just behind her. "Anger fires in you like gunpower. I was just trying to make you aware of a simple plan of action."

He followed her all the way to the kitchen and stood watching as she picked up the tablet without removing her gloves and tore out the page with the number twenty-one written on it.

"Less than three weeks before this tour of duty is over," she announced. "Good night, Captain."

Walker didn't move as she stormed into her bedroom and slammed the door. A few minutes later she returned in her nightgown. He noticed that she'd missed several buttons on her gown, leaving the collar to gape open at her throat.

The last thing he intended to do was mention the fact or say one word about how he could see the outline of her body as she stood between the lamp and him.

She retrieved the old Colt from where he'd left it on the table and walked back to her door.

Just as she reached the threshold, he said, "Would you rather I kissed you and not let you know of my intentions, madam?"

She turned slowly and stared at him as if he were a manner of animal she'd never seen. Finally, she said, "I don't know much about men, Captain. When I signed that paper marrying you, I'd never kissed a man, or even held hands. I don't know the first thing about how married people act or what they say to one another." She took a step closer. "But, compared to you, I'm an expert. So, let me make you aware of my plan of action for the remainder of our time together. If you step one foot into my bedroom, I'll make myself a widow."

She whirled and disappeared into the bedroom leaving the door open, but it might as well have been locked.

"I'll take that as a no," Walker muttered.

Chapter 11

Walker shoved a chair against the locked back entrance of Lacy's apartment and stomped downstairs to the print shop. He swore the tiny apartment shrank by the hour. They'd had a pleasant dinner, and a good night kiss had seemed like it might be a fine idea. To him anyway. Obviously not to her.

Walker paced by the front door. He must have been mad. At twenty-seven he should be far beyond acting like a fool. How could a woman have such big beautiful eyes . . . and a body all soft and begging to be held . . . and still fire up over nothing with the kick of a fully loaded flint-lock rifle? He needed to put a little distance between them. Hell! Across the Mississippi wouldn't be enough room as far as he was concerned.

He didn't have long to wait before Sheriff Riley walked across the porch.

Walker opened the door before the

sheriff had time to knock.

"Didn't figure you'd be ready for me." The sheriff looked more suspicious than surprised. "I finished my rounds a little earlier than I planned and thought I'd wait until you had time to say your good nights."

"We said good night. I'm ready," Walker answered, deciding one second longer than necessary under the same roof with Lacy was too long. "Where do I meet this man you think I need to talk to?"

Riley removed his coat as he ambled toward one of the cane chairs near the big potbellied stove in the center of the shop. "He didn't like the idea, but I told him this time a night the saloon would be a good place to visit. It's too cold to stand on the street corner and talk." The old man rattled an empty coffeepot and frowned. "He never has liked crowds, but I got him to agree. He's waiting for you now."

Walker didn't comment. The bar was fine. Anywhere sounded better than here. "I'll be back in an hour."

The sheriff laughed. "If you're talking to Carter McKoy, you'll be back sooner than that, but it don't matter. I'll be settled in here until you return. Take your time. I figure you and Carter might as well be

178

brother-in-laws because your wives think of themselves as sisters. So you'd need to get to know one another, even if Zeb Whitaker wasn't a threat. I already told him about the rumor that Whitaker's offered money for any man who'll bring one of the girls to him." Riley looked directly at Walker. "And there is not much some men won't do for a hundred dollars. Times are hard."

Walker agreed, but he prayed the rumor was just that, a rumor and nothing more. He didn't like the idea of Lacy having a price on her head.

He was halfway to the saloon before he thought that he should have asked for a description of Carter. Other than knowing the man didn't want to meet him in a bar, he had no information about McKoy.

Walker entered, circled the room, and saw only one man who looked like he'd rather be in hell than inside the saloon. He was a big man of about Walker's height and maybe a few years older. His clothes marked him as more farmer than rancher, and no gun hung about his waist. He stood three feet from the door, looking as if he might bolt at any moment.

Walker extended his hand. "Carter McKoy?"

McKoy nodded. "Captain Larson."

Walker watched the man Lacy talked of often. McKoy married her best friend, Bailee, the same night Walker's name was signed to a marriage license with Lacy. To hear Lacy talk, she considered McKoy the perfect husband. The man who could do everything from build houses to read his children to sleep. "Nice to meet you." Walker measured the man. He'd learned to size a man up fast in the army.

Carter only stared.

"Shall we take a seat?"

Carter nodded once more.

They found a table in the back where they could see the door as well as everyone in the room. Walker held up two fingers to the bartender as he sat down. "You don't come in here much." It was a statement to Carter, not a question.

"No," he answered.

Walker waited for the drinks while watching the crowd with McKoy. A saloon on a weeknight was pretty much the same in every town. Regulars came in to drink their troubles away, travelers to relax, gamblers to test their luck. Barmaids, days, or weeks away from a good bath, milled among the groups of men. Added to the local mix tonight were several cowhands returning from a fall cattle drive with too much money in their pockets and nothing but time on their hands until spring roundup. A poker game in the back provided background noise.

The bartender sloshed two whiskeys on the table and left.

Walker picked up his drink and leaned forward. "The sheriff said you needed to see me."

Carter didn't touch his glass. "My Bailee's worried about Lacy." The man acted like every word had to be forced out. "She . . . we think she should be with us at my farm. I've got three hands I can trust on round-the-clock guard, and it being winter, I can stay close to the house. She'd be safer with us than in town."

If any other man in the room had said that to Walker, he would have taken offense. But Carter stared at him directly, with honest eyes that indicated the man had never learned to lie. "That's kind of you —" Walker started.

"It's not being kind. Lacy's family."

Walker once heard the sheriff say that not a rabbit could hop onto Carter's farm without him knowing about it. Carter didn't look like a man who planned to argue the truth, and Walker was smart enough not to waste his time.

"Lacy's my wife," he said calmly. "Would you give up your wife to another to guard?"

A hint of a smile twisted the corner of Carter's mouth. "No. I wouldn't." He stood. The discussion was over. Each man understood the other.

Walker offered his hand to the big man once more. No words passed between them. None were needed. He knew Carter would be there if he needed him, and he knew he'd cover Carter's back any day. Walker almost wished he could stay around and get to know the farmer who found words so hard and loyalty so easy.

As Carter turned, Walker said, "Take care of your Bailee."

Carter's answer was barely above the noise of the crowd. "Take care of your Lacy."

Walker watched him leave, then sat down and drank the other whiskey. Bailee might be Carter's, but there was no possibility Lacy was his.

Walker didn't understand her temper any more than he understood her. She'd be happy, even laughing one minute and arguing with him the next. All his life he'd let reason rule his actions. He'd been a fool once at seventeen and swore he never would allow emotion to rule his actions again.

He was a big enough man to admit that he made a mistake with Lacy the day they met. She thought she was coming to a real husband, while all he'd thought about was getting her out of town.

Walker accepted a third drink from the bartender, something he never did, as he remembered their short time together. Maybe her leaving that day had not been all he thought about. He remembered how she'd looked as she took off her clothes in front of him as simply as if she'd done it a hundred times. There had been no show about it and the beauty lay in the simplicity of her actions.

One of the barmaids delivered a couple more glasses of whiskey. "Need some company?"

"I'm afraid I'm not much for company tonight," Walker answered, but she moved around and sat on his knee anyway. He downed the whiskey, feeling his mind start to cloud.

"Why don't you let me be the judge of that?" She purred like a kitten, but she smelled like cheap perfume. Her hand wound around his neck as she pressed one breast against his shoulder. "I bet you could be mighty fine company on a cold night like this, soldier."

He drank the other whiskey she'd brought, trying to remember how many he'd had and cupped the back of her head with his hand. His eyes blurred just enough that for a moment he couldn't see her clearly.

She gave no resistance as he pulled her mouth to his. He kissed her long and hard.

When he let her go, she moaned in an exaggerated pleasure he was sure she didn't feel. The taste of her mouth made him want to vomit. Maybe Lacy was right, and something was wrong with him. He'd wanted to kiss his wife and hadn't while he had no desire to kiss the woman on his knee, yet he had.

The saloon girl stretched, moving her body close to his face. "You want to go upstairs?"

The stiff lace on her dress scratched his chin.

Walker laughed without humor. "No thanks, I've already been up to the landing tonight, and that was enough."

She acted hurt. "Well, you find me when you're feeling like a little company. I can show you a few tricks that little wife of yours will never learn in the print shop."

Half the town must know who he was, Walker realized. "No thanks," he mumbled, feeling like he'd somehow dishonored Lacy by kissing the barmaid.

Not that Lacy wanted him as a husband, and he certainly didn't want her as a wife. Which left them where? Celibate till death?

Walker wished he could ride off. A good range war almost looked inviting. As far as he was concerned, he didn't want to see another female for the rest of his life. He'd never be drunk enough or dumb enough to consider the barmaid's offer, but he thanked her anyway. He'd also never be fool enough to ask Lacy again.

He stayed another half hour watching the crowd, having another drink, and trying to figure out why he had thought kissing Lacy would be a good idea. She'd been nice to him all day, but she was nice to Jay Boy and Duncan, too. She'd even touched him several times. Probably less than she petted her cats, he decided. If he had to pass a test on reading his wife, he'd be found illiterate within seconds.

Maybe he'd been on the frontier too long. Another five years at a fort without a woman, and he'd probably go so crazy towns would post signs saying he couldn't enter for fear he'd attack every woman on the street.

But it hadn't been a hunger for *any*

woman tonight. If it had, he'd be upstairs right now with the barmaid.

It was a hunger for one woman. A woman who was across the street promising to kill him if he stepped foot in her bedroom. Walker laughed to himself. It wasn't like he could have her in his bed and get her out of his system.

He'd already done that, and it hadn't worked.

Walking back to the print shop, he took a deep breath, trying to clear his mind. He was here to do a job. Nothing more. He'd always been able to concentrate on the mission. It was time he put the last seven years of training to work. In his early army days, he stood guard for twelve-hour shifts in all kinds of weather. Watching over Lacy for three more weeks couldn't be any more grueling.

After bidding the sheriff good night, Walker locked up and climbed the stairs. The apartment was quiet and dark as he knew it would be. Even if she were awake, she wouldn't be coming out to say good night to him. Not tonight.

Three feet into the room he stumbled over the corner of the quilting frame and lost his balance. Tumbling into one of her make-believe chairs, he shattered the box

186

below the quilts into splinters and rolled across the floor, slamming against the corner of the bookshelf. Andy flew off one of the shelves, yelled his protest, then disappeared under the other make-believe chair.

For a moment, he remained perfectly still, mentally checking to see if he still lived. Then he moved one limb at a time to determine damage. When he opened an eye, both of Lacy's cats stared at him from just beneath the chair. They looked disgusted.

Walker swore that the one-eared cat named Andy was laughing at him. A lamp flickered to life behind him. Walker rolled slowly over.

Lacy stood just outside her bedroom door, the lamp in one hand, her Colt in the other. "What happened?" She appeared worried and frightened as she moved toward him, holding both the gun and the light high. "Did someone try to break in?"

Walker sat up as she knelt at his side. "I tripped."

Her worry turned to anger. "You're drunk!"

The volume of her voice made his head ring, and he covered one ear, hoping to halve the sound. "I am not," he tried to answer in a normal tone while he mentally counted the drinks he'd had.

"And bleeding," she continued, "all over my new quilt."

Walker pulled his hand away from his head. Blood dripped off his fingers. "Well, maybe a little, but there's nothing wrong with my hearing. You don't need to keep yelling, madam."

Lacy stood and took the lamp with her. "Follow me."

He wasn't sure how he was supposed to do that in the dark with traps obviously waiting all over the room for him to fall into, but she didn't sound like a woman who would consider discussing her plan of action.

Fumbling his way to the kitchen, he sat in the first chair. His skull felt like it might split in two at any moment.

Lacy pumped a bowl of water and brought it to the table along with several towels. "Be still," she said as she plowed through his hair, searching for the source of blood.

With her standing and him seated, his face came breast level to her. He told himself he was gentleman enough not to notice.

He lied.

When she leaned across his shoulder to turn up the lamp, her side brushed against his temple.

Walker closed his eyes and wished he would bleed to death fast so the torture would be over soon.

"Be still, Captain." She handled his head with a none-too-gentle touch. "How can I find the cut if you keep moving around?"

Walker decided to follow orders and let her continue the cruelty.

One thin layer of cotton gown lay between his jaw and her breast. *Don't think about it,* he told himself.

As she worked, the material brushed his face from time to time, hinting at the softness that might be just beyond her gown. Unlike the barmaid's rough lace, his wife's gown had been washed soft and smelled, as she always did, of peach blossoms.

She dipped the corner of a towel in cold water and pressed it to the crown of his head. "I think it will stop bleeding if I press here for a while. Otherwise we could try stitching it closed." She leaned closer. "I've never tried sewing skin, but I think I could do it. I've seen the doctor do it a few times, and it didn't appear all that hard."

All the blood in his body could drip out, and he'd still be aware of her so near. "You know about nursing?" he managed to ask as he tried to sober enough to talk to her.

"Of course. I was once hired to be a nurse to an old woman. I did a good job, until she died."

Great reference, he thought and shifted in the chair. One of his knees brushed her leg as her gown bumped against his cheek, and he became totally aware of the fullness of her breasts.

"Be still," she snapped.

Walker tried to get his mind off her nearness. He stared down at her little toes sticking out from beneath her gown. "You think you're going to grow any more, Lacy?" he said before he thought.

Lacy stepped away as she thumped him against the side of his face with a fist full of wet towel.

Walker yelped and grabbed his throbbing head. After the pain settled, he said without looking at her, "I may be wrong, Nurse, but I don't think you're supposed to hit a man with a head wound *in* the head."

"How dare you comment about my bust!"

Walker realized his mistake and managed to raise his stare to hers. "I was thinking of your toes. Those are the smallest toes I've ever seen on a woman."

"You see a lot of toes, do you?"

"Well, no." Now he thought about it, he couldn't ever remember seeing any woman's toes. That wasn't what he usually looked at when the few women he'd seen were stripping down to skin.

"Then how do you know mine aren't huge?"

He guessed she laughed at him, but he didn't care. Better that than her thinking he'd been noticing the softness of her breasts . . . which was exactly what he had been doing a moment before.

She stepped back between his knees, no longer angry now that she understood he only studied her feet. "Lean your head over and let me check the cut."

He followed orders. While she worked, he added, "Are you sure they're not going to grow any more? Maybe toes are the last thing to develop on a woman. You're not that old, you know, you might not be finished."

Lacy laughed. "I'm twenty, Captain, and nothing's grown on me since I was fifteen."

He thought of telling her that her bust seemed about the right size, but he didn't know if his skull could take another blow.

Chapter 12

Lacy worked all morning, well aware of the captain guarding her. Wherever she went, he managed to be right behind her. Ever since he'd asked to kiss her, she'd been even more uncomfortable around him than before. She told herself that it wasn't so much that she would have minded the kiss but more that he'd thought about it. Planned it out like a field maneuver. If he'd just kissed her soft and light like he had the night before, maybe even on the lips this time, she wouldn't have objected. After all, he was her husband.

Eli came in and worked with Duncan on the press. The old man remembered Walker and spoke to him with respect, so whatever made Walker leave town hadn't been something that disgraced the family. She thought of asking Eli what he knew of the matter, but the old man had a love for gossip, which was always healthy in the news business, but never provided completely dependable information.

Besides, the men were busy with several orders for handbills that needed to be printed. The orders were small, but they would keep everyone working until the flat papers came in from Dallas. The big sheets were shipped in by train every Wednesday with national and state news already printed on them, headlines and all. The pages had blank space for local stories scattered in squares on each page. That way the small papers only had to set type for their ads and stories, then line up their press with the paper's gaps. The man who bought a paper on the street got an overall look at news from Washington and Dallas to Cedar Point. A story of a local farmer's sale on chickens might be placed beside the happenings in Congress.

Lacy wrote most of the stories, though Jay Boy loved to help when he had time. Eli did the ads. Not that there was much in the way of stories in Cedar Point. The weather was always important, weddings, funerals, and sometimes arrests. If any other news happened, Sheriff Riley or Willard the mercantile owner usually told everyone in town before Lacy could get it in print.

Late Wednesday afternoon, Walker tried

to talk her out of going to the station for the paper, but that had been her job since the first week she'd married. Walker's father had started teaching her the books the first morning they'd worked together, and part of the accounts included logging expenses. "This will be your responsibility soon, Lacy," the old man had said. "You have much to learn, but don't worry. I won't leave you until you know it all."

And he hadn't, Lacy thought. Even in the end when he took opium for the pain, he'd hold on as long as he could so they had time to talk. Then he'd swallow his medicine and float into a half-dream, half-dead state for several hours.

After more than two years, she still missed him dearly. She missed the way they'd talk for hours and how his crippled hand would pat hers and tell her she was a great treasure.

"My son is going to love you," he'd say, "like you got a right to be loved, Lacy." Then he'd fall asleep, and she'd dream about when her invisible husband came home and made his father's promise true.

The wind whipped cold and dry as she stood on the platform and pushed away the past along with a tear from her cheek. Why couldn't Walker have inherited an ounce of his father's kindness?

As the train pulled in, Walker leaned closer. "Stay behind me," he ordered without a hint of request in his tone.

Lacy nodded, but she couldn't resist leaning around him until she could see the train. An excitement rippled across the platform when the train pulled in. People going on trips. Folks coming home. The smoke and the noise. Like many in town, Lacy came sometimes just to watch it arrive.

She looked down the row of cars as passengers stepped off even as the train chugged to a stop. A tall young woman dressed in forest green swung from the steps with grace and yelled, "Lacy!"

Before Walker's arm could stop her, Lacy ran to meet the girl. "Nell!" she cried with pure joy.

They hugged, pulled apart to smile at one another, then hugged again. "It's been so long." Lacy laughed. "We weren't expecting you for at least another month."

"I know, but I couldn't wait. I've so much news I had to —" Nell stopped suddenly. "Lacy, there's a man standing just behind you staring at us."

Lacy didn't turn around. "Is he wearing a uniform and a frown?"

Nell whispered, "Tall, handsome, dark hair, big frown."

"Oh, don't worry about him. That's just my husband."

Before Nell could question her, Lacy stepped back and said, "Captain Larson, I'd like you to meet Miss Nell Desire, a dear friend of mine."

"Oh, Lacy, it's not Desire anymore. I'm almost of age now, and I need a more respectable name." The tall girl offered her hand to Walker. "Some of my friends call me Two Bits, but Lacy and Bailee insist on calling me Nell. I haven't decided on my last name yet." She laughed as if guessing she made little sense to Walker and not caring in the least. "When Fat Alice sent me off to school four years ago, she registered me as Smith. Imagine that, just plain Smith. But —"

"Pardon me, Miss Nell," Walker interrupted. "But I need to get my wife off this platform as fast as possible. Might you continue the discussion elsewhere?"

Nell grabbed her bag as the engineer handed Lacy her pages.

"See you next week, Miss Lacy." He tipped his hat.

"Thank you, Philip."

Walker took the papers and motioned

with his head toward the waiting buggy he'd insisted Lacy use instead of walking as she always did. "We need to be on our way, ladies."

Nell locked arms with Lacy. "Is he always so bossy?" she whispered.

Lacy glanced at Walker. From his raised eyebrow, she knew he'd heard. "I'm afraid so. But he'll be gone in nineteen days."

"That bad," Nell said a little louder. "Counting the days?"

Lacy didn't answer. She didn't have to. Her friend understood.

That night Nell joined them for dinner at the hotel. She kept Lacy laughing with her tales of school. It seemed the fine finishing school Fat Alice sent her to was not quite prepared for a girl who grew up in a whorehouse.

Lacy thought Nell appeared so grand in her proper dress, with her proper manners. But she remembered the little Two Bits who befriended Carter years ago. Lacy had sworn to be the little girl's friend forever, but to the McKoys, Nell had become family.

"When are you heading out to Carter and Bailee's place?" Lacy asked Nell over pie.

"First thing in the morning," Nell answered. "I was kind of hoping to see my ranger tonight if he's in town. It's been six months since I've had a letter from him. The man still can't get the idea that he belongs to me. He still thinks of me as a kid."

Lacy sighed. "He's not here, Nell. As far as I know, not even Sheriff Riley's heard from him for a few months." Ranger Jacob Dalton had put Zeb Whitaker in jail twice over the years. Lacy kind of wished he'd do it again. "If he knew Whitaker was out, I have a feeling he'd be headed this direction."

Nell patted Lacy's hand. "Don't you worry about Whitaker. He's probably too old to sit a horse by now. And I sent wires to Jacob to let him know what's happening. It may take a while for it to bounce around and find him, but he'll come as soon as he gets it."

Lacy tried not to appear worried. She didn't want to frighten Nell. "We think Whitaker shot out the windows of the print shop last week. Or maybe he just hired someone, thinking he'd scare me. Riley said he heard that the entire time he was in prison, Whitaker swore he'd get back the money we stole from him."

Nell glanced at Walker, who'd been silent while they talked. "Were the shots fired at Lacy, or just the shop?"

Walker shrugged. "I'm not sure." He leaned forward with his elbows on the table, suddenly interested in the conversation. "Why?"

Nell hesitated, not wanting to voice her fears.

"What are you thinking?" he asked.

"I was only a child, but I remember Whitaker coming to Fat Alice's place. This was before Lacy and Bailee clubbed him and thought they'd murdered him. He was nothing but trouble, left more than one of the girls beat up. Finally, Alice met him at the door with a gun and told him if she ever saw him again, she'd kill him on sight."

Nell shifted in her chair. "We didn't see him after that, but we still heard stories. If he thinks the three of you have his money, he might kill one of you to get the other two to give it up." She stared directly at Walker. "Lacy's right out in the open."

"I'm well aware of that," Walker said with the icy coldness of a soldier on duty. "Riley thinks she should go to someone named Sarah's place. Carter wants her to come to his farm, but she won't budge."

"This is my home," Lacy answered, knowing they wouldn't understand. She loved her home. She wouldn't just pick up and leave because Zeb Whitaker might be after her.

Nell leaned closer. "But Lacy, don't you see? You're the easiest for him to come after."

Lacy frowned. She really didn't need another person telling her the same thing. "Don't worry about me. I've got Captain Larson to protect me for nineteen more days and, who knows, so many people hate Zeb Whitaker, someone might shoot him by then. Or your ranger might be back to protect us." Lacy pushed her worries aside. "That is if he's not running from you." Everyone knew Nell had been crazy about the ranger since she was a child. She called him "my ranger," like the state of Texas had given him to her one Christmas.

"He can run, but Jacob Dalton can't hide. I'll catch up with him one of these days and make him marry me. I made him promise that he'd wait for me to grow up."

Walker leaned back in his chair as if the conversation had taken a turn that no longer interested him.

"Or maybe . . ." Nell winked at Lacy. "I'll just sleep with him and drive him mad with desire for me." She smiled innocently at Walker, as if the words she'd just said couldn't have come out of her mouth. "But if I do," she whispered to Lacy, "I'm making him pay the going rate."

Laughing, Lacy watched Walker try not to choke on his coffee. She'd long ago grown used to Nell and her talk. Her husband remained silent all evening, acting more as guard than host. He was polite but distant.

Lacy asked Nell to stay with her, but the young girl refused. She complained of living in a dorm all fall and longed to be alone for a few hours. She did ask to borrow Lacy's buggy and Dancer for a few days, planning to leave at dawn for the McKoy place.

Big silent Carter and a little girl everyone called Two Bits had sworn to be friends forever. Nell had kept her promise, as had he. Whenever she returned home, her first stop was always to Carter and Bailee's farm.

And if she were part of Bailee's family, Nell was also part of Lacy's. The little homeless girl who grew up in a house by the tracks had three adopted sisters. And they were all three in danger at the moment.

Nell gripped Lacy's hand. "Don't worry," she said. "Old Whitaker's not going to get to you."

Lacy tried to be braver than she felt. "That's right." She glanced at Walker. "The captain won't let him."

The corner of Walker's mouth lifted briefly as he gave a half salute.

The women said good-bye in the lobby. Walker offered his arm, and Lacy walked silently beside him. Any other time she would go with Nell to visit Carter and Bailee, but Walker wouldn't discuss the possibility. He didn't understand how dear Bailee was to Lacy. He'd probably never felt so close to anyone in his life.

Lacy decided being with Walker was lonelier than being alone. She'd given up hating him. She'd even stopped disliking him. Somehow over the past few days of his eternal politeness mixed with constant orders, she realized she felt nothing for him. He was a man without feeling, and he didn't deserve to be hated any more than an object did. He left home at seventeen, joined the army, and became a machine. He had no more heart than the printing press.

"Would you like me to carry you?" he asked, startling her from her thoughts.

"No, the ground is dry enough for me to walk without getting muddy."

They climbed the steps, remaining silent while he unlocked the apartment door. He stepped back, allowing her to enter, then followed her into the kitchen. As she had the nights before, Lacy tore a page from her tablet and dropped the number nineteen into the stove.

Walker watched her. "Am I really so intolerable?"

She looked up, surprised to find him staring at her. "I'm just used to having my time to myself."

Crossing his arms, he leaned against the doorjamb. "How can I make this easier on you, Lacy?" For once he sounded like he meant his words.

She smiled. "Eating out every night is nice. I've never had such a luxury."

He nodded. "I look forward to it, too. The food is far better than army mess."

Pressing her palm to her forehead, she tried to think of anything that might help the tension. She wasn't afraid of him. She knew he'd never hurt her, but having him forever near wore on her nerves. "Maybe if I knew you better, it would be easier to be friends."

Walker nodded. "I'm willing to try if it would keep you from jumping every time I step within three feet of you."

Lacy removed her coat and laid it over the back of her kitchen chair since he'd already used the only hook by the door. "We could start by having tea."

He grinned. "We could start by having coffee."

She put water on to boil. "How about one of each?"

He got the cups down, and she pinched tea into her cup. As soon as the water boiled, she filled her teacup, then dropped coffee into the remaining water.

She was halfway finished with her tea when the beans had boiled long enough for Walker to pour his coffee. He sat down across the tiny table from her and waited.

"Where do we start?" She sipped, letting the hot liquid warm her. In an odd way she felt she'd missed their talk at dinner with Nell there. Now seemed like a good time.

"I don't know." He leaned back in his chair. "We could set some ground rules, I guess, like we're playing a game."

She agreed. A game would be nice; otherwise it might sound like an interrogation. "How about I ask one question, any question, and you have to answer. Then you're allowed one question, but only one, and I have to answer."

"Fair enough. What subjects are off limits?"

"None," she answered.

"I accept the terms."

Lacy wanted to giggle. Though he acted as if he were negotiating a treaty, maybe this would work. They'd get to know one another better at least. There was no reason they couldn't be friends. "All right, something easy."

He waited.

"What is your favorite time of year?"

"Fall," he answered simply.

"But why —"

"Only one question. My turn."

She agreed with a nod.

"Why do you make quilts?"

"That's easy. My mother and grand-mother quilted when I was little. When I first started working with your father, there wasn't a great deal to do, so I'd piece together scraps on slow days at the shop. By the time he moved up here with me, I had several tops that needed to be quilted. He gave me half a closet full of old blankets to use as the stuffings." She realized she hadn't answered the question. "It's like painting for me. I feel like I'm creating something no one else has ever made."

From his look she guessed she gave far

more detail than needed. "My turn," she said. "Why did you join the army?"

Lacy watched him drink his coffee and guessed he was thinking about whether to tell her the truth. Finally, he said, "I loved another man's wife."

"Do you still?" That would explain so much. Why he didn't want to be married to her. Maybe if he couldn't have the woman he loved, he never wanted another for a wife. But how could he have loved another so young? He'd only been seventeen when he'd run away to join the army. Lacy frowned. This one question at a time thing wasn't going to work.

"The next question is mine," he answered. "Do you like running the shop?"

"Yes," Lacy answered simply. "Do you still love the other man's wife?"

"No," he said too quickly for it to be a lie.

They each took a drink. When he looked her straight in the eyes, she had the feeling they were no longer playing a game. "What happened the morning you met Zeb Whitaker?"

Lacy was up and moving. She made it halfway across the main room before his words stopped her. "Lacy, stop flying from reality and answer me."

"I don't want to."

"You agreed. You're the one who set the rules."

She couldn't bring herself to turn around. She didn't want to play the game anymore. Taking a long breath, she forced herself to calm. "All right. This mess has cost you a month of your life. I guess you've a right to know. Bailee, Sarah, and I were in a wagon heading south from Kansas. We'd been out of food for days when one morning a buffalo hunter came into our camp. He said he had to shoot his horse and wanted to buy our wagon. Bailee wouldn't sell. He reached in his saddlebags and produced a handful of gold, insisting that we agree. But it didn't matter how much money he had because if he took our wagon, we knew we'd be dead."

She heard Walker's boots tap the floor and knew he moved closer, but she didn't budge.

"When we wouldn't take his offer, he decided to take our wagon anyway. Since we were all half starved, I don't think he thought of it as much of a crime. At the last minute, he said he wanted to take me with him," She fought to keep from choking on the words. "He ripped the front of my dress open to make sure I was woman enough to bother with." She fought back tears. Even after five years, the night was too horrible to talk about.

"He slapped me until I was too scared to cry out and started dragging me to the wagon. He didn't even give me time to pull my clothes together. He was too busy talking about what he'd do to me every night on the trail and how he'd sell me once he got tired of feeding me.

"All of a sudden, Bailee hit him with a board, and we thought she killed him. She started crying, so Sarah picked up the board and hit him, too. And then I did. I hit him as hard as I could, praying that I was the one who killed him."

Lacy raised her chin. "We left him there, the gold from his saddlebags spilling out over his body, and made it to Cedar Point by the next night. We all confessed, and the sheriff told us we'd go to prison, but I didn't care. I would have killed him again if I'd had the chance."

"But the sheriff told me there was no body." Walker filled in the details as he moved to stand behind her. "He couldn't charge you, and he couldn't let the three of you go because you'd confessed. He had to find a body and prove you were guilty, or find Whitaker to prove you were inno-cent."

"But Zeb Whitaker had disappeared, it seemed. Riley couldn't stand to send us down state to a prison, and he couldn't afford to keep us here, so he charged us each a fine and married us off to anyone willing to pay it. I thought the nightmare would end, but Whitaker is coming after me again. He says he wants his gold, but I think he blames me for all his troubles. I think he hates me the most."

Walker had never considered the cruelty of what had happened. He'd only been thinking of himself when his father telegrammed him that he was now married by proxy. Lacy had only been fifteen; she must have been frightened out of her mind. She must be terrified now.

"Lacy," he whispered not knowing what to say.

When she turned to face him, he opened his arms.

Awkwardly, she moved into his embrace. While she cried against his chest, he held her close. "It's all right, now, Lacy. He'll never hurt you again."

He held her until the tears stopped. She thanked him and disappeared into her bedroom, but it was a long time before Walker could sleep. In the five years since they'd been married, he'd never thought that

Lacy might have been an innocent in what happened to her. At first he'd thought she'd manipulated his father; then, after she'd visited him, he'd thought that she was just a fool who must have gotten in with the wrong people. He felt more sorrow for her than anger.

He didn't consider himself to be an easy man to fool. If Lacy lied to him tonight, she was a master at it. He stayed up until almost dawn piecing all the details together.

The next morning, for the first time in years, he overslept. When he rolled over and smelled coffee, he awoke all at once.

Lacy's humming drifted from the kitchen, and he relaxed.

Stomping into his boots, he met her stare when he reached the doorway.

"You almost missed breakfast," she said with a shy smile. "Which, considering the way I cook, might not be a bad idea."

She put the food on the table while he washed up behind the blanket that had become part of the kitchen. With his hair still damp, he sat down to a breakfast of potato pancakes and eggs.

"Looks good," he managed to lie.

"Thank you. I wasn't sure how many you'd want, so I made lots." She scraped the last few pancakes out of the skillet.

Whatever had happened between them last night had worked. Both were more relaxed. She even buttered his bread and handed it to him as though they were some old married couple. He questioned her about her Thursday workday, and she went through all the details of what had to be done so that they'd have the paper ready by Friday afternoon.

When she'd finished her meal, Lacy leaned close and checked to see how his head was healing, then stayed a moment longer to comb his hair with her fingers.

Walker closed his eyes and relaxed, imagining what it would be like to have a woman, to have Lacy, so near, so comfortable around him that she'd touch his hair while she talked about her day. It seemed a foreign world, but peaceful, if only for a moment.

"No one will see the scar until you go bald." She laughed. "But with this much hair, it may take a while."

When she moved away, he felt the loss of her even before he heard her stand.

"Well." She cleared the dishes. "What do you think of my cooking, Captain?"

The pancakes were burned on the outside and a mush of milk and egg mixture on the inside. Walker couldn't lie. "You're a great quilter."

"Spoken like a man not afraid to die." She laughed and raised the rolling pin she'd used to toughen the biscuit dough.

They were both laughing when someone pounded on the kitchen door.

Walker leaned over, pulling her behind him as he reached for his rifle. "Who's there!" he yelled.

"It's Riley. Let me in, Walker."

The door swung open.

The instant she saw the sheriff's worried face, Lacy let out a little cry. Walker circled her waist with his free hand while he unsnapped the leather over his pistol with the other.

Riley hurried in. "It's bad." He shook his head. "I should have seen it coming, but I never thought —"

"Bailee? Sarah?" Lacy grabbed the sheriff's coat. "Who is it? Who's —" She couldn't finish.

Walker pulled her against him and braced her for what he knew would be bad news. "What happened, Sheriff?"

"Bailee and Sarah are fine." The old man swallowed and forced words. "It's Nell. She's hurt bad." He closed his eyes, not wanting to see the pain his words would cause. "Carter was coming into town to make his weekly delivery. He found your buggy all busted up down by the draw. Nell must have left before full daylight and been traveling as fast as old Dancer can run."

Lacy pushed away from Walker and jerked off her apron. "Where is she?"

Riley stepped out of her way. "At Doc's. But —"

Lacy didn't give him time to say more.

Chapter 13

Walker followed Lacy as she ran down the back steps, across the alley, and into the rear entrance of the doctor's home. He was one step behind her when she darted through a kitchen, across the front office, and to the door of the examining room.

When the doctor saw her, he hurried forward, blocking her flight. "Now, Miss Lacy," he started. "It's not as bad as it may appear. There's a lot of blood, but I have her breathing regularly. I was about to check for broken bones."

Lacy stopped so fast Walker almost ran into her. She took huge gulps of air and waited for the doctor to move aside. Walker knew she prepared herself.

"Let me see her, Timothy," Lacy ordered.

Walker had met the doctor a few days before and thought him an odd match for the town. Dr. Timothy McClellan looked like he belonged more in Boston than on the frontier. He was tall, in his early thirties, with thinning sand-colored hair. His body appeared too bony to look healthy, and his intelligent eyes missed nothing around him. He stared at Lacy with the expression of a man facing a firing squad.

"If you'll calm down, I could use your help." He tried to be firm. "The last thing she needs is someone panicking. Thank the Lord McKoy found her, or she might have bled to death pinned under a buggy."

Lacy took a step forward as if planning to walk right through him if he didn't get out of her way.

The doctor moved aside. "We've got to move fast. Can you stay with me and help?"

"Yes." She moved toward the table and whispered, "I'm here, Nell, and I'm not leaving."

Walker wasn't sure he wanted to go farther. He'd seen enough blood to last him a lifetime. But he didn't want Lacy to have to face the scene alone.

The doctor made the decision for him. "I'm going to have to ask you gentlemen to leave. Now that Miss Lacy's here, she can assist me with Nell's clothes, and I can get to work."

Walker glanced over his shoulder. He wasn't surprised to see Riley standing by the door, but he hadn't even noticed Carter seated in the corner. The big man had blood all over his chest and hands.

To Walker's surprise, Lacy crossed to Carter. She laid her hand on his shoulder and whispered, "You got her here, now it's time to let the doctor do what he can. I'll be right with her, don't worry."

Carter nodded once and stood. He didn't say a word, but all in the room knew how much he cared for the young woman he still called "the kid."

Walker followed Carter and the sheriff into the little office beyond the examining room. They both took seats on chairs that were too small for them in a room that seemed dingy even with sunlight shining through a big window that faced the street.

The sheriff stepped into the kitchen area and grabbed a towel. He wet it and handed it to Carter. "How do you think the accident happened? We all know Nell can handle a wagon good as any man."

"She tumbled, wagon and all, down fifty feet." Carter closed his eyes as if trying to remember details. "Must have tried to make that turn at the draw too fast."

Walker noticed Carter's hands moving at

his sides a few minutes before he said, "I had to put Dancer down. Two broken legs. If he hadn't been thrashing, I wouldn't have seen the buggy."

Carter rubbed off some of the blood, then looked directly at Walker. "I thought it was Lacy at first. All I saw was brown hair on a woman's body pinned below the buggy."

Riley shook his head. "It ain't like Nell. She's made that drive out to your place for years now. I remember when she didn't come to my shoulder she used to ride the train to town, borrow Lacy's buggy, and fly out to your place every time she got fired up about something." The sheriff leaned back and toyed with his pipe. "I remember when Fat Alice told her she had to go away to school, she ran off. Alice telegrammed me, knowing Two Bits would be heading to you. When I wired back that she was safe, Alice answered to let her cool off a few days and then send the ranger after her."

Riley smiled, unaware that no one seemed to be listening to him. "Jacob Dalton came in from your place with her thrown over his saddle like a bag of potatoes. He tossed her on that train heading north and swore he'd track her down if she climbed off it before Chicago. She was swearing and spitting fire. She swore that when her breasts came in she was going to be a lady of the evening so she was just wasting time on education."

Carter relaxed a little. "She wrote me Jacob threatened to climb on the train if she didn't clean her language up."

"Oh, he did," the sheriff agreed. "Said he'd paddle her all the way to Kansas City, but she just yelled back that when she went into business she wasn't planning on letting him in her bed, even if he paid double.

"I think if the train hadn't started, I would have had to arrest the ranger just to cool him down. I've never seen him as mad at any outlaw as he was at that little hellcat of a girl in there." He pointed to the closed door. "After Nell left, I had to get him drunk to make him stop yelling. He swore the kid's parents must have been a rattle-snake and a badger."

Walker saw what the two men were doing. They were reminding each other of what a tough young lady lay on the other side of that door. He wished that he knew her, wished he'd watched her grow up as these two men had.

Lacy leaned her head around the door, her eyes full of unshed tears. "Nell's awake. We've got the drape on her, but she won't let the doctor start until she talks to Walker."

All three men stood. The sheriff and Carter paid no mind that their names hadn't been among the requested. All three marched back into the room.

Dr. McClellan circled like a warrior ready to do battle. "Be quick. As soon as the water boils, I've got to get to work, and I don't want an audience."

Walker was relieved to see several pots of water by the fireplace in the corner. Most of the doctors he knew didn't bother to wash their hands, much less wounds, but he'd heard they were teaching washing everything in medical schools nowadays.

Carter moved to one side of the table, Walker to the other.

Nell was covered with a cotton drape Walker had heard some doctors use when examining a woman. He'd seen men nude while the physician worked, but propriety demanded doctors only see the part of a woman injured, never more. The thick, unbleached material insured modesty, but judging from spots of blood already soaking through the drape, there wouldn't be much of Nell that McClellan wouldn't see today.

Nell's hair, almost the same brown as Lacy's, looked matted with blood and dirt. She had a cut on her forehead, another at her throat, and bruises already formed along the side of her face. One eye had closed with swelling, but the other stared up at Carter.

The big man took her hand without saying a word.

Nell glanced from him to Walker and back. "Tell the sheriff," she whispered, "that I was chased by three men. I couldn't see who they were, but they started shooting as I neared the bend." She closed her eyes in pain. "I took a slug in my right arm and another in my back."

Walker developed a great respect for the young woman fighting back pain so she could say what had to be said. She didn't whine or bother to tell them how frightened she must be. He leaned closer, not wanting to miss a word and wishing he had time to tell her she would make a fine soldier.

The sheriff fidgeted at the foot of the bed, wanting to ask questions, but the doctor motioned him to be quiet as he circled, readying the room.

McClellan snapped orders at Lacy and, from the way she moved about, Walker had no doubt she'd helped the doctor before. They were frantically preparing to fight for Nell's life.

"Captain?" Nell whispered.

"I'm here," Walker answered.

"Once I tumbled, I couldn't move, but I heard them when they rode up to the overturned buggy. A man said, 'That's the first one down; let's move on to the next. When two are dead, the third will talk easy enough.' "

It took a second for the truth to hit Walker.

"Water's ready." The doctor broke the silence. "Everyone out!"

Nell's knuckles whitened around Carter's hand. "Watch over Bailee. They'll go after her next, now that they think they've got Lacy."

Carter's big hand moved beside Nell's fingers as if he sent her a private message.

"Don't worry about me," the girl said. "Take care of Bailee."

Carter nodded and headed out of the room as the doctor snapped at them to hurry so he could get Nell patched up.

Walker glanced at Lacy as she tied on a white apron and moved a table full of supplies close to Nell. McClellan poured drops of chloroform onto a cloth. Walker backed out of the room.

The sheriff had stopped Carter from leaving when he made it back to the office. "Now hold on there." Riley pulled on the big man's arm.

Carter appeared ready to fight his way out if necessary.

"He's right." Walker moved between the door and Carter. "We've got to take a minute and plan."

"I have to get home to my wife," Carter answered.

"I'm going with you." Walker's comment surprised the big man. "I want to see the wagon. Plus we'll be safer together." Whoever shot at Nell might still be on the road between town and the McKoy farm.

Carter nodded.

"You're right, we should all go out and have a look," Riley put in.

Walker looked at Riley. "Right now, whoever shot Nell thinks they killed Lacy. Let's leave it that way for a few hours. I know it's a lot to ask, but I need you to watch over Lacy and Nell until I get back, Sheriff. And no one, not even a deputy, is to know that it's Nell on that table and not Lacy."

Riley mumbled. Like an old hunting dog, he didn't favor the idea of being left behind, but they both knew Walker wouldn't miss a clue, and if there was an ambush waiting, the younger men would have a better chance of riding hard and fast to cover. The sheriff nodded.

"Thanks." Walker gripped the old man's shoulder. "It's good to have someone I can trust. I'll be back before dark."

Carter and Walker left out the back door with only a stray dog to notice them. Carter unloaded several bushels of potatoes at the back of the mercantile and was waiting by the time Walker saddled up. They headed out of town, Carter in his wagon, Walker mounted.

Carter took the lead, since Walker had no idea what direction to take. Walker followed close enough to keep the wagon in sight but far enough away to notice any movement beside the road when the wagon passed.

By the time they reached what was left of the buggy, Walker had outlined a plan.

Chapter 14

Lacy's back ached so badly she felt it might snap at any moment. They'd worked on Nell's injuries for hours. Dr. McClellan first checked her for internal damage, which many doctors wouldn't have bothered with because many women would have objected. Lacy saw a woman die once from a tumor rather than allow a doctor to touch her so intimately. She knew Nell had no such fears and told Timothy McClellan so, when he hesitated.

Once they realized no internal organs were damaged, they moved to Nell's head and stitched up the cuts she suffered when the buggy rolled over her. All but one were in her hair, and Timothy closed the wounds with stitches that would have made a quilter proud. The last wound only took a few stitches at her throat, but looked like it might leave a scar. A reminder that if the small puncture wound had been an inch over, Nell would have bled to death before anyone could have saved her.

Next, the doctor moved to her limbs. A bullet lodged just below the shoulder on her left arm, and her right arm was broken in two places. Nell had been right about a bullet in her back. It wasn't as deep, but it was in a far more dangerous location.

Lacy watched as the doctor tried to remove it with great care.

After almost an hour he tossed the instruments aside. "I can't get the bullet," he swore.

Lacy fought to breathe. "But you can't leave it in."

Timothy's worried stare met hers. "If I dig around her spine any longer, I could do more damage than the bullet did. I'll not cripple her to get it out."

He paced beside the table, cursing his lack of skill. "I went the full two years of medical school," he complained, "so why do I feel so incompetent?"

"Just do the best you can," Lacy urged. "That's all anyone expects." She had heard several people say Dr. McClellan was already ten times a better doctor than the old man he'd replaced.

"She can live with it inside." He made a

shaky judgment call. "Who knows, the bullet might not affect anything. It could just float around." He seemed angry at the world. "This isn't the war. Chances are good the gun the bullet came from didn't use black powder, so the possibility of blood poisoning is less than it would have been ten years ago." He walked over to a small cabinet and poured himself a drink, something Lacy had never seen him do.

After downing the shot of whiskey as if it were medicine, he straightened and apologized for his outburst.

She would have been more reassured by the doctor's words if he hadn't looked so unhappy.

"What is it?" she whispered later as he bandaged the incision.

"I saw a wound like this in the small of a man's back once when I was in medical school." He wiped the sweat from his forehead with the sleeve of his shirt. "The man never walked again. One small bullet put him in a wheelchair for life."

Lacy wanted to scream, but she bit her lip and kept working. When Walker's father had been ill, she'd spent many hours with the doctor. He didn't have a wife and couldn't afford a nurse, even if he could find one willing to help out. So, sometimes, he'd cross the alley and ask her to assist. Blood didn't frighten Lacy like it did some people, and she wasn't afraid of hard work. She knew he was being more honest with her now than he might have been if he hadn't trusted her.

The memory of Nell jumping off the train yesterday filled her thoughts. She tried to imagine what it would be like if Nell couldn't walk, but no picture came to mind. Lacy thought of telling the doctor to try again because she knew Nell would risk death, maybe even prefer it, over being crippled. But this was Timothy's call. He had to do what he thought was right. His job was to save a life, not gamble with one.

"I'll give her something for the pain." He tied off the bandage. "We've got to keep her as quiet as possible and pray infection doesn't set in."

The doctor had no bed to offer Nell except his own in a little room above his offices. Lacy knew getting her up the stairs to his room, or even her little apartment above the shop, would cause more pain for Nell. Most patients walked in and out of the office. The few who couldn't were usually treated at home, for it was much easier for McClellan to travel to them. Only now, a sickroom or even a real bed would have come in handy.

The doctor must have read her thoughts for he added, "She'll be all right here for tonight. We'll bank her on both sides with a rolled blanket and make her as comfortable as possible. If the bleeding stops by morning, we'll talk about where to move her." He touched Lacy's shoulder with a quick pat. "You need to get some rest."

"I'm staying right here. You go." Lacy washed her hands. "I need to clean the small scrapes and cuts, then I'll change the bandages as needed."

The doctor hesitated, struggling with the idea, then nodded as if he no longer had the energy to stand. For a young man, he had old ways about him, and she was reminded of how her mother used to say some people were like old souls walking this earth one last time.

"During the night, we'll change shifts." His sad eyes closed as if he prayed. "We'll know more by morning. Until then, there isn't much for either of us to do but wait."

Lacy left him standing by Nell's side as she went into the kitchen to make coffee. They had a long night ahead of them.

She heard Walker return and relieve the sheriff from guard duty. She continued to work as the captain's voice floated from a room away.

"It's a miracle the girl is still alive," Walker reported. "The buggy looked like it had been used for target practice. Once it went off the road, it rolled several times, too damaged to even try and repair. Carter found Nell beneath a pile of rubble."

Lacy glanced in the office as Sheriff Riley shook his head. "I need to make a report, but I'll be back by morning." He stood and moved to the door. "Jay Boy stopped by with the doc's paper, and I told him Lacy and you left town at dawn. I said I wasn't sure when she'd be back, but not to worry."

"Good. Leave Lacy's whereabouts in question."

"The boy said he'd tell Eli and Duncan and help them get out the paper. He said he thought a day or two away might do Lacy good and didn't seem concerned." The old man smiled. "He's a smart one. He'll keep that paper going."

Lacy reasoned that trips to the McKoy farm were frequent, and Jay Boy would know to feed the cats and lock up each night. In a few years he'd be man enough to run the paper. Even now he took more responsibility than most young men his age. His writing was almost as good as Lacy's and better than most of Duncan's work.

She turned back to the cookstove, waiting for the coffee, as she rubbed the back of her neck. As the last rays of the dying sun flickered through the tiny kitchen window, she leaned toward the light, stretching tired muscles.

Walker walked in and stood close behind her. She didn't turn around. She knew the sound of his boots and guessed he must be as tired as she. Too tired to even make an attempt at conversation.

He brushed the muscles of her back with his open hand and without a word let her know he was there if she needed him. Closing her eyes, Lacy smelled trail dust, horses, and leather, as if he'd been riding hard. The usual aroma of his shaving soap had worn off for the day, and in a strange way, she missed it. She leaned into the wind-chilled wool of his coat.

When his hand moved over her shoulder, she shifted with the sore muscles, but he didn't step away. His fingers spread out across her back while his thumbs moved along her spine, pushing into her hair and then down as far as her collar would allow him to go. The gentle, slow movements of his strong hands relaxed her.

Lacy knew she should step away, but his touch was magic. All the fear and worry drifted from her body.

"You all right?" he whispered.

She sighed, realizing that he might need to touch another as dearly as she needed to connect.

His warm hands moved down her back to her waist, then up again to her shoulders. "Tell me to stop," his voice was even closer to her ear, "if you don't want this."

She would never have been brave enough to tell him what she wanted, what she needed, but she would not tell him to stop. Slowly she leaned her head until it rested against his chest. For the moment he was more than just her husband on paper.

He took the weight of her body against him, moving closer, the warmth of him molding along her back as his hands circled her waist and pulled her to him. His head leaned forward and his chin brushed against her hair.

"It feels so good to hold you," he said low, his breath caressing her ear. "I've thought about . . . worried about you all day, wishing I could be this close to you . . . wanting to know you were safe."

She could guess what he'd been thinking

all day. The same thing she had. It could have been her on the table in the other room fighting for life.

Lacy couldn't voice her fears, and she knew Walker wouldn't, for it somehow seemed a great sin to thank heaven it hadn't been her, because by so doing they would also be saying they preferred it to be Nell who was hurt.

"I'd trade places with her if I could," Lacy whispered.

Walker's arms tightened about her waist, and she realized she'd said her thoughts out loud.

"It's not your fault, Lacy."

"But —"

He pressed a kiss near her ear. "None of this is your fault."

She crossed her arms over his, clinging to him as if he might let go and she'd fall. But his hold never lessened. His arms were the harbor she needed. The day of worry and work had left her spinning with fear. Now, he grounded her. She closed her eyes and drew from the strength of the man holding her.

He rocked her gently. The side of his face moved against her hair in a caress. Lacy tried to remember any other time in her life when she'd felt so safe. This captain of hers who had no heart offered her the very thing she needed.

"It feels so good to hold you," he whispered.

"I know," she answered, no longer able to guard her words.

When the coffee boiled over, she pulled away. He let her go with a groan, then straightened as if he'd somehow shown a weakness he hadn't intended to reveal.

Lacy took the doctor a cup, then found Walker in the office. He sat in the room's only comfortable chair behind the doctor's desk, reminding her of how he'd looked two years ago when she'd walked into his office at Cottonwood. She knew him better now, and after the way he'd held her, she knew there was warmth behind the straitlaced captain who had shown none the day they met.

"Dr. McClellan says she's resting quietly. That's a good sign." Lacy put her hands together in front of her, suddenly embarrassed at how she'd leaned so close to him only minutes before. "He's checking the bandages now. I told him I'd take the first shift so he could get some sleep. You could go —"

"I'm not going anywhere," he snapped, seemingly irritated she'd even suggest that he might leave her. "I'll be right here if you need me."

Lacy frowned. She should have known better than to recommend he do anything. The captain always had his actions planned out. But why did he make everything he said sound like a command? Why couldn't he talk with an ounce of the gentleness he'd shown her when he'd held her in the kitchen?

Without another word, she left the room. She was too tired to think about her husband's strange ways. In a few weeks he'd be gone, and she promised herself she'd never think of him again.

The doctor rolled down his sleeves as she stepped back into the room with Nell.

"Call me if there is any change," he said sounding exhausted. "And thanks for being here today. I don't know if your friend would be alive if you hadn't made it possible for me to move so quickly." He smiled. "We make a good team."

"Thank you," she said. "For everything." She almost added, *For being kind, for helping Nell, for not yelling at me.*

"I'll be right upstairs. If you need me, all you have to do is call. I'll take the next watch."

He walked out the door, and she heard

him speak to Walker. Then, all was silent. She wasn't surprised they had little to say to one another; they were as different as two men could be. The doctor fought to save lives. By profession Walker sometimes ended them. Timothy was gentle and soft-spoken. Her husband preferred to order or yell. Yet Walker's touch had been warm, caring, and the doctor's had been, as always, impersonal.

Lacy turned down the lamps, made sure the rolled blankets were tucked around Nell, and relaxed on the small settee by the window. The dainty piece of furniture was too small to lie down on and too long to serve as a comfortable chair.

Lacy glanced around. There was nowhere else to sit in the room unless she wanted to pull a chair in from the office. She wondered about Dr. McClellan's strange furniture. Except for the desk and one chair in his office, everything in the place seemed like it would belong more to a woman than a man. Maybe the doctor had a wife who was to have come west with him, but couldn't or wouldn't at the last minute. Also from the settee to the massive desk in the office, all the furniture appeared mismatched.

Lacy sighed, thinking it looked like he'd

picked up what everyone else had left behind when the wagons heading west were too heavy. She remembered a few places along the Santa Fe Trail where wagons had to be made lighter to make it any farther. The dumping ground was called the bone pile. She'd seen one with whole dining table and chairs tossed in and pianos amidst the forgotten boxes and trunks that families had first thought they couldn't leave behind.

Lacy wiggled, trying to get comfortable on the settee, but it was a waste of time. The arms were too far apart to sit and too close together to recline.

She glanced up and noticed Walker standing in the doorway watching her.

"What?" she whispered, irritated and too tired to care.

"I brought more wood for the fireplace," he said as if she'd asked politely. He lay it in a box without making a sound. "Do you need anything else?"

"No." She tried to put her arm over the end of the settee. One side was too tall, the other too short to work. "I just have to try to stay awake in case Nell stirs. This thing needs to be a foot longer to recline on or a few feet shorter to sit in. It is an absolutely ridiculous piece of furniture."

"Could I help? I have to remain awake to watch over you." He smiled as she wiggled, trying to get comfortable.

"Would you know what to do if Nell moves?"

"No."

"Then I don't see how you can be of any help, but thank you for the offer." Lacy tried scooting down to rest her head on the back of the settee, but her bottom almost slid to the floor.

Walker crossed the room to her, his coat hooked on one finger and thrown over his shoulder. "I've got an idea. How about I stay awake and you sleep? If Nell moves, I'll wake you, and you can take care of her. At least one of us can sleep then."

Lacy liked the idea but shook her head. "I won't leave the room, and this thing is too little to sleep on."

"Stand up." He offered his hand to help her.

She followed orders, for once too exhausted to argue.

He stepped around her and sat on the settee, then put his arms around her waist and pulled her down. There was enough room for her bottom to slip in between the padded arm and his body, and with her legs over his, she could lift her feet up. She leaned back enough to use the tall padding for a pillow and with his arm draped over her knees, she didn't have to worry about falling on the floor.

"Raise one foot."

She did, and his hand cupped the heel of her boot and pulled it off.

"The other."

He repeated his action.

Swinging his coat over her, he said, "Now sleep. I'll make sure you don't fall, and my coat should keep you warm enough."

"But won't you be cold?"

"I've got you over me." He grinned.

She was too worn out to think of an argument. In truth, she felt comfortable and warm.

Curling into the settee, she ignored the fact that part of her lay across Walker and drifted to sleep as his hand moved gently along her leg until he made sure his coat covered her feet.

Chapter 15

Walker watched Lacy wake slowly, struggling as if from a bad dream. She twisted, and he gently tightened his arm across her legs so she wouldn't roll off the settee.

"Lacy? Are you awake?" he asked, brushing the hair from her face.

She shifted again and opened her eyes, coming awake in degrees. "No. Yes. I'm awake. Has Nell moved?"

"No, but you've been asleep for four hours."

She swung her legs off him and stood. "Four hours! I have to check the bandages." His coat tumbled to the floor. "I shouldn't have slept so long."

Walker steadied her as she tried to balance while straightening her clothes and pushing her hair back. He couldn't help but smile. She looked adorable with her dress all twisted and her hair bouncing free around her shoulders. He couldn't hide a grin as he realized he'd never seen a woman wake up before.

She shoved her hair back and searched the settee. "I've lost —"

He opened his hand, and she saw her hairpins.

"My hairpins," she finished needlessly.

"I took them out," he said simply.

Lacy grumbled as she grabbed them. "You pulled my pins out while I was asleep?" She acted as if she was accusing him of something when he was standing right in front of her showing her the evidence. "You touched my hair?"

Walker shrugged. "Guilty."

Lacy arranged the pins in her hair as she walked toward Nell. "Do me a favor, Captain, and don't touch me when I'm asleep."

He thought of all the times he'd touched her in the past nine days, and she hadn't objected most times. Maybe she had a thing about him being near when she slept, or maybe it was her hair. He'd heard women can feel strange about such things. Or maybe she woke up on the wrong side of the settee. It didn't matter, he'd wait and ask her about it later.

She glanced back at him as if expecting him to argue.

He didn't say anything. He planned on

making no promise he couldn't keep. The woman slept almost on top of him. He saw no harm in removing the pins to make her more comfortable. If he happened to touch her hair, well, it was part of the service.

He barely hid his grin. In truth, he'd played with her hair most of the time she'd been asleep, enjoying the way it felt.

"Well, do you have anything to say?" she snapped.

"No."

Maybe he should not only stop answering her but stop talking to her altogether. They seemed to do better without words. He'd enjoyed every moment of watching her sleep, but as soon as she woke, she numbered the things he did wrong. Which, he'd decided, might be her favorite pastime.

After tossing another log on the fire, Walker ventured a few steps closer to Nell. The girl was as white as the sheets covering her. He heard her mumble during the hours Lacy slept, but she hadn't cried out. She must not have been in a great deal of pain. They had her packed in among so many blankets that she couldn't have been uncomfortable or cold. Now she looked even younger than her seventeen years.

For a few minutes he watched Lacy's

hand gently wrap a bandage across Nell's arm.

When Lacy looked up and saw him, she surprised him with a smile. "There's very little blood, and what's there is drying over the wounds," she whispered, her mood shifting like the wind. "Except on the shoulder where Timothy dug a bullet out." She pushed a stray strand of hair from her face. "I don't think that's anything to worry about. Timothy says the wound needs to bleed a little to clean itself out."

Walker touched the back of his hand to Nell's forehead. "I don't feel any fever." He acted like he knew what he was doing.

Lacy smiled again. "She's going to get through this and be just fine, you'll see. You wouldn't believe what she's gone through in her life. She'd never let a few bullets slow her down."

"I hope not," he added even though he wasn't as sure as Lacy seemed to be. "I don't like seeing her hurt."

"Me either." She touched Nell's cheek. "But she's in good hands. It won't be long before she's whole once more."

Lacy pulled the blanket to Nell's chin and tucked it in with care.

Walker picked up his uniform jacket and dusted invisible dirt off it. "It's long after

242

midnight, and I haven't eaten since those potato pancakes this morning," he said without looking at Lacy.

She tilted her head and watched him. "They're probably still on the table if the cats haven't eaten them. I'm sure they're still just as good."

"How about you stay here while I slip across the alley and check?"

Lacy nodded. "Please, I'm starving."

He placed his rifle at Lacy's side. "If you hear anything, lift this gun and have it already pointed before someone can get to the examining room door. I swear, I'll be back as fast as I can with food, but I need to know you're prepared to defend yourself."

She nodded, frightened by his warning.

A few minutes later he darted up the back stairs to Lacy's apartment. When he entered, he left the door open, despite the cold. Walker could see the back door of the doctor's place, and he didn't want to let it out of his sight even for a moment. The odds were no one knew Lacy was even in the doctor's office, but he still didn't like leaving his post.

Just as Lacy had suspected, her breakfast was still on the table. The cats had finished off the eggs but left the pancakes. Walker glanced at the one-eared Andy. "Traitor," he mumbled. "You could have eaten them, too."

The cat appeared only mildly insulted. Walker grabbed the plate and tossed the leftovers to the stray dog in the alley that had followed him without barking. Walker then collected an armful of food and rushed back to Lacy.

When he passed the dog, the animal was sniffing the potato pancakes.

"There just as good as they were yesterday," Walker mumbled in encouragement, but the dog only watched him pass.

Walker stepped inside the kitchen and set down his load.

"I'm back," he said, locking the door before he crossed the office to where she was.

He found Lacy cleaning the dried blood from Nell's fingers.

She talked to her friend as if Nell could hear. "Now don't you worry, you'll be right as rain in a few days, and then what a story you'll have to tell that ranger of yours who thinks he has all the adventures."

Walker cleared his throat and stepped closer. "You were right," he lied. "The cats finished off our breakfast, but I could scramble some eggs. I brought over the bread and eggs left in the storage chest."

Lacy nodded without much interest.

Walker went back to the kitchen. While the stove warmed, he checked the doctor's supply cupboard and found it empty except for three cans of peaches and a few spices. No wonder the doc was so thin.

Walker scrambled a half-dozen eggs and cut thick slices from a loaf of bread. He shoved the doctor's desk in the front office almost to the examining room's door so that they could eat and still see Nell.

The food was cold before Lacy washed her hands and sat down, but neither of them noticed. They ate in silence. Without asking, Walker stood and refilled her coffee, then pulled his chair closer to her so he wouldn't have to raise his voice.

"We have to talk," he began while she sweetened her cup. "Carter and I have a strategy."

Lacy raised one eyebrow.

"All right, I had a plan after seeing Carter's place, but he agrees with me."

She drank her coffee, waiting for him to explain.

"Right now there is a good chance that whoever shot at Nell thought that they were killing you. Maybe they even think you are dead."

"Maybe," she echoed, following his reasoning.

"Whoever it was may not even know about Nell. After all, she came to town and as far as we know only a handful of people even noticed her. It was your buggy, your horse, and Nell bundled up in blankets could have passed for you driving."

"So what do we do?"

"First we get you out of town and let them wonder. It might not be a bad idea if the ambushers think they got away with killing you. They might even come to town to find out, and all they'll hear is that you seem to have vanished."

"All right." She surprised him by agreeing.

"Then you'll go with me to Fort Elliot?" It was the nearest fort and, once housed there, she'd be safe. "And Carter thinks we should get Nell away as fast as we can."

"I agree, Nell would be safer there, but I'm not going to the fort."

"You have to, Lacy."

"No," she answered as casually as if he'd offered more sugar. "I want to stay close to Nell. I agree I need to disappear, but not so far from home."

Walker thought about arguing, but Carter had already told him Lacy wouldn't consider the fort. "You'll be safer at Fort Elliot."

"I could go to the gypsies who live on the land behind Carter's. They mostly keep to themselves, but I think they'd let me cross their settlement that backs up to Carter's land."

Walker was one step ahead of her. "Carter and I talked about that. He agreed Bailee will want Nell back at their place to recover. So, at the same time we make you disappear, we have to get Nell to McKoy's. The doc's not set up here as a hospital. She'd be safer at Carter's."

Lacy nodded. "Once I'm at the gypsies, I could cross the trees and join you at Carter's place. Between Bailee and me, she'll have the best of care."

He leaned closer, touching her arm with his hand. "Getting you out of town shouldn't be all that difficult. Knowing the way my father never threw anything away, I think I may still have some old clothes in the storage room at the shop. We can dress you up like a boy and slip you out of town after dark tomorrow night. Anyone seeing you will just think a kid is heading home. Once you're on the road, I'll join you and provide escort."

Lacy frowned.

"It'll work. No problem. But the next step is getting Nell out. As soon as the

247

doctor says it's safe, Carter plans to send his wagon to town with an old man who works for him named Samuel driving. He says Samuel comes to town for lumber all the time and drives so slow Nell will think she's still in her bed. They've probably already started building a sling that will fit in the bed of his wagon. We can put her in there, and she'll rock like a baby all the way."

Lacy didn't look like she was buying any part of the plan. "Why can't I ride with her?"

"We thought of that, but it would be risky. You're the one Whitaker wants. If someone did notice Samuel, or stop him on the road, he'd just explain that he was taking Nell, ill with a fever, to Bailee. That should keep anyone from getting close, but if you were in the wagon, it might draw more attention." Walker didn't want to add that whoever shot Nell might not hesitate to kill to get to Lacy.

"But, I —"

"Don't worry, the sheriff and I will stay in sight of the wagon the entire way. Carter said once we're on his land, he'll make sure the wagon isn't followed. Then I'll come back, wait until dark, and ride out again behind you dressed as a boy. Only, I agree, this time we take the south road to the gypsies' settlement."

The doc interrupted them as he tromped down the stairs, pulling his clothes on as he called, "How is she?"

"Better." Lacy stood. "But I want you to take a look at that shoulder."

Walker watched Lacy hurry off, no longer interested in his plan. An hour later, when they returned and sat down at the desk, the doctor surprised Walker by saying that he thought they should get the women out of town as fast as possible.

Now Lacy looked interested.

"Is it safe to move Nell?" Walker wanted to make sure.

"It won't be good for her," Timothy admitted. "But here in the center of town it will be impossible to keep her presence a secret for long. It's lucky that no one stopped by the office yesterday. As soon as word gets out, it's only a matter of time before the outlaws find out about her."

Dr. McClellan appeared to have given considerable thought to the problem. "Then they might come in to finish the job," he continued. "It would take several men to defend this place with a back door, two front doors, and windows easy to get to on the second floor. All anyone wanting

Nell dead would have to do is set fire to the businesses on either side of the office. This whole block might go up in flames before we could get her out of my examining room."

Walker agreed.

"It's a risk to move her, but it may be the only way to keep her alive."

Walker stood. "If you'll keep an eye on her for a while, Doc, I'll see if I can't find Lacy some riding clothes." He offered Lacy his arm.

The doctor waved them away as he poured himself a cup of coffee and returned to Nell.

Ten minutes later, Walker pulled an old trunk from the back shelf of the storage closet. He carried it to Lacy's little office and sat it atop her desk, then decided to risk lighting one small lamp. "I think we'll find what we need in here." He pulled down the shade of the office door, even though it only led to the shop.

"This won't work." Lacy shook her head.

"Put all your hair up while I search." He half expected her to argue or complain about being ordered, but she must have been too tired.

Walker tried to make out each piece of clothing while he watched her bend and brush her hair into a bundle of curls atop her head. "I think this is one of my old shirts," he said when she straightened. "I was a few sizes smaller when I packed these." He noticed several moth holes, tossed it in the trash, and reached for another piece of clothing.

"Don't throw that away. I can cut some squares from it." Lacy shook her head like some kind of windup toy caught in a wind. She'd given up trying to get her hair to stay up in favor of examining the old shirt.

Walker resented her total lack of faith in his plan. He and Carter had it all thought out. "You're short, but you can wear the clothes of a fifteen-year-old boy. If we stick a hat on you, no one will know."

He tossed her a pair of trousers. "Put these on while I find a good shirt."

Giving her plenty of time to follow his first order, he tossed back a shirt without turning around and told her to put it on also. If she had to change with him present, the least he could do was be gentleman enough to keep his back to her.

He heard her grumble.

"It will work, Lacy!" he snapped, frustrated at her. "You can wear a boy's clothes for a few hours." He couldn't imagine that she'd be so uncooperative about changing

251

into a man's clothes. She couldn't be so vain, or maybe she just hated his plan so much he'd have to drag her to safety.

When he turned around, she had her back to him. The pants he'd told her to wear were too big in the waist and tight across her hips, but once on a horse, no one would notice. She'd be fine. The shirt hung long from the shoulders and would cover up her waist and backside if left hanging out in back, so he saw no problem.

"Turn around."

She shook her head.

He leaned and put a hat on her head. "Turn around, Lacy. So what if you look like a boy. I'm not going to laugh."

"No," she answered.

"Lacy, stop being a fool about looking like a boy. Turn around." He was too tired to continue this game.

She turned around. He didn't laugh. She didn't look like a boy.

For a moment all Walker could do was stare. The boy's shirt that had been too big at the shoulders didn't come together to button across her chest. As she breathed, he saw her cleavage between the cotton and the rounded swell of each breast. The shirt might only lack an inch closing, but it was a very important inch.

She tried to pull the shirt together, but it was useless. There would be no hiding the fact that she was very much a woman.

"You're right." He admitted defeat. "No matter the clothes, you'll never look like a boy."

Her brown eyes rose to his, and to his surprise he saw no embarrassment in them. "I tried to tell you."

She laughed nervously, and he envied the cotton shirt that moved slightly over her body with each breath. "I may be short, but I'm a woman fully grown. I thought you knew that, Captain."

Walker saw no point in arguing. She was every inch a female, and somehow the boy's clothing made it even more obvious than her high-necked dress and wool vest. "I'll think of another plan."

"So, I can put my clothes back on?"

"Of course." If she stood there much longer, she'd probably catch cold.

"Captain?"

"Yes?"

"Turn around."

With great self-control, Walker followed orders.

Chapter 16

Lacy fought down a laugh. She'd finally made the captain speechless. She almost felt sorry for him. It occurred to her that maybe she should tell him that she'd never thought of herself as modest. But, after all, it wasn't as if he hadn't seen her before without her clothes.

Yet . . . if she didn't know better she would have sworn he must have forgotten she'd undressed before him once before. She felt the heat of his stare. The captain might be without a heart, but he wasn't dead.

"I'm finished." She buttoned the last button. "You can turn around now."

He did. Slowly.

"I tried to tell you back when you had the idea. Some women, even in men's clothes, don't look like men."

"I got the point." He stared directly at her face.

"Well, don't get mad about it. It's not my fault. My mother and grandmother were both well —"

"I understand," he said without allowing her to finish. "You didn't have to expose yourself in front of a man to prove your point."

"I didn't expose myself in front of a man. You're my husband. We've been living together for a week. Surely you noticed that we aren't built the same."

He didn't look like he wanted to be reminded of it. He straightened as if at attention. "I'm also a man, and your behavior just now was inappropriate. An hour ago you didn't even want me touching your hair."

The captain was back, she thought; no human remained.

Anger fired in Lacy. "Inappropriate? I'm sorry, Captain, but I don't exactly know the rules here. Maybe you should explain them to me. I first thought a husband should act like a husband, but when I demanded that, you acted as if I'd made the request at gunpoint."

She paced her little office, three steps left, three steps right. "It's hard to treat you like a stranger when you're breathing down my neck. We're not friends, but until this is over, we can't survive as enemies."

He closed his arms over his chest as if waiting out a storm. He didn't plan to budge an inch, and he looked like he'd turn to dust before he admitted he was wrong about anything.

Lacy planted her fists on her hips and decided she could be just as headstrong. "You demand I follow orders like I joined your army and, when I question them, you look at me like you plan to have me shot at dawn as a deserter." She knew both their emotions were raw with all that had happened, but she couldn't stop herself.

She blew out the lamp, casting them into shadow. "You seem to be the one with all the experience and all the rules. I've never even been kissed, and in this state of married-with-no-husband, it looks like I'll never know what it's like. I've been married but never courted, and bedded but never loved."

She tossed him the clothes he'd demanded she try on. "I give up! I quit! Shoot me if you like! I don't want to be in your army anymore." She turned to leave, then whirled back to face him once more.

"And one last point. I didn't tell you never to touch my hair, I said not to touch me while I'm asleep, and if you can't figure out the difference, I've married the dumbest man in Texas. So do me a favor and go back to wherever you came from and never speak to me again."

Before he could answer, she shot out the door of the office and flew toward the back stairs. She heard him bumping into tables as he tried to follow in the dark, but she had no intention of turning around to help him. He was the most self-righteous man in the state. Maybe in the country. She didn't care if he fell over the printing press and died. How dare he proclaim her behavior inappropriate?

Lacy paused at the landing. What if he hurt the press? For one moment she thought of going back down, not to save Walker, but to protect the printing press.

In that hesitation, he caught her.

Before she could fight, he shoved her into the wall and pressed his body against hers, making her immobile in a fraction of a second.

Until now, she hadn't realized how strong he was, or how powerful. His entire body must have been honed for years as a fighting machine. He didn't need a knife or a gun, he could kill her with his bare hands.

She shook with fear. His forearm rested

across her throat; one slight push, and he'd close her windpipe.

His warm breath brushed against her face as he fought to breathe. Then he said her name, low and angry. No matter how he was dressed, Lacy had no doubt a warrior's heart beat against her own.

A sob escaped before she could bite her lip and stop it.

A moment later, he stepped away as though her nearness had burned him.

She almost slid to the floor in relief. She wasn't sure if he'd been about to hold her or hurt her, and what frightened her even more was that she didn't think he knew either.

She saw his outline on the other side of the landing, only a few feet away. He'd braced his hands wide apart on the railing and took deep breaths as if he'd been fighting for his life.

Lacy didn't move. She didn't know where to go. The one person in this world who'd sworn to protect her had attacked her. Or had he?

Rubbing her arms, she felt no bruises. What if she had tried to fight back? Would he have only trapped her, or defended himself? What if, in his anger, he had hit her and not just caught her? Had he run to save her or catch her?

And the way he moved, she thought. The way he moved was too fast, too smooth not to have been practiced.

Suddenly she realized how cold it was in the shop. The fire had gone out downstairs, and she knew none still burned in the apartment. She'd left yesterday morning for the doctor's without her coat, and now the icy air seeped into her blood. But she didn't move. She wasn't sure what Walker would do. Just when she thought she was getting to know him, she realized how much of a stranger he was.

To her surprise, he faced her. His hard, powerful muscles were now tightly under control as his body stretched tall and straight as if facing a court.

"My action, madam, was inexcusable." The aloof manners returned without emotions, as if he'd practiced them over and over. "I only meant to catch up to you, not grab you."

Her husband was colder than the night. He couldn't use the reasoning that he was trying to help her like he did last time when he'd held her. She was thankful he didn't try. Anger had driven him this time, she reasoned, nothing more. And for her no-hearted husband, the loss of his temper was a flaw.

Lacy tried to stop her teeth from chattering as she slowly gained control of her own emotions. "You frightened me."

"It is with deepest regret I —"

She didn't want to hear the stiff formal talk of an officer, she wanted to hear him be a man, but she wasn't sure there was one left inside the soldier. "Stop calling me madam."

"If you wish." He wouldn't come out from behind his invisible wall.

"Since when has any of this been as I wish?" She climbed the steps, aware that he followed, but not too closely this time.

They went into the apartment, and he waited as she packed a few things in her tattered carpetbag and put on her new navy coat. Then, without a word, she prepared to leave her home, not knowing when she'd return. She didn't care what the captain's plan was, she had a plan of her own. She would stay with Nell, and somehow they'd get to Carter and Bailee's place. There she'd be safe, and she'd tell Walker he could go back to being a soldier forever. She wanted to stay at home and work, but she'd give that all up if he would forget this duty he seemed to think he had toward her. The only chance that might happen would be if she could prove that she was safe on her own.

As she gathered a few quilts and her tablet from the kitchen table, Walker lifted her bag and waited for her at the back door. He accepted each bundle she wrapped, never once commenting on how much she took.

They crossed the alley and entered the doctor's office just as dawn grayed the sky.

"Glad you're back, Miss Lacy," Timothy greeted her without seeming to notice the soldier standing in front of her. "I want you to take a look at something."

Lacy didn't say a word to Walker as she stepped around him and followed the doctor. It crossed her mind that life would have been so much better if she'd married a man like Timothy McClellan. He was kind and soft-spoken. He always asked, never told. She could have been a great help to him, and maybe he would have cherished her. There was no fire burning beneath the surface with the doctor, no bottled-up anger that threatened to explode, no hidden warrior ready to attack.

Blinking away the tears, Lacy realized all she'd ever wanted in this life was to be cherished. Not someone's duty or responsibility. She wanted to be of some value.

Because Walker's father had treated her so, she'd thought Walker would also when he finally came home. But she'd been wrong.

Dr. McClellan didn't comment on her silence as he talked about Nell's progress. "I've been careful to put her legs so there will be no pressure to her spine, but a few minutes ago I noticed her left foot."

Lacy moved to the table as he lifted the cover off Nell's feet. "Look!"

All she saw was Nell's leg.

"What?" Lacy realized the doctor was waiting.

"I think she may have moved her leg. It could have just been a jerk of muscles, but if it was her controlling it, there may still be feeling in her legs."

It took a moment for Lacy to digest the words.

Timothy laughed. "That's not the exact place I put her foot when I checked to make sure her ankles weren't swelling. If she moved, then there is at least some hope."

Lacy clapped her hands, then hugged the doctor. "That means she may be able to walk," she whispered, almost afraid to hope.

He didn't return her hug but smiled like a parent might with an excited child.

"We'll know more later, if it happens again, but the sign is a good one."

Lacy laughed and cried at the same time. All day and most of the night she'd worried that Nell might not be able to walk. She couldn't imagine the little girl who'd grown up running everywhere suddenly confined to bed or a wheelchair.

The doctor warned her not to get her hopes up, but this was the first good sign.

She stepped away from Timothy and noticed Walker standing at the door, his arms folded over his chest as he watched. Without a word, he turned and walked away.

An unexpected hollowness touched her heart. She wished she understood the man beneath the soldier, but she wasn't sure he'd ever unlock the prison he kept himself so tightly barricaded in.

For the first time she wondered what had hurt him so deeply that he'd rather live alone than let another person near. When they talked sometimes, his words didn't seem so guarded, but when he grew angry, he hid behind the part of him who'd turned all emotion off in order to be a soldier.

Without warning, the front door opened with a bang. Walker swung in one fluid movement, his gun drawn and pointed at the wide-shouldered figure of a man stomping into the office.

The intruder's coat collar was up and his hat pulled low.

Lacy held her breath as the trespasser slapped a pound of trail dust off his coat and removed his wide-brimmed hat. Dust flew from shoulder-length hair. He was filthy from head to toe and swearing as he looked into the barrel of Walker's Colt pointing right at his heart.

"Stop right there," Walker said almost calmly. "If you make a move for a gun, you're a dead man."

The stranger's eyes darted from Walker to Lacy standing right behind him. "Morning." He smiled without an ounce of fear in his dark brown eyes. "This must be that husband you're always talking about. Touchy fellow, ain't he."

Lacy cried with joy and ran past Walker into the arms of Jacob Dalton.

He laughed and swung her around, sending dust flying in every direction. "Hello, honey," he shouted as if he'd used the endearment a hundred times. "You're a sight for sore eyes."

"It's about time you got here!" Lacy cried as she messed his hair. "I almost didn't recognize you. You look like you swam through mud to get here."

"Pret near did. I've ridden through storms so bad the buffalo crawled in with the groundhogs to wait it out." He laughed, proud of his lie. "But Nell will see there's hell to pay for my not coming faster. She wired me you needed me, and in her mind there's no other job in the state more important."

Lacy glanced at Walker, still holding his pistol in place, as Jacob set her back down. Walker couldn't have appeared more bewildered if she were dancing with the stray dog in the alley.

She stepped back until she no longer stood between the two men. "Ranger Jacob Dalton," she said as if her husband didn't look like he were still considering shooting the man, "I'd like you to meet my husband, Captain Walker Larson."

Walker slowly holstered his weapon. "There's a Texas Ranger beneath all that dirt and mud?"

Jacob offered his hand. "Sorry, about the dust. I've been riding hard."

The two men shook hands, each watching the other closely.

"I've heard tell of you, Walker. It's good to see you in the flesh. I've a great deal of respect for you if half of what I've heard is true."

Walker nodded.

"How'd you find us?" Lacy asked.

"I didn't. Not on purpose anyway. I heard the sheriff had been in visiting the doctor yesterday, and no one knew where he was this morning, so thought I might catch him here before I head over to the hotel to clean up. Now that I know you're all right, a bath seems in order." He smiled at Walker. "Though I doubt you'll be needing me, now you've got the captain."

Lacy glanced at Walker. She realized Jacob didn't know Nell was hurt.

Walker nodded slightly, telling her he understood.

"Dalton," Walker took the lead. "There's something I need to tell you. There's been an accident —"

"Ranger," Dr. McClellan shouted as he opened the door. "Thank God you're here. She came to a few minutes ago and asked for you."

Jacob's questioning eyes looked from Lacy to Walker.

"It's Nell," Walker said, but the ranger was already storming across the room. "She was ambushed heading out to the McKoy place yesterday morning."

266

Jacob was at the operating table before Walker's words died in the air. Lacy didn't want to watch, but she couldn't help herself. She slipped into the room. She hated to see the ranger's pain, but she couldn't leave him alone.

The ranger tossed his hat and coat on the floor and stood at the foot of Nell's makeshift bed. He folded his hands in front of him and grounded like a tree.

Lacy knew he fought to keep from grabbing Nell and demanding she get up.

When the doc moved to his side, Jacob asked, "Can she hear me?"

"No, I don't think so. I gave her something to help her sleep a few minutes ago. But when she comes to, she'll be glad you're here. Right now she's just whispering your name while she's fighting back the pain."

"What happened?"

Lacy and the doctor backed away, neither wanting to tell the ranger what had happened to the kid he'd befriended for years. They already saw raw pain on his weathered young face.

Walker stepped forward and, in a much more caring tone than Lacy would have thought him capable of, he told Jacob every detail, including his plan to get Nell and Lacy to safety.

Jacob stood for a long while without saying a word. Then he thanked the captain and asked if he could have a few minutes alone with the kid.

Lacy thought she heard him choke back a cry as she closed the door, tears already streaming down his face.

Nell's ranger had finally come home, and Nell didn't even know he was there.

Chapter 17

Walker moved to the window facing the street and stared out at the morning. The rainy day reflected his mood. A window seat kept him from standing close enough to be seen by anyone passing. Part of him wanted to ride off and never look back at this town for as long as he lived.

The same feeling he'd had once before, he thought. His lifestyle in the army was hard on the body, but this place was hard on his heart.

Last time he'd been torn apart by love, and now he'd been pulled back because of duty.

The doctor walked to the front office, pulling off his bloody apron and reaching for his coat. He announced he planned to head over for breakfast at the café. "I've missed four or five meals, so it will take me a while to catch up. Don't expect me back soon, but tell the ranger he's welcome to make himself at home."

McClellan left without another word. Walker thought about asking him to bring back a couple of meals, but the fewer people who knew they were holed up here, the better.

Lacy moved about in the next room. The ticking of an old clock on the wall by the kitchen door seemed to be measuring time slower with each beat.

"Captain?" Lacy's voice drifted from just behind him.

He didn't turn around, didn't want to see the tears he knew were in her eyes. Without a word, he leaned back from the window, lifted his arm, and gently circled her shoulders.

She rolled into his embrace, crying softly against his chest.

For a long while he held her, glad that the room lay in shadow. Neither of them had slept much. The hours and emotions weighed on them both. Her nerves were raw, his control crumbling by the hour. But even with all the trouble around them, he closed his eyes and thought once more how good she felt in his arms. There seemed nothing better than Lacy willingly and warm in his embrace. The feel of her was addictive. Somehow, no matter how often they fought, she still returned to his shoulder when she cried.

He might never be more, but Walker knew he was one thing to her: a refuge.

Finally she stopped sobbing and stood next to him as if needing another's nearness.

Looking down at her, he wiped a tear from her face with his thumb. "Nell is going to pull through this, you'll see. That ranger won't let her die."

Her smile didn't reach her eyes. "And would you let me die?" she whispered.

The honesty of her question shocked him.

"No," he answered. He thought of adding something about it being his duty, but it was more than that. Somehow, through all the fights and danger, she'd become important to him. He'd stand in death's path if it rode for Lacy.

She stared at him for a minute, seeming to build her courage. "What happened to you back there on the stairs before dawn?" She glanced down at her hands. "I have to know what you intended. You don't seem like the type of man who snaps and not be able to explain his actions afterward." Her honest eyes met his. "Would you have harmed me, Captain?"

Without looking at him she added, "I have to know if I need to be on guard. If I have to walk softly until you're gone."

She didn't have to add that she'd lived near such a man before. That she survived once in the past.

"And if I had?" He hated asking. "Then you'll deal with it, because you can tolerate anything if you know it will eventually end, right Lacy?"

A strand of her hair swept across her face when she nodded, and he hated knowing that somewhere, sometime she'd felt a fist strike in anger.

"I would never hurt you." He wondered to himself if he lied. Hadn't he hurt her the first time they met? "I didn't mean to frighten you. I reacted out of training and anger when you took flight." And something else he didn't want to admit even to himself. "I ran after you to catch you. I meant you no harm."

"But if I'd fought you? If I'd pushed?"

"It wouldn't have mattered."

There was just enough light to see the worry in her eyes.

"You've no reason to be afraid of me, Lacy." All he ever did was try to convince her that they could stand the sight of one another. He was tired of trying, but this time he couldn't blame her. He had over-reacted.

He might not be able to admit it to Lacy, but Walker needed to be honest with himself. The lie would only fester inside. He was attracted to her. More than attracted, that was too weak a term. If she asked him to bed her right here, right now, he would not hesitate as he had the first time. There would be no clock ticking away the seconds.

If he had another chance with her, he would take it slow, letting her experience loving one step at a time.

Only his wife didn't want him . . . would probably never want him again. He lived in a hell of his own making.

She stared at him with those huge eyes full of mistrust. Maybe it was just because they were exhausted, maybe it was the strain they'd both been under, maybe he'd truly frightened her, but he had to make it right with her.

"I don't know a great deal about being around women," he admitted. "But I swear I would not have harmed you on the landing, no matter what you said or did."

She nodded, accepting his apology, even if he knew she didn't fully believe it.

"At least I know you don't fear all men.

You've hugged every man you've seen this morning *except* me."

Lacy looked surprised at his observation. "I wasn't aware you were a man who welcomed a hug."

He stiffened at the prick. "I think that I would." He didn't bother to add that having been raised by only a father and living most of his life in a fort, there had been very few times he'd embraced a woman even lightly.

"From anyone?"

"No." He smiled. "The doc's too thin, the ranger's too dirty, and the sheriff is too old. I guess that leaves my wife, if she were willing to offer the service."

She moved in front of him and squared her shoulders as though bracing herself for a task. "Well, since I seem to be passing them out this morning, it must be your turn."

He waited. If he took a deep breath, his chest would have touched her, but he had no intention of advancing.

She had to stretch to put her arms around his neck. The hug was awkward. "Help me out a little, Captain." She laughed shyly. "I feel like I'm trying to hug the garden scarecrow. You're too tall."

He leaned down and placed his hands at

her waist. "Maybe you're too short."

His last word brushed across her mouth by accident. When she didn't pull away, he kissed her gently.

Her bottom lip trembled, but she still didn't retreat.

Waiting, he hesitated.

She tugged on his neck and leaned her body against his.

Accepting the silent invitation, he kissed her again. Nothing in his life had ever felt so good. The light touch of her lips against his was newborn, washing away scars across his heart he'd lived with so long he thought them a part of him.

When she stepped away, he let her go. For a moment they stared at one another. Then she touched her fingers to her mouth. Without warning, she whirled and marched halfway across the room, then turned and hurried back, her hand still covering her mouth.

He sat on the window seat, crossed his arms, and waited, trying to decide if he should apologize for the hundredth time to her when she eventually came to a stop.

She stood in front of him once more. "Thank you," she whispered.

"For what?"

She lowered her hand. "For kissing me.

Now I've been kissed. I won't have to wonder."

Walker couldn't hide his grin. "You're welcome. Any time I may be of further service, let me know."

She brushed her hand over her lips once more. "I like the way it felt, Captain. Not at all like I thought it might."

"And how did it feel?" he asked knowing firsthand exactly how the kiss had felt.

"Nice." She smiled. "Butterfly soft at first and then warm."

While he fought the urge to pull her to him, she did the strangest thing. She reached over and ran her fingers over his mouth.

He unfolded his arms slowly so he wouldn't frighten her.

She moved closer, touching his face, tracing the line of his jaw with her fingers. "You haven't shaved today."

"I will." He gripped both sides of the window seat so he wouldn't reach for her.

Her fingers crossed his lips again, then she leaned closer and touched his mouth with hers, not kissing, only feeling. "How do I let you know?" Her words tickled across his face.

"Know what?" he answered, trying to think with all the feelings shooting through him.

"That I'd like to be kissed again, please." Her words brushed over his mouth.

"This will do." He was no longer able to resist. He hugged her to him. This time his kiss grew bolder, spiced with a need for her that surprised him.

When she leaned away, it was harder to let her go, but he knew if he didn't want to frighten her, he had to allow her to set the pace.

She pulled her bottom lip into her mouth as if tasting his kiss. "That was nice. Thank you, Captain."

"Stop thanking me, Lacy," he said sharper than he'd intended.

"Stop ordering me," she answered, but her eyes were dancing with pleasure.

He would have closed the space between them once more, but a rider passed the window. They both leaned farther back into the shadows on either side of the window.

"I meant no order," he whispered from the other side of the window. "I also hadn't realized it was getting so late. People are already on the street. We'll have to be more careful if we're near the windows."

She nodded and hurried back into the office, but the sunlight followed her, as did his gaze.

Walker noticed the blush across her cheeks slowly cool and knew reality had returned. Part of him wanted to go back to the kiss they'd shared in the shadows, but he knew there were many things that needed to be said. Their game of kissing, no matter how pleasant, had to be pushed aside to allow full attention to be given to problems.

He followed her into the kitchen. She handed him a bucket, and he pumped water as she talked. "I've got a plan that will get me to the farm, and I don't have to pretend to be a boy."

"All right."

She handed him another bucket and continued, "I told you about the gypsies' place. I could go there without playing dress-up."

Walker filled a third bucket and wondered how long this plan might take to discuss or if she would simply talk until the well ran dry.

"One of the girls, Cozetta, comes in to cook and clean for the doc. Judging by his food supply, I thought she must be overdue, so I asked. Timothy says if the weather doesn't keep her away, she's due today."

Walker saw where she was going, but he

waited as she set the kettles on to warm, then grabbed her bag.

"She comes to town in a little two-wheel cart. One of the old women from the village always rides along as chaperone, otherwise there'd be talk about a young girl cleaning a bachelor's place. I've heard Timothy complain that he has to pay the old woman for doing nothing, but that's the only way he can get Cozetta."

Walker almost asked her to shorten her plan to a few hundred words.

She continued, "Maybe I could wear the old chaperone's shawl and ride back with Cozetta. From the village, it's not a far walk to the river. Once I cross that, I'll be on Carter's land and in his orchard."

"What do we do with the old lady?" Walker followed her through a side door off the kitchen he had never noticed before. He tried to listen and not slosh the water all over his legs.

Lacy frowned. "I don't have all the kinks worked out yet."

"How about leaving her here with the doc?"

Lacy shook her head. "He's always saying one of the old women makes his flesh crawl, and he thinks another one has fleas."

"Could she stay with someone in town?"

Lacy shook her head. "If these women had any friends or family, they wouldn't be living out at the settlement."

She set her bucket down. "Bailee told me once that the gypsies never turn anyone away. They may have to invent a job, like chaperoning, but they find a way on one side of the law or the other."

Walker got the feeling Lacy didn't quite trust all those who lived in the gypsy village, but he didn't say anything.

"The doc complains one old woman stares at him as if she thinks he'll murder her if she isn't watchful." Lacy pulled a tub from the corner to the center of the little room and poured water in it.

"Could you fit in the back of the wagon?"

"Maybe, but it would be tight. Cozetta takes home the doc's laundry, and I've seen Mosely load in harnesses that need work. The men in the settlement will mend them cheap, then Mosely doubles the price when people come to pick up their leather."

Walker smiled. She was doing it again, adding in facts that didn't need to be there.

Lacy got the hint. "I could probably hide

amid the bundles if nothing else goes into the cart."

She tested the water and added, "Nell and I would both be safer if I could get Cozetta to take me, because we wouldn't be traveling on the same road. If I could get to the gypsy camp, I know I could find Carter's orchard, but it wouldn't be an easy journey, and the trees are so thick in spots a horse couldn't even get through."

"I could go with you." He emptied his last pail.

"No. You wouldn't fit in the cart, and if you were riding along behind us, anyone on the road would suspect something."

Walker collected the buckets. "I presume this is for the filthy ranger smelling up the other room." He pointed to the tub.

Lacy smiled. "No, it's for me. I'll be finished before you have time to heat water for the ranger's tub."

Walker looked around. The place was more storage room than bathing room, but he could see why the doc would keep a tub placed in it. The room was warm, with no outside walls and no windows, and the advantage of being close to the kitchen for a source of hot water.

"You bathe here often?" he asked before he could stop himself.

Lacy pulled the pins from her hair. "Sometimes. When Cozetta's here, she'll keep watch at the door, and I'll bathe and wash my hair. Dr. McClellan used to sit with your father until I returned to the shop, but now he makes a production of saying he's going out whenever he sees me talking to Cozetta in the kitchen."

Walker felt guilty for asking. Lacy must have had very little time to herself while she was watching over his father. He stepped back into the kitchen and waited for the kettle to boil.

He could hear her humming and realized how such a simple thing seemed to relax her.

"Ready for the hot water?" He stood outside the door.

"Ready," Lacy answered.

When he entered, he was surprised to find her in her undergarments, her shoes and stockings already off and her hair down.

"What is it?" she asked when she saw his face.

"You're not dressed." He felt like a fool stating the obvious.

"We're not going to start that again, are we?" She giggled nervously. "I have to do this as fast as possible and go back to Nell.

I've yet to figure out how to soak in a bath with my clothes on." She twisted her hair and pulled it into a knot at the top of her head.

He knew better than to say more.

He poured the water and planned to leave, but as he turned, she stood near. When he met her gaze, he couldn't resist. Without touching her, he leaned and kissed her full on the mouth.

"Oh," she said.

"Do you mind?" He smiled, knowing her answer.

"No. I just didn't think about people kissing anytime."

"You're right, we'll reserve such behavior for greetings and farewells. And of course train stations —"

She leaned up and kissed him, stopping the list. He circled her shoulder with his arm but didn't pull her closer. When she stepped away, he felt sure more than hot water steamed the room.

"I'd better hurry," she whispered a little out of breath.

He nodded and left the room, knowing that if he stayed longer, there would be no time for her to bathe. Walker pulled a chair up against the door and tried not to think about Lacy on the other side.

An hour later, the ranger made use of the tub. Walker stood by the front door as Lacy dried her hair near the fireplace in the room where Nell slept. He told himself from his vantage point he could see the street, but he spent most of his time watching her.

Riley showed up with milk and a basket of biscuits from Mrs. Abernathy. He didn't seem the least surprised that the ranger had found Nell and explained that even when Nell was only a half-grown kid, the ranger saw himself as her guardian angel.

Walker almost didn't recognize the man who walked out of the storage closet with his hair still wet. Without a pound of dirt and mud on him, Jacob Dalton looked far younger, and his hair wasn't brown, but sun-whitened blond. He wore his double-holstered Colts far too easy not to be a man who made his living by them.

Walker told them of Lacy's idea, and Dalton agreed with the plan. Except he insisted that he ride with the wagon Nell was in. He explained that, unlike Walker, he knew what Whitaker looked like. If he spotted the man, even from a distance, he'd know the old buffalo hunter.

The sheriff suggested both Cozetta's wagon and Samuel's carrying Nell leave at the same time. That way Whitaker couldn't follow both and, with the ranger guarding one and Walker checking the progress of the other, chances were good Whitaker would do nothing.

"Zeb Whitaker is a coward at the core. He'll wait until he thinks he can get to them without anyone shooting at him. Or," Riley drew on his pipe, "he'll get someone else to do the dirty work."

"Where do you think he's hiding?" Dalton asked as he wiped soap from his ear.

"No telling. He knows these parts better than anyone. Old Mosely over at the livery used to be a friend of his, but he swears he hasn't heard from Whitaker since he got out of jail."

"If I can link him to Nell's attempted murder, I'll have him back behind bars." Dalton's jaw set.

Walker's respect for the ranger grew. Most men in his shoes would be talking of killing whoever hurt Nell. Jacob Dalton put the law first, at least for now.

The day stayed dark and cloudy. The rain stopped, but no one came by to see the doc. Walker watched the street. Most townsfolk stayed inside by their fires. Cozetta showed up as expected with an old woman along for the ride. The young girl seemed shy around the ranger and Walker, but she whispered to Lacy and the doctor.

Lacy crossed to the men as if she were the appointed translator. "Cozetta says you three make her friend nervous, so two of you have to leave." She grinned. "The biggest two. Cozetta's friend says the sheriff's small enough to fight off if he decides to try to ravish her."

All three men leaned to look at the tiny old raisin of a woman who sat by the fire wrapped in shawls.

"So you two big ones had better be on your way."

"Did you tell the gypsy about riding back with her?" Walker asked, ignoring her request.

Lacy nodded. "She says she only goes as far as the first set of cabins, but the old woman said she'd take me all the way to the orchard's edge. I told her you'd be following. She said for you not to come close until she turns toward the trees."

Walker frowned.

"Don't worry, she says she knows a spot where the river is shallow. Once you join us at the tree line, we'll cross and find our way to Carter's."

Jacob mirrored Walker's worried look. "I was back there on the other side of the creek once. It's not easy crossing in day-light, much less at night. You might be wise to wait till daybreak."

Lacy shook her head. "The women said I'm welcome to stay, but they want no part of inviting in a stranger like Walker. She didn't even like the idea that you would be following the wagon at a distance. She tried to convince me to tell you to ride with the ranger."

When neither man spoke, Lacy added, "What do you think?"

"I'm riding with you, but she won't even know I'm there."

Walker met Jacob's stare, and knew the ranger agreed with him. Lacy might trust this old woman she hardly knew, but Walker planned to be near.

Lacy sighed. "All right, I won't tell her, but you two better get out of here. We need to change the bandages and be ready to leave in an hour. We should get there before dark. Timothy says Nell can travel if we pack her in with blankets, so Jacob, climb my back stairs and take every quilt in my house you need for Samuel's wagon. If I know Carter, he's already sent the old man to wait at Mosely's livery until we're ready. Use all my quilts if you need to; we want her protected and warm for the ride."

She turned to Walker. "You'll need something besides that uniform. And I need my new thread box and wool from my bedroom. While we're at Bailee's I might have time to sew." She took a quick breath. "I've repacked my carpetbag if you want to strap it to your horse."

The doc called, and Lacy hurried back to Nell.

Jacob winked at Walker as he stood. "Bossy little woman, ain't she?"

Walker reached for his coat. "My commander gives fewer orders."

Riley chuckled. "You better get going, boys. Now, me, I didn't hear her tell me to do one thing. I'm going to stay right here all warm and have myself the last biscuit."

The thump of a cane announced the old woman coming near. She walked past the table as if she didn't see the three men standing around it and headed toward the kitchen. She grunted with every other step, as if hiccupping in baritone.

When she disappeared around the corner, the last biscuit vanished from the basket. All three men had been within three feet of her, and none had seen her lift her breakfast from under their noses.

The ranger and Walker hit the door laughing as Riley swore.

Chapter 18

An hour later, Lacy watched Jacob Dalton carry Nell carefully through the doctor's house and out the back door to a wagon waiting in the alley. The tough ranger, who'd lived in the saddle and slept on the ground for so many years he thought it home, couldn't quite keep the tears from falling. If anyone asked him, he'd swear he didn't cry, but Lacy knew his heart was broken. Even if Nell lived, she might never walk, for they'd seen no further movement in her legs.

The child Dalton had checked on and looked after and cared about since the first day he became a ranger no longer answered when he said her name.

No one paid attention to the soupy fog or the bitter cold. They held their breaths while he lowered her into the quilt-covered wagon bed and kissed her cheek as though she were only resting and not near death.

Nell didn't make a sound as they layered

first blankets, then a tarp over her in case it rained before Samuel could get home. Finally, the men lifted boards Samuel had hammered together to make the wagon bed look like it was only a load of lumber. He'd even tented the front so that Nell would be covered but still be able to breathe beneath the layers.

Walker stood at one end of the alley, the sheriff at the other, just in case anyone ventured near. But no one but the stray dog paid them a call. For some reason the mutt growled at Walker.

Lacy decided it was probably because the captain had changed into civilian clothes. Though in truth, he looked no less a military man. It hadn't surprised her that he'd chosen a dark brown coat and trousers. Walker must get tired of always wearing blue. But the Stetson amazed her. He'd picked a hat almost as dark as his hair with a finely tooled leather braid around the brim. He'd also packed his army issue pistol in favor of a weapon that hung lower beside his hip.

"She's ready." Jacob signaled to Samuel as he swung up on his horse. "Slow and easy now, old man."

The carpenter nodded and made a clicking sound that started the horses moving.

The ranger tipped his hat to Lacy. "See you at the McKoy place, honey. Take care crossing the orchard. If I get there in time, I'll set a lantern you'll be able to see from the river to guide you in."

"Thanks." Lacy touched Jacob's big gloved hand. "Take care of her."

"Don't plan to stop now." The ranger disappeared into the fog.

For a minute Lacy stood listening to the sounds of his horse and Samuel's wagon rolling away. She wanted to go with them. More than anything, Lacy wanted to demand to stay with Nell, but she knew Nell was safer without her. The fog cloaked them now, shielding them from anyone who might be watching the road. If it rained, Samuel would still guide the wagon safely to Carter's place. The path they traveled would be easy, not as rugged as the one Lacy faced, but tonight, they'd all be back together at Carter. Tonight they'd all be safe.

Cozetta and the old woman hurried down the steps with bundles of the doctor's laundry. They stuffed a few bags into the cart and left the others to be loaded after Lacy climbed in the back. The girl seemed worried, but the old woman had a determined set to her jaw as if she wanted this chore over as soon as possible. Lacy heard them whispering earlier, as if arguing, but she couldn't make out any words.

She buttoned her coat, pulled on her gloves, and moved toward the little wagon as Cozetta climbed in front and sat on the bench covered by a crude bonnet of sun-bleached rags. The old woman took the reins.

Walker met Lacy at the back of the cart. He draped the quilt she'd made for him out of his father's suits over her head and shoulders. "I know you said use all your quilts for Nell, but this happens to be mine. It'll keep you warm."

He lifted her into the wagon, and she squeezed between the bags. Tossing one bundle to her left, he leaned until the brim of his hat touched the top of her hair. "Take care," he whispered. "I'll be right behind you. You won't see me, but know I'm there. No harm will come to you."

Lacy nodded. He'd been over the plan ten times already.

"When she turns toward the trees, I'll catch up to you. We'll cross the river and the orchard together."

"But your horse?" She looked past him to the magnificent animal pawing the ground, ready to go. Walker's saddlebags as well as her carpetbag were tied to the back of a military-style saddle.

"I'll tie him near the river if it's too dark to lead him through the trees and come back for him at daybreak. He'll be all right. Trooper has a habit of throwing anyone who tries to ride him but me, so he won't be easy to steal."

Lacy snuggled, trying to get comfortable and finding it hard to believe Walker had found an animal who liked him. The cats avoided him. Even the stray dog growled at him. She grinned. Come to think of it, humans didn't warm up to him all that fast either. But this devil of a horse that looked like he'd gladly stomp on her, waited for Walker's command.

The old woman twisted around enough to give them both an angry, hurry-up glare.

Leaning close to Walker, Lacy whispered, "She doesn't think you're following. Told me to tell you that if you even think about it, you'll be putting me in more danger."

"I'm not —"

Her fingers on his lips stopped his protest as she whispered, "She doesn't need to know."

Walker met her eyes and nodded.

The old woman turned around again and scowled at them.

Walker didn't pull away. He had something to say and planned to say it no matter how long the old lady glared.

Lacy waited, wondering what last order he had in mind. He'd been acting nice ever since she'd kissed him, but she knew it couldn't last.

Finally, he pushed his hat back and leaned an inch closer so that his words brushed the side of her face. "I know this isn't the time, but . . . if we were alone, I'd be tempted to kiss you again."

She shivered at the intimate tone in his voice. "If we were alone, I'd be tempted to let you."

Chuckling, he straightened. When he glanced back at her, she was surprised at how an honest smile changed his face, making him look younger. He tossed in two more bags of laundry over her. Lacy couldn't stop the grin that spread across her lips. The strange captain had more difficulty with his last words than he ever experienced yelling orders at her.

Completely covered, Lacy listened and waited. The old woman slapped the reins, and the mare pulled the wagon forward, rocking Lacy gently against the bags. She shifted as they turned, heading out of the alley. She counted the bumps moving down Main Street. As they rattled out of town, all sound vanished but that of the wagon crushing against frozen earth and the jingle of harnesses.

Lacy listened. Voices were too muffled to understand. Walker's blanket kept her warm as she curled into a ball. She wasn't afraid. She knew he would be close enough to help if they encountered trouble. The rocking of the wagon lulled her to sleep.

Her last thought before dreaming was the memory of her first kiss. It has been so nice, soft and light, but the kiss in the storage room would warm her blood for hours to come.

It was dark when the bags were pulled from around her. Lacy blinked, expecting to see the circle of cabins of the gypsy village or Walker waiting to help her down. But only blackness surrounded her.

At first she thought the fog must be hiding the lights from windows and fireplaces. Surely she should be able to see a hazy glow in the distance. She allowed her eyes time to adjust. Finally a shadow, black on black, moved toward the back of the wagon.

Boots shuffled in the dirt. The sound of leather creaking popped in the night. Another figure joined the first.

"That her?" A stranger's voice shattered the night's silence.

Lacy turned to the front of the wagon, now able to make out the shawled shadow of the old woman sitting alone on the front bench of the cart. She must have been asleep when they dropped off Cozetta. If so, they must now be close to the river.

The old woman hopped down with far more energy than she'd climbed in with. "Of course that's her. You don't think I'd bring you the wrong woman? She's the one Whitaker thought he killed on the road to the McKoy place."

Almost all of the woman's thick accent had vanished. "Now, where's my twenty in gold? We only have a few minutes before that captain of hers I told not to follow probably catches up to us. This one said he wouldn't trail us, but I know he's back there. I saw it in the way he looked at her. He didn't plan to let her go alone."

Lacy squinted, trying to make out the two shadows standing behind the wagon. One was so thin he appeared more tree-shaped than human, and the other couldn't have been much taller than her yet carried at least three times her weight. Even in the dark, they didn't look all that threatening. The thin one jerked with nervous energy, and the fat one whined as they tried to decide what to do.

"Who are you?" Curiosity outweighed fear in Lacy. "What do you want?"

The short shadow removed his hat. "We want you to come with us, Miss Lacy. We got someone who wants to have a talk with you."

"I don't think so." She tried to place the voice, but he didn't sound like anyone she knew. She pushed back against the bench of the cart as far away from the two men as possible.

The tall shadow sprang like a snake, grabbing her, blanket and all, and tugging her out of the wagon. "You're coming with us, miss, whether you like it or not. You're worth a hundred dollars."

"Put me down!"

The old woman snorted. "I thought you said you were getting fifty. If you're getting a hundred, I want forty. After all, I did all the work, even lied to the girl."

The short shadow and the old woman argued while the thin man's arms wrapped around Lacy, pinning her within the folds of the quilt.

"Put me down!" Lacy ordered, more angry than frightened.

She kicked and tried to break free. When she screamed, the short shadow stopped arguing and covered her mouth. It took him several tries, but he clamped his fat hand over her face and shut her up.

"Gag her, Gray. You want her screaming and waking up one of these gypsies?" the short man hissed at the tall one holding her. "They'll come after us."

"You gag her. I'm not turning loose. If she gets three feet from me in this blackness, we'll never find her."

"I can't gag her. I'm keeping her from screaming." He squealed as Lacy sank her teeth into one of his fingers.

"I'll gag her," the old woman complained. "But, you'll pay me fair. If anyone finds out I helped you, I'll be homeless again."

Lacy fought wildly, trying to jerk free from the thin fingers before the old woman got what smelled like a rag tightened around her head. She only managed a short scream before the rag tightened into her mouth. The old woman tied the knot in back, pulling Lacy's hair without care.

"All right. You win." The tall man stepped away and wiped his hand on his trousers. "I'll give you forty, but you have to slow that captain down you claim is following."

The woman swore a curse at both men as they pulled Lacy into the blackness.

"He'll be riding full-out if he's close enough to hear those screams. So you don't have much time."

Part of the quilt covered Lacy's head and engulfed her. She could no longer hear what the men were saying, yet she still kicked at anything that came near.

She thought she heard one of the men groan just before they tossed her forward. She hit hard against the floor of what felt like a wagon bed, but when she tried to move, walls were on either side of her. Arms no longer imprisoned her, but something did. Then suddenly she was moving with the roll of a wagon, bouncing against the sides of what felt like a box as she struggled to free her arms from the blanket. She had to pull the gag out of her mouth and call Walker before it was too late.

Gasping for breath, she finally pulled her head away from the blanket. She was so surrounded by blackness at first she didn't think the quilt could be off her face. Slowly, fighting the folds and the confined space, she pulled her hand free and touched her face, jerking the rag from her mouth. Then, with terror rising, she reached above her, encountering rough wooden boards.

Lacy traced the space with her free hand as her heart pounded wildly. Wood all around her. Complete darkness.

She pushed on the sides, the top. Nothing gave. She pounded, screaming, but no one answered. Deep down where even nightmares fear to go, she knew.

Not just a box imprisoned her, but a coffin.

Chapter 19

A moment after he realized the wagon had turned away from the river and not toward it, Walker heard a scream. He watched the tree line just across the water, expecting trouble to come riding in hard and fast.

Another scream, quickly muffled, echoed from beyond where the old woman must have turned. Walker felt cold, hard fear in his gut. Not for himself — he could fight off whoever waited in the night — but for Lacy. He kicked Trooper into action. The land grew uneven as he neared the bend. Huge rocks shadowed the path, and mounds of dirt high enough to hide a wagon rose on either side.

He urged Trooper forward and thought he heard voices, but they circled in the icy wind like carolers on a merry-go-round. The moonless night, thick with fog, hid the ruts of the old woman's cart from his view. If he wasn't careful, he'd accidentally move away from Lacy instead of toward her.

Trooper's head rose, his ears alert. The horse had sensed trouble before Walker many times over the years. Shuffling whispered in the wind, and Walker rode toward the sound. Voices echoed again, angry and hurried, too distant to make out words. Then he thought he heard a wagon roll away.

He needed to get to Lacy. She must be terrified. But the night twisted sounds.

Footsteps suddenly hurried toward him.

He stilled Trooper with a pat and raised his weapon. Though his heart prayed that Lacy ran toward him, Walker's experience taught him to prepare for the worst.

The steps grew nearer, muffled by the damp ground.

Walker swung down from the saddle and prepared for an attack. As always, Trooper stood the ground behind him. He'd trained the animal to stay put, even if gunfire sounded.

Suddenly, the old woman burst through the fog. By the time he saw her clearly, she stood five feet from him, her shawl flying in the wind, her hair wild around her.

She opened her mouth to scream, then froze as she stared at the rifle pointed at her head.

Walker lowered the gun a few inches, but stayed ready in case something or someone followed her.

"Help!" she cried, her accent so thick he barely understood the word. "Help me. I've been attacked." She flung herself against him, holding on tight as if she thought the devil chased her.

"Lacy?" he tried to push her away. "Where's Lacy? What happened to my wife?"

The old woman pointed into the darkness and spoke in a language he didn't understand. He knew she could speak English — he'd heard her — but she must be frightened too badly to think clearly.

"Show me!" Walker shoved her in the direction she'd just come from. "Take me to Lacy."

She shook her head wildly and refused to budge or let go of his coat. If he planned to advance, he'd do so with her anchored behind him.

Walker grabbed her by the arms. "What happened? Where's Lacy? Show me!" She was of no help, hysterical.

The woman crumpled like a pile of rags.

Walker pulled her to her feet. Her body wasn't nearly as frail as he would have guessed it to be. He swore he felt tight muscles on her arms beneath the shawl. He wanted to shake an answer out of her, but the old woman had passed out cold.

Leaving her crossed his mind. If he carried her back in the direction she'd come from, he might find Lacy, but who knew what else? With the old hag in his arms, he wouldn't be prepared to face trouble. Leaving her seemed cruel; carrying her would be foolish. He did the only thing he could think of. He lifted her onto his horse.

"Easy now, Trooper," he whispered as the woman slumped on the saddle, conscious enough now to hold on to the horse's mane.

Walker took the reins and calmed Trooper. "Easy, boy," he whispered again, knowing the animal didn't like anyone but Walker on his back.

They'd gone thirty feet, maybe more, when Walker made out the outline of the cart. He glanced back at the old woman, but she still leaned over the saddle, mumbling something about being robbed by devils.

She wasn't calm enough to answer his questions. Something had frightened her, but doubts gnawed at the back of his mind. Something wasn't right. She'd run fast toward him. Both her arms and legs were muscled, not frail. She mumbled and cried as if she were frightened mindless, but she had the sense to stay on the horse. She was acting!

He tried to lead her closer to the cart, but she mumbled, "No, no," as if too frightened to go farther.

Walker gave up the effort, looped the reins across Trooper's neck, and ran to the cart. He'd worry about the old woman later. "Lacy!" he yelled. "Lacy!"

He tossed several of the bags out of the back but knew he wouldn't find her. He circled the wagon once, rage pounding blood through his veins. Just as he'd feared, she had vanished.

He grabbed the lantern swinging from the bonnet railing over the seat and fumbled for a match in his pocket. A moment before he lit the flame, he thought he heard the slap of leather, like reins being used as a whip. He glanced up in time to see the old woman straighten and kick Trooper into action like a seasoned horseman might.

The highly trained horse bolted into a full run into the night.

Walker turned up the wick and listened, already knowing what would happen.

The old woman must have made it a hundred yards before Trooper balked. He knew the animal well. The horse would buck until he was free of any rider but Walker.

A moment later, he heard her scream and knew she was no longer on the animal's back. He didn't know if she were hurt or dead. He didn't care. Walker knew he'd been tricked, and his trained mind began to organize. The night was far more to his advantage. They couldn't be more than a half mile ahead of him. He'd have Lacy back in a matter of minutes, and anyone involved would pay dearly.

He whistled once, and Trooper galloped toward him.

Lowering the lamp, Walker studied the dirt around the cart, reading the signs as easily as he might a book. He fought the temptation to hurry, knowing that a mistake would cost him time. Two sets of boots, one long and thin the other almost small enough to be a woman's, marked the earth. Between them in spots were prints of Lacy's new boots. She'd been half carried, half dragged across the damp ground, then tossed in the back of a wagon. He knelt, touching the ground with his fingers. No blood. They wanted her alive.

He let out a breath he'd been holding since he'd heard the scream.

After following for ten feet, he reached softer ground and saw the ruts of a wagon that must have been hidden.

The tracks were easy to follow from there, thanks to the recent rain. They traveled over the land for about a mile, then headed onto a rough road wide enough for only one wagon. Walker guessed it must be the same road, only farther south, that the old woman had used before she'd pointed the cart toward the gypsy land. If so, it linked Cedar Point to Fort Elliot and the settlement of Mobeetie. He'd traveled the road a few times as a boy.

Walker twisted the light out and mounted. His eyes grew used to the night. If he planned to catch up with the wagon, he needed to make some time. The road was too well traveled to pick out the signs he'd been following over the land, and there would be few places to turn off. He would take the chance that they were moving straight and fast.

Walker rode for an hour, stopping now and then to listen for the sound of a rig in front of him. Nothing. Years of training served him well. He didn't panic. He knew Lacy's life depended on it. Each time he passed a place in the road where ruts had turned off, he lit the lamp and studied the tracks to make sure they hadn't been made recently.

As time passed, the temperature dropped lower, but Walker hardly noticed. All his energy focused on finding Lacy. He realized on top of all the anger and worry, his arms ached for her. He felt as if he might die if he didn't hold her again.

Walker rode until almost midnight with no sign of the wagon or Lacy. He told himself over and over that she'd been kidnapped and not harmed, for whoever met the old woman had no time to kill, and he'd seen no blood spilled in the dirt. Someone had gone to a great deal of trouble to capture Lacy. If they'd wanted her dead, they could have shot into the bags of laundry. So, he reasoned, the men who took her were probably not the men who shot up Nell and the buggy.

He also reasoned that whoever the kidnappers were taking her to wanted her alive, at least when she arrived.

The possibility that two groups, one killers, one kidnappers, searched for her bothered him. How did they know Lacy was in the cart? Whoever shot up the buggy thought Lacy was dead. They wouldn't be lying in wait for her. Somehow the two men who'd taken her had not only learned that she was alive but also where she would be.

The memory of something Sheriff Riley said echoed in his thoughts. "If there's a price on her head, there are men around these parts who'll do about anything for money."

And women, he thought. The old woman. She'd left the doctor's office twice to his knowledge. Once out the back way to visit the privy, and again saying she had to buy more soap at the store. Both times she'd been gone long enough to talk to someone, maybe even plan. She'd driven slow, far slower than necessary, Walker remembered. That would have allowed the kidnappers time to get into place.

Walker tried to remember if it had been the old woman or Lacy who had suggested Lacy ride in the cart. Lacy had been the one to tell him, but had it been her idea, or someone else's? He couldn't remember.

She was all right, he reminded himself over and over as he rode. Only, he'd promised to be near. He promised he'd be there if she needed help. He'd let her down. Harm had found her on his watch.

Walker pushed on. It was almost dawn

when he finally spotted a wagon on the side of the road in a place where several others had pulled off before to camp and rest. Leaning his head forward as if he were sleeping in the saddle, Walker neared. He saw two men, but no sign of Lacy, and wondered if he'd come upon the wrong wagon. Two men were often needed to haul freight along these roads. One to manage the horses and the other to ride shotgun in case trouble came near.

A thin man squatted, building a roaring fire, while another slept on the ground close by. From the look of their horses they couldn't have been camped long. The one standing seemed nervous, breaking branches and tossing them into a fire already big enough for their needs.

Walker kept the wagon between him and the campfire just in case one of them was observant enough to notice his military saddle. "Mind if I join you?" he asked in what he hope sounded like a sleepy voice. "I've been riding all night." His words frosted the air as he swung from the saddle.

The thin man didn't look like he wanted company. "Ain't got no food!" he yelled.

"Neither do I." Walker walked around the wagon. If these weren't the men, he was wasting his time. If they were, what had they done with Lacy? "But, if you'll share your fire, I've got cigars. I thought I'd smoke one while I stretch my legs."

The thin man fell for Walker's reason for stopping and accepted the cigar eagerly. "I don't usually smoke a cigar like this." He twisted the thin tobacco in his fingers. "What'd you have to pay for this, mister? Two bits?"

"Four." Walker lit a match and offered the man a light. He noticed the stranger was unarmed. If these men were hired kidnappers, they were the worst he'd ever seen. They should have camped off the road, posted a guard, not let anyone near.

While the thin man drew on his cigar, Walker studied the area. No sign of Lacy. Only a short man huddled next to the fire snoring, and a coffin in the bed of the wagon.

"Transporting a body?" Walker pointed his cigar to the wagon.

"No, just the box." The thin man took a long draw and smiled. "This is a mighty fine cigar. You're welcome to warm yourself. I swear it's so cold I felt like I was moving through snow and not air."

"You been here long?" Walker squatted by the fire.

"No, maybe an hour. I was for moving on, but figured Sneed might nod off and fall out of the wagon." The thin man laughed. "It's better to let him sleep a few hours than have to keep stopping to put him back in the wagon. That man can eat more and sleep sounder than any man I ever met."

Walker knew he could ask no more questions without the thin man getting suspicious, so they smoked the cigars in silence. They couldn't be traveling far without provisions, but he had nothing to connect them with Lacy. "Well, thanks for the use of your fire." Walker stepped away. "I'd better be getting on to Fort Elliot." He raised an eyebrow and studied the man. "How much farther is it?"

The thin man shrugged. "Don't know for sure, half a day, I guess, maybe less."

"You're not heading there?"

The man shifted nervously. "No, we're on our way to Mobeetie. It's just beyond the fort."

"I hear it's a rough town."

"Wouldn't know," the man answered. "This is my first time there."

Walker walked away. "Have a good trip." Something wasn't right, but it wasn't all that unusual for a man not to be too friendly in this country.

"You, too," the stranger answered. "And thanks for the cigar."

As Walker moved back toward his horse, he spotted a corner of a quilt hanging out of the coffin. His blood froze. He knew of only one quilt made with the browns and blues of a man's suit.

Walker tightened the cinch on Trooper's saddle and kept his voice conversational. "You wouldn't want to sell that coffin would you?"

"No. We've already got a buyer."

Walker weighed his options. If he opened the coffin too soon, Lacy might get between him and the two men. But he had to get her out. He couldn't stand the thought of her in that box a moment longer than necessary.

He pulled his rifle from the saddle and leveled it on the thin man. "Wake your friend!" Walker ordered. "Or you're a dead man."

The thin man dropped his cigar and lifted shaking hands. He kicked at the body beside the fire. "Wake up!"

The little man came awake like a bear, all rage and roar. He made a step toward the thin man before he woke up enough to realize what happened. When he saw

Walker's rifle, he moved his hand toward his holstered gun.

"You pull that from leather," Walker promised, "and I'll have a bullet in your brain before you can aim."

Sneed was smart enough to move his hand away. "If you're robbing us, we ain't got nothing, mister. We been out of work most of the winter."

"Spread that blanket out." Walker pointed to the scrap of wool the chubby man had been using for a bed. "And unbuckle your gun belt. Slow."

Sneed followed orders while Walker reached beneath the wagon's bench and retrieved a rifle. He unloaded it and tossed it on the blanket.

"Wrap your weapons."

"These ain't worth nothing, mister," Sneed grumbled as he wrapped. "I got them secondhand, and they ain't even worth stealing, I oughta know."

Walker picked up the guns and clipped them to his saddle. "Now, your clothes and boots."

Both men looked shocked, then jumped as Walker fired a round between them. They started undressing, jumping around like puppets, just in case Walker fired another round.

"You can't take everything. Without the wagon and no clothes, we'll die before we can walk anywhere," Sneed begged. "We're half a day or more from Cedar Point or Mobeetie."

"I'm not taking the wagon, only what's in it. You should be able to make it back to Cedar Point before dark." He watched them shiver. "Toss the clothes in the fire."

Both men hesitated.

Walker took aim. "And the boots better hit the center of the fire, or one of you will be bleeding."

The two men watched as their clothes caught fire and their boots began to smoke.

Walker took a step closer to them. "You forgot your underwear."

Sneed looked offended. "You don't expect us to be bare naked to the world." He crossed his arms, standing his ground. "I haven't had my long johns off since September."

"It's that or death, gentlemen. Take your pick. I don't think there's a court in this country that will find me guilty of killing two snakes who kidnapped my wife."

The tall man glared at Sneed. "You didn't tell me she had a husband. I never would have gone along with this if I knew she had a man who'd come after us. All you said we had to do was get her to Mobeetie. Nothing dangerous, you said. Just take her for a little ride and make a hundred dollars."

"The underwear." Walker didn't want to listen to their argument. "In the fire."

Both men stripped, then shivered in the cold, their pale bodies looking mismatched to their tan hands and faces. Sneed only wore one sock, and he did his best to try to hide it. His partner had both socks still on, but the toes were out.

"Stay close to the campfire until I get my wife." Walker climbed in the wagon, then unlatched the casket. "Take one step toward this wagon, there'll be more than your clothes burning in that fire."

He raised the coffin lid, fearing what he might find. If she was hurt or even bruised, both men would die.

There, curled inside her blanket, slept Lacy. She blinked away the light and huddled farther into the quilt.

"Sorry to wake you. I know how you hate mornings." Walker smiled, loving the way she looked when she first woke. "But we really need to be going."

She finally focused on him. "I knew you'd come. I've been waiting for you."

Without another word, she came into his

arms and eased the ache he'd had in his chest since the moment he'd realized she'd been kidnapped.

He carried her, quilt and all, to Trooper and sat her sideways before swinging into the saddle behind her. She hugged him so tightly he feared he might not be able to breathe. He could hear her laughing and crying all at the same time. He knew he'd have more control if she rode behind him, but he liked the feel of her with her hip pressing against the inside of one of his thighs and her legs over his other.

Walker kissed her head and held her close with one hand as he kept his rifle pointed in the direction of the fire. "Lacy, do you trust me?"

She nodded.

"Then tuck your head against my chest and don't look up. I don't want you to see what I had to do."

Lacy followed orders. "Is it the two men who captured me?"

Walker pulled Trooper away from the wagon and glanced back at the two kidnappers trying to stand close enough to the fire to stay warm without burning. "Yes," he whispered against Lacy's ear, breathing in the smell of her that he'd hungered for all night.

"Is it an ugly sight?"

"One of the worst I've ever seen," Walker answered honestly, knowing he'd have to tell her the truth later.

Lacy pressed harder against him. "Don't tell me about the blood or what you had to do. I don't know if I can bear it."

"All right," Walker answered as they rode away. She might be all tough and yelling when she was mad, but he knew she must be the gentlest soul on earth. "Just know that I did what I had to do." He knew no matter what settlement the two men wandered into, they'd be noticed by the law.

Lacy rubbed her cheek against his coat, and neither said a word for a while.

The sun tried to fight through the clouds but only succeeded in casting a gray light across the fog. When the ground turned more uneven and rolling, Walker guided Trooper off the road and into a stand of trees. The winter grass grew tall, almost brushing Trooper's belly at times. They crossed beneath ancient cottonwoods on a carpet of leaves, moving slowly now, letting the horse find his own footing. The day seemed to darken as branches overlapped.

Finally, Walker stopped. "We're another three, maybe four hours from the fort. I need to rest the horse for a while." He swung down, then lifted her to the ground. "I hear a stream over in the thick of those cottonwoods if you want to wash up."

She walked toward the water without a word. He removed the saddle and brushed down Trooper with dry grass. As he tossed the old scrap of wool Sneed had been sleeping in earlier over the horse's back, he noticed her standing behind him. Watching. Her clothes were wrinkled, and her hair a mess, but he couldn't help but smile. Lacy was safe. He'd felt like someone ripped out part of his insides when she'd disappeared.

He built a fire and tied Trooper in the small clearing banked on three sides by trees. Lacy retrieved her bag from where he'd strapped it and pulled out a brush.

"Aren't you afraid someone will see the smoke?" She brushed her hair as if it were something important to do.

"The fog's thicker than the smoke. I'm more afraid we'll freeze." He could feel the temperature dropping and knew they needed to keep moving, but Trooper had to rest, and now that Lacy was safe, the two nights he'd spent without sleep were starting to catch up to Walker. He needed to be alert when they neared civilization.

He spread his bedroll on the ground beside the saddle and motioned her to sit. "Why don't you relax."

"But, I've been asleep," she answered as she sat on a corner of the blanket and leaned back against the saddle. Absently, she braided her hair in one thick cord. "There was nothing else to do inside the box while I was waiting for you."

"Good." He rolled onto the bedroll and handed her his rifle. "Then you keep guard."

Without another word, he spread the quilt atop them both, lay on his back, and pulled his hat down over his face.

Chapter 20

Lacy waited for him to say more. Surely he didn't plan to sleep out here in the middle of nowhere? They could have both walked and let the horse rest. There was no need to stop. She wanted to get to Bailee. Nell must be there by now, and they'd all be worried sick about her.

"Captain?" She tried to see under his hat.

He didn't move.

"Captain?" She tapped his arm that rested a few inches from her leg.

Walker raised his hat slowly. "Yes?"

"Shouldn't we be moving on? The others will be worried by now. Maybe we could make it as far as Carter's place by nightfall. If you're worried about me, I can go farther. I'm not all that tired."

He seemed to think about her plan for a minute. "Carter and Jacob know you're with me. They'll assume you're safe." He put his hat back over his face, apparently planning to end the conversation.

"But," Lacy hurried to add, "if it's three or four hours to the fort, it must be even farther to Cedar Point. I've never been down this road, but I've heard it's a hard day's journey on a good horse."

"Your point?" Walker said without raising his hat.

"My point is, we'll be forever getting home as it is, and you're taking a nap."

He didn't answer, so she poked him. "Captain?"

The hat slowly rose from his face, and to her surprise, he looked angry. "I've had no sleep for two nights. In fact, I'm not sure I've had much in the way of sleep since I got ordered to come watch over you. Trooper needs a few hours' rest. I wasn't aware we planned to visit during the time."

Lacy lay the rifle at her side and leaned down so that she could see his eyes better. "I slept most of the time I was in that coffin. There wasn't anything else to do while I waited for you to show up."

"You seem to have the ability to sleep anywhere." He raised one eyebrow. "Whereas I need someplace quiet." His last word echoed across the small clearing.

"I understand." She straightened back

up, lifted the rifle, and resumed her guard. The man had held her so tight when he'd saved her. He'd even brushed the top of her head with his chin as if loving having her back with him. Only now she was here, he seemed to have little interest in talking to her.

He moved the hat back in place over his face and pulled the quilt to his shoulder.

Lacy waited, trying to be still. The fire warmed the air a little and the saddle kept her back from the cold, but she wasn't comfortable. She pulled off one glove and felt her nose. Cold. She tried to rub it warm, then gave up and decided just to let it freeze off. After all, Walker probably wouldn't notice.

"Captain?"

"Yes," he mumbled.

"I'm sorry to bother you again, but you haven't had time to get to sleep. I still don't understand why you think we're going to the fort. If we're not going to Bailee and Carter's place, we should be heading home."

"We're not going back to Cedar Point. You'll be safer at the fort."

"But —"

He raised his hat again. "Cedar Point is not safe. This was the third time someone's tried to do you harm. I'll not take the risk again."

"But I don't want to go anywhere. We'll take precautions. I have the paper to get out and the cats to feed. I can't just leave."

"Lacy, we're going to the fort." He closed his eyes, ending the discussion.

She poked him in the shoulder once more, anger building. "So what you're saying is I have no choice. You saved me from those two idiots only to kidnap me again."

"I'm not kidnapping you," he mumbled through the hat.

"What do you call taking someone by force where they don't want to go?"

Walker tossed his hat, giving up on the idea of sleeping as he rose to one elbow and swore.

As always, Lacy's temper exploded first. "Take me back to the mismatched morons. At least they kept me warm in the box. If you left them still breathing, maybe they'll take pity on me and agree to rekidnap me. As least when I was with them, I was heading somewhere, not sitting in the middle of nowhere."

She tossed aside the quilt he'd spread over her legs and tried to pull her skirt away so she could stand, but she'd wiggled so much, her legs were tangled in yards and layers of material.

Walker sat up and placed his hand over her arm. "Lacy, settle down," he said, trying not to make it sound like an order. "I'm not making you go to the fort. It's the closest place from here where I know you'll be safe. Once there, we can telegraph the sheriff, and he'll get word to Carter and the others that you're all right."

She didn't comment.

"Besides," he continued, "if Whitaker thinks you're dead, he won't expect the paper to be up and running. Look at it as a little time off."

She stopped struggling. He was right, of course, but she wasn't ready to admit it.

Walker dragged his fingers through his hair. "Look, Trooper's carried me most of yesterday and all night. He needs to rest for a few hours."

She nodded, guessing he'd figured out she'd never let an animal suffer. "All right. We'll rest. Then I'll go to the fort. But only long enough to plan how to get back home."

"Good." He relaxed back on his elbow and spread the blanket over her. Then, as casually as if he'd done it a thousand times before, he lay his head in her lap and rested his arm across her knees.

Lacy sat very still. She wasn't sure if he were just getting comfortable or making certain she didn't try to bolt while he slept. His breathing grew slow and regular as she watched his features relax in sleep. He shifted once, pressing his cheek against her coat.

"Captain?" she whispered.

"Mmm?" He didn't open his eyes.

"Thank you for coming after me."

He didn't answer. She knew he fell asleep.

Cuddling against the saddle, Lacy let her hand move into his dark hair as she tried to relax. She liked the coarse feel of it. She knew he only thought of her safety when he insisted on going to the fort, but he didn't understand that she needed her home. Her things around her. She'd never be one of those women who could live out of a trunk. If she'd had any other choice, she wouldn't have traveled west. It didn't matter that she had little and her furniture was mostly made out of crates. She had a place where she belonged. Lacy realized how important that was to her.

And, she thought, in a very small way she had him also. After a few weeks he'd be gone, but she'd have his memory. People would ask about him. She could dream about him someday coming home as if he were a real husband. Even though he didn't know it, he made her life less lonely. He was a part of her world, though she'd never be a part of his.

An hour passed in the calm of the clearing. She knew she didn't have to be on guard. The only way someone would find them would be if they happened to stumble over them in the fog. The air thickened, and snow began to swirl. When Walker rolled to his side, Lacy scooted down so that the quilt covered her shoulders. He moved once more in his sleep, circling her with his arm, pulling her to him.

Lacy closed her eyes, pressed her nose against the warmth of his chest, and relaxed, letting the horror of the night slip away. Her body warmed next to his, and she listened to the beating of his heart.

An inch at a time she slipped her hand into the folds of his coat, seeing if she could feel his heart. Part of her wanted to make sure he had one, this man of duty and honor.

Sure enough, there it was, pounding slow and steady as he slept. She wanted to be closer to that heart and believe if only for a few days that it beat for her.

She let her hand rest there, as she dreamed of what might have been if he'd wanted her for a wife. She used to say she'd have so many children she'd have to number them, for there would be no time to think of names. But now she knew there would be no children. People lie in the same bed and get pregnant. Lacy knew how it happened. She'd even done it once, and a baby didn't come.

She was broken, she thought, just like her mother had been broken after she was born. Her grandmother told her once that her father had been angry that there would be no sons. She hadn't gone on to say more, but Lacy knew that he'd left because her mother could never have more babies, and his only child had been a girl.

Maybe it was for the best that Walker didn't want her for a wife. Since she couldn't have children, she wouldn't be much use to him.

Pulling back a few inches, she looked at him and let herself wonder for the first time in a long while what it would have been like to have a husband. A real husband.

She stretched, feeling his body along the length of her. She moved her hands to his hair and brushed it gently from his sleeping eyes. Very carefully, she leaned forward and touched his mouth with care. When he didn't move, she ran the tip of her tongue along his bottom lip, tasting him.

He shifted in sleep, and she found herself even closer. Slowly, so he wouldn't wake, she moved her cheek along his, feeling the whiskers tickle her skin. She pressed her nose into the collar of his coat and felt the strong pounding of pulse at his throat. Her hand spread across the wall of his chest as she unbuttoned his coat and warmed her face against his skin.

Without warning, he rolled atop her, pinning her to the ground. "What do you think you're doing, Lacy?" He didn't sound like he'd been asleep.

She didn't want to look at him, but there was no way to look away. "I was smelling you." She might as well confess to everything. "Tasting you, too, I'm afraid."

He appeared confused for a moment, then a slow smile spread across his face. "Were you touching my hair?"

"Yes," she admitted. "Strictly out of curiosity."

"Didn't I tell you not to ever do that while I'm asleep?"

"No. I told you." She blushed.

He lifted himself above her so that he could see her better. "So, let me get the rules straight, you can touch my hair, smell me, taste me, but I'm not to touch you."

"Well, yes, Captain. You can also get off of me now. I didn't mean to wake you."

"It's not easy to stay asleep with you next to me." He rolled to his side but left his arm still draped over her. "And just out of curiosity, would you mind if I tasted you?"

She could hardly say no. Closing her eyes, she waited for the kiss.

But he didn't start with her lips. He unbuttoned the top few buttons of her coat as if opening a gift.

She lay very still as he did the same to the top of her dress, exposing her throat. Then as lightly as she'd touched him, he moved his cheek down her neck, stopping every few inches to open his mouth and taste.

Lacy shivered in pure delight. She'd never felt anything so amazing. The roughness of his jaw moving over her skin, the softness of his lips. A sigh escaped before she could stop it.

Walker raised his head. "Quiet please. I'm not finished." He undid another button. "Are you cold?" he whispered, brushing her ear with his words.

"No," she answered as his fingers pulled the material away so that he could touch the hollow of her neck.

Slowly, he inched up her throat until he reached her mouth. She'd expected his kiss to be soft, teasing, like those across her skin, but it came bold and hungry to her. He opened her mouth and kissed her as she'd never dreamed a kiss could be.

The cold, the fog, the hard ground, none of it mattered as he wrapped his arms around her. For the first few kisses he taught, then they learned together what the other liked. He'd lie perfectly still and let her kiss him, then she'd try to do the same. They kissed until they were both out of breath, then laughed and kissed again like teenagers.

Finally, she stretched beside him, thinking of what pleasure kissing could bring, when she looked up to see him watching her. Without a word, he spread his fingers beneath her coat and moved his hands along her body. His eyes never left hers as his hands crossed over the cotton of her dress, molding his fingers to her curves.

She knew she could have stopped him with a word, or even if she'd looked away, but she didn't. When he lowered his mouth to hers once more, she tasted passion in his kiss.

He gave her the kind of kisses she wanted as his hands stroked her gently, greedy for the feel of her.

Trooper stomped in the clearing several feet away, and Walker reluctantly pulled away and looked up. For a moment, he listened, then lowered his face beside hers and groaned in pure agony. "Lacy, we can't do this now. The fire's almost out. It will be dark soon. We'll freeze to death." Even as he said the words, his hands stroked her body as if not getting the message from his brain that it was time to stop.

Lacy wanted to say she didn't care. She'd never felt anything like this in her life. Her body boiled from the inside out. Her stomach hurt with a hunger she didn't understand. Her breasts ached, wanting to be touched. She wanted something she'd never had, never even known existed. Until now. She wanted the passionate man who'd lost himself in kissing her only a moment before.

But that man was disappearing, pulling himself under control, pulling them both into reality, and he hadn't even moved an inch away from her yet.

He kissed her forehead, then rolled to his feet. "We'd better go. I'll saddle the horse."

Lacy felt like she'd been tossed in cold water. She sat up and tried to straighten her hair, but she couldn't make herself stand. A moment ago she'd been floating on a cloud, and now all the problems came crashing down on her.

He stood above her and offered her his hand. When he pulled her to her feet, he held her tightly for a moment. She wasn't sure if he wanted to apologize for letting them go so far, or if he, like her, longed to return to what they'd been doing.

"Are you all right?" he whispered, and she thought she heard the need for her in his question. "I didn't go too fast?"

"Yes. I'm all right." She thought of screaming that he was going too slow as far as she was concerned, but she wasn't sure exactly what he was talking about.

"No regrets?"

She started to say that they hadn't done anything to regret, but she simply said, "No, Captain."

He laughed. "Lacy, when are you going to start calling me Walker?"

"When I know you better," she answered, thinking if they lay back down, that might have a chance of happening.

"All right, we'll work on your knowing me better later. Right now, I've a duty to get you to safety before we both freeze." He didn't say another word as she folded the quilt and he saddled the horse, but he held her tight against him as they rode toward the fort. Once in a while he'd move his chin against her hair, and she knew he remembered, just as she did.

She didn't want to talk. She needed time to think about what had happened. Lacy relived everything, tried to remember the way she'd felt, the way he'd tasted. The fact that the captain could react with such tenderness surprised her.

When they were within sight of the fort, he leaned close to her ear and whispered, "When we get to the fort, I think we should check in as man and wife."

She nodded. That made sense. They were married. If they tried to be anything else, it would look strange, a woman traveling with a man not her husband. Lacy doubted the fort would even allow her to stay.

"Which means," he added, "that we'll get married quarters if they're available. We'll probably be sharing one room and have meals with the officers."

Lacy didn't see any problem. They'd been sharing three tiny rooms for almost two weeks.

He shifted as if he had more to say. She waited, knowing he'd eventually get whatever it was off his mind. "When we get to the fort, I'd like our stay there to be together. If you've no objection. I promise, Lacy, I'll take it slow and easy."

She knew what he asked. They would be sharing a room, maybe even a bed. At least that's what she thought he meant. She wasn't going to embarrass herself by asking and find out he'd only been explaining the workings of the fort to her. So she said the only thing she could think of. She said, "I've no objection."

They crossed into Fort Elliot without another word.

Chapter 21

Lacy held tightly to Walker's lapel as he rode past the guards at the gate. The fort reminded her of an old medieval castle looming out of the darkness, lording over the flat land around. Trooper danced through the entrance, as though sensing that their journey might be over.

Walker maneuvered the horse up to a long building with one end marked as headquarters. "We're home," he whispered.

He dismounted slowly while the guards watched him. "I've traveled across half the forts along the frontier, but I've never visited this one."

Lacy wasn't sure he talked to calm Trooper, or her. The guards seemed poised and ready for trouble. They watched, sizing up both the rider and his mount. This was a place only a man like Walker would call home. To her it seemed colorless and stiff.

Walker looped the reins over the hitching post. "Fort Elliot holds the distinction of being the most northern post in Texas." He patted the horse, his voice level and low. "I always wanted to see this place."

A sergeant, a few years younger than Walker, stepped out of the first door and walked along the wide porch. He smiled a welcome but didn't salute.

"How can I help you, mister?" the sergeant asked. "All civilians have to be off the grounds before the gates are closed at sundown, so I'll have to ask you to state your business and leave."

Walker lowered Lacy from the saddle before he faced the sergeant. "I'm Captain Walker Larson presently stationed at Fort Davis but on assignment at Cedar Point. I'd like to speak with the commanding officer."

"Did you say Captain Larson?" The younger man tilted his head as if having trouble hearing.

"I did." Walker shot the words. "And I'm waiting, Sergeant."

The man straightened. "Of course, sir. I'll tell the major you're here."

Walker stepped onto the porch. "Have someone see to my horse. Sergeant?"

"Yes, sir, and it's Hayes, sir."

The sergeant opened the door to the main office and moved aside while Walker led Lacy inside. He held a chair by the fire for her without taking his eyes off of Walker and then hurried to follow orders.

Once they were alone in the office, Lacy asked, "Do you ever say please?"

"No," Walker answered. "And you, madam, were a perfect army officer's wife."

"How's that?"

"Silent." He grinned, proud of his joke.

She started to argue, but she treaded on strange territory here. A fort was a place she knew nothing about, though she'd seen soldiers from time to time come to Cedar Point to meet a shipment sent by train. Once in a while they caused enough trouble in the saloon to have the sheriff mention something about having them sleep it off in jail for the night, but for the most part she remained ignorant of the army. Maybe she'd be wise to listen until she understood. For all she knew, the general, or whoever ran this place, might kick them out if she did something wrong.

The door opened, and a tall man with graying hair rushed in. She'd expected him to salute, or something, but he hurried forward and grabbed Walker's hand, then slapped him on the back. "Welcome,

Larson. Great to have you here. An honor, a real honor."

Before Walker could say a word, the man added, "You're out of uniform." He said it like Walker had grown horns.

"I'll explain." Walker turned toward Lacy. "But first, Major Garner, I'd like to present my wife."

To Lacy's surprise, Major Garner bowed low and kissed her hand. "Madam, it is a pleasure to meet you. Please know that I'm at your service." The major was quite handsome in a stiff kind of way. "I've had the honor of meeting your husband a few times but was unaware he had a wife. Your beauty graces our small fort."

"Thank you," she managed to say, noticing that his fingers were long and thin, made more to play a piano, she thought, than do combat.

She expected him to turn back to Walker and act like she were invisible, but to her surprise, he asked about her health and wanted to know if she needed time to freshen up.

When she said yes, he shouted for Sergeant Hayes.

Still holding her hand, Major Garner turned to Walker and demanded why he'd never been told that Walker had such a lovely wife. "It's an oversight worthy of court-marshal."

Lacy realized the compliment came at full volume and sounded more like a challenge. She felt overwhelmed and thankful when the sergeant arrived to show her to their quarters.

Hayes escorted her down the long porch to a line of doors each about ten feet apart with a high window next to each entrance. "These are the single officers' quarters, but right now we have several empty. Our married housing is due south of the barracks, but it's full at present. If you've no objection, Mrs. Larson, I've had a room readied." He opened one of the doors. A light already glowed from a newly lit fireplace.

"I've taken the liberty of putting the captain's and your things in here. Meals are served at the mess hall at seven, noon, and six, but I'll be glad to bring you a tray. Mrs. Garner always takes her lunch alone in her quarters and, of course, the married housing have their own cooking stove."

Lacy was glad to hear other women stayed within the walls of the fort, but before she could ask about them, the sergeant continued, "There's a privy out back. It's reserved for the wives from ten to eleven a.m. and from seven to eight p.m. No man will enter between those hours."

Lacy stepped inside. "Thank you." She looked up and smiled. "I've never been to a fort before. What do I call you?"

He seemed to relax a little. "Hayes, ma'am. Sergeant Hayes. My office is the first door, and if you need me, you'll find me there most of the time."

"I'm Lacy Larson."

"Yes, ma'am. You're Captain Larson's wife. I never met him until now, but I've heard tell of him. It's a real honor to see him in the flesh. I was beginning to think he was just a legend." Hayes appeared nervous, as if he'd said too much. "I'll be right outside this door when you're ready. I'll escort you back to your husband."

"I can find my own way, thank you." Lacy smiled. The offices weren't thirty feet from her.

Hayes straightened slightly. "Begging your pardon, ma'am, but no woman, not even the major's wife, is allowed to walk alone on the grounds after dark."

"I understand," Lacy lied. "I'll let you know when I'm ready to return."

He closed the door, and Lacy looked around the neat little room. It couldn't have been more than ten feet wide and twice as long, with a door and window at each end. Everything had an order. She'd be willing to bet the other officers' quarters looked exactly the same. A desk to the left, a small table with two chairs near a fireplace, a bed and a dresser with washbowl and pitcher atop it. An eight-day clock ticked away on the mantel, sounding as if it had just been wound.

Quickly washing and changing into her only other dress, Lacy hoped no one would notice the wrinkles. She put her shawl over it and opened the door, not at all surprised to find Hayes waiting for her.

When she returned to the office, she noticed a cloth had been spread over one of the desks where a simple meal of meat and potatoes waited. The captain and Major Garner were seated, but they stood as she entered, and Walker held a chair for her. But he didn't touch her as she hoped he might.

"Your quarters are satisfactory, madam?" he asked impersonally as if he weren't sharing them with her.

"Yes, thank you," she answered, wondering what he would have done if she'd said no. Or, worse, thrown her arms around him and begged to go home. But she couldn't . . . wouldn't . . . embarrass him by showing an ounce of the fear she felt in this place he thought of as safe.

While they ate, Walker explained about the kidnapping attempt. The major asked one question after another, while Walker filled in the details of Zeb Whitaker and his attempts to kill Lacy. She didn't miss the facts he left out. Like their arranged marriage, or that he had only seen her once before twelve days ago.

"Of course you'll stay here. In fact you may be a godsend to a dilemma I'm facing." The major's statement held no doubt he welcomed them. His entire face softened as he turned to her. "My wife will be back tomorrow morning, and she'll enjoy the company of your bride." He smiled at Lacy. "You'll be safe here, madam." With those words he seemed to think he'd solved her little problem of being kidnapped and almost murdered. He moved on to what he considered more important matters.

She wondered if any of the army wives ever went nuts being called madam. The men talked about a problem in transporting some prisoners, and Lacy fought to stay awake.

Finally, Walker noticed her nodding off and stood, saying he needed to see his wife to quarters.

The major stood and bade her good night, but as Walker opened the door, he added, "We'll continue this discussion over maps and port in my office."

Walker nodded and took Lacy's arm.

As he walked her along the porch, she said, "You must be exhausted. Tell the major you'll visit with him tomorrow."

Walker opened their door and stepped back, waiting for her to enter. "You don't understand. That wasn't a request, it was an order. I have to return."

Lacy nodded, but he was right, she didn't understand. When she looked into the room, she saw a tub full of water by the fireplace.

"I took the liberty of ordering you a bath, madam."

"How long will you be?"

"You'll have plenty of time. Don't wait up for me. Go on to bed. I'll not wake you if I'm late." His words were formal, but she saw the warmth in his eyes.

She leaned up and kissed him on the cheek. This strange man she knew so little about was her only friend in this place. She wanted to keep him close, and even if he couldn't stay, it felt good knowing that he wanted to.

She took her time bathing, then warmed

by the fire before climbing into bed. Walker had been right. She did feel safe but not just because of the fort.

She knew he was near. It felt odd to depend on someone else, to know they were close if needed. Even when she'd been kidnapped, she'd been mad more than frightened, because she knew the captain would find her.

As she fell asleep, Lacy wished she was more than just a mission he was on in Cedar Point. Why couldn't he have told the major he'd come home to visit his wife? The answer was simple, she decided: because it wasn't true.

When Walker quietly slipped into the room an hour later, Lacy was sound asleep. He walked over to her side of the bed and stared down at her. She seemed so peaceful, so beautiful. He wanted to wake her and tell her all that the major had said, but he couldn't bring himself to disturb her. The past two days had been hell on her, and she deserved the peace of sleep. Besides, he wasn't sure he wanted to face the questions she'd ask if she knew what the major planned.

Jerking his uniform from his saddlebags, Walker hung it outside the door, knowing it would be pressed by the time he needed it in the morning. He then pulled off his shirt and washed. In truth, he'd enjoyed wearing civilian clothes and would miss them come morning.

He thought of stripping off his remaining clothes, but he wasn't sure. The last thing he wanted to do tonight was frighten Lacy. Despite how casually she'd acted when he'd seen her in her undergarments, he had no idea how she'd react seeing him.

Tugging off his boots, he stood them by the fire, then pulled back the covers and lay down on the other side of the bed. For a while he didn't move, thinking this would be the first time he ever slept with a woman.

He thought of touching her, of holding her, of making love to her. After all, she'd agreed to stay here with him as husband and wife. She could hardly complain if he bedded her. He'd done it once before.

Walker realized he didn't want to just bed her. He wanted to make love to her. He wanted her to come to him, as she had this morning, with her arms stretched toward him not out of duty but out of desire. It took no genius to realize she knew nothing of making love. The first time they'd been together must have frightened her half out of her mind. She'd never even been kissed when he took her virginity. That one fact gnawed at him more than he wanted to admit.

Walker put his arm over his eyes. If she'd give him a chance, he'd make that day up to her. He'd show her how it should be between a man and a woman. He'd take it slow and teach her step by step. He'd spend days waking the woman in her.

If she'd allow him? Not likely, he reasoned.

Reaching to put out the light, he noticed the notebook she'd brought with her. She'd ripped off another number. Now the number fourteen was scribbled across the top page. Fourteen more days until he left. Fourteen more days of tolerating him.

Frustrated, Walker picked up the tablet and threw it across the room. He didn't want to think about the countdown anymore. He didn't want to be reminded that he had only two weeks left before he'd have to keep his promise to ride out of her life forever.

When the tablet hit the wall, Lacy started from the noise and sat halfway up in bed.

"What was that?" she whispered sounding afraid.

"Nothing. Go back to sleep." Angry at himself for waking her, he turned his back to her. If she was still counting the days, she wasn't likely to welcome an advance from him.

But it wasn't Lacy's way to follow orders. "Captain?" she whispered.

"Yes," he said wondering if she planned to ask him to leave the bed. He could demand to stay. It was his right. But he knew he'd leave if she wanted him to go. He'd put his bedroll by the door and do what he'd been ordered to do: protect her.

"I'm glad you're back," she answered with a yawn. "Good night."

He rolled to face her. "Lacy, what is it you want?" He had to know where he stood. He wasn't sure he could survive their days in these quarters if he didn't know the rules. He also knew fort life well enough that if he slept anywhere but here, everyone on the place would know it by morning.

She opened sleepy eyes and looked at him, as if considering going back to sleep and not playing his game. Finally, she said, "I don't want to be afraid anymore. I'm not brave like Bailee and Sarah. I try to act like I am, but I guess you've already figured out that I'm not."

An exhausted sigh escaped her. "I'm tired of fearing shadows."

Walker opened his arm and she cuddled beneath it. "Do you feel safe now?" he whispered into her hair. Dear God, but she smelled good.

"Yes, thank you."

"I'm glad, but I meant to ask what you want from me?"

"I don't want —"

"I didn't ask what you don't want," he replied, then cringed realizing she'd probably list that she didn't want him to yell at her anymore. "Tell me what you want from me other than to feel safe."

She didn't move, and for a while he wasn't sure she planned to answer. Then she laid her hand over his heart.

He covered her fingers with his and waited. The fire crackled low now, setting the room in a golden glow. He felt her warm and soft against his side, but her fingers were cold.

Finally, she whispered. "I want you to make everything go away except the two of us. I don't want to think or worry about anything — not the army, or Whitaker, or even what's happened before between us." She brushed her fingers over his chest as if dusting off his heart. "I want to know the man with this heartbeat."

Of all the things she could have requested, he never expected that. She asked the impossible.

He tried to think of how to tell her no . . . that he wasn't brave enough to open his heart again. He'd never survive another blow. Before he could think of the right words, she did the strangest thing. She rose up a few inches and leaned over him until her lips touched his.

Her kiss wasn't light, or playful, but filled with purpose. She kissed him as she'd learned to, just as he liked to be kissed.

When she finished, she didn't pull away but whispered against his cheek. "Make there be no more world but this bed, Captain. A neutral ground where there is no fear and no orders to follow. Hold me while we sleep as if we were the only two people alive."

He dug his hand into her hair and held her head as he rolled, pinning her against the pillows. "I'll try, Lacy. Dear God, I'll try."

He kissed her then, deeper than he ever had. The taste of her flowed like a drug through his veins. His heart pounded so hard he thought it might explode. She stretched beneath him, wrapping her arms around his neck and pulling him even closer.

And as she kissed him back, the impossible happened. All the world melted away.

Chapter 22

Lacy slept on Walker's shoulder feeling warm and protected all night. He made no advances beyond a few passionate kisses, and she didn't understand why. She knew he wanted more from her. She could see a hunger in his eyes, but for some reason he held himself in check.

Now that she'd discovered what it could be like between a man and a woman, she would have welcomed another lesson, but she'd not try to talk him into more, or trick him. She'd done that once before and hated herself for it. He might be attracted to her, but that didn't mean he wanted a wife any more than he had when she demanded he take her to his bed two years ago.

When she sat up and pushed the covers away, he was gone. For a moment, she wondered if she'd dreamed him lying down beside her during the night. For so many years she'd thought about what it would be like to have a husband at her side. There had been a few lonely nights when she'd talked to him as if he were beside her in the darkness of her little apartment. She'd say "Good night" out loud, knowing there would be no answer.

No, he'd been there. They'd talked last night and touched. She could still almost feel his hand resting just below her waist on her hip as he slept. Over and over in sleep he'd tightened his hold around her as though fearing that she might slip away before he woke.

She liked the warmth of his hand touching her and would have told him so if she could have found the words. She liked hearing his steady breathing and the way he pulled the covers over her when she rolled over. He protected her like he thought she might vanish at any moment if he didn't stand guard.

But in the end, it had been he who slipped away without waking her.

She glanced around the neat little room. His civilian clothes hung over a chair near the fire. His saddlebags were folded by the washstand.

Lacy relaxed. He was still near. He hadn't abandoned her in this strange place.

She tiptoed to the high window and opened the shutter.

Blinding sunlight greeted her. She blinked. For a moment Walker seemed to be everywhere. On guard, riding a horse near the corral, walking by the flagpole. Then she realized all the men were in uniform, and they all looked very much alike. As her eyes adjusted to the bright light, she eliminated most of the men. Slightly too short, not enough hair, too fat, too thin.

A knock sounded at her door. "Mrs. Larson?" someone shouted.

Lacy jumped back from the window, not sure what to do, but since she stood in her gown, she said, "Yes?" rather than asking whoever it was to come in.

"I've been instructed to bring you breakfast in ten minutes. Will that be acceptable?"

"Yes." She almost laughed. She'd landed on another shore where they all spoke Walker's language. All proper and stiff.

Lacy scrambled into her clothes and managed to straighten the bed before the knock came again, exactly ten minutes later.

"Come in." She stood straight, waiting.

A soldier entered, his head down as he walked to the table and left a tray of food.

He didn't look to be much older than Jay Boy, but he wore a uniform.

"Thank you," she said.

He smiled briefly. "You're welcome, Mrs. Larson. Will there be anything else?"

"No, thank you." She wanted to ask if he'd seen her husband, but she wasn't sure that would be proper.

The young soldier backed out of the room and closed the door.

With one smell of the food, Lacy realized she was starving. She pulled a chair close to the table and uncovered a breakfast that would have fed a family. Before she could take a bite, the door opened again. She didn't have to look up. She recognized her husband's stomp.

He marched across the room, retrieved his saddlebags, then walked to stand on the other side of her table. Impatient, he set the bags down with a thud.

Lacy glanced up from her food, noticing the captain was back in all his proper uniform and his frozen features. "Good morning," she said, remembering the man who'd taken slow pleasure in kissing her fingers the night before.

"More correctly, good afternoon."

She didn't argue. "All right, good afternoon." His uniform had changed to that of a soldier without any rank, and she wondered if he'd borrowed it. "What time do we leave for home?"

Widening his stance, he clasped his hands behind him. She wasn't sure if he planned to address the troops or brace for a blow. "We'll have to delay. I've orders to accompany a prisoner south. I'll return in a few days."

Lacy was up and moving toward him. "You can't leave me here for days. Turn down the order. I can be ready before you can saddle Trooper. We can leave now. I have to get back and make sure Nell is all right. I have the paper —"

He picked up his saddlebags as if she'd finished talking. "You'll be safe, just stay within the walls. I've sent the telegram to Riley. Everyone will know you're safe with me. As for Nell, I'm sure she's in good hands."

"I'm not staying. I want to go home."

"That's impossible." His words hit like ice water on her face.

She swung at him in pure frustration, but he caught her hand and put it behind her as he pulled her near with a powerful hold.

Struggling, she pushed against him with her free hand. She saw the crack in his armor and stopped. She might be angry, but he seemed to be enjoying her temper. She had no intention of allowing him the satisfaction of thinking she played some kind of game of power with him.

"Turn me loose."

He did at once.

She didn't step away, letting him know that she might be angry, but she was not afraid of him.

Smiling down at her, he understood her silent message and whispered, "Lacy, I have to go."

He placed his hand gently on her waist, then spread his fingers across her back and down to her hip.

She met his gaze and knew he was remembering the night.

"Should I step away?" he smiled, reading her pleasure.

"No," she said as his hand moved up her back and then low once more. She wished she could find the words to tell him how she felt when his hands moved gently over her.

His hands traveled up once more, molding lightly against the sides of her breasts as he kissed her softly, then whispered, "I can't explain now, Lacy. There's not time. But you have to trust me.

Promise me you'll be here when I get back." He tilted her head up as he moved a few inches away. "I have to know you'll be here when I return."

She moved from his touch.

Turning toward the fire, she said, "So, I'm a prisoner here."

"You're my wife." His words suddenly had an edge of anger to them.

She picked up the tablet and ripped out another page. "I'm a prisoner for thirteen more days and then no more."

"If that's the way you want it." His words grew cold. "But I want your promise that you'll be here when I return."

"You have it, Captain." She felt like she talked to a stranger once more. Where had the man gone who held her so close last night?

Without a word, he walked out of the room and closed the door. She rushed to the window and watched him swing up on Trooper. Five men waited for him at the gate. They rode out of sight. He didn't look back.

Lacy straightened, refusing to cry for him. Just about the time she thought he was human, he proved her wrong. Whatever he had to do was more important than her. He'd seen to her safety, then he'd left her here, his duty completed.

She ate breakfast alone and then unpacked her things in the dresser and shoved her carpetbag under the bed. She paced for a while, then got out the new wool and thread. Sewing always calmed her, but today her hands seemed clumsy as she tried to piece together why he'd left so suddenly. Had he allowed her too close last night? Was he afraid he might become a man and not just a soldier if he lay beside her one more night? His departure didn't make sense. Maybe it was as he said, simply an order, nothing more. And there for a moment, before he'd issued his last orders, she'd almost thought he wanted her.

She tried to recall the conversation Walker had with the major the evening before. She'd been tired, and at some point it almost seemed as if they'd been talking in some kind of code.

The sergeant interrupted her hours later to ask if she would take tea with the major's wife. Lacy had a feeling it was more an order than a request and thought of turning it down, but in truth she needed to leave the tiny room for her own sanity. If she couldn't go home or depart the fort, at least she could explore the workings of such a place. She'd probably never be inside another one.

The major's wife looked nothing like Lacy expected. She was as short and plump as the major was tall and lean. Her hair had streaks of silver in it, and tiny spectacles, just like Lacy's reading glasses, sat on her nose. She seemed genuinely glad to have company.

Lacy silently thanked Bailee for the lessons in how to have tea as she sat down. Marianne Garner's kindness quickly made Lacy comfortable.

"You know," she said after the tea tray was removed, "your husband is a legend on the frontier line. My husband would love to have him here at Fort Elliot."

Lacy had no idea what the woman was talking about. Walker had never mentioned anything about his life in the army. If he were known for anything, she felt sure it would be for following every rule.

Marianne leaned over and patted Lacy's arm. "It would be wonderful having you here. I don't see many wives, and men like your husband are rare." As if sensing Lacy's discomfort, she changed the subject. "One of the many things I love about life in the army is how quickly we wives bond like family. Maybe it's the close quarters, or the worry over our men, but you'd be welcomed here, my dear."

Lacy couldn't help but wonder what another one of the "things" could be that the major's wife loved. She'd bet Marianne's list of likes wasn't as long as the list of hates Lacy thought about. But it wouldn't have been polite to debate the woman.

They talked of canning and travels, of families and friends, and eventually of quilting. There they found a match. Marianne showed Lacy a trunk full of quilt tops and pieces, clarifying that she lacked skill in the final step.

Lacy laughed, explaining how the last stage of quilting could be the most fun. When she offered to help put a quilt together, the major's wife seemed delighted. Within minutes they both sat on the floor trying to pick the first top to become a real quilt.

Marianne called Hayes in, and Lacy explained what she'd need to build a simple frame. The women agreed they'd start after breakfast tomorrow and quilt all the next day.

As Hayes walked her back to her quarters, Lacy realized how excited she was at the thought of finishing one of Marianne's quilts. She'd never had anyone to work with. Sewing had always been something she'd done alone.

She ate her dinner in her room and wondered where Walker slept tonight. Though the major's wife had been chatty about everything else, she didn't say a word about where Walker went.

The major had stepped in to say hello just before Lacy left. She thought she saw worry in his gaze as he forced a smile and bade her good day before she could ask any questions about Walker. That was another thing she hated, Lacy thought; she hated not even knowing which questions to ask.

Now, sitting alone in her little room, Lacy's thoughts turned to Nell. Walker had been right when he said she was in the best of care; Bailee always seemed to have everything organized. The ranger was probably camped out on their doorstep in case he was needed, and if she knew the doctor, he'd be out making a call every morning until he knew Nell was out of danger.

But Lacy wanted to be there. Somehow Nell's troubles were partly her fault. She wasn't sure how, but if Nell hadn't known Lacy, she would not be fighting for her life right now.

Lacy tried pacing, then sewing on her

wool dress, but nothing helped. Finally, she curled into bed and wished Walker lay beside her. "Good night," she said aloud. "Wherever you are."

The next morning she overslept and had to dress quickly. She wasn't surprised to find the sergeant waiting for her when she stepped out of her quarters.

"Mrs. Garner has decided to set the frame up in one of the empty single officer's quarters so the quilt will be a surprise for the major." Hayes walked her two doors down to an open doorway. "Though not much happens around here that he's not fully aware of."

Lacy glanced at Hayes, trying to figure out if he were simply talking or issuing some kind of warning. Her years of collecting the news had made her develop an ear for what people sometimes didn't say.

Hayes didn't meet her eyes as he ushered her inside.

There stood a quilting frame rigged together by rope and boards in a room exactly like her own. Four women and Mrs. Garner were having tea by the fireplace and waiting to start. The major's wife introduced each woman by name and by her husband's rank.

Millie and Grace were both young lieutenants' wives. They were shy and looked to be away from home for the first time. Millie said she'd helped with quilting before, but Grace admitted she'd never even tried.

The other two women were older by ten years. January's husband was a captain like Walker. She said they'd even served together a few times along the fort line, but she couldn't remember ever meeting the mysterious Captain Larson.

Lacy let the odd comment pass and turned to the last woman in the group.

Theda, a thin woman of about thirty, was January's sister and had come to stay through her sister's pregnancy, which judging from January's girth wouldn't be much longer.

Since the others knew one another, conversation flowed as they set to work. Marianne acted as mother hen over the group and called Hayes to run so many errands that the others giggled every time she yelled the sergeant's name.

Lacy could never remember having so much fun. She explained steps and found most of the ladies already knew the basics but loved learning new stitches that slowly sewed the layers of material together. Grace's stitches were big, almost childlike in skill, but Lacy found it easy to cross over the area Grace thought she had finished and lace tiny stitches in between her huge ones without the girl noticing what she was doing.

By the time they'd turned the quilt on the board twice, there was more room in the quarters, and Grace had learned enough so that her work looked smooth and even.

By noon they were all laughing and joking as they sewed. Though Grace was shy, Millie loved to talk once she warmed up to everyone and told them all about being courted by her husband.

When she took a break to breathe, Marianne asked, "How did you meet your Walker, Lacy?"

For a moment Lacy acted like she pulled a knot out of her thread and tried her best to be casual. "I met him in a little town called Cottonwood."

"Was it love at first sight?" Millie batted her eyes.

"No, in truth, I fell in love with his letters first." She'd almost forgotten those days when she'd been fifteen and read his letters to his father, never dreaming the man who wrote would be nothing like the soldier she met. "He has a way of writing that almost makes you believe you're with him." For the first time in two years Lacy wished she hadn't thrown the letters away the day she rode back from Cottonwood.

"That's so romantic," Millie chimed in, having no idea of the real story.

Hayes delivered a tray of sandwiches. None of them wanted to stop long enough to eat. The cold winter day outside seemed far away as they worked and talked.

When the mantel clock struck five, Marianne announced it was time that they all returned home. She invited Lacy to join her and the major for dinner, but Lacy declined. Marianne didn't seem to mind, so Lacy guessed it had truly been an invitation and not an order.

She hugged all the women good-bye and started to return to her quarters. On a whim, she decided to take a walk. It would be sunset in an hour, and she'd once more be a prisoner, not allowed out.

There was such organization to the fort. It seemed to run like a well-oiled machine. Everything seemed neat and clean, unlike towns where no two buildings were the same size or had the same roofline. Lacy could see why her proper husband would feel at home in such a place.

As she passed Hayes's office, the sergeant stepped to his door. "Is there something I can do for you, ma'am?"

"No. Thank you for all your help today."

"You're welcome." He seemed pleased that she'd noticed.

"I just thought I'd stretch my legs." Lacy stepped off the porch.

"Would you like me to accompany you?" He glanced back at the stack of papers on his desk.

"No. I'll be fine. I'd like to walk to the corral and watch the horses. Is that allowed?"

"Of course. Though you'll find no mount as fine as your husband's horse. We do have a few fall colts that are fun to watch."

He went back to his desk, and Lacy circled the grounds. The place was like a little city. She walked by the corral and watched the colts for a while, then crossed to the main gate. She thought of walking down the road a piece to see what the wild town of Mobeetie looked like. She'd read that the town bore the Indian word for Sweetwater as its name and bragged that a saloon had opened the day it was founded.

On second thought, she decided to go no farther than the huge gate. After all, she'd told Walker she wouldn't leave, and if the gate closed at sunset, she might get locked out. She stood just inside and watched the late sunlight play across the tall grass, making it look almost like the prairie was on fire.

It was near dark when she circled back by Hayes's office and stopped at the door to say good night.

He jumped up from his desk when he saw her. "Oh, Mrs. Larson, I have a telegram for your husband that came yesterday about an hour after he left."

"He'll be in tonight," Lacy hoped more than knew. He'd said a few days. Had he meant two nights also?

"Would you mind giving this to him?"

"Of course not." Lacy accepted the envelope. "I'll be happy to. Good night, Sergeant."

"Good night, Mrs. Larson."

Lacy walked down the porch to her quarters and closed the door just as the last rays of the sun faded. She thought she heard the sound of the gate closing.

Standing by the fire, Lacy flipped the telegram over in her hand. Written on the outside were the words, "For Captain Walker Larson, From Sheriff Riley, Cedar Point."

Lacy tore the envelope open, knowing it

had to be news from home. Walker had told her he'd let the sheriff know she was all right, and now he must be telling them of Nell's progress. She almost tore the paper opening it. All last night and most of today, Nell had been in the back of her mind. A part of her was with the girl if only in spirit.

Glad Lacy is safe stop Nell is improving stop Dalton informs me you are to wait before riding out stop Rangers are on the way from Fort Worth stop Repeat do not go after them alone stop

Lacy read the message over and over, trying to figure out what the sheriff meant. He wanted Walker to wait. That could only mean one thing. Riley and Dalton knew Walker rode into danger.

She shoved the telegram in her pocket and headed toward the door, but when her hand touched the knob, she froze. Where was she going? Who could she tell? Hayes could do nothing. The major was the one who gave the order. He must know of the danger.

Pieces began to fit together. The way Marianne kept saying that Walker was so brave. That he'd be able to do things no one else would even attempt. That the major believed in him.

Memories of how Major Garner had looked at her. Nervous. Sad. Almost as if he felt sorry for her. She'd thought it was because he sensed that something was not right between Walker and her. Now she knew it was because he feared she might be a widow soon.

Lacy paced. Whatever Walker had ridden into had been dangerous. Everyone at the fort probably knew it except her. Walker had known. That's why he'd been so cold, so formal. That's why he'd made her promise to stay at the fort.

Maybe that was why he'd touched her so gently yesterday morning. Could he have thought it might be the last time?

Time ticked by as she tried to think of something, of anything she could do. But there was no one to ask, no one to turn to. Hayes wouldn't tell her anything. He might not know anything. The major would probably be angry at Walker for marrying such a fool if she ran down to his quarters and cried that Walker was in danger. Of course he was in danger; it was the nature of his job. She had no way to contact anyone until morning and no horse or buggy to get home in, even if she was foolish enough to try to make the journey alone and at night.

Her nerves unraveled as the hours passed and she heard nothing. If Walker planned to make it back tonight, surely he'd be here by now. It would be foolish to even think of going to bed. She knew she'd never sleep. On restless nights at home she would have moved close to the fire and quilted until she could keep her eyes open no longer.

Quilt! It might be the only thing that kept her sane. It had saved her when Walker's dad had been dying. Working on square after square of fabric somehow kept her life together as she sat beside the old man's bed and watched him slowly pass away.

She hurried to the window and looked out.

The grounds were deserted. The light in Hayes's office no longer shone out on the porch.

Lacy put out her lamp and opened the door. Silently, she slipped two doors down. The shadow of the long porch hid her from view of even the guards at the gate. Within a few seconds she hurried inside the empty quarters with the quilting frame.

Making sure the window was shuttered, Lacy lit the lamp, built up the fire, and began to work. Her nerves slowly calmed as she stitched.

Chapter 23

It was almost dawn when Lacy finally put down her needle. She'd worried and sewn her way back and forth across the quilt and finally grown too tired to see the stitches. She stood and stretched, feeling as though she'd aged a year during the night. Opening the shutter, she watched the sun lighten the sky, afraid of what the day might bring. Walker said he'd be back in a few days. Had he meant two, or three? If he didn't return today, she couldn't bring herself to think of what that might mean.

Walking to the dying fire, she tossed the telegram Riley had sent onto the hot coals. The sheriff's message had come too late. Walker rode out without the warning and without knowing Rangers were on their way.

She turned down the lamp and slowly stepped out onto the porch. It might be early, but the fort churned with activity.

For a moment she watched, thinking of what it would be like to live in this small town where each man and woman had their duties. She almost laughed. This place would never do for her; she'd never be able to get up so early and start her day. Now, if the fort opened about ten, she might consider it.

"Mrs. Larson?" Hayes ran toward her. "Is the captain all right?"

Lacy faced the sergeant, confused by the question.

Hayes reached her. "I heard he ordered bandages sent to his quarters when he rode in."

Lacy moved toward her door. "When was that?"

Now it was Hayes's turn to look confused. "Fifteen minutes ago." Hayes fell into step with Lacy. "Major Garner just rode out for that big meeting he has in Mobeetie every month, and he yelled for me to have Captain Larson report to his office at noon if he was able. I asked how bad he was hurt, and all the major would tell me was that the captain refused to see the doctor."

Lacy flung open the door to their quarters and saw Walker standing beside the table that was covered with medical supplies. He'd stripped to the waist and was trying to tie a knot in a bandage across his arm using his one free hand and his teeth.

Slamming the door, she hurried to him. "What happened to you?"

He dropped the bandage. "What happened to me! What happened to you? I thought you'd left. I was changing clothes and trying to stop bleeding long enough to go after you."

He was bloody and dirty, and she'd never seen such anger in his eyes, but she couldn't help but run toward him. He was alive. She'd worried for nothing.

Walker took her wild embrace with a groan, but he didn't let her pull away when she realized she'd hurt him. He held her tight with one arm as if he had to know that she was really beside him.

She wiggled within his hold, her heart still threatening to pound out of her chest. "I thought you were hurt, or killed. I feared you'd never return." Her words came fast, running over one another. "I couldn't sleep, so I quilted all night."

Walker buried his face in her hair and took a deep breath. "The guard said he'd seen you by the gate last night."

She stared up at him. "You thought I'd leave after I gave you my promise to stay?"

"I only knew you were gone, and I had to go after you, even if it meant deserting."

Lacy opened her mouth to argue, then saw the blood dripping down his arm from the bandage he'd tried to tie on. She forgot what she'd been about to say. "You're hurt."

"It's only a scratch."

"Let me see." She pushed on his shoulders, and he folded into a chair. She'd expected him to protest or give her a lecture about not staying in her quarters, but to her surprise, he simply watched her.

She cleaned the wound, which was only a scratch, a very deep scratch where a bullet had peeled off flesh for a few inches halfway between his shoulder and elbow.

As she dressed the arm, she asked, "Are you going to tell me about where you went and how you got this?"

"Do you really want to know?"

Lacy thought as she tied the bandage. "Yes." If this life were a part of him, she wanted to know.

"Can it wait?" he surprised her by asking. "I haven't had any food or sleep since I left."

Lacy opened the door, not the least surprised to find Hayes waiting just outside. "Sergeant, would it be possible to have a tray of food brought for my husband?"

"He's going to be all right?" Hayes tried to see past her into their quarters.

"He'll be fine, but he needs rest and food."

"I'll be back in five minutes. Will there be anything else, Mrs. Larson?"

"Yes, please tell Mrs. Garner that I will be late today for the quilting."

Hayes smiled. "I'll do that."

"And would it be possible to have water for a bath delivered?"

He nodded once and hurried away.

As promised, five minutes later, Hayes delivered a tray loaded down with food and a pot of coffee. He deposited it on the table and disappeared.

They ate in silence, both hungry for food and for the sight of each other. Walker asked her to help him put on his shirt before they sat down, but she'd insisted on him leaving it off so that she could see if the wound would bleed through the bandage. They compromised with her draping the shirt over his shoulders for, as he informed her, a gentleman doesn't sit at a table in a state of undress.

As they ate, she found herself spending far too much time studying his bare chest and little time watching for bleeding. He seemed a different man than the one she'd known before. He appeared exhausted, with dirt on his clothes as well as his face. Much less proper, she thought. Much more likeable.

By the time they finished eating, the tub was ready. Walker hesitated. "There's no blanket for privacy."

"I'll turn around, Captain." She almost laughed, surprised at his need for privacy. He must have lived in the barracks at some point. But then, undressing with men around was a great deal different than removing all his clothes in front of a woman.

With her back to him, she heard him undress and splash into the tub. "Sorry," he said, "I can't depend on my left arm just yet."

She turned around. The tub was big, but it looked so small with him sitting in it. Squaring her shoulders, she moved forward. "Allow me to help."

He turned down her offer, then demanded she leave him be, then swore, but she paid him no mind. He needed help and, unless he wanted her to call Hayes, she was the only one available.

She was right, of course. He needed her. They reached another compromise. She washed his shoulders, around the bandage, and his hair while he pouted. Walker might have been able to sit down in the tub with only one good arm, but he'd turn the water over if he tried to get out. With a towel wrapped around him, she helped him stand. Lacy felt sure the idea that he needed her help bothered him far more than his wound.

"Enough." He stepped from the water. "Turn around, Lacy."

She did and listened to him fumble with his clothes. If she waited for a thank-you, she'd die of old age.

When she turned back, he'd managed to pull on a clean pair of trousers. Without asking, she helped him with his undershirt, sliding the cotton gently over the bandage. Then she rubbed his hair nearly dry while he complained.

"What next, sir?" she asked when he combed his hair back with his hand. "Shall I shave you?"

"Get in bed," he mumbled with the temperament of a wildcat who'd been forced to bathe.

Lacy crossed to her side of the bed, unbuttoning her dress as she walked. She slipped it over her head and dropped it on the floor without a thought as she crawled under the covers. Now that she knew he was safe, lack of sleep caught up to her.

Walker threw the bolt on the door and joined her. He stretched out his good arm and waited for her to roll against him.

When she did, he pressed a kiss on her forehead. "This is what I thought about for two days. No other world. No other time but here."

Lacy yawned and placed her hand over his heart. Her captain had returned to her.

They both fell asleep with no other words between them.

Hours later, she awoke with him kissing her, and her dreams slowly moved into reality.

She gently pulled away and sat up. "Let me check that bandage."

Walker relaxed. "I wasn't thinking of my arm. It's time I got back in uniform. The major will be expecting a full report." He smiled. "But first, I thought I'd get reacquainted with my wife."

She leaned over him and studied the dressing. No blood spotted through. "Good." She ran her hand gently along his injured arm. "It may heal nicely."

"Do that again," he whispered as he tucked a pillow beneath his head and studied her.

She brushed his arm again, from

shoulder to his hand, then stared down at his face. His eyes were half closed as he watched her move. Looking down, she noticed the first few buttons of her camisole had pulled free, revealing part of each breast. She stilled, not knowing what to do. The last time he'd seen so much of her, he'd accused her of exposing herself.

"You're beautiful," he said.

She started to deny it or to say that he'd seen her before, but something in the way he looked at her stopped her. He wasn't just observing, or watching, or staring. He was worshiping.

Straightening her back, Lacy lifted her hands and undid the remaining buttons, then waited, unsure what to do next.

Walker lifted his hand and slowly pulled the thin cotton away from her breasts. For a while he didn't move, he only stared, then he whispered, "I think you are perfection."

She'd never felt beautiful in her life, but she did now.

He leaned up and gently kissed the tip of each breast before buttoning the top button of her camisole back in place.

"Thank you." She closed her eyes as fire rushed in her blood.

"For what?"

"For making me feel . . ." She didn't know the words to describe her feelings. She sat in a quiet room, but inside she was running full speed into the wind. "I liked you looking at my breasts," she admitted. "Maybe I'll show them to you again sometime?"

He laughed knowing she was teasing him. "I would be honored."

Then he pulled her down to him and kissed her soundly, only this time, his hand slipped beneath the cotton of her camisole and brushed over her. When she moaned in pleasure, he tightened his hold on her just enough to send lightning shooting through her veins.

The clocked chimed the quarter hour. Walker raised his head. "I could stay here in this private world of yours forever, but duty calls. It's almost noon. If I'm not in the major's office in a few minutes, he'll come after me." He smiled. "And there are things in this room I'd rather no other man see."

She wanted to pull him back, but she knew he was right. They'd had the morning together in peace; she could ask for no more.

He kissed her cheek. "Will you meet me here, madam, before midnight tonight?

There are a few things I'd like you to show me."

"I will," she whispered as he kissed her one last time before leaving.

This time the kiss was filled with a promise.

Lacy joined him, helping him dress as she pulled on her own clothes. He no longer acted angry and accepted her fussing over him, touching her as she touched him, enjoying her closeness as she helped him.

By the time she buttoned his jacket, he appeared strong as ever. No part of the wounded man who'd returned from battle remained. The bloody uniform with no rank on it lay in a pile on the floor. He now wore a uniform tailored only for him with his rank in plain sight.

"Tell me what happened while you were gone, Captain. Why did you wear those clothes?"

"Some other time, Lacy. I promise." He smiled as if they shared a secret. "But not in bed. I never want to talk of what I do in the army when we're in our private world."

"Fair enough," she agreed as she opened the door.

He brushed her bottom with his hand as he passed her and walked out.

She smiled. His touch had been light.

She stepped out on the porch and watched him salute Hayes, then turn and march to the major's office without a backward glance.

Lacy folded her arms and turned to see what Hayes needed.

"I had to be here to see it," Hayes whispered to Lacy. "I heard about the captain, but I wanted to see it for myself."

Lacy stared at the sergeant. "See what?"

"I saw him come in all wounded and bloody. He was barely able to sit the saddle. Then he walks out a few hours later right as rain."

Lacy almost told Hayes of the bandage and the pain Walker was in but decided not to. "What exactly do they say about my husband, Sergeant?"

Hayes looked at her in surprise. "Well, they say he's indestructible. Like a machine." The sergeant glanced down, no longer looking her in the eyes. "They say he has no feelings. That he don't feel nothing, not even the pain of a bullet."

"Sergeant Hayes, did it ever occur to you that they might be wrong?"

"I wouldn't know, ma'am."

"No, but I would." She smiled and left him standing on the porch.

Chapter 24

Walker gave his full report to major Garner. Just as the major feared, there had been an ambush before the prisoner could be delivered by six of the fort's best men. Walker had followed procedure, disappeared from the escort just after leaving the fort and rode ahead, out of sight.

He'd been trained years ago to move across the land like a shadow. He came upon the ambush before they'd mounted. He managed to capture two of the men planning to rush the detachment and killed another in a fight. Three other outlaws lay in wait in the narrow part of a canyon, planning to pick off the soldiers as they moved through a ravine. The ambushers were unaware Walker had taken out their point men. It had been a fiery battle, but all six soldiers returned to the fort with only minor injuries, and the prisoner was now under federal marshal's guard.

The only thing Walker left out of his report was his disappointment in not finding Zeb Whitaker among the group of outlaws. Walker had done the major a service, commanded a dangerous mission, but as far as he was concerned, he'd wasted his time.

"If you hadn't been here, six of my men would be dead right now." The major shook his head. "They're good soldiers, but they don't know the land like you do. They wouldn't have known the direction to ride to get out of the canyon."

"Don't give me too much credit. I did what I've been trained to do. They're good men. They might have made it without me."

"Not without casualties."

Walker changed the subject to news of the old buffalo hunter.

Zeb Whitaker had been spotted in several locations in the Panhandle. He might even be in Mobeetie, but no one, not the rangers, or the marshals, nor even the army seemed to be able to find him. Besides Nell's attempted murder, there had been two killings connected with him. It seemed he got out of prison planning to even the score with every man or woman in the country he thought had wronged him. Rumor was he'd killed a whole family over by old Tascosa so there would be no witnesses. The country was full of outlaws looking for a leader, and Whitaker campaigned for the spot.

If someone didn't stop him soon, every crime in the state would be tied to Whitaker, if only by tall tale.

Walker crossed back to the officers' quarters wondering how he could explain to Lacy that he'd almost gotten himself killed over a prisoner transfer. He'd also figured out that they couldn't stay at the fort much longer. Major Garner was in dire need of officers. He had fine troops with many who'd fought during the Indian Wars, but few officers. If Walker stayed, he'd be away from Lacy most of the two weeks he had left of his leave. Major Garner needed him too badly to allow him to sit around in the fort.

He also had a feeling Garner only sent six men as escorts because he wanted to test Walker. That bothered him. Garner should have never risked his men to prove Walker's skill. He could have easily sent a dozen men or waited for the marshals to pick up the prisoner at the fort. But the major had played Walker like a chess piece, and that rubbed the wrong way. The sooner he and Lacy left, the better.

He wasn't surprised that Lacy had vanished when he stepped back in their room. She might just be one little woman, but he had his work cut out for him keeping up with her.

Walking out on the porch, he noticed Hayes standing guard two doors down.

The sergeant silently pointed to the door, knowing Walker's question before he asked.

Walker opened the quarters and was surprised to find probably every wife on the fort sitting around a quilting frame. Lacy sat in the middle of them, laughing.

"I beg your pardon." He straightened. "I didn't mean to interrupt."

The major's wife waved her hand. "Oh, it's all right, Captain. We were just breaking up to go home and bake for the dance tonight. Lacy showed a few of us some fancy stitches yesterday, and everyone else wanted to learn them today."

Lacy stood and collected her things as she said her good-byes.

"Your wife tells me you two will not be attending the dance." Marianne Garner left a hint of a command in her tone. "I'd really love to have you join us. We've all grown quite found of your bride."

"Of course," Walker answered and noticed the panicked look Lacy shot him. To her credit, she didn't open her mouth until they were alone.

"We can't go." She faced him without fear.

"We're going." He didn't understand her anxiety. It was only a dance, one of the few fun nights at a fort.

"First, we need to get back to Cedar Point. I'm worried about Nell, and you said we'd only stay long enough to rest."

"If you'll accompany me tonight, I'll work on getting you back home."

"When?" She didn't trust him compromising so quickly.

"Tomorrow."

"Fair enough, but I have nothing to wear —"

Walker raised his hand to stop her. "Wait just a moment. I can solve that problem." He opened the door, and Hayes almost fell in.

"You need me, Captain?" Hayes looked like he'd been just about to knock. "Mrs. Garner told me you might be wanting the ambulance."

"Yes, Sergeant, I do need you. Go to Mobeetie and buy my wife a new dress. Something she can wear to a dance." Walker had no idea why Mrs. Garner would request an ambulance wagon for him. He could only solve one problem at a time, and Lacy wouldn't budge without a new dress.

The sergeant paled at the simple request. "Respectfully, begging your pardon, sir. I don't know anything about buying a dress. I ain't even got a sister, and as far as I know, my mother hasn't bought anything new since I was born."

Walker unfolded bills. "Don't worry. There won't be much of a selection. Just pick one of the ready-made they always have dressing up the mercantile windows."

Hayes shook his head. "What size do I get?"

Walker glanced at Lacy as if he'd never given it a thought that women might come in different sizes. "What size, madam?"

"I have no idea. I've never bought a ready-made dress before. This is insane." Lacy paced her three steps to the right and three steps back, even though she had more room. "I don't want to go to the dance. I could work on the quilt while you go. It's you, the hero of the day, that everyone will want to see, not me."

"I'm not going without you, Lacy." When she frowned, he added, "It's not open to discussion. The only question here is what size of dress will do."

Walker pulled one of her spools of thread from the open box and circled the thread around her waist. "She's about five foot, Sergeant." He clipped the thread and handed it to Hayes. "And her waist is this size. That should help."

"What about the other measurements?" Hayes stammered.

Walker wasn't sure which of the two, Lacy or Hayes, turned the deeper red. This wasn't going at all the way he planned. He wasn't about to measure his wife's chest size in front of the sergeant, or her hips, for that matter.

Lacy took a deep breath and pulled the string from Hayes's hand. "How about I go with you? I can pick out my own dress if I'm to have one."

"I'll be glad to drive you, ma'am." Hayes relaxed.

"We can't take her into town." Walker hated putting down her plan, but it would be too dangerous. "Someone might see you."

Hayes smiled. "That's why Mrs. Garner must have wanted me to bring the ambulance. We can close it up, and I'll get a few guards to go along. They'll volunteer just to get to meet you, Captain."

Walker thought they were going to a great deal of trouble for one dress, but he saw no other choice unless he wanted to decline the major's wife's invitation. "All right. Get the guards, and I'll let the major know we're taking the ambulance off grounds."

"Oh, he won't mind. I take the ladies to church on cold days and sometimes the folks in town borrow it when they have several going to catch the train." Hayes walked out the door. "The ambulance hasn't been used to haul wounded since we've been here."

When he'd left, Walker turned to Lacy. "Thank you for agreeing to accompany me tonight, madam."

"I'm not aware that I did, but you're welcome. We leave for home tomorrow."

"Of course."

She didn't look the least bit happy about the idea of a dance, but at least she agreed. Walker decided he'd compromise and tell her that they could leave after the first few dances, if she liked. He knew she thought him unyielding, but he could bend.

Ten minutes later, they rolled out of the fort and down the road to Mobeetie. The town had started off as a hide town twenty years ago when men needed a place to skin buffalo. Though it was now the county seat, it still held to its wild roots.

The sergeant pulled the wagon to the side door of what he said was the best mercantile in town. One corner of it had been converted into a ladies' dress shop by the owner's wife. "I heard the major's wife say it's even got a dressing room," Hayes said proudly.

When they walked in, a stout little woman greeted them, though she didn't look too pleased to see all the men stomping into her shop.

"How can I help you?" She puffed up like a toad as if preparing to order them out.

Walker moved aside so the toad could see Lacy hidden in their circle. "My wife would like a gown."

The owner smiled and offered her hand to Lacy. "Of course, dear. I'm Mrs. Deeds, and I'm sure we can find something." She pulled Lacy behind her, then turned on the men. Her smile melted so quickly, Walker wasn't sure it had been there.

"There's chairs over by the stove if you all think you need to wait," Mrs. Deeds said. "I'll not have you in this part of the store knocking over my nice things, so make sure you stay put. The crackers are free, but I'll expect a nickel on the counter for any pickles or candy you eat."

Walker straightened, preparing to inform the toad who she addressed, but Lacy's laughter stopped him. He winked at his wife and followed the round little woman's orders.

They waited for twenty minutes before the woman leaned out of the space and motioned Walker near. "I understand this is a dance your wife is attending?" she whispered.

"Yes."

"You'll be wanting evening clothes with all the necessaries?"

"Yes." Walker didn't understand why she hadn't asked Lacy these questions. He had no idea what "necessaries" were and wasn't about to ask.

"And is there an amount you wish to spend?"

Now Walker understood. Lacy had argued with him about every dime he spent, from their evening dinners at the hotel, to buying her such fine boots. He grinned at the store owner. "My wife followed me here with only a small bag. She needs everything. How about the budget be as much as you can talk her into spending."

The woman's whole face lit up. "Yes, sir."

A few minutes later, Lacy walked out wearing an evening dress.

Walker couldn't make himself form words. All he could do was stare. The dress of dark green started just off her shoulders and floated to the floor in yards of velvet. Her hips swayed with the material, her waist looked tiny, and her breasts . . .

Walker straightened. The top of her cleavage was exposed. He could see the creamy white tops of each rounded breast. Part of the dress must have been left off.

"How do you like it, Captain?"

"It's too low," he managed to answer.

"Oh, no. It's the newest fashion. Mrs. Deeds says so. Even the patterns coming in are off the shoulder for evening wear."

"It's too low," Walker repeated.

The stout little toad appeared beside Lacy. "It is not too low; don't be a fool. I've sold several similar to it for tonight's dance." She raised her head, trying to look down at him, even though she was a good foot shorter. "Only none were as nice as this one. Every woman who's come in the shop tried it on, but your wife is the first one it fits. This dress was made for her figure."

As if to prove her point, Mrs. Deeds pushed the material a little farther off the shoulders, showing off an inch more of Lacy's creamy skin.

Lacy smiled. "I feel like a princess in it."

Walker turned to Hayes, who'd moved up beside him and was staring at Lacy. "What do you think, Sergeant?"

Hayes smiled. "I think you look beautiful, Mrs. Larson. There won't be a prettier wife in the fort. You look —"

"That will be enough, Hayes," Walker snapped, suddenly not wanting to know what the sergeant thought.

He glanced back to Lacy. "You'll catch cold."

Mrs. Deeds had been waiting. She pulled a matching shawl from a box. "I have just the thing. It would be nice if she had jewelry for that delicate neck, but all I have are some cameos. She could wear one on a choker."

Mrs. Deeds paraded behind the counter and pulled the most expensive cameo from a glass case, jerking the price off before handing it to Lacy to inspect. When Lacy smiled, Mrs. Deeds showed it to Walker as if daring him to reject it.

"Is that the best you have?" He watched her mouth twist at the knowledge that she could have made a larger sell if she'd had the merchandise.

"It's perfect," Lacy insisted, already looking like she thought Walker was spending too much money.

He smiled at his wife. "Then it belongs on you."

She blushed, and he was proud of himself for thinking of the right thing to say for once.

Walker watched as Lacy lifted her hair and let Mrs. Deeds latch the choker around her throat. He caught himself being jealous of someone else touching her.

"What do you think, Captain?" Lacy smiled as she turned, her eyes dancing with excitement. "Will I be presentable?"

He managed a nod, but when she turned back to the dressing area, he mumbled under his breath, "I'll have to go unarmed, or I'll kill every man who looks at her."

Hayes laughed at his side. "The curse of a beautiful wife, sir."

Walker studied her, trying to figure out when she'd become beautiful. He remembered when he first met her, how he'd thought her short and decided he liked his women tall and lean. He'd liked her hair when he watched her comb it and loved the way her eyes expressed every emotion she felt. But when had the little woman who was his wife become unforgettable?

An hour later, they piled into the ambulance, and Hayes drove them back to the fort. Both the guards who'd accompanied them carried boxes, and Walker realized he'd handed Mrs. Deeds money and accepted change without asking how much the bill had been.

As soon as they were back in their quarters and alone, Lacy said, "And two," as if their conversation two hours before could be picked up again so easily. 'I can't go to the dance because I've never been to one and have no idea how to dance."

"You could have told me earlier," he commented, as if he hadn't been the one to stop her from finishing.

"Well, I have the dress, so we can go. Maybe I can say my husband is injured and we'd best not dance."

"You'll have every man at the fort lined up to take my place on the floor if you use that excuse."

"They'll soon learn I can't dance."

"They won't care." He smiled. "We'd better get to work on teaching you a few steps."

Twenty minutes later, Walker was sure both her feet were left. She had no rhythm, couldn't count the steps, and kept bumping into him.

"Lacy, pay attention. You can do this."

"I'm worried about you moving that arm too much."

He hooked his thumb in the waist of her skirt. "If I rest it here and don't do any fast moves, it doesn't hurt so badly. If you concentrate on not going the opposite direction, maybe my arm can rest, almost like it's in a sling. If we move together, it might not be jerked too much."

They started once more, but they banged together, then she twisted the wrong way, pulling his thumb from her waistband.

He groaned in pain before he could pretend it didn't matter.

She tried to act as if she wasn't about to cry. "I didn't think it would be so hard. I saw couples dancing one night when we stopped with the wagon train. It didn't look all that difficult. I went out on the prairie in the moonlight and tried it."

Walker released her hand and went to the window. He closed the shutters, throwing the room in shadows. "Was it this dark that night?"

She nodded.

"Then close your eyes and pretend you're still on the prairie. Only you're dancing with me, not the moon."

To his surprise, she relaxed and swayed as he hummed. He stopped concentrating on teaching her to follow steps in a pattern and moved with her as if they were swaying in the wind. The clock ticked away their steps.

After several minutes, she opened her eyes and met his stare. "We're dancing," she whispered. "We're really dancing."

He leaned and kissed her, pulling her off the floor and into his arms. Their feet might have had trouble matching, but there was no such hesitation in her kiss. When he finally set her down, her lips were slightly swollen and wet.

"I like doing that," he said before he thought.

"Me, too," she admitted as she stood on her tiptoes and brushed her mouth over his once more, silently asking for another kiss.

He smiled and granted her request. It felt so good knowing how she liked to be kissed.

When he stepped away, she moaned with delight, and he had to fight the urge to repeat his actions.

"I'll leave you to dress." His hand moved along the side of her body for one last touch. "I can bathe and shave in the barracks," he whispered as he kissed her neck, loving the way she tasted, "I'll not be thinking of the planned evening, but of the night we'll have together." His mouth couldn't resist covering hers once more.

He thought of bolting the door and forgetting the dance. The idea surprised him, for following protocol had always been his policy. But the need to hold her made his arm ache far more than the wound, and holding her on the dance floor would not be nearly enough to satisfy him.

"Will you touch me again when you kiss me tonight?" She asked so innocently that he was reminded of how little she knew of lovemaking.

"If you like."

"I would like that very much."

It took every ounce of his determination to turn and leave her.

Chapter 25

Lacy never spent so much time getting ready for anything in her life. She had her first new dress to wear and her first dance to attend. There had been barn dances now and then at Cedar Point, but no one ever asked her to go along with them. She could hardly let a man take her, and unaccompanied women usually went with their parents. Walker's father would have escorted her, but she knew the dance would only remind him of how crippled his limbs were.

This might be her only chance to attend anything so grand. For one night she wanted to forget all her worries and just enjoy. Zeb Whitaker seemed a million miles away, and Nell was in the best of hands with Carter, Bailee, and Ranger Dalton to look after her.

Walker knocked on their door just after dark as though he were her escort picking her up. He offered his arm, and they walked across the parade grounds to the dining hall. He told her she looked nice and reminded her twice to keep her shawl around her so she wouldn't catch cold.

A crowd of men stood on the porch smoking. They parted as Walker led her through them. Walker spoke to a few as he passed.

Inside, people hurried around making last-minute adjustments. Most of the wives were on the committee and had drafted their husbands into helping set up. The chairs in the big, open room had been shoved to the walls. The back side was lined with tables of food, and a far corner held a five-piece band.

"It's not all that fancy," Walker commented.

"It's grand," she answered noticing all the white tablecloths and rows of candles along each window. Though the surroundings had little color, the women in their gowns rainbowed the room.

She slowed as they neared a group standing near a wide fireplace decorated in dried flowers and purple sagebrush.

Walker covered her hand with his gloved fingers. "Relax, Lacy," he whispered.

She thought he used the same tone he'd used with Trooper, but she didn't want to comment on it and spoil the evening. It occurred to her that he might be a little nervous, too; though this was a fort, it wasn't his fort.

"I'm not sure of the rules." She'd been so excited thinking about the dance. Now that they were here, all she felt was fear. She had lived a lifetime of not being accepted, and the thought that she could just walk into this group and they'd welcome her seemed impossible. Lacy had lived in Cedar Point for five years, and some of the old-timers still looked at her as if she were new in town.

"Just stay beside me. If someone asks you to dance, it's polite to say yes; then you'll be escorted back to my side when the music stops." Walker squeezed her fingers. "These things are usually quite boring. We may want to leave early."

"But I don't want to dance with anyone but you."

He glanced down at her and smiled. "Don't worry about your skill. A gentleman never dances above his partner's level. Any man who asks you will take it easy. Believe me, you'll probably do as well at following them as they do at dancing."

Lacy wasn't sure if he reassured her or insulted her. She didn't have time to ask before Walker began introducing her to people. There was no way to remember all the names, but Lacy smiled and relaxed as she recognized the women of the quilting circle scattered among the others. Before Walker could stop them, Millie and Grace, the two youngest quilters, pulled her away from his side and raved about her dress.

Millie swore it was the most beautiful dress she'd ever seen and, when the major's wife joined the circle, she agreed with them.

"Walker thinks it might be a little low," Lacy admitted.

"Oh, no," they all chimed at once.

"Only a husband would think so," Marianne whispered and winked.

When the dancing started, Walker pulled her back to him and joined the others, ready to start the grand march. It was a simple dance where couples lined up in rows of four and stepped their way across the floor. She laughed. Everyone, even those without partners joined in the line of half dancing and half marching that officially started the ball. Her dress covered most of her steps, so no one knew if she were truly following the others.

When the song changed, couples turned to one another, and those without partners hurried off the floor. A violin started a slow tune, whispering across the air as if calling all lovers, then the other musicians joined in.

Walker smiled down at her, his hand touching her back. "Close your eyes, Lacy, and dance with me on the prairie in the moonlight."

She followed orders. He whirled her around the floor. Slowly, she relaxed and let his gentle guiding tell her where to move. When she grew brave enough to open her eyes and look up at him, she was surprised to see him smiling at her.

"Thank you," she whispered.

"For what?"

"For this night."

"But, it's just started, Lacy."

"I know, but it's already the best night of my life. No matter what happens, I'll always have this one night that I danced with my handsome captain at a grand ball with white tablecloths and candles all around the room."

He pulled her a few inches closer and whispered, "No matter what, we'll have this night."

When the music stopped, Walker seemed reluctant to let her go. As they walked back to the others, he said, "I have to ask Mrs.

Garner to dance. It's considered protocol. Will you be all right if I leave you with the ladies?"

"I'll be fine." Lacy couldn't help but wonder what kind of trouble he thought she'd get into surrounded by the army.

Theda, January's old maid sister, smiled when Lacy walked over and sat down in the chair next to her. January and her husband, Adam, danced, leaving the sister alone. "I'm afraid I don't know enough people to mingle like my sister told me to do," Theda said in her shy way, her hands already knotting and wrinkling her dress.

Lacy agreed. "How about we just sit back and watch? If anyone asks, we'll be busy mingling with each other."

Theda laughed. "I'd like that."

"This is my first dance," Lacy volunteered. "It's a little frightening."

Theda looked like she might cry. "This must be my hundredth, and to tell the truth, they only get worse. Every year I make the rounds to all my married sisters' homes, and at almost every stop there's a dance or a social I have to go to. Most of the time I spend the night just watching. There aren't that many single men over thirty that might ask me, and those who do usually turn out to be single for a reason."

Lacy felt sorry for the woman. Theda would never be the type to catch a man's eye, and Lacy wasn't surprised no one asked her to dance. Theda stood almost a head taller than most of the men in the room.

"How many sisters do you have?" She tried to change the subject.

"Five," Theda answered. "I'm the youngest, and the plainest." She shrugged, as if the fact didn't bother her. "So, while the others married, I stayed home to take care of my parents. I didn't mind. My father was a doctor, so I helped him after mother died, for as long as he practiced. Now, I'm alone. I have a little money to travel, but where can a single woman go, except to visit family?"

Lacy almost told her that when she was single at fifteen she went West, but instead, she said, "I took care of Walker's father until he died. I know how that can take all your free time, but in the end, it's worth it. I felt good about what I did for him."

Theda nodded, as if they'd just become comrades. "That explains it," she said. "Everyone wondered why Walker never had his wife with him. It certainly couldn't be for lack of love, I've seen the way he looks at you. Now, I understand."

Lacy thought of correcting her, but the

music stopped once more, and she noticed Walker returned Mrs. Garner to the major's arm. She'd watched them dance, and from what she could tell, Mrs. Garner never moved more than a few inches and then only in a circle. They stood in the center of whirling couples and talked, more than danced.

When Walker returned to Lacy's side, he didn't sit down but stood in front of Theda. "May I have the honor of this dance, Miss Theda?" he asked in his formal way.

Theda seemed delighted as she accepted. "I'm a little rusty, Captain, but I'll try to keep up with you." She stood, eye to eye with him.

Walker glanced back at Lacy and winked, making Lacy have to cover her mouth to keep from laughing out loud.

She watched as Walker took Theda's hand to dance. To her surprise, the tall woman followed his every move. She watched as his steps grew bolder, and Theda followed in time. When the music finally stopped, several couples had paused to watch the handsome captain and the tall old maid conquer the dance floor. By dancing in long steps, he'd made Theda look graceful, willowy.

When the old maid would have left the floor, Walker bowed and asked for another dance.

Theda glanced at Lacy, and when Lacy nodded her approval, the old maid smiled, making her look not nearly so homely.

This time Walker knew her skill and danced with Theda as if they'd danced together a hundred times.

Lacy stood as they walked back to her. They were both out of breath and laughing. She remembered what Walker said about a gentleman matching his steps to the lady's skill and was proud of him. He stepped close to her but took Theda's hand and kissed it. "Miss Theda, it was a pleasure. Promise you'll have time for another dance before this night ends."

The old maid blushed and thanked him as men lined up behind Theda, waiting for the captain to leave so they could ask for a turn.

Walker guided Lacy onto the floor.

"That was nice of you," she whispered, well aware of what the moves had cost him in pain.

"She's a good dancer," he answered, holding his arm still as his left hand rested on her back. "But it's you who feels right in my arms."

They sat out the next round and filled their plates, Lacy with tiny sandwiches and the captain with sweets. Before Lacy could eat, an officer asked her to dance. She looked to Walker for help in saying no, but instead he nodded slightly.

Only Walker had been wrong about her being escorted back to him after the song ended. She didn't make it off the floor before another asked her, then another, and another. Lacy tried her best, but didn't feel comfortable with the men who all appeared cut from the same cloth. At her height all she noticed were blue wool chests and shiny buttons. She tried to concentrate on following them but in so doing wasn't able to listen to their conversations. She wanted to freeze in midstep and say, "Do you want to dance or talk? Make your choice. I can't do both at the same time."

By the fifth dance, she decided she would say no even if it was impolite. Only the next soldier didn't even give her a chance, he grabbed her hand and whirled her against his chest.

She opened her mouth to protest, when she looked past the wall of blue to his face and relaxed. "Thank goodness," she whispered. "It's about time you saved me."

Walker laughed. "I had to finish eating."

She tripped on his foot. "You didn't eat mine, did you? I'm starving."

"That's what took me so long."

She tried again for his foot, but he moved too fast, and she laughed. Without a word, she settled into his arms.

After a while, she whispered, "Shouldn't we stop? Your wound must be giving you great discomfort."

"The pain in my arm from dancing is nothing compared to the frustration I feel watching another man hold you. It's easier to dance than plot the murder of every man in this room."

She glanced up, surprised at the warmth in his eyes. He gave no hint that he might be kidding.

They didn't leave the dance early as he'd said they would. Lacy thought he might just be making sure that she remembered her one social. It seemed impossible to believe that the captain actually enjoyed himself. When the band announced the last waltz, he pulled her outside and onto the parade grounds. There, in the moonlight, they danced with only the guard from the gate watching.

When the music stopped, she thought he might kiss her, but he offered his arm, and

411

they walked in silence back to their quarters.

After an evening surrounded by music and laughter, the silence of the little room seemed deafening. Walker bent and built the fire, but neither lit the lamp. She moved to her side of the bed, he to his, and they began undressing as the clock struck the midnight hour.

Lacy wasn't sure what to wear. She thought of changing into her nightgown, but it looked so plain compared to the undergarments she'd bought to go beneath her new dress. She pulled the dress over her head and laid it carefully over a chair. Tomorrow she'd brush it and pack it back in the box. She'd save the dress forever, and someday when she was very old, she'd make it into a quilt so that she could sleep beneath it and dream of this night.

She untied her first petticoat and let it drop to the floor. She took a step. The next petticoat fell.

Walker, who was removing his boots, watched her. "How many of those do you have on?"

Another dropped. "Five. Mrs. Deeds said that was the absolute minimum." Another puddled on the floor.

Walker had lost interest in his boot and

412

simply stared as the last one fell. She stepped out of it wearing her silk pantaloons with lace and ribbons tied just below each knee and white stockings beneath.

When she leaned to pick up the petticoats dotting the floor, he said, "Lacy, come over here."

She walked to where he sat, wondering if he might be having trouble taking off his left boot. The bandage around his arm was stained in blood, but it appeared more dried than fresh. "What's the matter?"

"Do you have any idea how adorable you look?" He smiled, letting his hand brush from her waist to rest on her hip. "I can't stop watching you."

"Let me change that bandage while you're doing all this watching. If the blood dries, it'll be really painful pulling the old cotton off."

The strap of her camisole fell from her shoulder, leaving her breast exposed almost to the nipple.

"Forget it." His voice sounded low, and for a second she thought angry, until she saw the fire in his eyes. He tugged at her strap and pulled the silk down until he freed one full, rounded breast.

Drawing her suddenly between his legs, he opened his mouth over the tip of her breast as his hands slid down over the silk of her undergarments.

Lacy cried out in surprise and pleasure. But this was no gentle game of kissing and touching. She wanted him to touch her, but slowly. She didn't want him to take her, she wanted to give herself to him.

His arm pulled her down in his lap, and his kiss moved to her mouth savage with need. She suddenly felt like they were doing battle, and he planned to win.

"Wait." Lacy tried to push away. "Wait!" She needed him to go slow. His haste made any pleasure vanish. All she felt was panic. She pushed harder. "Stop!"

He released her so fast she almost fell backward.

For a moment he stared at her, breathing hard, pulling himself under control. Lacy stood, stepping out of his reach. She turned her face away, embarrassed, even though she wasn't sure what had happened. One minute he'd be polite, loving, and the next it had been all fire and hunger. She wasn't sure if it was his fault or hers; all she knew was that something hadn't been right.

"If you're waiting for me to say I'm sorry," he said as he jerked off his boot, "you'll wait till hell freezes."

Lacy raised her chin. "I only wanted you to slow down. This is new to me. I need time."

"How much time! A week? A month? Five years of marriage?" He plowed his fingers into his hair and looked down, angry more with himself than her. "You're driving me completely mad, Lacy. You're every inch a woman. A woman made for loving if there ever was one, but sometimes you're like a child. You make it seem like the passion I feel for you is somehow dirty."

He tossed his boot into the corner. "You were fifteen when we married, and part of you is still fifteen. You want me to hold your hand and kiss you and sleep next to you and not make love."

"And you're old and worldly at twenty-seven?"

"Well, I've had some experience. Who lives to be twenty and never even kisses a man? I didn't think that was possible for even women like Theda, much less a woman like you."

"I was married at fifteen. I didn't think I was supposed to go around kissing men. Within months I had a paper to run and your father to care for. That didn't leave a lot of time to run around town kissing any man who bumped into me." She made herself take a breath and added, "I thought my husband would teach me all about it, not get angry at what I don't know."

She reached for her coat. "I'm not a child. But if I'm so behind in years, I can fix that in one night. How many men are there on this fort? Three hundred, maybe more. If I kiss a hundred, will that help even our score? Or maybe I'll expose myself to a dozen. You seemed to like the view; I'm sure they will."

"Calm down, Lacy!" he yelled.

She headed toward the door. "If they're as fast at bedding as you, I might be able to sleep with several before dawn. Then maybe I'll be caught up to you, and you'll stop treating me like an idiot."

"Lacy, don't you dare leave this room." His words rattled the air.

She turned back to him. "Or what?"

He moved toward her until he stood a foot away. "I swear I don't know whether to paddle you or make love to you." He kept his hands at his sides as if forcing himself to use words and not actions. "I didn't mean that it's wrong not to know how it is between a man and a woman. I meant that it's hard on me seeing you and wanting you and . . ." He rubbed his forehead. "Oh, I don't know what I mean. You've succeeded in completely destroying my peace of mind."

Lacy almost felt sorry for him. "You haven't been easy on mine, Captain."

They stared at one another, then both smiled, knowing each gave as much as they got. She knew a fire burned between them, but she had no idea what to do about the flame.

"Truce," he said, watching her as if he still feared she might bolt.

"Do you think we'll kill each other before your tour of duty is over at guarding me?"

"We might," he answered honestly. "But I've always wanted to die an interesting death."

He moved behind her and gently helped her off with her coat. She thought of saying she was sorry for flying off the handle when he'd kissed her so boldly. She knew he hadn't intended to harm her. "Maybe making love is like dancing." She turned to face him. "A gentleman never dances above the lady's level of skill."

He bowed. "I stand corrected, madam." The need for her still reflected in his gaze, but he'd managed to check his hunger.

She moved toward the dresser. "Captain,

how many women have you been with?"

"That's not something a man talks about to a woman, and especially not to his wife."

"But I see it as only fair. You know I've had none."

"All right, I'll tell you numbers, no more."

"How many?"

"Two, and both were paid for." He studied her as if trying to decide how much to tell her. "Since you came to me that day in Cottonwood, none."

"None, paid or unpaid?"

"None, period."

She turned, surprised. "Why? I knew you wanted no part of our marriage. I wouldn't have held you to a vow another made for you."

"Because I didn't want another woman. I tried a few times to go upstairs with a woman for an hour but couldn't talk myself into climbing the steps. None of them looked like you . . . smelled like you . . . were you. You came into my office that day and changed the way I saw women."

She poured water in the basin. "I'll clean that dressing now."

When Lacy turned, he'd sat at the table without arguing. He seemed relaxed once more, but she knew he still wanted her. Maybe in the doctoring, they'd find a common ground to stand on once more.

As she worked, he moved his finger along the inch of space between her camisole and pantaloons. His touch brushed light, teasing, and she was glad something took his mind away from the discomfort she caused in pulling the bloody bandage from his arm.

She cleaned the wound, noticing his fingers had gently tugged her drawers down an inch until they hung lower on her hip.

When she made no comment, he unbuttoned the last button of her camisole so that his hand could slide along the skin exposed at her waist.

"You don't mind this?" He moved his hand over her flesh.

"No," she answered, closing her eyes and letting the pure pleasure of his touch wash over her.

"Because I'm your husband?"

"Because it feels good to have you touch me like this," she answered.

"Me, or would any man do?" He watched her as if testing the waters.

"Well, the doctor's too thin, the ranger's too dirty, and the sheriff's too old. I guess that only leaves my husband. You."

He moved his hand over her skin like a blind man memorizing details. When his fingers brushed the thin scar just below her belly button, he stopped. "What's this?"

"It's nothing." She tied the clean bandage in place on his arm.

His hand crossed back over the tiny scar. "How'd you get it?"

Lacy didn't answer.

He waited, crossing back and forth over her flesh.

She tried to step away, but he held her with a hand at her back.

"Tell me, Lacy." Worry crossed his face, but the words sounded more like an order than a request.

She squared her shoulders. "Your belt buckle cut into me that day in Cottonwood."

She couldn't have shocked him more if she'd slapped him.

Chapter 26

Walker watched Lacy pick up her petticoats and fold them into a box. She moved about the room that had suddenly become small and confining to Walker's way of thinking. The whole fort wouldn't provide enough space between them right now with the way he felt about her.

He studied his wife as she brushed her hair out, trying her best to act as if nothing had happened between them. They hadn't said a word to each other since she'd told him about her scar. He didn't know what to say, and she seemed to think she'd said too much. Silence stretched between, endless and void.

He tried to remember the details of those few minutes they'd been together in Cottonwood. She'd looked wrinkled and dusty when she entered his office, like she'd spent days traveling. And then, once she informed him who she was, she had insisted she would not leave until they were man and wife.

He thought that she kidded, played a game with him. Walker called her bluff. Only when she removed her clothes, he didn't stop. He wasn't proud of what he'd done. The fact that she'd wanted it, even demanded it, didn't make his actions lie any easier on his conscience.

He hadn't raped her. They hadn't made love. He didn't know what to call the mating, but one thing for sure, what they'd done was nothing like what he wanted to do now. He wanted to make love to her, not just to satisfy a raging hunger within him, but to satisfy her. He wanted a mating of more than just bodies. He ached to be so close to her that he no longer knew where he ended and she began.

Leaning forward, bracing his elbows on his legs, he lowered his head into his hands. Part of him wished he'd never seen her before. If she had never come to Cottonwood that day . . . if he hadn't been forced to return to protect her . . . would he know any peace now? Or would he be even more lost than he felt?

Part of him knew he'd see her every day and night he had left of this earth whether they were together or not. And it was a sure bet they wouldn't be within a hundred miles of one another in two weeks. He'd made her a promise to leave, and judging from the count on her notebook, she planned to make sure he kept his word. Not that he would ever break it, but she didn't know. She didn't trust him enough not to fear him.

He knew forever could never work between them. She hated the fort, and he knew no other home. She was crazy about that little nothing town, and he could hardly breathe there. They spent more time yelling than they did talking since he'd been forced to come back to her. Nothing matched about them; even their sleeping patterns were different. He rose early, she slept in. If they were ever together for a time, they'd miss half the days watching each other sleep. They didn't fit together dancing, she loved animals while he didn't want to even be on a first-name basis with cats.

Walker stood, realized he had nowhere to go, and sat back down. This was insane listing all the ways they didn't go together. It only reminded him of how they did match.

He closed his eyes trying to forget how good she felt in his arms, how her lips tasted, how much he wanted her.

Nothing changed the fact that they were married, or that they'd started off all wrong. He thought they were mending, getting used to one another. He knew she was attracted to him, or at least she had been before he frightened her. He'd messed everything up tonight, and he wasn't sure how to make it right between them again.

If he wanted to start over, he had to be honest. He had to tell her who he was. Who he really was. Walker figured it was the only way. If she were going to pull away from him, she might as well do it for real reasons and not something she feared might be true.

"Lacy, we need to talk. There's something you've a right to know." He didn't lift his head. He didn't want to see her face when she found out what her husband did for a living. He took a breath and started at the beginning, "I left Cedar Point when I was seventeen because I thought I was in love with Samantha and found out she'd only been playing with me while she planned to run away with my brother. After they'd gone and I swore I'd never tell another woman I loved her, I discovered Emory had taken all our father's savings he kept locked away in the bottom drawer of his desk."

He expected Lacy to ask a question, but she sat silent as he continued, "I was putting money of my own back when my father caught me in his office. He thought I was taking it. We had a fight, and I left. Later, he figured out the truth and promised he'd make it up to me, but by then I was in the army.

"I'd always been the younger son, the one who was never good enough. I don't really blame the old man. Emory was the child born in love. I was the son of a marriage of convenience, nothing more."

He watched her eyes, seeing emotions floating liquid and raw in their depths. "So when I enlisted, I taught myself how to be the perfect soldier after the army taught me how to kill a man without a weapon. I thought if I could make everything perfect when I wasn't on a mission, no one would see the ugliness in what I did in the name of duty."

He forced himself to face her. She sat in front of the fire with her brush in her hand, but she'd paused, listening.

"When I joined the army, I really didn't care much if I lived or died. They asked if I wanted to go through a training they gave very few men. Within a year I could scout with the best Comanche and had learned to move so silently I could walk up behind a man without him knowing it until he felt the blood drip from the slash I'd made across his throat."

Lacy's eyes widened, and he knew he'd go into no more detail about his talent.

"Most of the time I go about the duties of a soldier, but I have a very valuable skill that the army needs to make use of once in a while. When I return to the forts, I always make sure everything I do, everything I wear, everything I say, is perfect. I even had another captain's wife teach me to dance once. All so none of what I did would show." He prayed she'd understand. "Even though what I do is necessary, I don't want any part of it lingering on me."

"So," Lacy whispered, "that's why you stomp around me. You're making sure I know where you are."

"I never want someone whispering about me as if I'm not like a regular soldier, as though they're afraid of me or afraid of what I might do."

"They respect you," she said. "I can hear it when they say your name."

He tried to smile, but he knew she'd see through him. "Somewhere in all the

426

training, I've forgotten how to be gentle. I don't know how to touch you like you want to be touched. Like you deserve to be touched."

Looking away from her, he couldn't bear to see the pain he knew would be in her face. She deserved a man who could love her like he'd never be able to. "This time, I can't fight for what I want . . . because what I want is you."

He thought he'd keep her safe this month, then give her the print shop and a divorce if she wanted. Somehow in his mind he'd decided that seemed fair. But now he knew her and she deserved so much more than he had to give. Living in such close quarters, being together all the time, she'd seen through his armor, and she'd been afraid. He'd never meant that to happen. He'd made her feel inadequate when all along it had been him, not her, who didn't know how to love.

He felt her fingers touch his hair, and he turned. She'd moved to his side silently, leaning so close he could feel the warmth of her even though they weren't touching. "I can't hurt you again," he whispered.

"You didn't hurt me, the buckle on your trousers did. I'm the one who refused to leave that day in Cottonwood. You had no choice. We were racing the clock."

"But tonight, you pulled away."

"I know. I was afraid you'd go too fast." A tear bubbled from her eye and slid down her cheek. "Even though it's been five years since that night Zeb Whitaker grabbed me, I still have nightmares about it sometimes. I knew it was you holding me earlier, but for a second that fear returned. That sickening feeling of being trapped. It wasn't your fault; there's something wrong inside of me."

He grinned. It seemed they were both laying fears and nightmares on the table, leaving them both unarmed and vulnerable.

"Nightmares aren't anyone's fault. We could fight them together, if you're willing. The question is, do you want me, or are you afraid of me?"

Her fingers moved into his hair, brushing it back in long, lazy strokes. "You're my husband. You're the only man I've ever wanted. I'm more afraid of waking without you than sleeping with you."

If he lived to be a million, he'd never understand this woman. She smiled at him, and there was nothing innocent in the look she gave him.

"It's cold outside." She moved closer. "Would you mind terribly if I got my experience with men in this quarters? In less than two weeks when you leave, I'd like to have enough memories to last me the rest of my life."

She lowered her mouth to his and kissed him gently. "I want to be your wife tonight. Your real wife."

"My only wife," he said against her mouth as the kiss deepened.

When she stepped back, he let her go, knowing she was testing him. He leaned and kissed the scar, wishing that he could remove it.

She cupped her hands around his face and raised his mouth to hers once more. This time her body swayed against him as they kissed.

For a long while he gripped the chair, afraid to hold her as she continued to torture him with her nearness. When he could stand it no longer, he swung his arm behind her knees and lifted her up against him as he stood.

She pulled from his kiss and laughed. "I'll have your clothes off this time, Captain."

He placed her atop the covers and pulled off his socks and trousers.

"All of them," she demanded.

He tried not to let her see how embarrassing it was stripping completely in front of her. When he faced her, she surprised him by studying him boldly. There was no doubt she liked what she saw.

"And yours?" he asked.

"No." She shook her head. "I'll not take them off. If you want my underthings removed, you'll have to take them off yourself."

When he leaned toward her, she whispered, "Only slowly, Captain, gently. One kiss at a time."

He folded down beside her and began at her shoulder, moving the material an inch at a time as he removed her camisole. He was careful not to touch her skin except with his lips as his fingers worked the material away.

When her top slipped away, he brushed his hands over her, loving how she moved, following his light touch. She closed her eyes and stretched as if she'd been waiting for him forever.

With each stroke along her body, he swept her silk garment down from her waist. The fabric finally slipped beneath her hips, and he pulled away the last material separating them.

Then he slid beside her, touching flesh to flesh all along their bodies. He lay still for a while, waiting to see if she'd yet bolt, but her skin warmed against his. Even the slight movement as she breathed drove him mad.

His control slipped, and he fought to concentrate on her. A step at a time, he awakened each part of her, kissing, touching, worshiping. The need to pull her against him made his muscles ache, but he knew if he planned to love her this night, she'd have to be the one who came to him. And she'd come with nothing between them, not even an old nightmare.

At times she seemed shy, but never reluctant. She wanted his touch. Even demanded it. Her hunger pleased him greatly.

When he finally moved above her, she was ready for more and accepted him willingly.

He paused, pushing the hair away from her face and staring into her eyes. He saw fire and passion mirrored there. A thousand thoughts came to mind, words he could say, words he needed to hear, but somehow in the depth of her brown eyes he knew all he needed to know. She wanted him, needed him.

Slowly, he began to move within her, taking her with him into desire's fire. He'd thought he'd known passion before, but now he knew he was as naive as she was. Nothing compared to the fire burning inside him. A sweet, all-consuming hunger without loneliness, as they moved into this mating, this loving, together.

She moaned and lifted to meet him, but he didn't hurry their journey. If they were to have a few short days together, he'd give her what she asked for, enough memories to last a lifetime.

Again and again, he pulled away, driving her mad with need. He took his time tasting her body, running his hands over every curve, feeling the warmth of her waiting for him.

Finally, when she cried his name, he pushed deep inside her and heard her cry out in pleasure. They were lost in passion's fire for a while, then floated gently down, wrapped in one another's arms.

Chapter 27

Deep in the night, Lacy felt Walker moving his hands through her hair. He brushed it over her shoulder and kissed the back of her neck. His fingers circled around, becoming entrapped in her curls.

"What are you doing?" she mumbled, half asleep as she stretched beside him. Their bodies had warmed against one another, and she couldn't believe how quickly she'd become accustomed to the feel of him beside her. She loved pushing softly into the wall of muscle and hearing him groan as if her light touch tortured him all the way to his soul.

"I found a spot on you I must have missed." He ran his tongue over her shoulder, nibbled along the side of her throat. "And you know I can't be less than complete in my duty."

Lacy rolled over, bumping her breast against his arm as she moved. "No, I remember; you've already kissed that spot." She giggled as his mouth moved up her throat and worked its way slowly across her cheek.

"Oh, sorry," he answered as he continued tasting. "Now I'll have to give all the other parts equal attention, since I've accidentally done this area twice." His chin slid between her breasts, tickling her skin with his unshaven jaw as he dove beneath the covers.

"Captain?"

He made a sound that told her he listened, even though his mouth was now fully occupied.

"I'd like to touch you."

Walker lifted his head. "What?"

"I'd like to touch you, if you don't mind."

"Where?"

Lacy laughed. "Everywhere."

He moved back to study her face.

The fire was too low to see him well, but she knew he raised one eyebrow and decided to act before he had time to think of a reason to refuse her request. "Lie back on your back." She pushed him in encouragement. "Just relax." She laughed. "And let me have my way with you."

He reluctantly followed her request. "I

don't know about this. My body's not soft like yours. I wouldn't think you'll get much pleasure from touching me. I've been stitched up so many times I look a little like one of your quilts."

She rose above him and paid no mind to his protests. "Now, put your hands down at your sides and keep them there." She shoved his shoulders down as if she believed she had enough strength to keep them in place. "There will be no touching of me until I'm finished."

He grumbled but didn't say a word as she moved her hands down his body. With each scar she stopped, examined it with her fingers, and then kissed the marked flesh as he'd done with her tiny scar.

His body was warm and muscular, with no softness about him. His skin tasted slightly salty as she moved over him and planted kisses first down his throat, then down his chest. She thought the pleasure of her actions would be in the giving, knowing how little he'd been touched in his life, but the pleasure was also in the taking, for she enjoyed the feel of him. She liked the way he drew in his breath when her mouth moved across his chest and smiled when he knotted the sheets into his fists to keep from raising his hand to touch her as her breasts slid over his ribs.

When she passed his waist, he drew in a breath and whispered, "A wife is not supposed to be so bold."

Lacy raised her head and tried to see his face. "How do you know? I'm the only wife you've had."

"True," he managed to say before she continued.

Amazed at the control she had over this powerful man, Lacy laughed. He reacted to the slightest brush of her fingers, and he sounded as if he were suffering. But he didn't try to stop her, and she knew he could have pushed her away with one hand. This only wife he had planned to know her husband quite well by morning.

Strangely, instead of satisfying her desires, she only needed more. The longer she touched him, the bolder she wanted to be, and the more she longed for his caress. She felt an ache deep within her she knew of only one way to cure.

Finally, frustrated, she leaned over his chest and whispered against his ear. "Can we do it again?"

"What?" he said between clenched teeth.

"You know. It."

"No," he answered. "I think another time tonight would kill me."

Lacy laughed, showing no care for his life as she wiggled against him. "Well, you always wanted to die an interesting death."

He closed his arms around her and rolled her beneath him, no longer caring if he died from the attempt. He made love to her boldly, freely knowing that she wanted him as deeply as he wanted her.

When they lay exhausted, beside one another on their stomachs, she rose to one elbow and continued touching him, running her hand over his backside.

"Go to sleep," he ordered, but he made no attempt to push her hand aside.

"All right." She leaned back down on the bed, but her hand stayed on his hip as if she planned to leave it right there the rest of the night.

Walker was preparing to risk death again an hour later, when someone pounded on their door. Before Lacy could react, he swung from the bed and lifted his Winchester.

"Who is it?" he demanded.

"Theda," came a shrill voice.

This time Lacy reacted before Walker. "Just a minute," she cried, and they both scrambled for their clothes. Neither managed to find underwear, but Lacy wiggled into her old dress and fought with the buttons in the dark, while Walker pulled on his trousers and shirt.

Lacy opened the door, and Theda rushed in as Walker lit the lamp.

"You've got to come," she cried, her words tumbling over one another. "January's in labor, and the doctor had to go to town to patch up several men involved in a fight at the saloon." She pulled Lacy along as she rattled, "We've got to help her, and I can't do it alone."

To Walker's amazement, Lacy remained calm. "Run back to your sister and tell her I'm on my way," she said, "then get all the pots you can on the stove full of water. We'll need hot water and lots of it and all the towels in the house. I'll be there before the water boils."

Theda nodded, calming now that someone was telling her what to do.

Hayes banged against the open door, looking like he'd dressed on the run. "Miss Theda, you can't be moving about the —"

Walker cut the sergeant off. "Hayes, go with Miss Theda and help. I'll bring my wife as soon as we're dressed. Also, send a rider to Mobeetie to tell the doctor to get back as soon as possible."

Hayes nodded, relieved that he wasn't somehow in trouble for letting women wander the fort before sunrise. He offered his arm, but the tall old maid only ran past him. He sprinted to catch up to her.

Walker closed the door. For a moment, they stared at one another. The world had found them, and there was nothing they could do about it.

"Lacy . . ." he started, realizing he needed to say a hundred things to her but not knowing where to start.

She pulled on one of her stockings. "I know," she answered as if she'd heard all of them while they'd made love.

They dressed, helping each other find clothes that had been tossed around the room and shoes that were scattered. Within minutes, the proper captain stood before her.

She pulled on her coat. "Ready?"

He lifted his rifle and nodded.

They walked out into the dark predawn. She didn't feel the cold, for her thoughts were still in his arms. She could still taste him on her lips, and the ache for him inside of her had already begun anew.

When they stepped onto the small porch of the structure marked as married officers' housing, his hand reached for hers.

They could hear people moving about in the house and knew a guard might be watching them from only yards away. There was no time for just the two of them any longer, but he had to touch her, and her hold was tight.

Walker leaned close and whispered as he knocked on the door, "I didn't get enough of you."

She smiled, already hearing someone running to answer. "Nor I you."

"It'll be dawn soon." He let go of her hand as he heard someone turning the knob.

"But eventually we'll have the night again."

The door opened, slicing light over them. Walker only had a second to look into her eyes, but he swore he saw a hunger there.

Then she was gone, pulled into the bedlam of birthing.

Theda had watched her father bring twins into the world, but he'd limited his patients to the elderly by the time her mother could no longer assist him in the office. Lacy had delivered babies twice, once on the wagon train and one time when Timothy was out of town. That made her the expert, so Lacy took the lead.

Luckily, Theda's panic hadn't spread to

January. She might be the one screaming, but she also knew exactly what she wanted them both to do. She'd had nine months to collect notes from every woman she knew about what to do when the time came.

With the first cry from pain, Adam, the prospective father, Hayes, and Walker were out the door to guard the house. Lacy worried that they might be cold on the porch, but they insisted they were comfortable.

Millie rushed in a few minutes later, but she was too excited to be of much help. Her job quickly became darting back and forth from the bedroom to the porch with reports.

By dawn, a baby's cry came from the bedroom, and Millie ran to yell, "It just popped out!" She had to make another run to announce the sex, a boy, because the men knew better than to leave their post before called.

When January was all cleaned up and tucked among pillows, the men were allowed to come in. Adam went right to his wife, but Walker waited at the door. Hayes said he still felt more comfortable on the porch.

Lacy watched Walker, wondering what he was thinking. Did he envy them, or was he glad that it would never be him pacing the porch while she screamed?

She collected pots and towels and left the bedroom. Walker followed her to the kitchen. When he realized they were alone, he pulled her into his arms, and for a long moment they just held one another.

"That was fast," he whispered against her hair. "I thought birthing took days."

"It does sometimes. January must be one of those women that delivery comes easy to. The last woman I watched took forty-eight hours to deliver, and most of that was at full volume."

His forehead wrinkled. "Do you think it will come easy for you?"

Lacy closed her eyes for a moment, then lifted her chin and looked up at him. "I can't have children. I'm broken."

Walker raised an eyebrow. "How do you know?"

"I didn't get pregnant when you bedded me in Cottonwood. I've heard of some women who can never have children. I guess I'm one of them."

"Did you ask a doctor?"

"No." Why would she do such a foolish thing? She could never see herself sitting down with Timothy and asking him such a personal question.

To her surprise, Walker smiled. "I think

it sometimes takes more than doing it once, Lacy."

She shook her head. "How would you know? You don't even know how long it takes to deliver a baby."

His hands spread over her tummy, but he didn't answer.

Chapter 28

To Walker's surprise, Lacy suggested staying one more day at the fort. She wanted to make sure January was all right. She wouldn't leave the baby until the doctor arrived and said all was well.

Walker took one last glance into the new parents' bedroom. January and her husband had the baby between them on the bed and were whispering. Theda worked silently in the corner, cleaning up.

He spent the day trying to stay awake during boring meetings with the major. Garner even talked him into assisting with the training of recruits. Though he worked with them, Walker never stepped beyond the standard manual of training. He would teach them all he could about defending themselves, but he'd promised himself a long time ago that he'd never teach another man to kill.

When he finally made it back to his

quarters, he wasn't sure he could stay awake long enough to eat supper. He hoped Lacy had managed to find time for a nap, but he doubted it. Hayes had said the women all went to see the baby around noon, then planned to spend the afternoon finishing the quilt.

When he finally made it back to his quarters, dinner waited on the table by the fire, but Walker didn't see his wife. He came full awake with alarm before he spotted her curled atop the covers, still dressed, but sound asleep.

He smiled, guessing she'd done her best to wait up for him.

He undressed and knelt beside her. "Lacy," he whispered. "It's time to go to bed."

She stretched and reached for him.

Walker laughed, lifting her up as he pulled the covers down. He tugged off her boots while she curled around a pillow.

"Lacy?" he said kissing her. "Would you mind if I help you?"

He'd planned only to pull the pins from her hair and removed her dress, but as he worked, he felt like he was opening the best present he'd ever had. He'd planned to stop at her underthings, but he didn't. He'd planned to let her sleep, but he couldn't.

She awoke nude in his arms and laughed

as if she were dreaming. They made love slowly and gently, floating on the pure pleasure of being back together. Now that they knew each other's body, no shyness slowed them as they touched and caressed.

"This day was endless not seeing you," he whispered as he kissed her. "I want to get you alone. I don't feel like sharing you with the world right now."

She moved her hands along his back. "I know," she whispered, telling more with her touch than with words how dearly she'd missed him.

"I thought of being here with you like this all day."

"I know," she added.

"I ached to hold you. Half the time I didn't even bother to listen to what others were saying."

"I know." She sounded preoccupied with exploring him.

He smiled. "Lacy, what do you know?" He stopped her hand from touching him until she answered.

She looked up, bothered that her pleasure had been interrupted. "I know you'd better stop talking and start making love to me, Captain."

He gave in. "You sweet-talked me into it."

When they were both satisfied, he held her close as they drifted into sleep. The last words he whispered promised they'd leave for home tomorrow.

Just before dawn, a pounding sounded on their door as it had the morning before, short, rapid-fire knocks.

Walker rolled, grabbing his rifle, and yelled, "Who is it?"

Lacy pulled the blankets around her and tried to rub the deep sleep from her eyes as she stood.

"It's Theda! Open up. I have to talk to Lacy!"

Walker laid the weapon aside and shoved his hair back. "I may have to kill that woman," he mumbled as he looked for his trousers. "Maybe I'll leave orders to shoot any female over six feet seen roaming the fort after dark. That should discourage her from her nightly run to our door."

Lacy giggled and reached for her gown. "I'm coming," she shouted.

Walker managed to get one button on his shirt fastened before Lacy threw the lock.

"Come in, Theda." Lacy stepped back. "Hurry, before Hayes sees you and sounds an alarm or something."

Theda rushed in. "I stayed in the

447

shadows away from the guard's sight. I don't think anyone saw me."

Walker frowned. The army should think about recruiting this tall, thin woman for his job. If no one saw her, she'd outsmarted three hundred trained men, proving their fortress not as safe as he'd thought. And apparently she'd done it unarmed and wearing a skirt.

Theda pulled the hood of her coat away from her face. "I couldn't wait any longer, Lacy. I had to talk to you."

The old maid glanced at Walker and blushed. "I'm sorry to have disturbed you, Captain, but I was afraid you might be leaving at dawn, and I'd miss Lacy."

He nodded once, accepting her apology and noticing her tearstained cheeks. "Please, Miss Theda, have a seat." He motioned toward the table by the fireplace where two chairs and the dinner they'd forgotten waited.

Walker moved to the chair at the small desk by the door and pulled on his socks, then boots. He noticed Theda lowered her eyes. Apparently, the sight of a man putting his shoes on was too personal a sight to see.

The women kept watching him, and he got the hint. He grabbed his coat. "If you ladies will excuse me, I think the cook will have coffee on over in the mess hall by now." He turned to Lacy.

She nodded, telling him he'd guessed right. "Please, Captain, take time to eat breakfast."

He understood. "I will, and I'll bring some back when I've finished." He watched Lacy's face. "It should take me half an hour."

His wife nodded slightly.

"Just coffee," Theda managed to say. "I don't think I could eat a thing. Worrying always upsets my delicate stomach."

They turned away from him. He felt like a waiter who'd been dismissed. Walking out of his own quarters into the cold morning, he tried to figure out what had been so hell-fired important that the woman couldn't have waited until daylight, but deep down he decided he already knew. He'd seen it all in the one glance yesterday morning. The old maid was no longer needed, or wanted, for that matter.

Walker wasn't surprised to find Hayes having an early breakfast with several men already dressed to travel. Walker sat down with the men in the mess hall's kitchen, and after a few minutes they relaxed and talked while they ate. He knew having an officer among them was strange, but he didn't feel like eating alone in the empty, cold officers' mess hall at this time in the morning.

Four of the soldiers were riding to Cedar Point at daybreak. They were excited about spending the night in town before picking up a payroll off the train and riding back the next day.

Hayes commented that since the weather was good, he might ride along and pick up a chair the major ordered from Dallas that had been stored at the station for a week now. He also talked about a lawyer in town who'd ordered a box of books, and if they were in, he'd promised to pick them up for Temple Houston.

"I owe the son of Sam Houston a favor, and it wouldn't be no trouble," Hayes added. "If I'm picking up the chair, I might as well get the box of law books."

"Would you have any objection if I ride along with you as far as the ranch a few miles before you reach town?" Walker couldn't believe his luck. He'd be taking Lacy to the McKoy place with an escort. "I'll need to borrow a horse for my wife. If you wouldn't mind bringing it back?"

"I'd be honored to have you along," Hayes answered. "But since I'm taking the wagon, she's welcome to ride with me. She'd be more comfortable."

Walker tried to consider whether she'd be safer on horseback or in a wagon. He'd like to have her double up with him on Trooper, but it wouldn't be the safest way. If trouble came, he needed to be able to move fast, and if Lacy were with him, she'd be in greater danger. But the thought of holding her all day in his arms was appealing.

"I heard her tell the ladies while they were quilting that she hates riding a horse." He laughed. "She said with her short legs she's always afraid of falling off and not being able to jump back on." Hayes suddenly looked embarrassed that he'd mentioned the captain's wife's legs. He hurried to add, "But Miss Lacy said she could drive a buggy as good as a man. Said she drove a wagon all the way to Texas once."

Walker took a long drink of his coffee, resenting the fact that Hayes had managed to find out something about Lacy that he knew nothing about. While he drank, he watched Hayes squirm a little. The sergeant was hoping Walker had let the comment about Lacy's legs slide.

Walker might not have, but he got to thinking about those legs and how good

451

they felt. The inside of her thigh was soft as butter and —

"More coffee, Captain?" The cook interrupted Walker's thought.

Walker almost spilled the remaining grounds in his cup as he looked up. "Thanks," he managed to say as he pulled his mind back out of bed.

When the cook moved away, he realized Hayes was waiting for an answer. "How about I ask my wife which she prefers," Walker said. "We'll be ready to leave in less than an hour."

Hayes nodded. "If you don't mind, I need to make a quick stop at Temple's place in Mobeetie and let him know I'll be picking up his box. Otherwise the man might think I'm stealing it and sue me."

"All right." Walker didn't like the delay, but he agreed.

"I could take the ambulance wagon if you like. We've got a bench seat that fits in back. That way Miss Lacy could be out of the weather for the day."

Walker smiled. Hayes was going out of his way. "That would be better." He knew the sergeant was aware of his wife's kidnapping and the reason they'd come to the fort in the first place.

Walker stood and collected a hot pot of

coffee and three cups, thanked the cook, and left. As he walked away, he overheard something he'd never heard said before about him. The cook mumbled, "Nice fella, for an officer. Wouldn't mind if he joined us early again some morning."

When Walker made it back to the quarters, he wasn't surprised to find Lacy fully dressed and packing.

He glanced around as he set the coffee down. "She's gone?"

Lacy accepted a cup. "Poor thing, January doesn't mean to, but she has her new family now, and they want some time together. In a two-room house, that doesn't leave much room for Theda." Lacy continued as she followed Walker around the little room while he packed, "January's also got the other women around to offer all the help she could need. The wives feel a real bonding here, and Theda isn't really a part of that either, even though everyone was really nice to her. I think being around them makes her even more lonely."

Walker poured her coffee, knowing somewhere there was an end to this conversation. For a woman who didn't want to waste time talking in bed, she sure did her share of it outside the covers.

He was thinking about telling Lacy that

they had an hour before they had to meet Hayes, and maybe if they hurried, they could spend half of it in bed, when Lacy added, "So, I asked her to go back with us."

"What!" Walker almost spilled the coffee for the second time today. At this rate, he'd be permanently scarred before the pot was empty.

Lacy looked at him in surprise. "I asked her to go back to Cedar Point with us. From there she can take the train."

When he frowned, she added, "You don't expect her to travel alone?"

"Of course not, but she's not my problem. Adam's her brother-in-law. Let him take care of her."

"Well, she can't ask Adam to take her; after all, he has a wife and one-day-old baby to consider. If she doesn't go with us, it could be days, even weeks, before she could go. Theda can't just ride over with the men picking up the mail. It wouldn't be proper, her being single and all."

Walker raised an eyebrow as he sat down at the table. Lacy's words sounded like they'd probably come out of Theda's mouth a few minutes before. "Where is Miss Theda?" He feared he already knew the answer.

"She's packing and saying her good-byes." Lacy sat on his lap. "She says her brother-in-law will loan her a horse."

"I've got Hayes rigging up the ambulance wagon for you now." Walker had trouble concentrating on looking angry with her sitting on his knee. "Theda can ride inside with you."

"Oh, that's great. You've thought of everything." She kissed him then, what he'd been waiting for since the moment he walked in.

He thought of telling her that Hayes had the idea for using the ambulance wagon but decided against it as her kiss turned from thank you to desire.

He moved his hand along her leg, pulling up her dress as he kissed her. The need to touch her flesh burned like a hunger he'd never known. But layers of cotton blocked his progress. Finally, he pulled away from the kiss and groaned in frustration.

She cuddled against him. "What is it?"

"I want to touch you."

"You are touching me." He had one hand lost in the material of her skirts and another circled around her just below her breasts.

"No." He stared down at her. "I want to

touch you, just you. I need . . ." He didn't know how to tell her that he needed to feel her with a desire so strong he feared it might consume his body completely.

"Can it wait until tonight?"

"No," he said honestly, knowing he was admitting a need for her that gave her the advantage.

To his surprise, she made no bargain. She stood, pulled off her boots, and turning her back to him, let her petticoats and underthings fall to the floor, then walked back to her place on his lap.

Walker was speechless as she curled into his arms and began kissing him again as if she'd only paused.

It took him a minute to realize what she'd done so easily. Her skirt still covered her completely, but when he slipped his hand beneath, he felt first the silk of her stockings, then the bare velvet of her thighs.

He would have thanked her if he could have torn his mouth away from hers, but as he touched her, the kiss grew deeper. She played no game but let him touch her boldly, as if caressing a woman beneath her skirt was the most natural thing to do in the world.

When he touched her most private part,

she jerked in surprise, but she didn't pull away, and he knew — all the way to his soul, he knew — that she belonged to him. Not just on paper. Not just in his dreams. But forever.

Chapter 29

By the time Walker helped Lacy into the ambulance wagon, everyone else looked ready to ride. Even Theda sat in the back, rearranging her bags so that her hatboxes didn't get crunched. The old maid traveled with two trunks, three hatboxes, and a huge umbrella. They were lucky to be taking the wagon, or she would have needed a train of packhorses to move her.

The quilt Lacy made of Walker's father's old suits now lay over the bench like a cushion. It seemed to welcome her, as if the old man still lingered near. Though the canvas walls of the wagon were tied down, wind whistled through. If the day didn't get warmer, the blanket would be needed.

Lacy smiled, wondering if any of the blush on her cheeks still showed. She watched Walker. He looked so commanding in his uniform. No one would ever believe he'd sworn less than an hour ago that he would die if he didn't touch her.

They hadn't had time to make love, but the warmth of his hands still lingered on her legs, and the promises of tonight excited her. He'd looked so surprised when she'd removed her petticoats and pantaloons. He didn't understand how dear his touch was to her, she realized as she shoved her tablet farther into her carpetbag. That first day she'd written the days out one by one, counting down the time until he left.

She'd rip the number eleven out tonight. Eleven more days until he disappeared from her life. Eleven days to have a husband. She wanted to experience as much of him as possible, for there would never be another man in her life. He might have been trapped into this marriage, but she'd been there when the paper was signed. She might have only just turned fifteen, but she knew what she was doing, and she'd done it willingly.

"Ready?" Hayes leaned in to see that they were both seated.

"Yes." Theda wore a brave smile, but her cheeks were moist with tears, and fear flickered in her eyes. In a whisper she added, "This was the first time I've ever gone anywhere that one of my sisters didn't see me off at the train station and another was waiting for me when I reached my destination."

Lacy patted her hand. "Well, I guess this will be a grand adventure. We'll stop at my friend's place before dark. They'll be happy to see you. Then, in the morning, one of the men will take you to the train."

"I'm afraid," the old maid whispered. "I told my sister I was going home, but there is nothing for me to hurry back to there. But I'm afraid if I take one step off my routine, no telling what may happen."

Lacy cringed, almost hearing Walker yelling, as she said, "Would you like to stay with me for a few days at Cedar Point?" With all that had happened lately, Lacy wasn't sure if she offered her shelter or trouble, but at least it would be interesting. "Walker and I would be happy to have you."

"Thank you," Theda said. "That's very kind."

Lacy had no idea if that was a yes or a no, but she figured it could wait.

"I've never been very brave," Theda admitted.

"Me either."

Theda shook her head. "I'd think you'd

460

have to be brave being married to Captain Larson. He frightens me a little, but then most men do."

Lacy realized that Walker no longer frightened her at all. Somehow, she'd learned to trust him. He could yell, and order her around, and demand his way, but when they were alone together, he couldn't say no to her. She smiled. Her real problem lay in the fact that she couldn't say no to him either.

"We're stopping in Mobeetie for just a few minutes, if you ladies need anything," Hayes yelled back.

Lacy looked at all the boxes stacked by her old carpetbag. She couldn't think of anything except a nightgown. The mercantile in Mobeetie might have something with lace. It occurred to her that she didn't have any money with her. The only logical thing to do would be to ask Walker to loan her money until she could withdraw some from her account and pay him back. It seemed extravagant to spend maybe as much as two dollars on a gown and robe, but Lacy wanted to. She'd wear them for Walker and then pack them away with the beautiful dress from the dance.

"I'd like to buy a pair of gloves, if there is time," Theda said. "I left mine with January. Hers were wearing out, and I knew winter would be over before she could get out to find more."

"No problem. I'll drop you ladies at the mercantile side door and leave the wagon there. By the time I check with the lawyer upstairs, you'll have your shopping done." Hayes slapped the reins, and the wagon moved away from the fort.

Mrs. Deeds greeted them a few minutes later when Walker led the women into the shop, then turned to order the four men traveling with them to spread out along the front of the store.

While Lacy looked at nightgowns and Theda at gloves, Lacy heard Mrs. Deeds lean over to Walker and say, "Same rules apply as before, Captain?"

"Same rules," Walker answered, and Mrs. Deeds smiled.

A moment later, the owner of Mobeetie's best and only ladies' shop pulled out a box from beneath the counter. A matching gown and robe she swore had just come from Dallas.

Lacy shook her head. "Oh, that's far too expensive."

"What price range did you have in mind, dear?"

"One dollar, maybe a few bits more."

The old woman smiled. "Well, you're in luck; this fits within your needs."

Lacy couldn't believe it. She'd never seen anything so nice. Mrs. Deeds tossed in slippers for no extra price.

While she boxed up her purchases, Lacy turned to Walker. "I'll pay you back, Captain."

He raised an eyebrow as if he planned to argue, but said only, "Of course."

Lacy found herself pacing a few minutes later as Theda tried on every glove in Mrs. Deeds's collection. She wanted to be on her way. She'd had no word about Nell in three days, and she was starting to worry.

Walker also seemed uneasy, maybe because they were no longer protected by the fort. When she asked, he didn't take his gaze from the street as he tried to reassure her that nothing was wrong.

Theda paid for her gloves and slipped out the side door. Lacy started to follow but paused, waiting for Walker, who watched the windows, searching, as if sensing trouble. He motioned the men to mount up as Hayes came down the stairs.

Walker touched her arm. "We're ready. Go, quickly, once you leave the store."

"What's wrong?" She knew something had to be. She also guessed he wouldn't take time to tell her, and she was right.

When Lacy darted from the side door, she saw Theda swing her umbrella at a man trying to exit the back of the wagon as fast as possible.

"How dare you touch my things!" the tall woman yelled. "Get out of here immediately."

Lacy had seen the man when she'd been in town before. He'd sat outside the saloon looking too drunk to walk. She'd felt sorry for him then, not realizing he was a thief who must steal whatever he could in order to fund his habit of drink.

She smiled. She almost felt sorry for him again today, for Theda was dealing out justice with a mighty swing of her umbrella.

Walker rushed past Lacy to help the old maid, but Theda had already handled the situation. The thief darted away, screaming in pain. Two of the soldiers took off in pursuit, but Walker ordered them back.

Lifting Lacy into the wagon, he said, "Wonderful job, Miss Theda. I'll have you in my regiment anytime."

Theda, who a moment before had been raging mad, now looked like she might faint. "I can't believe my heart didn't stop with terror." She crumpled onto the bench as Hayes took up the reins. "When I climbed in and saw him picking through my boxes, I just reacted." She looked up at Lacy, her eyes wide with fear. "He might have killed me."

Lacy doubted it. The man was much smaller than Theda and looked too poor to even own a gun. But Lacy said, "You were so brave."

Theda smiled and calmed. "I was, wasn't I."

Within minutes they were clear of the town and riding hard. The bench seat inside the ambulance wagon would have been comfortable at a normal rate, but at this speed, Lacy and Theda rocked from side to side.

With a sudden dip in the road, Theda's elbow hit the iron of the bench side and she yelped, then quickly insisted it was nothing, but Lacy didn't miss the way she babied her arm.

After another five minutes, Theda was too frightened to talk.

Lacy feared she couldn't endure a day at this speed. She also knew it would be a waste of time to ask the men to slow down. There was a reason for their hurry, and if they knew what it was, Theda might be even more nervous than she already was.

Pushing off the bench, she gripped the

canvas sides and crawled forward. Beneath the driver was a stack of army-issue wool blankets. Rising to her knees, Lacy spread them out on the floor of the wagon. Then she motioned for Theda to join her.

Theda spread Walker's blanket over them both, and they cuddled in the bed of the wagon. Here, the ride was smoother, and they didn't feel like they might fly off in one direction or the other at any moment.

Theda laughed. "This is exciting. How'd you know to get low like this?"

Lacy told her the story of how she came to Texas. Now that they were away from the fort, she felt she could tell everything, including how Walker and she were married and what it had been like on the wagon train. An hour passed as Theda asked questions, forgetting all about how fast they were traveling.

When the wagon slowed, they heard a tap on the side canvas and Walker's voice. "You two all right in there?"

"We're snug as bugs." Theda laughed, high on the adventure. "Why'd we slow down?"

"I thought . . ." Walker paused. "Lacy, is it rough on you?"

"No, dear," she answered, giggling at

Theda's face. "We're tough enough to take it. Let's make some time."

She heard Walker give an order, and they were off again. In less time than she thought possible, they slowed to turn onto Carter McKoy's farm.

Lacy poked her head out and watched as Walker rode up to the gate and fired two shots, then waited for an answering two shots before opening the gate and motioning in the wagon.

The four mounted soldiers waited at the entrance, while Hayes drove the wagon up to the house. Lacy was out of the wagon and running to Bailee before Hayes had even brought the horse to a stop.

The two women hugged wildly, then Lacy stepped back and introduced first Theda, and then Walker. Hayes had finished unloading the wagon by the time she got around to him. The sergeant tipped his hat, then saluted Walker and departed without a word.

Walker dismounted and moved to where Carter stood.

Ranger Dalton stormed out the door. "Hello, honey," he shouted to Lacy. "How was army life?" When he set Lacy down from a hug, he offered his hand to Walker. "Captain."

Walker straightened, and Lacy held her breath. "My wife's name is Lacy, Dalton. I'd thank you to remember that."

The ranger grinned. "I was wondering when you'd care enough to notice." He turned to Lacy. "Nell's waiting to see you inside, Mrs. Larson."

Everyone but Walker and Carter moved.

Just before Lacy stepped inside, she thought she heard Walker say low to Carter, "Fill me in?"

The big man nodded as they both walked toward the barn.

Part of her wanted to know what was going on, but right now, she had Nell to see about.

The doctor had waited with Nell while the others ran outside to greet the wagon. He stood when everyone returned, but in his usual quiet way, he made no greeting.

Lacy saw the worry in his eyes a moment before he masked all expression from his tired gaze.

She forced questions down. They could wait until she could talk to him without anyone overhearing. She moved beside the bed.

Nell smiled up at Lacy. Her color was better, and the cuts on her body were beginning to heal, but, she didn't move.

"How you feeling?" Lacy kissed the girl's cheek and took her hand, which felt cold in her grip.

"Weaker than a kitten," Nell admitted in a whisper. "But the doc says I'm getting stronger every day. I guess I lost a great deal of blood." She blinked back a tear. "I wouldn't have made it if Carter hadn't come along when he did."

Lacy looked around. Nell had been set up in a corner of the huge main room and, from the location of the ranger's gear, Dalton was sleeping a few feet away on a long couch. The location was practical but offered Nell little privacy.

"You're going to be just fine," Lacy whispered.

"I know," Nell answered. "I know." She sounded as if she were trying to convince herself.

Timothy motioned with his head that maybe they should move away. "She needs to sleep. She's been waiting up until you got here, but it's time for more medicine."

Lacy kissed Nell again and stepped away as Dalton and the doctor pulled a wooden divider to offer Nell some privacy.

"She's still needing a lot for the pain," the doctor whispered when he joined them a few minutes later. "She'll sleep for a while now, and then I'll check on her before I head back to town."

Lacy noticed Theda standing by the door looking totally out of place. "Timothy, could you look at my friend's elbow? She hurt it on the ride here and is trying to act like it's nothing, but I know it pains her."

"Of course." He grabbed his bag.

To her surprise, Theda didn't argue when she introduced the doctor and suggested he examine her elbow. Lacy insisted they use the small bedroom at the front of the house.

In a few minutes, Timothy's kind manner had won Theda over. Her sleeve was too tight-fitting to allow him to see unless she removed her blouse or he cut the material. He stepped out of the room while Lacy helped the old maid pull her arm and shoulder free of the dress.

When the doctor returned, he was as professional as Theda was nervous. But as Lacy encouraged her to talk about helping her father, she relaxed. To Lacy's surprise, Timothy had heard of Theda's father. He'd been a great doctor during the war and was still talked about at medical school for some of the things he'd pioneered in field hospitals.

Three hours later, when everyone sat down to dinner, the doctor and Theda were still talking. Dalton filled his plate and moved behind the divider to have his meal with Nell, even though she still slept. Carter looked like there were far too many people in the house, but Bailee kept him busy helping with his sons. Walker, Lacy realized, was the watcher in the group. He was polite, even helpful, but never a part of the group.

When Bailee announced that Theda and Lacy would share the only bedroom and Walker was welcome to bunk in the main room by the fire or in the workshop with old Samuel, Lacy was the only one who caught the disappointment in Walker's eyes. He looked straight at her.

Dalton laughed. "I tried the bunkhouse the first night. I'd rather sleep with a dozen bears than listen to Samuel snore all night again."

"I'll take my chances by the fire," Walker said, but Lacy knew he wanted to be closer to her.

To everyone's surprise, the doctor asked if Bailee would mind if he stayed the night. He claimed he wanted to keep a close watch on Nell, but everyone wondered if it might have something to do with the tall old maid. She'd followed him to Nell's side every time he'd checked on the girl, assisting him.

When the house settled down, there was no private time for Lacy to talk to Walker. He walked her to her bedroom door and said good night, formally, but she saw the need in his eyes.

The world had closed in around them. There would be no time for them to be alone tonight.

Lacy fought back tears as she closed the door and put on the gown she'd planned to show off to Walker. Tonight, only Theda would see it.

Chapter 30

Walker swore as he unfolded his bedroll by the fire.

The ranger laughed from ten feet away. "Stop complaining, I've been sleeping in this room for a week now. It ain't so bad. You're the last one to get to sleep, and the kids wake you up by dawn coming down from the loft like a herd of buffalo smelling fresh water. Add to that, Carter patrols the house a couple times a night checking the locks like someone might sleepwalk and unlock a door, and Bailee checks on Nell every few hours like I might not be doing the job."

Dalton continued, as if Walker cared, "But tonight should be interesting with the doc sleeping on a cot in the kitchen. No telling how many times he'll be in and out of here. If Miss Theda thinks he's doing doctoring, she'll be running out to stand by his side. Then there's your wife, Mrs.

Larson. She'll probably wander out here to check on Nell just in case me, the doc, and Bailee are all falling down on our jobs." Dalton sighed. "I'd get more sleep in a stampede."

Walker had little sympathy. "At least your wife isn't sleeping in another room. After tonight, I'll only have ten days of leave left."

"It's not like you only have ten days of marriage left." Dalton tried to help.

Walker groaned.

Dalton sat up. "It *is* like you only have ten days left! Larson, maybe no one's ever explained this to you army guys, but marriage is for a lifetime. That's why they put that 'till death do us part' line in there, so the husband won't accidentally throw out the wife with last year's calendar."

Walker didn't want to talk to the ranger about his marriage, but he knew Dalton would be around long after he'd gone. The ranger's shoulder would probably be where Lacy cried, if she missed him, which he wasn't at all sure about, since she still carried that tablet around and marked off each day.

He poked at the fire, mumbling as much to himself as to the ranger, "I gave Lacy my word that if she'd let me protect her,

I'd leave in twenty-four days and never come back. The time's over half gone, and she hasn't said a word about my not keeping that promise."

"Have you?"

"No."

Dalton swore. "That's crazy. You're her husband." He stood and walked over to the fire. He rubbed his hand through hair a month past needing to be cut. "You are her husband, aren't you, Captain?"

"I'm her husband."

"Her real husband . . . in every way? Not just on paper."

"In every way."

"Then don't go. Or at least take her with you."

"I gave her my word I'd leave, and she wouldn't go with me, even if I asked her."

Dalton shook his head. "Then you got one hell of a problem. Tell me, Captain, just for the record, do you love her?"

"Yes," Walker answered without hesitating. The question had not entered his mind before, but when asked, he could give just one answer, the truth. Even to say he thought he did, or he might, would have been a lie. There was no doubt; he'd loved her since that day in Cottonwood. Not because of her body, or what they'd done, but he loved her for being so brave. In those few minutes they'd been together, she'd become his wife in body as well as in his heart. "I love her," he said again, letting the words roll around in his mind.

"Have you told her?"

"No."

The ranger looked bothered by the captain. "I'm no expert, but I think you oughta tell her. It might make some difference."

Bailee tiptoed down from the loft, having put her boys to sleep. "Good night," she said to the men as she passed through the main room and headed downstairs to where Carter had built a bedroom underground.

She paused at the opening of the trapdoor and glanced back at Walker. "I agree, Captain. You should tell her." Laughing, she disappeared.

Jacob also laughed, but Walker rubbed his forehead. Everyone on the place would know he loved Lacy before he even had a chance to tell her. She was going to kill him. He might as well load the Colt for her.

An hour later, Dalton was snoring when the doc crossed the room to check on Nell. Walker woke enough to reach for his rifle, before he recognized Timothy's lean shadow moving through the room.

Walker froze as the doctor crossed the main area and tapped on Lacy and Theda's bedroom door. He thought of lifting his rifle and asking the doctor a few questions. It took a pretty foolish man to tap on another man's wife's door with the husband not ten feet away and armed.

But Walker waited silently.

When Lacy opened the door, Timothy whispered, "Could one of you help me change the bandages? I'd rather not go underground to wake Bailee, but I could use another set of hands."

"Of course," Lacy answered.

"I will," Theda shouted, waking the ranger. "I'll be with you in a moment, Doctor."

Walker watched the old maid hurry from her bedroom a few minutes later and disappear behind the divider separating Nell from the rest of the room.

"Now might be a good time to have that talk, Captain," Dalton whispered from his bed on the couch a few feet away. "She's already awake."

"Mind your own business, Ranger," Walker grumbled as he stood.

"Yes, sir," Dalton chuckled and pulled the covers up over his shoulder.

Walker marched to the door Theda had just run out of. He didn't bother to knock as he turned the knob and stepped inside.

Ten minutes later, Theda came out from behind the room divider. "The wound is healing nicely," she said. "You're a wonderful surgeon, Doctor."

"Timothy, please," the doc said.

Theda swayed like an elm in the breeze. "All right, Timothy. I'll say good night again, but if you need me, you've only to call. I know how a doctor's day sometimes can be long, and the work goes smoother with an assistant by his side."

She made it three steps toward the bedroom door before Dalton's voice stopped her. "I wouldn't go in there just yet, Miss Theda."

"Why not?" Fear widened her eyes. "Is there trouble?"

"No, the captain's just talking to his wife. I think he's trying to negotiate for a life sentence with no time off for good behavior." The ranger laughed at his own joke. "Maybe you should give them a little time."

"But . . ."

The doctor stepped up. "I could use a cup of coffee. Miss Theda, would you like to join me?"

"Well . . ." Theda looked flustered. "I guess I could, only taking coffee with a gentleman in one's nightclothes is most out of the ordinary."

"I'll chaperone, Miss Theda," Dalton offered. "I'm a sworn officer of the law."

Theda still looked unsure. "Well, um, I guess it would be all right."

Timothy offered his arm as if he were taking her on a walk through the park on Sunday afternoon and not for coffee a few feet away in the kitchen. "I'd be honored," he said. Neither of them seemed to notice that he didn't have his jacket on and stood in his stocking feet.

"Thank you, Timothy." The old maid took the doctor's arm. As they neared the kitchen, she looked back. "Aren't you coming, Ranger Dalton?"

Dalton had already replaced his hat over his face. "I'll chaperone from in here."

The couple disappeared into the kitchen as Theda's shy laughter drifted back into the main room.

Chapter 31

Lacy opened the window's shutter and looked out into the night. The moon shone, a lantern of light in an almost clear sky. The wind had settled for the night, but the breeze still chilled her. Winter hung in the silent air, pausing, waiting.

A guard stood in the small window of the barn. From his lookout post he could probably see half the farm. She was safe here, surrounded by the people she loved most in this world, yet tonight she felt restless, lonely. Her world had changed so completely in the past few weeks.

The bedroom door opened, and she whispered without turning, "How's Nell? Any change?"

"The same." Walker's voice echoed in the room. "But I may be dying."

Lacy turned around, surprised at how good his voice sounded to her.

She studied him. "You look all right to

me, Captain. No blood showing, no wounds."

"But I'm not. I need you with me. The door between us is too much of a wall. I need my wife."

The hunger in his eyes warmed her as no fire could. "But we've no time."

He shoved the door bolt in place. "We'll take the time."

Moving toward him, she whispered, "So, I'm a prisoner again? You plan to lock me in."

He didn't even bother to argue as he watched her every move.

When she reached him, she brushed her fingers across his heart, and he closed his eyes, taking the light touch like a blow.

"We need to talk," he said as she played with the corner of his mouth. When her tongue slid along his bottom lip, all he could manage was a moan. He pulled her close and kissed her.

Lacy loved the way he always hesitated as if afraid of moving too fast, but when passion flowed through his veins, he didn't bother to hold back the desire for her. He was a man starved for the taste of her, the feel of her. His hands moved along the soft cotton of her gown, trying to touch her all over, all at once.

"How do you like my new nightgown?" she whispered as he moved down her throat with kisses.

"I'd like it off." He pulled at the strings.

"But I thought you —" He stopped her with another kiss that made her body shake with longing.

When he shifted away, he whispered against her ear. "Let me get this conversation over fast. I like, I want, I need what lies beneath your gown. I need you." He opened the front of her gown. "Did you really think I could sleep one door away from you? All I could think about was how good you feel and taste."

"Walker," she whispered as he tenderly touched her breasts. "Can we do it again?"

"No," he answered without stopping the caress. "There's not time and in this house little chance of privacy."

She leaned back so that he could see what he'd been touching.

He drew in air sharply as if she'd punched him. "We'll make time, and I'll find a place."

While she closed her robe, Walker picked up his blanket from where it lay at the foot of the bed and threw the bolt. He grabbed her hand and walked out into the main room.

Dalton raised his hat and lifted to one elbow. "Evening, Captain," he called as if they passed him on the street.

Walker looked around, then headed for the door. "We're taking a walk," he announced as if it wasn't the middle of the night.

The ranger smiled. "I'd go with you, but I'm busy at the moment acting as chaperone."

"You weren't invited." Walker draped the quilt over Lacy's shoulders and opened the front door.

"Lacy?" the ranger shouted. "You agreeing to this walk?"

"I'm insisting on it." She laughed as Walker lifted her into his arms and carried her onto the porch.

Walker first turned toward the barn, than reconsidered and took a few steps in the direction of the workshop. He stopped once more.

"I'll show you a place," Lacy whispered. "Head toward the orchard out back."

"You take a lot of walks in the middle of the night?" he teased.

"Only in my dreams," she answered.

They traveled across winter grass until they reached the peach orchard Carter's parents had planted before he'd been born.

The old trees weren't tall compared to most fruit trees, but their wide branches crisscrossed one another in spots.

"Bailee showed me a safe place to hide if trouble ever comes. Carter's parents were killed in a raid when he was little, and he survived because of this hiding place."

Walker stepped carefully over the roots, ducking low branches until they came upon a hidden spot, protected on three sides by earth and covered on top with branches. The opening would have been impossible to see from more than a foot away, but the ground suddenly twisted and turned, then opened.

"It's a cave."

"Not exactly, the roof is open to allow light in. But the place almost seems to have been created in the middle of the orchard as a secret world."

Walker slowly twisted through the darkness until he came to where the space opened up to the size of a small room. The faint smell of peaches blended with rich dirt. The place was so silent it felt like a church.

Walker lowered Lacy to the ground and watched as she spread the quilt. When she sat down, he moved behind her and lowered so that his leg braced her back. The air seemed warmer in the cavelike room, but he pulled the corner of the quilt over her lap.

She untied her robe.

His hand moved to stop her. In the pale moonlight, he could see her confusion.

"I thought you wanted me?"

"I do," he answered without letting go of her hand. "I never thought I'd ever want anything in this world as much as I want you. You come to me so easy sometimes. I know I frighten you, but you always give me another chance. Each time you step into my arms only makes me want you more, for the gift you give me is priceless."

"You're my husband," Lacy answered.

"Is that all it is to you, Lacy?"

She could wait no longer, she leaned and kissed him, pushing him down as she moved above him.

Walker knew he had to tell her how he felt, but showing her seemed so much more interesting. The feel of her atop him made thinking difficult and talking impossible. He was lost in her nearness.

Laughing, they managed to strip off their clothes and roll up together in the quilt. Their loving came natural now, no hesitation. She was his mate, and whether he said the words or not, it didn't change a thing. Lacy was his wife, and he was her husband. No amount of time together or apart would ever alter that fact.

In the silence of the night, he loved her slowly, taking his time with each level of desire. When he entered her, it was more giving of pleasure than any taking, and she responded as he knew she would, with sighs of satisfaction.

They lay wrapped together for a long while, both awake, both not wanting to shatter their joy.

She cuddled down in the blanket, pressing her cold nose to his chest, and he laughed. "I get the hint," he whispered. "It's time to take you back."

She didn't move. "Do you think Jacob will know what we've done?"

Walker laughed and lied, "No, he'll just think we went for a walk. A very long walk."

Lacy doubted the ranger was ever that naive, but she didn't say a word as Walker slid from her side and collected his clothes. When he knelt, fully dressed, he whispered, "Would you like to put that beautiful gown back on, or shall I carry you back wrapped in the quilt?"

Lacy sat up, the moonlight caressing her bare skin. "I thought you didn't like the gown."

"I love the gown," he corrected. "But not as dearly as I love the woman beneath."

Lacy's heart stopped. Was he just saying words to be polite, or worse, saying what he thought she wanted to hear? Or did he mean what he said? Did he love the woman beneath? If so, it would change everything between them.

She reached for her gown. She wasn't brave enough to ask.

He moved closer to the opening while she dressed, and he tried to figure out how to put his feelings into words.

When she finished tying the robe, she picked up the quilt and joined him in the blackness at the front, deciding to say nothing and see if he ever used the word *love* again.

Her hand touched Walker first, and even in the dark, she felt his tension. "What is it?" she whispered as he pulled her close.

"Someone else is in the orchard." His words brushed her ear.

Her heart matched his as they both froze, listening to something shuffle through the trees.

Chapter 32

Walker ordered Lacy to stay in the cave as he handed her his uniform jacket.

"But it's cold." She tried to give the coat back to him.

He tugged off his boots and pulled a long, thin blade from a hidden pocket on the inside of his left boot, then slipped it up the sleeve of his shirt. When he saw her watching him, he explained, "I want nothing to reflect the light. One gold button could be the death of me. I'd rather be cold than dead."

Touching her cheek, he rubbed a tear away with his thumb. "Stay here, no matter what happens, no matter what you hear. Know that I'm all right and I'm near. Stay in this place until I come after you."

Lacy nodded, near panic. They were alone in the orchard with someone who wanted her dead. There was no other reason anyone would cross the stream and sneak through the trees in the middle of the night.

Carter and Jacob could help if they knew, but there was no way to contact them. Walker had to face whatever moved out there alone. She didn't know how many men circled above them, but she knew he'd be outnumbered. They'd be well armed, and he had only a knife.

She blinked and he was gone, disappearing into the night as soon as he stepped one foot away from her. Hugging his still-warm jacket to her, Lacy moved back into the little shelter. There, she had light, even if it was only the pale moon, and she could hear what was happening above her, even if she saw nothing but branches.

He had little more light, for the trees blocked the moon's glow. Someone might be only a few feet in front of Walker, and he wouldn't be able to see them.

She knew Walker hovered near, but she couldn't even make out his footsteps. Once she thought she heard leaves moving, but it was probably only a breeze.

Fighting pure panic, Lacy wanted to run back to the house and warn the others. If the trespassers got past Walker, they might make it to the house. Except for the guard at the barn window, everyone would be asleep. They wouldn't have a chance.

Her blood slowed as her heart forgot a beat. If they got past Walker, he'd be dead.

She wanted to scream for him to come back. Whatever was out there, they would face it together. She didn't want to think about tomorrow without him.

But he was trained, she reminded herself. A legend, the major had said. He knew what he was doing; she had to trust him. This was the kind of work he talked about being good at, even though he hated it.

Listening, she heard a thud, like a body hitting the ground. Then feet shuffling and whispered voices too far away to make out words.

The minutes ticked by like hours. Lacy unfolded the blanket and sat on it, forcing herself to be still.

Leaves rustled. A branch snapped. Someone moved closer to the opening above her.

Gunfire shattered the night, sounding like it rolled all the way to heaven and back. Sleeping birds took flight, screaming in protest.

Lacy's knuckles whitened as she gripped the sides of the blanket and fought to remain still.

Movement again, closer. Not the sure

steps Walker would have made, she decided, but the hurried steps of someone frightened.

"You shot Sneed!" came a high, panicked whisper only a few feet above her. "Damn it, you shot Sneed!"

"I thought he was that devil, Larson," another man whispered back. "He's already took out two of my men, and I swear I can almost feel his breath on my back. When I saw movement, I shot."

"Well, you took out one of your own men with that shot," the panicked voice complained. "Didn't you know that if you heard someone move it couldn't be Larson? They say no one hears him until it's too late."

"Shut up. He's just a man."

The high voice mumbled, "I knew better than to go along with this plan. Sneed said it wasn't a good idea. We're lucky Larson didn't kill us the first time. If he sees us now, we're dead for sure. I'm seeing if Sneed's still alive, then I'm leaving back the way we came. I want no part of your plan tonight."

The other man bellowed in anger. "If you're not with me, you're against me, Gray, and I don't take kindly to those against me."

Lacy didn't hear Sneed's friend answer. She choked with fear. She knew the other voice. She'd heard it five years before: Zeb Whitaker.

Jumping up, she began to pace. Three steps forward, three steps back. At least the guard, and probably Jacob, must have heard the shot. They'd be on their way to the orchard now. Only, they'd have to cross the open field to get here, and in so doing, make themselves targets. Whitaker could wait in the trees and pick them off, then go after the women. Nell was too weak to fight, Theda would be too scared, Bailee would try to protect the children. She had no idea what the doctor would do, but he didn't look like he'd ever lifted a gun.

They could all be dead soon — everyone she loved except Sarah — and Whitaker would go after her next. If he found Sarah, she'd have no one to protect her except her husband.

Leaves rustled as if being kicked aside. Branches snapped. Horses whinnied. Somehow, they'd brought horses across the river. Lacy remembered the old woman and figured out how Whitaker and his men made it this far. The old woman had brought them.

"Where do I tie the horses?" a woman's

voice sounded, little more than a whisper on the breeze.

"Over by that thicket," Whitaker answered. "And crawl down in those bushes. I don't want Larson finding you."

A few heartbeats later, Lacy heard the snap of branches and something tumbled down from her see-through roof. As she watched in surprise, the bundle of rags jumped to her feet. The old woman!

She prepared to fight when she saw Lacy backed into a corner but recovered when she realized Lacy had no weapon. "Well, what have we here?" The woman no longer sounded old, and her voice had lost the accent. She wasn't one of the gypsies who lived next to Carter, but she must have played her part well to get them to take her in and trust her.

Lacy would have given anything for a gun or even a club, but there was nothing. She had to face the woman alone. Even the dried branches that had fallen in were behind the intruder, out of Lacy's reach.

The woman's smile shone in the moonlight as she pulled a knife. "I owe that husband of yours, and I'm about to even the score."

When she lunged, Lacy tossed Walker's coat at her and darted into the blackness of the entrance. For a few steps she saw nothing, but she kept running, feeling her way. Then she was back in the orchard, in the open air.

Gunfire sounded to her left and was answered in the distance. The men were coming. Lacy ran toward the firing, stumbling over roots in her bare feet, jerking away as branches pulled at her robe, trying to slow her down.

She stumbled and fell, rolling until she hit something that gave slightly. Scrambling to her feet, she touched what had stopped her. A body! Her hands brushed across damp clothing, and the smell of blood filled her lungs. She turned and ran back in the direction she'd come. Twigs cut into her feet. Branches grabbed at her hair and ripped her gown, but she didn't cry out.

Without warning, a trunk of an arm grabbed her, swinging her off the ground in a hold that cut off her air.

Lacy fought as she heard the deep laughter of a man she'd once confessed to killing.

"Got you, little rabbit," he said. "Let's see if you make a sound when you die." He raised his arm, and Lacy saw the wide blade of a hunting knife coming toward her. "I'd like to take my time killing you after all the grief you've caused me. How about I gut you so you'll be able to talk while you bleed to death?"

She closed her eyes, refusing to scream.

"You'll be surprised how much blood is inside of you, little rabbit." Whitaker laughed. "I'll kill you fast, if you tell me where my gold is."

Lacy bit her lip. She couldn't bargain for her life. She had no idea where his gold was. What did it matter if she died fast or slow? She'd be just as dead. The pain of leaving Walker would be far greater than anything Zeb Whitaker's knife could do to her.

The blade slid along her abdomen as if looking for the perfect spot to slice through her flesh.

"Tell me!" he demanded.

Lacy squeezed her eyes tight, trying to picture Walker in her mind. She wanted him, not the old buffalo hunter, to be her last thought.

Gunfire exploded from a few feet away at the same time a knife whistled through the air, inches from her ear. Whitaker coughed as if choked and loosened his hold. Before Lacy could break free, he tumbled to the ground, taking her along with him.

She opened her eyes, then scrambled away from him. It was too dark to see much, but it looked like a bullet had hit the side of his head and a knife had pierced the center of his throat.

He jerked once as if trying to fight off death, then stilled, his eyes staring up at the sky.

Steps ran toward her from different directions. Several yelled, and her name seemed to be echoing off the trees. Walker reached her first, swinging her up into his arms. Jacob, Carter, and three of his men followed close behind.

Lacy cried, finding her voice for the first time since her husband had left her. "The old woman . . . she's back there . . . she has a knife."

"It's all right," Walker said as his hands moved over her. "She's tied up. I saw her follow you out of the cave."

Jacob holstered his gun. "I shot one on the way into the orchard." He knelt, making sure the old buffalo hunter was finally dead. "Did you leave any more for us, Captain?"

Walker ignored his comment. "Anyone hurt?"

"Carter's arm was grazed by the first shot at us. Can't believe they missed him.

He stormed the orchard like a bull. But with that first shot, I knocked him down, and after that, we didn't give them a chance at any more target practice."

Lacy raised her head. "Who's guarding Nell and the children?"

"Bailee's got the kids playing underground, and Theda's watching the back door while the doc watches the front." Dalton stood, satisfied Whitaker was dead. "When I tossed the rifle at the doc, he caught it like a man familiar with weapons."

Walker sat Lacy down and touched her hair. "Are you all right? I heard you take a fall." His hands moved gently over her once more as if he had to know that she was unharmed.

"I'm fine," she lied.

"Good. Go with Carter back to the house and make sure he has that arm seen by the doc. I'll help Dalton round up what's left of Whitaker's gang." Though his words had ordered her to leave, his hands still lingered for the feel of her.

"I don't want to leave you," she whispered before she thought.

"I know," he answered. "But I need to know you're safe. We'll finish here as fast as possible."

"If the talk about you is true, Walker," the ranger swore, "it's going to be a regular egg hunt finding bodies tied up and dead all over this place. I've heard tell a dozen to one is about even with you."

"I only killed one, Whitaker. He shot one of his own men, but the fellow is still breathing."

Dalton straightened. "I killed Whitaker. Shot him in the head."

Carter moved to Lacy's side and lifted her up with his good arm. She didn't protest as he carried her out of the orchard. She knew he was hurting, though he didn't say a word. She also knew it would be hard for her to walk. If Carter didn't carry her, Walker would see that she was hurt. The sooner she let Walker do his job, the sooner they would be together.

Lacy held to Carter as he walked across the field toward the house. She heard Dalton and her husband arguing, and she had to smile. No matter who killed Whitaker, it was all over. The nightmare that had followed her for five years would never bother her again.

Two hours later, the outlaws were loaded into a wagon. Carter's men rode along with Dalton to take them to town. There had been some talk about waiting till morning, but no one wanted the trash on Carter's farm any longer than necessary.

The doctor and Theda took care of Carter, then Sneed, who looked like he might make it, and last Lacy, whose feet were soaking in cold water while she waited.

As Theda cleaned Lacy's wounds and bandaged her cuts, she whispered, "I've had so much excitement tonight, and I haven't died from it." The old maid seemed surprised to be still alive. "I asked Timothy about it, and he said my parents must have told me never to get excited as a way of disciplining me since they were so old when I was born, but as far as he can tell, there's no medical reason for it."

"Timothy?" Lacy smiled.

Theda blushed. "He said he wishes he could afford a nurse like me. He said I'm a natural as an assistant. He says he wishes I'd stay a while."

"And are you?" Lacy swore she saw years dropping away from the old maid's face.

"I think my heart could stand just a little more adventure."

Chapter 33

Sheriff Riley's voice could be heard inside the house, even though he was on the porch. "I'm getting mighty tired of having folks confess to killing Zeb Whitaker. It's getting to the point I probably couldn't put together a twelve-man jury without at least one of them swearing he killed the man."

Lacy looked out the window. Walker and old Samuel had taken the wagon she'd driven into Texas five years ago down to the orchard and picked up the buffalo hunter's body. Carter had fixed the wagon when he'd first married because it belonged to Bailee and he figured she'd want to keep it.

Lacy thought it interesting that Whitaker would be taking his last ride in the very wagon he'd tried to steal.

The sheriff had ridden back with the men after they took the other outlaws into Cedar Point. He'd locked them up, woke one of the deputies to watch them, and came out to check for himself what had happened.

"So, whether Whitaker died by a knife in the throat or a bullet in the brain don't matter. The man is double dead. He was a fool to walk onto Carter's land, and going after the captain's wife was downright crazy. I think I'll just list the cause of death as suicide."

Dalton laughed. "The tough old hunter would hate that."

Walker agreed.

Theda walked onto the porch with a tray of coffee mugs. "The doctor says you men can come in now; everyone's been seen to. But I'll have to ask you to keep your voices down. We've sick people inside."

Lacy smiled. Theda was a natural.

The men accepted their cups and moved indoors. It was long after midnight, but no one seemed to want to call it a night.

Dalton crossed to sit next to Nell. She was awake enough to ask questions. The ranger quietly told her the story of all that had happened, including the part about him saving Lacy with one shot.

Nell laughed softly, but everyone in the huge room stopped and listened. The girl was coming back to them one painful inch at a time.

Sheriff Riley sat at the kitchen table visiting with the doc about Sneed. As soon as the man could be moved, he'd need to go to jail. Riley wasn't sure exactly what Sneed's crime was, being in the wrong place at the wrong time, maybe. He wouldn't be tried as one of Whitaker's gang, since Whitaker was the one who shot him, but it didn't seem right to set him free. He'd been showing some rather strange behavior lately, including showing up in town totally nude.

Bailee came down from putting the children back to bed. She moved behind her husband's chair and touched his shoulder. He pulled her hand to him and moved his fingers over her open palm. She smiled and nodded. Without a word they walked toward the trapdoor. Bailee smiled and waved good night as they disappeared.

Walker crossed to where Lacy sat by the fire, wearing one of Bailee's gowns that was far too long for her. Without asking if she needed help, he lifted her in his arms and carried her to the small bedroom.

He placed her on the bed and returned to the door. "Miss Theda," he asked with formal politeness, "would you mind if my wife and I had a few minutes alone?"

Lacy almost giggled, wondering what the

captain would do if anyone refused his request.

"Not at all," Theda answered. "I've already told Timothy I'll be sitting up with the injured tonight. Please, feel free to get some sleep."

"Yeah," Dalton yelled from behind the divider. "Get some sleep."

Lacy watched Walker's face harden, then relax. "Thanks, Ranger, I think I will," he said in a none-too-friendly tone.

She heard the ranger's laughter as Walker bolted the door.

He pulled off his shirt as he walked toward the bed. But instead of going to his side, he moved to hers and lifted her feet while he pulled the covers from beneath her. For a long moment, he stared at the bandages.

"It's nothing," she answered his unasked question. "I only have a few cuts from running."

"Where else are you hurt?" he demanded, and she realized he hadn't noticed that her feet had been cut in the orchard.

"I'm fine, Walker."

His frown didn't lift. He knelt above her and began to unbutton her nightgown.

"I'm fine," she insisted. "Just a few

bruises and scratches, nothing more." She stopped his hand. "I'll not be examined."

He relaxed, sat on the edge of the bed, and pulled off his boots and trousers. "But, dear, you know that's one of my favorite things to do."

She laughed. In truth, he'd spent a great deal of time touching and kissing every part of her body. But tonight, she didn't want him to worry over all the bruises. She didn't want to relive what had happened.

"Could you just hold me tonight?"

He brushed her hair back from her face as he stretched out beside her. "If that's what you want. I'd love to."

She cuddled against his arm. "It's all over, isn't it, Captain?"

"It's all over," he whispered into her hair.

She pulled away and rose up so she could see his eyes. "You have ten days left." She didn't know how to say what needed to be said. She wanted to beg him to stay and spend the time with her, but she knew tomorrow or ten days from now, saying good-bye to him forever wouldn't be any easier.

"I've already thought about that." He watched her closely. "I thought we could go on a honeymoon. Away from people."

Lacy couldn't have been more surprised. "But why? Where?"

"Why? Because we never had one. And where, I thought maybe a little town called Cottonwood. It's calmed down since the range war, and I'd like to make right a mistake I made there."

"A mistake?"

Walker moved his hand over her shoulder and slowly down to her hip. "You see, I met my wife there, and I did the wrong thing. I made her hate me when I should have made her love me."

"I never hated you." She realized that even in the darkest hours after she'd returned, she couldn't put the blame for what happened on Walker.

"But could you learn to love me?" His fingers played with the buttons at her throat.

"Perhaps," she answered, knowing she already did.

"And would you be willing to be my wife? My real wife? Every day, every night?" He moved his hand beneath the cotton of her nightgown and touched her breast.

"I already am, but it would never work. Where would we live? I don't belong at the fort, and you could never settle down to life in Cedar Point."

He tugged her gently to him, kissing her neck. "We'll fight about it later," he whispered. "Somewhere there's got to be a compromise."

Lacy forced herself to pull away. "Captain, I want the words."

"What words?"

"I want to hear the words if I'm your real wife." A tear threatened to spill over and betray her fear. She wasn't sure she wanted him to know how important the words were to her.

"Is that an order, madam?" he asked, his emotions under tight control.

"Yes," she answered.

Walker raised an eyebrow, watching her closely. "All right. I want you."

"Try again."

"I need you?"

"No." Lacy had to have the words, had to believe that he felt them, had to know that he didn't say them by accident.

"I love you."

She smiled. There, that was what she'd been waiting to hear. The words she'd never heard. The words that would forever command her heart. Lacy curled down next to him.

His arm moved around her tenderly as

he whispered, "I love you," once more in her ear. "I love you, my one and only wife, and will till the day I die."

"I love you, too, Captain."

His arm tightened around her shoulders.

She smiled, knowing what he wanted. "I love you, Walker."

Epilogue

Fort Davis
The Frontier Line
Texas

Walker stormed out of his office. "Peterson!"

"Right here, Captain." The thin sergeant moved from the shadow of the porch and stood at attention.

"Have a half-dozen men ready to ride in fifteen minutes. I think the stage may need an escort."

Peterson smiled. "I've had them ready since dawn, sir. Just waiting for you to say the word."

Walker raised an eyebrow in question. Peterson had been with him for years. Sometimes he swore the man read his mind.

"Always do when the captain's lady's coming." Peterson pulled on his hat and stepped into the warm sun. "Mind if I ride along with the escort this time, sir?"

Walker shoved on his gloves, frustrated with himself. "Do I always send an escort?"

"Every time. Mrs. Larson's been coming out every other month all spring, and you haven't missed one yet."

Walker didn't argue. In truth, he had trouble concentrating the few days before she came back to him . . . and the few days after she left . . . and every night when he faced sleeping without her by his side. The woman had gotten in his blood, and if she didn't change her mind and come live with him for good instead of spending four weeks with him then four weeks in Cedar Point, he feared he might go crazy. Every time she left his quarters, a little more of her remained behind. Maybe only a quilt, or a few more books, but something. Something to remind him. Something to make him miss her more.

Peterson fell into step as they marched toward the horses. "Will she be bringing the animals with her again?"

Walker nodded. Pets were frowned on at the fort, but no one said anything. She wouldn't leave the cats behind, and he liked the dog.

"You know, Captain, if we searched, we

could probably find a dog and two cats as mangy as those she hauls halfway across Texas. That dog you call Alley is the ugliest mutt I've ever seen. He makes a cow dog look handsome."

Walker didn't argue, but he liked the alley dog and feared it would starve to death if it didn't get army food every other month. Lacy might have left him behind, but Walker insisted if the two cats got to visit, Alley came along as well.

"Mount up, men," the sergeant yelled, then added to himself, "We're going to ride like the devil until we get to that stage."

Walker didn't know how to explain that he could wait no longer for Lacy. He swung into the saddle and shot out the gate at full speed. Every time he swore he'd wait for her to come to him, and every time he rode a little farther down the trail to meet the stage. At this rate, within a year, he'd be riding all the way back to Cedar Point. She wouldn't leave the paper until she thought Jay Boy could handle it, and he couldn't end his career with a promotion due any day.

Something was going to have to change. She would either come to her senses, or he'd completely lose his. On days like this,

Walker didn't care which, he just knew he needed her. Living in Cedar Point wasn't what he wanted, but without Lacy, he didn't seem to be living at all. He had no idea what it would take to make her think of his quarters as home and not that tiny apartment over the shop.

An hour later the stage came into view, bouncing across the dusty trail. The driver waved and pulled the reins when he spotted Walker.

Lacy was out of the coach by the time he reached her. Walker told himself he'd be cold when he greeted her; after all, she'd been away for a month when she should have been here where she belonged.

But when he saw her, his heart ached to hold her, and all he saw before him seemed perfection. He ran the last few feet and swung her up in his arms, pulling her as close to him as he could. He laughed as she kissed his face and cried his name as if she'd been starving for him. He held her near, breathing for the first time in a month. The world never seemed real without her close, and he knew he'd never get tired of having her at his side. This little woman he swore he'd never love held his heart.

"This happen every other month?"

Walker heard one of the men ask Peterson.

"Yep. It's like witchcraft; every other month the Captain turns into a man."

The new soldier shook his head. "Can't they work it out?"

"Oh, they will one of these days. Right now, I think they're having too much fun fighting about it."

Walker carried Lacy to his horse and lifted her up. As he climbed behind her, he waved the stage on. The men would escort the now-empty stage to the fort, and he'd take his time riding back. He wanted to get used to the feel of her once more.

When the coach, loaded down with her things, rocked past him, Walker noticed something new amid the cages of animals.

A cradle.

He pulled her closer, loving the way she felt so right against him. "You staying longer this time, madam?"

Lacy laughed. "I thought I might."

"Welcome home, my love."